MW01128402

WHO WANTS TO MARRY A
MILLIONAIRE?

Also by Sophie Ranald

*It Would Be Wrong to Steal My Sister's
Boyfriend (Wouldn't It?)*

A Groom With a View

*You Can't Fall in Love With Your Ex
(Can You?)*

WHO WANTS TO MARRY A MILLIONAIRE?

SOPHIE RANALD

Who Wants to Marry a Millionaire? © Sophie Ranald 2014

Previously published as The Frog Prince

All rights reserved in all media. No part of this book may be reproduced or transmitted in any form by any means, electronic or mechanical (including but not limited to: the internet, photocopying, recoding or by any information storage and retrieval system), without prior permission in writing from the author and/or publisher.

The moral right of Sophie Ranald as the author of the work has been asserted by her in accordance with the Copyright Designs and Patents Act 1988.

ISBN-13: 9781515373063

This book is for my darling Dad, Ranald 'Mac' Mackenzie.

CHAPTER ONE

A ll girls dream about falling in love, don't they? I did, anyway, for years and years. And then I went one better. I fell *on* love. I suppose I was lucky to find Julian that way – luckier, at any rate, than my mate Wizzy, who instead of falling on to Julian, as I did, landed on concrete and ended up in A&E with a compound fracture. My descent was certainly more comfortable than hers – although, unlike me, Wizzy wasn't still experiencing the impact of her fall a year later.

But I'm getting ahead of myself. This should start at the beginning, like all good stories do – like the fairytales I was addicted to writing and illustrating as a teenager used to.

If I were writing a fairytale, I'd go with something like this:

Once upon a time, there were three beautiful princesses. One of them had hair as black as a raven's wing, and she was called Princess Polly. The second, Princess Wizzy, had hair the colour of chestnuts in autumn. And the third had golden hair, and her name was Princess Stella. One day, the three princesses set off on a journey…

That's pretty much how the Brothers Grimm or whoever would kick off our story – you get the idea, anyway. It all started with Wizzy's twenty-fifth birthday (her real name's Isabella, but Wizzy was her pet name as a baby, and it stuck because it suits her – she's one of those people who seem to exist in fast-forward, darting through life like a swallow, making the rest of humanity look somehow slower and duller than she is). Or, perhaps more accurately, it started with her deciding that she wanted to spend that weekend, or Birthdayfest as she termed it, in London. Or maybe what sealed our fate was her sister Martha's idea of booking afternoon tea for four, with all the prosecco we could drink, as a surprise.

Yes – on reflection, it's most definitely the unlimited fizz I blame for events taking the course they did.

We all put on floaty frocks and heels and got the Tube from Martha's house in Balham to a posh hotel with a view across the river to the London Eye. We sat down, exclaiming excitedly to one another about how fabulous it all was, and in no time the first sandwiches, cake and free bubbly began to arrive. We did not stint.

"Rare roast beef with horseradish," Martha said. "That's the good stuff, right there."

"Chocolate cake with actual gold!" I said. "Do you eat it? Or keep it for later to wear?"

"Lemon curd!" Polly said. "Gimme."

"Could you top up my glass, please?" said Wizzy.

Three hours later, stuffed with food and distinctly pissed, the four of us reeled out of the cool, dim hotel foyer into brilliant sunshine.

"Oooh," Martha said. "That's bright. Shit. Isn't it weird how daylight makes you feel much drunker than you felt inside?"

"True, dat," I nodded earnestly.

Polly, who'll be the first to admit that she's a bit of a lightweight, said, "I'm feeling sick. And my head hurts. And did I mention that I feel sick? Why did I have that third scone?"

Wizzy said, "Come on! No slacking, it's my birthday! What are we going to do next?"

"A little lie-down in a darkened room?" suggested Polly hopefully.

"A brisk walk to clear our heads?" Martha said.

"I'm not walking anywhere briskly in these heels," I said. My strappy yellow stilettos, purchased at vast expense in the Kurt Geiger sale, were slicing cruelly into my toes. If we went dancing later, as planned, I'd have to keep caning the drink to get through the pain.

Wizzy said, "I want to ride on the lions in Trafalgar Square!"

"I'm not riding anything, I'll get car-sick. Lion-sick. Whatever," said Polly.

"Brilliant idea!" I said.

"Stupid idea," Martha said. "But you're the birthday girl, sis, so if you want to ride on lions you must ride on lions. Don't expect me to, though, I'm a Londoner now and I have put childish, tourist things behind me."

Wizzy stuck her tongue out at her, and we all laughed and trooped down the Strand and into Trafalgar Square.

"There they are!" Wizzy said, and dashed over to the nearest lion and somehow scrambled up, sitting astride it, the hem of her flowery skater dress rucked up around her hips, her long bare legs stretched over the lion's hot bronze flanks. "Come on, Stella!"

I looked up at her, doubtfully. Wizzy's five foot nine and has a serious gym habit. I'm five foot three and have the upper-body strength of a goldfish.

"Come on!" she said again, leaning over and offering me her hand to help me. Tentatively, I took it, she gave an almighty heave, and the next thing I knew, I was up.

"Woohoo!" all four of us went, Wizzy and I giddy with excitement, the other two presumably giddy with relief that they'd remained on terra firma.

"What now?" I said.

"Lion selfie! I'll post it on Shutterly," said Wizzy. "Chuck me my phone, Martha."

Martha was far too sensible and grown-up to chuck hundreds of pounds-worth of fragile technology anywhere, but she found Wizzy's phone in her tiny handbag and passed it up to her.

"Smile, Stella," Wizzy ordered, and we both grinned like mad into the lens. Wizzy clicked the shutter and inspected the result. "Hmmm. Good, but not good enough. We'll get a much better shot if we stand up."

"Are you fucking crazy?" I said.

Wizzy shrieked with laughter. "Maybe a bit. Come on. It'll be grand, this guy's got a wide back." Carefully, swaying just a little, she got to her feet. "See? It's easy."

Reluctantly, I shuffled forward to the lion's head and leaned one hand on its mane, edging up on to my knees and then on to my feet. The metal of its back felt horribly slippery under my shoes and the ground looked a long, long way away. I felt sweat break out on my palms and snake down my back.

"Hurry up!" I said. "I want to get down."

I'm not sure exactly what happened next, and nor do I know how Wizzy managed to hold on to her phone and keep her finger on the shoot button, but she did. The resulting series of photos, which she posted all over social media and still makes everyone she meets admire, show her joyful grin and my forced smile, which dissolves into a rictus of terror as I lose my balance, grab Wizzy's hand and pull her off kilter too. Then all you can see is the tops of our heads, the background blurring, and the horrified face of a man coming closer and closer, his arms raised in a vain attempt catch us, or perhaps just in self-defence, his mouth forming a silent howl of, "Nooo!"

I knocked him off his feet, landed on top of him, and heard a horrible thud as his head hit the pavement. A second later, I heard Wizzy say, "Jesus fucking Christ," and I realised my eyes were closed, squeezed tight shut in terror.

I opened them, and saw Wizzy's face, grey with pain, her mascara smudging in long black runnels down her cheeks. Martha and Polly came dashing over to us and helped us to our feet, and the man I'd landed on stood shakily up as well.

"I'm probably okay," I said. "Wizz, are you okay? Are you okay?" I asked the stranger who's cushioned my fall. "I'm so sorry."

"I think I've bust my wrist," Wizzy whispered. "But look! I didn't drop my phone!" And she gave a feeble giggle, then started to cry in earnest.

"I… I'm not entirely sure," the man said. "I hit my head. I'll live, but I've felt better."

"Right, taxi to A&E," Martha said. Admirably calm, she shepherded us all away and hailed a cab. "You'd better come too and get your head looked at, concussion can be nasty. What's your name?"

"Julian Mason," said Julian, obediently following. Martha is just as irresistible a force of nature as Wizzy, in her way.

Fifteen minutes later, we were all seated in a bedraggled row on plastic chairs at St Thomas's hospital, next to a small, subdued group of men who'd come second in a fight after a football match. Wizzy and Julian had been handed tickets and told they'd be seen shortly. Polly was trying not to cry. I kept apologising to Julian, and he kept saying it was fine, it was an accident and not my fault. Then a few minutes later

I'd apologise again, rinse and repeat. Martha was looking anxiously at her phone.

After a bit Wizzy was taken off to be x-rayed and Julian was taken off to recite the months of the year backwards and touch the tip of his nose with his eyes closed. He was the first to return.

"I'm officially fine," he said. "I'll have a lump on my head but my brain power is unimpeded. So I think I'll head off."

Just then, a nurse approached our sorry little group.

"Mrs King?"

"That's me," said Martha.

"Your sister's x-ray results are back, and it's a fracture but not a complex one. We'll need to keep her in for a few more hours until there's a consultant available to set the break."

"Thanks ever so much," said Martha, then she looked at her phone again. "Look, I'm really sorry but Paul's just texted me again and Harry's having a total meltdown. I've never been away from him for this long before, poor little chap. I really have to get back." She looked at Polly, who was visibly wilting and kept nodding off in her chair. "And you ought to come with me, Polly. Would you mind awfully waiting for them to sort Wizzy out, and then bringing her home? I'll give you my Addy Lee account number, you can just get a cab straight back to Balham."

"That's fine," I said. "Of course I'll stay."

"I can wait here with Stella," Julian said.

"Oh, would you? That's awfully kind. Right, then, I'll see you later, Stella. Here are Wizzy's keys, let yourself in, don't worry if you wake us, and please ring if you need me to come back." Polly in tow, she swished off, her red hair and red dress the only spot of colour in the drab waiting room.

"How about a coffee?" said Julian.

Sitting opposite him in the café, a cup of too-hot, too-weak vending machine Nescafé steaming in front of me, I took a proper look at him for the first time. He wasn't very tall and he was very lean, lithe almost, with sloping shoulders and long, elegant hands like a pianist's. His eyes were a dark, brilliant green and his hair was dark brown, but shone like mahogany where the harsh strip lighting caught it. His skin was pale and flawless, and his teeth were perfect too. I realised that the man I'd fallen on was seriously beautiful.

I don't know if it was just us, or the circumstances that had brought us together, but it seemed impossible for me to make any of the normal small talk you do with someone you've just met. I didn't ask him where he lived or what he did for work, or anything like that, and he didn't ask me.

Instead he said, "I saw the most amazing picture today. It was painted six hundred years ago, but it could have been yesterday. I was thinking about that, when I was walking to the Tube station. How people now are just like people have always been, and the spaces where we live are different, but the same."

I said, "Was that the thing at the National Gallery? About the Italian Renaissance? I'd love to see it."

"There was a woman in a one of the paintings who looked a bit like you," Julian said. "Small and fair and kind of still. But of course people in paintings are always still."

"They aren't!" I said. "You can often see them move, if you look hard enough. And anyway, I was definitely moving when I knocked you flat."

Julian laughed, and we talked for a bit about fourteenth-century painting, and I tried not to be all obvious about knowing more about it than he did. Neither of us drank our coffee.

Then I said, "I suppose we'd better go back," and we went and sat in the waiting area again, in two different hard chairs.

Julian took out his ipod and scrolled through it and said, "How about a bit of Royal Blood?"

"Cool," I said, and he passed me one of the speaker buds and I plugged it into my ear and we listened to the music together, like teenagers on the bus on a school trip. After a while, I felt his hand touch mine and I folded my fingers around his. And that's how Wizzy found us two hours later when a nurse escorted her out, groggy with painkillers.

We stood in an awkward little cluster, waiting to say goodbye.

I rang for a cab. The nurse gave Wizzy a supply of good strong drugs and a lecture about keeping her cast dry.

Julian said, "Would it be possible to see you tomorrow?"

I said I didn't know, but I'd see, and he gave me his number, and as we were leaving, Wizzy dug me in the ribs with her elbow, the one that wasn't immobilised by plaster, and said, "You pulled!"

I did see Julian the next day, and the day after that. I wasn't going to, but my friends insisted.

"Ring him! You have to ring him! This is, like, the most romantic meeting ever!" were Polly's parting words before she got the train back to Edinburgh and Angus.

"Are you sure you don't want me to stay and keep you company, Wizz?" I said. "You know, bro's before ho's, or whatever?"

"If you don't ring him, I'll beat you to death with my cast," Wizzy said from the depths of the sofa, where she'd spent the morning watching *Frozen* with Mia, Martha's little girl.

So I did. I rang him, and we met for lunch, and I couldn't eat any of my sushi because somehow I felt that there wasn't room inside me for anything except the thrilling bubble of desire I felt for him, and anyway he was holding my right hand across the table and I couldn't manage my chopsticks with my left. But I did have three glasses of pink wine, and we chatted about trivial things, delighting in each experience of common ground.

We talked about the music we liked (Julian was the first person I'd met who was also into Rumour Cubes) and hated (he was delighted to learn that I couldn't stand Katy Perry). We discovered that we were both bored by sport but loved games (him: Minecraft; me: Candy Crush – okay, my choice was perhaps a little more lowbrow than his, but still, it seemed to bring us closer).

This time I did get around to asking him what he did for a living, and he told me he was an academic, a mathematician, and currently working on a project to model the way leaves changed their colour in autumn. This struck me as so fascinating and beautiful that I asked him to explain to me how it worked, and he did, and half an hour later I was still listening, none the wiser but loving the passionate way he talked about his work and the spidery notes his pencil made on the paper tablecloth as he talked about datasets and bell curves.

We talked about our families, and learned that we were both only children. Julian told me he'd never really known his father, and his mum had recently married a man who Julian couldn't stand, and so he rarely saw them. I said I didn't get on with my mum either, and rarely saw her. He didn't ask me why, but I could tell he got it.

We lingered for hours over our lunch, sharing a mango ice cream (which, luckily, I was able to eat one-handed) and several pots of tea. Eventually, having thoroughly outstayed our welcome, we drifted away and walked along the river in the sunshine, past unfamiliar, gleaming glass buildings, still holding hands. I felt elated and dizzy with possibility, and when Julian said, "Want to see the most amazing view?" I immediately agreed.

He led me into one of the sleek riverside towers, into the elevator that whooshed us ear-poppingly upwards, and into an apartment, all polished concrete, pale leather and glass.

"Look," he commanded, and there was London, spread beneath us in the fading afternoon sun. Tower Bridge; a glittering pinnacle that Julian said was called the Shard; the river snaking through it all, almost too bright to look at.

"Is this place yours?" I asked, amazed.

Julian laughed. "Unfortunately not. It's my mate Will's, he's just letting me crash here for a week while he's away with work and I'm out here for a conference."

"Out here?"

"I live in Canada," he said. "I told you, didn't I?"

But before I could answer, he'd pulled me into his arms and started kissing me, and then we had sex, and after that it was too late, the damage was done – I'd fallen for him as hard as if he'd shoved me off the balcony.

Looking back, that weekend was the start of more than just Julian's and my relationship – and it was the end of so much that I'd come to take for granted. In fact, the day Wizzy rode the lion changed everything for all three of us. For Julian too, of course. And for Will, who I hadn't even met.

When Polly got back to Edinburgh, she found Angus waiting for her at Waverley station. He had a huge bunch of pink roses in his hands, and he had something he needed to ask her and something else he needed to tell her. The first was whether Polly would marry him. He'd done a lot of thinking over the past two days, he said, and although they'd only been going out for a few months, he was absolutely sure – more sure than he'd been about anything, ever – that Polly was the woman he wanted to spend the rest of his life with. When Polly had finished crying and they'd finished snogging passionately and the small crowd that had gathered around them on the concourse outside the Bagel Factory had dispersed, Angus told her the other thing. It was that his bachelor uncle Andrew had died, leaving his house in the Highlands to Angus and his brother Gray.

Wizzy was signed off work for four weeks, and after about the first three days she was climbing the walls with boredom. She developed an obsessive interest in reading travel websites and following people's blogs about their round-the-world journeys, and she decided that as soon as her plaster was off and she'd saved enough money, she was going to do that, too. Wizzy had been snapped up a few years before by the graduate recruitment programme of a huge multinational company and was proving to be the best thing that had ever happened to fabric-softener marketing, so at the end of that quarter she received a fat bonus for which she thanked her employer by handing in her notice.

And I was in love. In the space of just a few hours, I went from wondering if I was ever going to get over Declan, who'd recently dumped me and left my heart bruised if not actually broken (he was an art critic who I'd met through work, and although I adored his brooding grey eyes and deep, insightful conversation, I'd begun to think that if I never heard the phrase 'ontological oeuvre' again in my life, it would be too soon), to being utterly dizzy with love and longing for Julian. When I woke up in the morning, the first thing I did was pick up my phone and check for email from him. Before I went to sleep, I texted him to say goodnight. I couldn't concentrate at work, because I kept drifting off into fantasies about what it would be like when we could eventually be together. And it goes without saying that I dreamed about him almost every night.

This went on for seven months. I couldn't eat and lost a stone, which given I'm pretty scrawny anyway was not a good look. I almost drove Polly and Wizzy mad talking about Julian, how much I loved him, and whether we would ever see each other again. When, at last, he sent me the longed-for email saying that he'd applied for and got a research fellowship at UCL in London, I think my flatmates were even more relieved than I was.

After that, it seemed like everything happened at once. Polly and Angus went off to Inverness-shire to try and turn Uncle Andrew's falling-down mansion into a hotel. Wizzy shouldered her backpack and jetted off to Thailand to work on her tan on the beach before starting her travels in earnest.

And I gave our flat a final clean, returned the keys to the letting agent, and got the train to London to start living happily ever after with Julian.

CHAPTER TWO

But when Princess Stella awoke in the enchanted castle, it was not as she had dreamed it would be. Giant spiders lurked in their webs in every corner of her turret bedroom. Although she put on her apron and swept and swept, it seemed the magical dust could not be cleared away. There were mice, but they did not turn into footmen. And the prince had saddled up his horse and ridden away into the forest...

It was the day I'd dreamed of and longed for – the day Julian's and my life together properly began. But it didn't work out quite as I'd hoped. There was certainly a promising start, when I woke up on our lumpy mattress, which had come with the furnished flat and bore a faint but unmistakeable smell of sick, opened my eyes, and saw his face on the pillow next to mine.

Maybe, I thought, there would come a time when I was tired of looking at him, but I simply couldn't imagine it ever happening. His lean jaw was relaxed in sleep, his lips faintly smiling as if he was dreaming of something that made him happy – me, perhaps. Or more likely quadratic equations. One hand rested under his cheek, which was darkened with the beginning of a beard – the stubble that had rasped my skin last night when we made love, again and again, making up for all the months we'd been apart. A lock of soft dark hair had flopped down over one of his eyes.

13

I lifted a hand to brush it away, as gently as I could, but my touch still woke him.

"Shit, Stella," he said. "What time is it? Why didn't you wake me up?"

"It's half seven," I replied drowsily, reaching out to pull him towards me. "And I just did."

"Jesus. I'll be late for my nine o'clock meeting with Ken, that bastard 59 bus takes forever. Way to fucking go, Mason, that's how you impress people in the new job."

And he swung his feet over the edge of the bed, giving me a tantalising glimpse of his long legs and taut buttocks as he hurried to the bathroom, still muttering to himself.

I rolled over on to my back, closed my eyes and listened to the unfamiliar sounds of Julian's morning routine, smiling as I wondered how long it would take before they became familiar. The click and hum of the electric shower starting up; the discouragingly feeble patter of water hitting the bathtub. The buzz of his razor. A crash and another shout of, "Fuck!" as he opened the wardrobe door and it fell off its hinges.

"God, this place is a tip," he said, stepping over the door to pull a shirt from its hanger. "Everyone told me it would be impossible to rent anywhere decent in London on my budget but I thought they were exaggerating. Guess not."

I sat up against the pillows, which were as flat as pitta breads and not much softer. "I'll ring the landlord today and ask him to buy a new one," I said. "And I'll clean the place and have a delicious dinner waiting for you this evening. I'll be a proper fifties housewife, you'll see. And once I find a job we can move somewhere nicer."

"Mind you have my slippers and a sherry waiting when I get home," he said, leaning over the bed to kiss me. His tweed jacket smelled a bit of mothballs, I noticed. Then I heard the scrape of his key in the lock and the rattle of the letterbox as he slammed the front door behind him, and he was gone.

It was quarter past eight, and the thought of the empty hours stretching ahead of me felt suddenly daunting. I picked up my phone and started to make a list.

Buy screwdriver

Fix wardrobe

Google removing sick smell from mattress

Hang pictures

Then I remembered Julian telling me that the land-lord had strictly forbidden any nails to be banged into the scruffy magnolia walls. The watercolours I'd painted and framed for my degree show, which I'd displayed so proudly on the wall of my bedroom in Leith, would have to stay in their box. I felt a wave of homesickness – for Edinburgh, for my cosy, chaotic single life and for my flatmates. But it was pointless thinking about my old home – strangers would be living there now. Polly was in the Highlands, probably frying bacon and eggs in the hotel kitchen. Wizzy was in Bangkok doing whatever intrepid backpackers do. And I was in Streatham, embarking on life with Julian – the man I'd been in love with for months but who, I realised, I barely knew.

I didn't cry until I opened the oven door. I'd been through almost an entire bottle of bleach cleaning the bathroom. I'd put myself at risk of developing housemaid's knee scrub-bing the floor – which was a particularly hideous laminate meant to resemble limed oak, peeling away from its base in some places and uneven and wobbly in others – and it still felt sticky when I walked on it.

I'd unpacked all two thousand seven hundred and ninety-one of Julian's books (yes, I counted) and arranged the ones that would fit in the second-hand bookcases, which, judging by the sag they'd developed in the middle of the shelves, weren't going to be up to the job. I'd folded up all our clothes, burying my face in Julian's jumpers in the hope that they might smell of him, not just of Ariel, squeezed everything into the rickety wardrobe and tried and failed to reattach the door to its hinges.

I'd explored the little corner shop and the too-expensive Tesco Express down the road and bought the ingredients for a lasagne, cooked the value minced beef with loads of garlic and herbs and made a white sauce on the canting spiral hotplate, and assembled all it in a beige stoneware dish from Poundland. Then I had a shower and put on some make-up and made a cup of tea, and I was ready to sit down and watch *Don't Tell the Bride* when I thought, "I'll just check the oven."

I should have been prepared for it, of course. But I wasn't, and when I saw the decades-old, crusted black grease, heard the screech of rusty metal when I tried to move the single, buckled rack, and inhaled the sickening smell of what I could have sworn was dead mouse, it was too much for me. I slammed the oven closed again, leaned my back against its chilly enamel door, my arms clasped around my knees, and had a good old howl.

Then I remembered that Julian might be home any minute, and I wanted him to find a smiling, serene Stella and not a sobbing wreck, so I wiped my eyes, changed my pale-pink T-shirt for a moth-eaten grey jumper, blew my nose and wearily pulled my Marigolds back on. *Don't Tell the Bride* would have to wait – I wanted everything to be… not perfect, there was no hope of that, but as close to acceptable as I could make it. And mouse al forno wasn't going to hack it.

I was bending over the oven – which had rapidly overtaken the floor as my arch-enemy in our new home – scraping away at the grease with steel wool, my hair and my jumper already splattered with bleachy water and black gunk, when the doorbell rang and I sprang up, cracking my skull against the top of the oven. He must have mislaid his keys – but he was home!

I ran to the front door, twisting open the lock with my soapy, rubber-gloved hands.

"Angel!" I said, "I'm so pleased you're... Oh."

It wasn't Julian. It was a man I'd never seen before, a tall, rangy blond man with impossibly long legs in faded denim jeans. In his hands, at about my eye level, he was holding a bunch of yellow tulips and a bottle of champagne. I gawped in confusion for a moment while the bottle and the flowers dripped on to the greige rag that served as our doormat, then I looked up into his face, and was met with an amiable smile.

"Stella?" he said. "I'm Will. Will Turner. Julian's friend. I'm so sorry, you're obviously..."

"No, no, it's fine," I rubbed my soggy hands on my jeans. "It's just... we only moved in yesterday and Julian's still at work and it's all a bit chaotic."

"I know," Will said. "I rang Julian earlier to ask how it was all going, and he invited me over. He didn't tell you, did he?"

I hesitated. Would it be worse to give Julian's oldest and best mate the impression that I was a disorganised slattern who greeted her guests in rubber gloves, wearing dirty jeans and with the telly blaring in the background, or risk hurting

SOPHIE RANALD

his feelings by telling him that Julian hadn't mentioned a thing about this planned visit? "Well, he…" I began.

"Course he didn't tell you," Will laughed and shrugged. "That's Julian for you. At university he memorised pi to ten thousand places, but he still couldn't remember where he was supposed to go for tutorials. Shall I come another night or can I give you a hand?"

"Oh, God, how rude." I felt myself blushing, realising I'd kept him standing in the doorway with his tulips and his fizz. "Please come in. I'm so sorry the flat's a bit of a state."

Will followed me through to the postage-stamp living room, with its stack of empty boxes against the wall and teetering piles of books that hadn't yet found homes, and I parked the flowers in the kitchen sink and finally shook his hand, cool and damp from the cold glass.

"I'm Stella. Obviously. Lovely to meet you at last," I said. And then our voices sort of collided in mid-air as we said at the same time, "I've heard so much about you," and I laughed, and felt a bit less awkward.

It was true – Julian had told me loads about Will. How the two of them had met at uni and instantly clicked, bonding over their shared ability to understand fractals and algorithms and all the other stuff, and their mutual passion for online poker. He'd told me, slightly disapprovingly, how Will had turned his back on a highly promising PhD when he'd had the idea for a social media start-up, and spent the next two years working on it with his business partner, Louise. Shutterly had gone on to be enormously successful – of course, I use it all the time, you probably do too – and now Will was CEO of Ignite Digital, with a swish HQ just off the silicon roundabout and an army of geeks all coding away like mad developing new apps. Samsung had bought into

18

the business, Apple were rumoured to be sniffing around and, basically, Will was beginning to get seriously rich.

My memory of what he'd said was a bit vague, because it had been on the night after we met, when we'd first made love. At the time, I hadn't really concentrated. But now it all came back to me – I remembered lying in the tangle of dove-grey sheets, listening as Julian told me that Will had only recently bought the flat, because his accountant had told him there was no safer bet for surplus cash than property. Of course, while Julian was telling me all this, I'd still been reeling with post-orgasmic bliss and with the news that the man I'd fallen in love with was about to bugger off back to Canada.

But anyway, Julian wasn't in Canada any more, he was here, home, with me. And I was standing in the kitchen of our new flat, staring stupidly at his friend, remembering having sex in his bed.

"Would you like a cup of tea?" I said, blushing furiously. "I'm sure Julian won't be long, and I'm really sorry, but I was just cleaning the oven. It's grim, but if I don't finish it now I don't think I'll ever be able to face starting again."

Will looked at me and at the state of the kitchen, and I suppose he must have seen my smudged make-up and guessed I'd been crying.

"The place looks amazing," he said. "I can't believe you only moved in yesterday. I bet you're shattered – Julian is one of the finest minds of our generation but unless he's changed a lot he won't have given you much help. Why don't I pour you a glass of this and you drink it while I finish cleaning up?"

It was an offer I couldn't refuse. I watched Will squeeze his hands into my washing-up gloves and fold his long legs up and stick his head into the grimy recesses of the oven, and I sipped my champagne and we chatted about this and that, although to be honest I couldn't hear any of his replies to my polite getting-to-know-you questions about his job and where in London he lived, because he was talking into the cooker. Not that it mattered, really, because I had remembered most of the answers.

Eventually, straightening up from the floor, he said, "I reckon that's as good as it's going to get."

"Thank you so much," I said. "That's so amazingly kind. I can't believe you did that. You've totally earned your dinner."

But when I turned the knob to switch the cooker on, there was a flash and a bang, and all the lights went out. I dropped my glass, which Will had just topped up with champagne, and then started to cry again.

"Come on," Will said. "Text Julian and tell him we've gone to the pub."

Fifteen minutes later, I'd changed back into my pink top and repaired my face, and was sitting at a table with a huge glass of white wine, and Will. It felt weird that this man, who I'd only met that afternoon, had already scrubbed my oven, mopped champagne off my kitchen floor and given me a few tentative pats on the shoulder while I sobbed like a gibbering loon.

But, somehow, I couldn't feel uncomfortable with him. He seemed to have taken it all in his stride, and because he wasn't embarrassed in the slightest by the situation, nor was I.

"So," he said, taking a gulp of his pint. "You and Julian – together at last. Living happily ever after?"

"I hope so." I smiled, conscious that my face was taking on the gormless, blissed-out look Wizzy had told me I assumed whenever I talked or thought about Julian. "It feels really strange, to be living together after months of having this totally long-distance relationship. And even today, obviously, I've hardly seen him because he's been at work."

"You'll have to get used to that," Will said. "Julian's a natural workaholic. Maybe when he gets made a professor he'll slow down a bit, but I doubt it. How did you two actually meet? You're not a mathematician as well, are you?"

"Oh, God, no. I'm rubbish at anything to do with numbers. I'm an artist – well, I want to be one, one day. I read fine art at uni, and painted quite a bit and even sold a couple of things, to people who must have been really kind or had really bad eyesight. But when I lived in Edinburgh I worked at a gallery, doing customer service stuff, mostly. Pouring wine at private views, persuading people to buy pictures, putting the decimal point in the wrong place on price stickers, all that stuff. I met Julian at my flatmate Wizzy's twenty-fifth birthday party."

I told him all about Wizzy and the lion, and us ending up in A&E, and he laughed and said it would make a great story to tell at our wedding. I felt a glow of excitement and pleasure, realising that Julian must have talked to Will about me in terms serious enough to make him think of that. Me and Julian, married. I'd thought about it before, of course I had, during the months without him. And it sounded as if Julian may have done, too.

"It's certainly not your average way of meeting someone," I said. "I was mortified. But he was really nice about it, and only a bit squashed. And then we got talking and we kind of hit it off, and we spent the next couple of days together, before he had to go back to Canada and I had to go back to work. And that was it. Apart from one weekend together in New York, our relationship has basically been brought to you courtesy of email and Skype. And Shutterly, obviously."

I meant it all to sound light-hearted, romantic and fun. And a lot of the time, those months of falling in love with thousands of miles between us, had been fun. I'd taken a selfie every day and sent it to Julian so he could see what my life was like, and, I hoped, remember what I looked like. The three nights we'd spent in New York had been unalloyed joy – walking together in Central Park in the sunshine, drinking overpriced cocktails at the Rainbow Room, eating greasy hot dogs in the street and licking ketchup off our fingers. And, mostly, hurrying back to our hotel room and having sex.

But I didn't tell Will about the horrible parts. The days I'd spent at work scratchy-eyed with exhaustion because we'd been Skyping until four in the morning. The week when all I got from Julian was radio silence – not a text, not an email, not a word. By the second day I was frantic with worry; by the fifth I kept having to sneak off to the loo at work to cry; by the seventh I was just furious. And then he'd called, quite calm, and told me he'd been finishing a paper for the *Canadian Journal of Mathematics*, and he was so sorry, he just hadn't been able to focus on anything else at all.

And of course the time when he arranged to come to Edinburgh for my birthday, and I'd spent weeks twitching with excitement and longing, trying on outfit after outfit and wondering if he'd think I looked beautiful in them. Then, when he called to tell me he couldn't come after all, because a colleague had lost his ten-year-old daughter to leukaemia and Julian had to cover his time off for bereavement, not even being able to be angry because a child had died and that was infinitely worse than how I was feeling.

"But it can't have been easy," Will said, as if he'd read my mind. "You must be bloody relieved he got this job in London and you can get on with having a normal life together."

I nodded. "Exactly. I just need to find a job too, make loads of friends, figure out how the Tube works and get Charles Saatchi to make an offer for one of my paintings. Then I'll be sorted. But what about you?"

I realised Will had been sitting patiently, listening to me bang on about myself, even buying me another glass of wine without me really noticing, and I'd hardly found out anything more about him at all. I snuck a look at his face. All I'd really noticed about him when we met was his height – he must be about six foot four, I thought. But he had a nice face, too, sort of angular – he'd be amazing to draw. I liked the way his blond hair stuck up in places, as if he'd tried to tame it but it had had other ideas. And his eyes… were they blue or green? Anyway, despite being absolutely not my type, I could see that he'd appeal to a girl who was in the market for someone tall.

Someone like Wizzy, when she got back from her travels, I thought. She's constantly bemoaning the dearth of men who she doesn't tower over in her beloved high heels. Since my spectacular success introducing Polly to Angus, who I'd met in my art history class, I'd become rather proud of my skills as a matchmaker. I imagined Wizzy and Will, Julian and I, a cosy foursome together. We'd have dinner parties, our kids would be best friends at school…

"What about me?" Will asked, jolting me out of my daydream just as I'd got to the bit about us holidaying in the South of France, our children playing hide and seek in the garden while we sipped rosé on a stone terrace with a view of olive groves.

"Have you got a girlfriend?" I blurted out.

"Yeah, kind of," said Will, dashing my hopes. "Charlotte. She's an intern at the PR firm we sometimes work with, but she's trying to break into modelling. We've been going out for about four months, although we had a bit of a blip last week. But we're back together. I think."

He thought? What did that mean? I was itching to know more about the beautiful Charlotte – as a model, I supposed, her being beautiful was a given, along with her being tall.

"What kind of a blip?" I asked, adding hastily, "or would you rather not talk about it?"

"It's okay." Will shrugged. "She's quite sensitive, that's all. And I guess I don't always get the boyfriend thing right. And work is a bit full-on, and she resents that, and gets upset. It's what you might call a volatile relationship."

I thought, that must mean that either Charlotte is a high-maintenance nightmare, or Will is flaky, unreliable and a bit of a dick. I knew which I wanted to be true.

"I'd love to meet her, anyway," I said. "You guys must come round some time. I can make dinner, if I ever get the cooker to switch on without tripping all the lights."

Will was in the middle of saying politely that that sounded like a great idea and we must get a date in the diary, when my phone buzzed, and it was a text from Julian saying he was about to get off the bus and would be there in five minutes. So I dashed off to the loo and combed my hair and put on more pink lipgloss, and bought us a round of drinks, including a beer for Julian, and when I turned to take them back to our table, there he was. In the flesh, in his tweed blazer, which I'd seen in so many photos but hadn't known the smell of until today. There was his hair, curling over his collar. There was the shirt I'd seen him pull out of the dodgy wardrobe just a few hours ago. And underneath it all was the body I'd revelled in last night, and would get to enjoy again tonight. Him! All mine! I still couldn't quite believe it. My heart gave a wonderful lurch of excitement and joy at seeing him, and I couldn't have cared less that he was two hours later than he'd said.

"Will's nice," I said to Julian later that night, as we lay in the too-narrow bed on the too-lumpy mattress, our heads on the too-thin pillows, all of which were beginning to become familiar, and even loved, because they were Julian's and mine.

"Mmmm," said Julian, running his fingertips over my left nipple. Even though we'd just fucked, my flesh went 'ping!', instantly on red alert at his touch.

"What's with Charlotte then?" I asked, trying to distract myself from the delicious, insistent pulse that had started again between my legs.

"Haven't met her," Julian said. "But from past experience, she'll be horrible."

"Really?" I said, intrigued.

"Yeah, since Will sold out and made his money, he's become some kind of walking honey pot." Julian turned over on to his back, so the beautiful, pale arc of his ribs was illuminated by the street lamp outside our window. Curtains, I added to my mental list, or blinds. I leaned over and kissed the place where the ivory smoothness of his abdomen just started to be dusted with copper hair. He smelled of me – of us.

"But why would she be horrible? Will seems so nice."

"That never stopped him getting knocked back. When we were undergrads together, Will couldn't pull to save his life. I got the girls. I got the firsts, too."

I felt a pang of jealousy. What girls? How many? But it didn't matter, I told myself. What mattered was us, here, now.

"And then the last few years, he was all about work," Julian went on. "Now I guess he's back in the game, but the only women he seems to meet are in it for his bank balance. His last girlfriend was a gold-digger, and a bit of a psycho to boot. I haven't met this Charlotte, but that's what she'll be like, for sure. Some vacant stunner who doesn't care about him, only about what's in it for her. Not like you, my gorgeous, darling Stella. You're as kind and clever as you're exquisite, and I am just so, so glad you're here with me at last, and we're going to be together forever."

He rolled over, propping himself up on one elbow, and the light from outside now illuminated his high, beautiful forehead and his perfect, smiling teeth.

"God, I want you so much," he said, and I wanted him too, and I let him, and I loved it, even though it hurt because of all the sex we'd had in the last twenty-four hours, to make up for what we hadn't had before.

CHAPTER THREE

The prince and the princess were very happy, but they were very poor.
Princess Stella's meagre store of gold was running ever lower, and
she did not know what they would do when it was all gone. 'If only
I had a fairy godmother,' she sighed...

Over the next few weeks, Julian and I began to get into
a routine. Each morning, I'd wake up with his arms
around me and his warm breath on my neck. I'd turn over,
still half asleep, and rest my head on his chest, feeling the
drowsy warmth of him, breathing in the smell of his skin.
Then we'd be interrupted by the fierce buzzing of his phone,
followed almost immediately by the beep of its alarm.

I got used to the frantic rush of him getting ready for
work – when I suggested setting the alarm fifteen minutes
earlier, he said, "What, and have less time in bed with the
most beautiful woman in the world?" Which was hard to
argue with, of course, especially as he almost always had
time to bring me a cup of the tar-like instant coffee he likes,
while I luxuriated under the duvet.

He kissed me goodbye, grabbed the battered leather
satchel he used as a laptop bag, and went crashing out of
the flat. And then the silence descended, and the long day
stretched ahead of me, needing to be filled with things
other than waiting for him to come home.

It wasn't too bad at first. I scrubbed every inch of the flat, until my hands were dry and sore, my nails broken and my cuticles a mess. I finished unpacking all Julian's books and the rest of my clothes. I went for runs on the common and met the huge, fearsome swan who guarded the pond and pecked my feet until I learned to bring bread for him, his demure wife and their cygnets. I made friends with Hussein who ran the corner shop, and sometimes he gave me free Turkish delight and dolmades. Quite often, I'd go and buy random things there that we didn't need – a lemon, a can of Sprite, a box of matches – just so I'd have someone to talk to for a few minutes.

I read the jobs section of the *Guardian* religiously every day, sending off what felt like hundreds of CVs in response to ads that said, "We carefully consider each and every application. However please be aware that interest in this position will be high. If you do not receive a response within thirty days, we regret that your application will have been unsuccessful on this occasion. Please do not contact us as feedback will not be supplied." I sent long emails to Polly and Wizzy, telling them how happy I was and how wonderful it felt to be living with Julian at last.

And once I'd done all those things, and had a cheese sandwich and an apple for lunch, I'd look at my watch and realise that Julian wouldn't be back for at least six hours, and the afternoon stretched ahead of me, as empty as a blank canvas and even more daunting.

I tried to paint. I remembered how, when I was a teenager, I'd discovered the escape it gave me – the joy of losing hours in front of my easel, realising that I was creating something I could be proud of and other people might even think was good. I remembered the relief of finding that hours had passed during which I'd been, if not actually happy, at least not thinking about not being happy. They weren't much, those little watercolours inspired by the fairytales I'd read obsessively as a child and returned to at thirteen, but I loved them: the princesses in their elaborate dresses, the enchanted castles, the horses (those were a bastard to draw, and I never got them quite right).

So now, I took my sketchpad and sat in the park and drew the swans, but when I got back to the flat and put my sketchpad on the tiny fold-out dining table in the corner of the living room, it felt dark and oppressive. My brush couldn't seem to capture the sunlight, the limpid water, the sparkling white feathers of the birds. I checked my bank balance obsessively, alarmed at how quickly the deposit on the flat, the new pillows and the stock of cleaning products were eating into my meagre savings.

Anything I could think of to do seemed like an extravagance – getting the bus into town and having a cappuccino, walking to Primark and buying a scarf, browsing the charity shops for cushions to hide the cracks on our brown pleather sofa. Even the cost of my afternoon forays to Tesco and the gas I used cooking our dinner frightened me. I'd never not had any income – even as a student, I'd funded my art supplies and boozy nights out with friends by working nights in a bar.

I knew I needed to build a new social circle, but I couldn't think how. London was so huge, so teeming with strangers – where would I even start? I couldn't afford to join a gym or go to art classes. And I was conscious that, even if I did somehow conjure up a group of lovely new friends, I'd always be the one who was too skint to go out or, worse, who drank only tap water and ate only a starter, and then insisted on calculating her individual share of the bill instead of splitting it equally.

There were a few days when, in the middle of the afternoon, at a loss for a way to fill the hours, I just went to bed, pulled the covers over myself, even though it was October and still warm, and let myself slide into a deep, almost drugged sleep. I was only jolted awake when I heard our neighbour returning home after picking her baby up from nursery, which meant it was after six and I hadn't even thought about cooking our supper.

And there was another thing. With nothing to do all day, I was focused entirely on Julian. He was the one working – my job was to make our home as nice as it could possibly be. So I cooked, I cleaned, I ironed his shirts, I longed for him to come home in the evening. But he didn't really seem to notice. There were a couple of nights when he didn't get in until after eleven, saying he'd been distracted by something at work and eaten a takeaway, or not, he couldn't remember, but he wasn't hungry and why didn't we just go to bed? And then, after we'd had sex and I was drifting off to sleep, I'd be woken by the light of his laptop screen as he worked and worked into the night.

I didn't mind – Julian's work was his passion as well as his career, and it was his new job that had allowed us to be together. But did his genius and his brilliant prospects really mean he was incapable of putting a shirt into the laundry basket instead of leaving it on the floor for me to pick up, or replacing the lid on the jar of coffee? I loved him, but there were moments, when I was scrubbing the loo or emptying the hoover bag, when I found myself wondering, "Is this it? Is this what I signed up for?"

One night, as I was putting the finishing touches to a particularly uninspiring fish pie, made from value mackerel and prawns that were on offer because they were about to go out of date, I heard the familiar sound of Julian's feet on the stairs, accompanied by an unfamiliar thumping. I paused, a mashed potato-laden spoon in mid-air, and listened. He was early, which was in itself unusual, but it sounded as if he was bringing home a live goat.

The thumping stopped, and Julian's key scraped in the lock. I dropped the spoon back in the pan and ran to open the door.

"Hello! What the hell have you... Oh my God."

Julian was flushed and sweating, and standing next to him was a full-sized, paint-stained easel.

"I'll tell you what, this is one heavy bastard," he said. "I hope it inspires you, because it's nearly killed me. They were having a clear-out at the art school, so I grabbed this and brought it home on the bus. I thought a bit of kit from the Slade would make you paint even better than you do anyway."

I felt tears sting my eyes, and a huge grin break out on my face.

"We can put it by the window," I said, flinging my arms around his hot, damp shoulders. "The light there's so much better than at the table. I don't think anyone's ever given me a nicer present."

But later, as we ate our dinner off chipped plates on our knees, my mind drifted back to our precarious finances, and I said, "You can't carry on supporting me forever, you know. It's bonkers."

Julian put down his phone, which he'd been tapping away at intently, sending an email while he ate with his other hand.

"Of course you'll find a job, my little star," he said. It was the pet name he'd started calling me all those months ago, in his lovely, passionate emails. Twee, certainly, but a huge improvement on Declan's habit of calling me 'reassuringly expensive'. Hearing him say it made me feel a warm jolt of love somewhere deep inside me. "Anyone in their right mind would snap you up. But it might take a little while, and until you find something, I'll look after you. Academia isn't exactly lucrative but I won't let you starve, I promise. And if there's anything else you need, anything that'll make you happy, you must just say. Clothes, paints, a diamond ring, anything."

A diamond ring? I looked at him. He was smiling, looking pleased and almost shy. He didn't mean it, I told myself. We'd been together for no time at all. I loved him, of course – I was dizzy with love for him. There was a part of me, the sensible part, the part that was like my Mum, that warned me against passion, against rushing into things. But, at that moment, I knew that Julian wasn't just the best thing in my life – he was the only thing.

I put my fork down, suddenly not a bit hungry any more. Although the fish pie was, to be fair, decidedly minging. Julian took my hand.

"I adore you, Stella. You're everything to me. Since I met you, I've only really felt alive when I'm with you. I think about you all the time. I walk around in a daydream at work, longing to be back here with you. Little things like money are nothing when you've got the kind of love we have. True love, once-in-a-lifetime love. And we're so lucky to have found it. So many people don't – they go through life with good-enough marriages, cold marriages. We're not like that."

"No," I said. "We're not." I looked at him, his perfect, pale skin, his green eyes that were like chips from a broken wine bottle, sometimes dark as moss, sometimes brilliantly sparkling. I pushed back the lock of hair that flopped over his forehead, which I never tired of touching. "I can't believe how lucky we are."

"We are lucky," he said gravely. "I don't ever want to forget just how fortunate I am to have you. And I don't want your happiness to be spoiled by worrying about the little things. I'm going to take care of you, always, I promise."

He took me in his arms and I felt the familiar, delicious, melting desire for him. It was stupid even to think about feeling trapped. What did a bit of boredom matter when, every evening, I had this?

"I love you so, so much," I whispered. He took me in his arms, pressing all the doubt and uncertainty out of me. Later, we fell asleep there on the horrible sofa, and when I got up the next morning I had to scrape the crusted, congealed remains of our supper off the plates before I could wash them up.

The next day, I did the rounds of all the pubs and coffee shops within walking distance of our flat, asking whether they needed waitresses. Four said no, they'd had to let people go recently because business was so slow. Another couple said the managers weren't in, but took my name and number, promising to call me back (I'm still waiting).

The manager of one pub said, "You've come at a good time, blondie, I've just had one of my chicks walk out. Come through to the back and let's have a chat." The chat took the form of him gazing at my chest and stroking my arm repeatedly, and telling me I'd need to 'show a bit more flesh' if I wanted to make good tips. Skin crawling, I made my excuses and left, saying my phone contract was new and I couldn't actually remember the number, but I'd call and give it to him (he's still waiting).

By lunchtime, only one other bar had said they were looking for people, but they'd informed me quite matter-of-factly that there was an unpaid training period, a fee for the uniform, and all the tips went to making up the minimum wage for the bar staff and the people working in the kitchen. I decided that times might be hard, but I wasn't quite desperate enough to subject myself to such blatant exploitation, so I said I'd give it some thought, and turned for home and my cheese sandwich.

As I ate, I tapped out a despondent email to Wizzy.

Hey babe

Wish I could say I was bringing you exciting news from sunny Streatham. But a) it's pissing with rain, and b) the only news I have is that things with Julian are good – we are sick-makingly loved up and he gets more amazing every day, but you knew that already so it's SO not news.

I CANNOT find a job. It's shite, you'd think there'd been a recession or something. Have sent off spam-worthy quantities of CVs for proper jobs and resorted to looking for bar work, and even then am getting knocked back. What's next? Cleaning? Stringfellows? (NOOO!)

How are you, gorgeous girl? And more importantly, where are you? Is it Tibet still or have you crossed the border into China (cue dramatic James Bond theme music)?

Write soon, I need you to make me laugh!

Mwah

Sx

Not for nothing had Wizzy been a rising star in Unilever's marketing department. Whatever she did, whether it was studying, getting plastered and dancing until seven in the morning, or falling off lions, she did it wholeheartedly. So it shouldn't have surprised me that, despite being on the other side of the world, she threw herself into solving my employment problem. That same evening, I got a reply to my email.

Stella Griffiths, how many times have I had to tell you off for being DEFEATIST? Of course you will find a job, and we've been out of recession for months. Anyway, why didn't you ask me earlier? You need to talk to Martha – she's opened a cutesy café in Balham and apparently the yummy mummies are loving it. I have no idea if that's anywhere near Streatham but I've sent her your details and she will get in touch if she needs a hand slinging cheese toasties at her insufferable clientele.

On Sunday I am running the Great Wall of China half-marathon! (When I say running, I may be crawling by the end...) There will be blisters in my future!

Love you

Wizzy

PS – I shagged an Aussie boy last night. He was hot, but I realised halfway through that his eyebrows looked like they'd been put on upside-down. Freaked me right out.

Not for the first time, I felt a pang of envy for Wizzy's insouciant attitude towards men. It's not so much that she's slept with lots of people, although she has – more than me, anyway. It's that she manages to have and enjoy all these casual flings without them leaving the slightest dent in her self-belief. Wizzy would have kissed upside-down-eyebrow man goodbye and strolled away without a backward glance, and with a funny story to add to her repertoire.

When I was single – before Julian, that is – if I met someone I liked, I'd spend days in agony, boring my flatmates and myself by mooning around going, "He hasn't texted. He's not going to text, is he? I shouldn't have slept with him. Oh God, why did I sleep with him, and now I like him and he hasn't texted and I saw he posted on Facebook so his phone's definitely working…" and so on. Which is why I ended up having a succession of boyfriends who I didn't even like all that much – if they did seem interested in me, I was so overwhelmed with relief and gratitude I'd go out with them and not notice for months that they were rubbish in bed or popped their collars or read *Zoo* magazine on the loo.

I pondered on this for a while, thinking how amazing it was that Julian and I had found each other and I'd never have to sleep with a *Zoo* reader or collar-popper again, or worry about whether my phone was going to ring. Then I sent Martha an email, and spent the rest of the afternoon waiting for her to ring me, obsessively checking my phone every five minutes just like the old days.

Eventually evening came, and I gave up waiting for Martha's call and started waiting for Julian to get home. Long after I'd eaten my jacket potato and chucked his in the bin, I heard his feet on the stairs.

"Hello, my little star," he said. "God, I'm shattered. Got caught up at work, I didn't realise it was so late. Were you worried? Shall we go straight to bed?"

"Julian," I said, much later, as we lay in each other's arms. "Aren't you bored?"

"Bored? How could I be? I've got work, and I've got you."

"Okay," I said. "But I haven't. Got work, I mean. I get lonely, being here all day on my own."

"You mustn't feel lonely," he squeezed me tighter in his arms. "Not when I'm here."

I looked at his face in the dim light. He looked concerned, but also puzzled, and I realised that he genuinely didn't get it.

"Having you is wonderful," I said. "But I need other people, too. I'm used to being with people all day at work, seeing my flatmates in the evenings, going out. I miss that. Can't we go out sometimes? Go to a club? We're in London, there's so much to do and I feel like all I'm seeing is the inside of the flat and the highlight of my day is going to bloody Tesco." My voice cracked.

"I'm not stopping you from going out," Julian said. "You don't need my permission to make new friends. And you're coming to my work end-of-year thing next month, remember?"

I tried to make myself sound as reasonable as he did. "No, obviously you're not stopping me from doing stuff, but it would be fun to do more things together, wouldn't it? Meet Will and his girlfriend for a drink? That kind of thing. We could even invite them round for supper."

I remembered the long, chaotic evenings in our flat in Leith, sitting round the kitchen table with Polly and Angus and Wizzy and whoever she was seeing, and our other friends dropping in for drinks, and later heading out into town in a big, lairy crowd and dancing until late, and happily comparing hangovers the next day while Polly fried great mountains of bacon and eggs.

"Okay," Julian said. "Good idea. I'll text Will tomorrow."

"Brilliant!" I said. "That would be amazing. Get them to come over soon, maybe on Friday? It'll be a whole one hundred percent increase in my social life, from no plans to one."

"You can't express zero as a percentage, little star," Julian said, but before he'd finished explaining why, I'd fallen asleep.

The next morning, when I checked my email, and there at last was a message from Martha.

Hi Stella

Thanks for your email – Wizz told me you might get in touch. I'm sorry the job hunt isn't going so well. It's tough out there, isn't it? I don't need any help in the restaurant right now, but there's another idea I'd really like to discuss. Any chance you're free next Wednesday? Come and meet me at the café and have some lunch and we can chat about it. I'd love to see you again.

Mx

I accepted and excitedly entered the date in my diary. Dinner with Will and Charlotte, and now lunch with Martha to talk about some mystery project – this was beginning to feel like progress.

Chapter Four

Once upon a time there was a handsome prince who had journeyed for many years in distant lands, seeking his fortune. Now, his purse swollen with treasure, he returned to his homeland, ready to seek a fair lady and offer her his hand in marriage. He began courting a princess who was as regal as she was beautiful, thinking that he would make her his bride. But she was not as she had seemed…

"Are you sure I look okay?" I asked Julian for the hundredth time, balancing precariously on our bed so I could see most of my body in the tiny mirror above the chest of drawers.

"You look amazing. You always do, but when you're dressed like that… Mmmm." He put his hands around my waist and lifted me carefully down. "In fact, as they're not due to arrive for ages yet…"

He pulled me close, his hands pressing insistently into my hips, pulling me closer to him. It took a supreme effort of will, but I said, "As if! I haven't just spent an hour and a half getting ready for you to smudge my make-up and unstraighten my hair."

I realised that it had been weeks since I'd bothered to do much more with myself than clean my teeth and keep the reforestation programme that nature had introduced on my legs more or less in check. Make-up, nice clothes – it just didn't seem worth the effort when there was no one but Hussein at the corner shop to see the slap, I had no money for clothes and the extent of Julian's and my social life had shrunk to watching reruns of *The IT Crowd* together before bed.

But tonight was different – tonight Will was coming for dinner with the mysterious Charlotte, who Julian and I had yet to meet. Of course, it wasn't like we were going anywhere fabulous, and I was all too painfully aware that our flat didn't warrant dressing up. But still, it was an occasion worthy of more than boyfriend jeans from Primark and a vintage Nirvana T-shirt appropriated from Julian's side of the wardrobe. I wanted him to be proud of me, fancy me even more than he normally did, so I'd put in some serious effort.

The thing is, because I'm slim and I've got long blonde hair, people, especially girls, tend to look at me and at first glance assume I've struck it lucky in the looks lottery. But this just isn't true. I've got short legs and a chest that no amount of mega-boost silicone inserts in my bras can redeem. If I'm tired, or stressed, or don't lavish on it the kind of care you'd give a particularly fragile bonsai tree, my skin freaks out and goes red and flaky and spotty, all at once. My eyelashes and eyebrows are so pale you can hardly see them, and I have horrid nails. And just in case I wasn't aware of all this, Melinda Massey, the school bully, and all her cronies used to chorus, "Nice from far, far from nice," when I walked past them in the corridor.

So my preparations for our dinner party had taken a bit of time and a lot of effort. I'd been to TK Maxx and rummaged around in the beauty section and found a tube of Elemis face mask for a fiver, and lain down with it smeared all over my face and cucumber slices on my eyes, praying that Julian wouldn't come home unexpectedly early. I'd shown no mercy to my cuticles, filed my nails and painted them a pale, matte pink. I'd straightened my hair, ironing out every last trace of frizz. I was wearing one of my less shabby pairs of jeans and a sparkly, backless black top that had seen good service on many nights out with Polly and Wizzy in Leith.

My own preparations were complete, and it was time to turn my attention to the food.

"Would you mind just wrapping the garlic bread in some tinfoil?" I said to Julian. "And then doing the dishes while I make a salad?"

I felt like a bit of a slavedriver, especially as Julian had already tidied away his books and papers, which seemed to spread like weeds over every available surface, and been to Tesco to buy ice. However, I'd realised that if I didn't chivvy him like mad, he would slope off to the bedroom and I'd find him there half an hour later, glued to his laptop and claiming he hadn't heard me calling him. So delegation it was – after all, he'd offered to help and Will and Charlotte were his friends.

As a child of the nineties, I was pretty much brought up on microwaved cottage pies and those chicken Kiev things that spurted lava-hot garlic butter into your mouth and made your breath smell for days. The most actual cooking Mum ever did was cutting up chips and deep-frying them in a wire basket encrusted with old oil, to go with our fish-shop battered cod on Fridays. She always said that takeaway fish was one thing, but buying chips when you could make them perfectly well yourself was wanton extravagance.

So, anyway, I never learned to cook from Mum when I was growing up. During my short-lived career as a Brownie, I attained my cookery badge by learning useful skills like baking rock buns, assembling a crack-free Swiss roll and cooking eggy bread over a campfire. And then I moved in with Wizzy and Polly. Wizzy was permanently on a diet and lived on salad, and I was quite happy to eat jacket potatoes, or toast and marmite, or nothing. It was Polly who was the gourmet in our household. On our first night in the flat, I came home to a delicious smell that literally stopped me in my tracks, and I said, "Oh my God, what are you doing?"

"Making a Thai prawn curry," said Polly airily. "I thought we should have a housewarming dinner. There's puréed mango in the fridge and a bottle of prosecco, so we can make sort-of-bellinis."

"How do you know how to do this stuff?" I asked her, awe-struck, and she told me she'd done a cordon bleu course during her year out, and worked as a hostess in a swanky London cocktail bar, and 'just sort of learned as I went along'. Over the next few years I picked up quite a bit from Polly, but my repertoire was still awfully limited – as was our kitchen. So, following a Facebook consultation with Polly, I'd decided to play it safe and make spaghetti carbonara, garlic bread, salad and tiramisu for dinner. According to Polly, it was so retro it was right back on the cutting edge of foodie fashion.

When the expected knock on the door came and I ran to open it, there was Will, alone, holding an Uncorked carrier bag clanking with posh wine and a box of Godiva chocolates. We ushered him in and sat him down and Julian gave him a beer, and then I suppose we must have looked questioningly at him, because he sighed, took a gulp of his drink and said, "Charlotte's on her way. She texted to tell me she was running late."

He didn't quite roll his eyes, but the guarded, pissed-off expression on his face told me quite clearly that running late was business as usual for Charlotte, and that Will was none too pleased about it.

I left the two of them chatting about a new biography of Alan Turing that Will had read and Julian wanted to, and went through to the kitchen and started frying pancetta and separating eggs. As I watched the whites running through my fingers, anticipating the moment when the yolk would try and escape too, I wondered what possessed a man like Will to go out with a girl he didn't appear to like very much.

I didn't know him well, of course – a few drinks down the Five Bells isn't much of a basis on which to assess someone's character. But Will, in spite of his success and his flashy apartment, seemed like a genuinely nice person. Anyway, he was Julian's friend by definition that must make him thoughtful and kind – so what was he doing with the sort of gold-digger Julian had suggested Charlotte might be?

Just then, the door-knocker crashed again, startling me so much that I almost squashed an egg yolk. By the time I'd washed my hands, Charlotte had arrived and my questions were answered.

She was the most stunning girl I'd ever seen in the flesh (and that includes the time Wizzy and I spotted Camilla Thurlow buying knickers in Topshop on Princes Street).

She had the kind of expensive, flawless glamour that takes far more than an afternoon's titivating to achieve. Her hair was glossy, a rich, deep brown with shades of chocolate and chestnut and a hint of gold running through it – the sort of colour that takes hours in an expensive salon to achieve, yet looks perfectly natural (I know, because Wizzy told me all about it when she was working for Unilever and going through what she called her Corporate Brunette phase). Her skin glowed, literally glowed from within like a pearl, whether from some sort of magic shiny make-up or chemicals or lasers or just being able to sleep as much as she wanted I couldn't possibly say. Her dress was the particular shade of chartreuse that was right in fashion, right then, and would stop being in fashion in about three days' time.

I watched Julian taking her coat with a sort of reverential air, as if Bayonetta had just walked into our flat, and suppressed a flare of jealousy. But I couldn't help imagining what my Mum would say about her: "Face like a bulldog chewing a wasp." I also noticed that she'd arrived empty-handed, apart from her tiny violet handbag, from which she extracted a packet of Marlboro Lights and lit one without asking. Although Julian can't bear smoking, he said nothing, and I felt my resentment level ratchet up a notch.

"So this is, like, Streatham," she said. "Oh my God. I didn't even realise it was an actual place. I thought it was made up, like Walford, or whatever. SouthwestEnders." And she laughed merrily at her own joke, puffing smoke from between her pouty scarlet lips. "The Uber man who brought me looked totes terrified, I think he feared for his alloys. But I made it!"

Charlotte paused for a second, so we could all appreciate just how thrilled we were that she had, indeed, made it.

"And you must be Julian. Will says you're, like, an actual genius. I've never met a genius before. And Stella, Will says you're from Edinburgh."

I waited for her to say she'd never met an actual Scottish person before, but she didn't.

I said, "I'm from Dundee originally. I just went to uni in Edinburgh, and then stayed because I liked it."

Charlotte said, "Oh my God, the festival! That is like, so cool. My friend Marcus did a thing there this year, or it might have been last year. But I'm sure you know him. Everyone in Edinburgh does. Marcus Urquhart?"

I tried to channel Wizzy, and the kind of hilarious yet crushing reply she'd come up with, or Polly, and how her easy kindness would have totally defused the situation. But I couldn't. I looked at Will's stony face and Julian's rapt one, and said, "I'll open some more wine and put the pasta on."

The hiss of the boiling water hitting the hot pan drowned out whatever Charlotte said next. I chucked in some spaghetti and went back into the living room with a few plates and some knives and forks.

"Can I give you a hand with anything, Stella?" Will offered, but I said, no thanks, I'd be fine, and slammed the plates down on the table together with a new bottle of wine, and leaned against the door frame so I could listen to the conversation without actually having to participate in it.

"So, Charlotte," Julian said, bright spots of colour appearing on his cheeks when he said her name, "Will tells me you're a model."

I remembered what Will had told me, which was that Charlotte was actually working for free at a PR company while she looked for modelling jobs, but I didn't want to appear bitchy and jealous (even though that was exactly how I felt), so I said nothing.

Charlotte inspected her fingernails. "Yah," she said.

Will said, "Charlotte's just got back from Milan. She's had a hectic time recently with all the fashion weeks."

"Yah," Charlotte said again, yawning hugely and displaying her pretty white teeth. "It was totes tiring. I was networking all day, and you have to start at like five a.m. if you want to go to the gym, which I do, natch, and then you're networking, like, all day, and then there are parties all night and that's what you're there for really, isn't it?"

She gave Julian a sidelong glance under her sweeping fringe and bit her thumbnail. Julian actually squirmed in his chair, and I wished with all my heart that I hadn't been too well brought up to throw the salad over her head.

"The Prada afterparty was awesome," Charlotte went on, flicking her hair over first one shoulder, then the other. "Kim and Kanye were there and I was talking to Carine Roitfeld when they arrived and she was like, 'Darling, her shoes are so Fall 2013.' I literally pissed myself."

"Why don't we have some food," I said, "before we all *literally* starve to death?"

I escaped back to the kitchen and busied myself draining the pasta and adding beaten egg yolks, butter and pancetta. I tasted it, then added a huge chunk of extra butter, on the basis that a moment on Charlotte's lips would mean a lifetime on her hips. But my efforts were in vain, because when I returned to the table carrying the steaming bowl of spaghetti – which smelled absolutely gorgeous – Charlotte was standing up and Julian was helping her put on her coat.

"Yah, so, like, soz, but we can't stay," she said. "My agent just texted me and she's been totally let down by some girl who was meant to be doing this launch tonight at Chinawhite. She needs me there, like, half an hour ago. Coming, babes?"

Will pushed back his chair and took a large gulp of wine. "Nope," he said. "I'm staying, seeing as we were invited for dinner and Stella's gone to a lot of trouble. I'll see you out."

The two of them walked to the front door and I listened agog as they had a fierce but whispered row. I couldn't make out anything they said, until Charlotte said, "Well, fine, be like that then," and the door slammed.

Will came and sat down again. "Right. Sorry about that."

There was an awkward silence, during which I spooned some spaghetti on to our plates.

"Is she going to be okay?" I asked.

"She's fine," Will said. "There was no work emergency. That was just Charlotte-speak for a better offer. She never has work things if I'm taking her to Nobu or the Chiltern or away for the weekend."

Julian gave a sort of manly grunt that I supposed was meant to indicate sympathy.

Will said, "Anyway. I think it might be about time to pull the plug on that, but I'm not going to let her spoil our evening. I'm starving and this looks great."

I suppose it was the novelty of having someone to talk to who wasn't Julian, and the fact that I'd had my first glass of wine five hours ago, to celebrate putting the tiramisu in the fridge to set, and not really stopped. Or it might have been that the lovely Sancerre Will had brought was just so delicious compared to Tesco Simply Soave. Or maybe it was missing Polly and Wizzy, and thinking how much better it would be if Will's girlfriend was there, but not vile Charlotte – someone who'd ask me about my painting, and suggest we meet for coffee, and become a friend.

Anyway, I drank far too much, way more than I had for ages, and when we'd finished the pudding and Julian was making coffee, I said to Will, "You know what I reckon is the problem?"

"Problem with what?" he asked, topping up my glass.

"With you," I said. "Well, not with you, obviously, because you're lovely. But with you and girls?"

Will looked a bit embarrassed, but I didn't care.

"The problem," I said, "is you're too good on paper. I know it's rude to talk about money. But nice women, ordinary women, meet you and just assume you're out of their league because, as everyone who reads the *Daily Mail* sidebar of shame knows, rich men only date hot models. Actresses. Whatever. Not just because you're hot – although you are seriously hot."

Will was looking increasingly mortified, but I ploughed on regardless.

"Properly hot. And you're lovely. I think you are, anyway. But the thing is, you're rich too. So you end up with a girl like Charlotte, who, I hate to say it, will never love anyone as much as she loves herself."

Will laughed. "I'm not rich! As my financial advisor keeps telling me, I'm one dotcom crash away from the JobCentre. You're making me sound like I'm Mark Zuckerberg, and I'm so not. And anyway, look at George Clooney – he's loaded and he's married to a human rights lawyer."

"But she could be a model, if she wasn't clever enough to be a human rights lawyer," I objected. "It's, like, the law of unintended consequences. Or something." I sensed that I was losing the thread of my argument a bit, so I said to Julian, who'd come back with three mugs of instant coffee and a pint of milk, "I'm right, aren't I?"

"Right about what?" said Julian, and I wondered if he'd actually been listening to our conversation.

"That Will needs to find a nice girlfriend, not someone horrid like Charlotte who's only out for his money. Or like whatshername, who you said…"

Julian squeezed my thigh under the table, quite hard. I shut up.

"I guess what Stella's saying, mate, is that Charlotte is a bit materialistic. Nothing wrong with that, necessarily, but it's not what you want in a partner, is it? Look at us, we're brassic skint and we don't care, because we have each other."

He stroked my face and I kissed him lightly on the lips, and we looked at each other for a long moment. I could see four of his eyes, swimming blearily in and out of focus, but that didn't make it any less romantic.

"Being in love is so... It's wonderful. Being together. Knowing someone cares about you more than anything else," I said. "We just want everyone to be as happy as we are, especially you, because you're so nice. You're the nicest man I've met for ages and ages, apart from Julian."

I saw Will catch Julian's eye and give a small, wry smile.

"I'm made up for you two," he said. "But I think it's time for me to go back to being single."

"But you meet people at work, right?" said Julian.

Will laughed. "Like, no. Do you? How many women in the maths department at UCL?"

"Well, there's Francine," Julian said. "She's the faculty administrator. And we've got two post-docs who are women. But I take your point. If I was single, I wouldn't think work was the obvious place to start looking."

"Exactly," said Will. "We're huge about getting more women into STEM, Louise had this total thing about it, rightly so. So we try to recruit female developers when we can, but as soon as there's a talented graduate on the market it's like a gold rush, everyone wants them and sometimes we lose out. So the company's still eighty percent blokes. And I couldn't date anyone at work, anyway, it would be totally unprofessional."

Julian, apparently relieved to have the chance to change the subject, launched into a discussion about the challenges of achieving gender diversity in science, technology, engineering and maths, and I gathered up our plates and started washing up.

Swaying slightly, up to my elbows in hot, soapy water, I thought about living happily ever after, and how wonderful it felt to be doing it. I imagined the sort of woman who Will might fall in love with, who'd love him back like he deserved. I imagined someone pretty, funny, clever and kind – someone like Wizzy, except of course Wizzy had never met him, and wasn't likely to for months, by which stage he'd be unhappily ensconced with another Charlotte. Then I had an idea, and it struck me with such force that the glass I was rinsing slipped straight out of my hand and on to the floor. Happily, being a sturdy Ikea glass designed to take far worse punishment, it just crashed and bounced, and I picked it up and went back to the table, armed with a bottle of our cheap and nasty wine from the fridge.

"I have it!" I said. "I know exactly what you need to do. You need to go undercover."

"What?" said Will.

"Under. Cover." I thumped my glass on the table for emphasis. "You know that story, right? About the princess who kissed a frog, and then he turned into a handsome prince. That's what you need to do."

"What, so if Charlotte's a frog and I kiss her, then she won't be horrible and I won't have to dump her?" Will said. He'd had rather a lot to drink too.

"No! Not that at all. You meet a lovely girl, somehow. Someone who doesn't care about money, and material stuff. Someone who loves you for yourself. Because she doesn't know you were voted one of the UK's top 100 most eligible bachelors by… anyway." I paused, not wanting Will to know how extensively I'd Googled him.

"So you meet this girl, and you fall in love, because she's just nice and genuine, like you. But she doesn't know who you are because you're operating in deep cover. And then, when you're sure, you show her your bank statement, or take her to the Maldives, or something, and you're like, 'So you get me, and the luxury holidays, and the Mulberry bag and the car and the VIP pass to Glastonbury, and… well, me.' And she goes, 'Ohemeffgee, I kissed a frog and he turned out to be a handsome prince.' And voilà – you live happily ever after."

Julian said, "My little star, that's the stupidest idea I have ever heard."

CHAPTER FIVE

"Charlotte. Please, Charlotte, for God's... Charlotte. Calm dow..."

But Will's protestations were useless, or at any rate too late. His girlfriend was already reaching towards the stainless steel, hourglass-shaped object that stood on the floating shelf behind her. In his office in Shoreditch, Will had a cabinet bulging with trophies, but he kept this, the first award he'd won and the most precious, here at home.

Charlotte gripped the trophy in her Shellac-manicured hand. It looked a bit like a dumbbell, Will thought, as she swung back her toned, slender arm, took aim and prepared to launch it at him.

"You fucking bastard!" she screamed. Will had noticed before that when she was angry, she dropped her husky smoker's drawl and her voice became harsh and shrill. He'd also noticed that when she knew she was in the wrong, her strategy was always to go on the offensive. It was a tactic he'd successfully adopted when playing Minecraft, but relationships, he felt, ought to be different from online gameplay. Surely?

"You fucking showed me up," Charlotte went on. "How do you think I felt, turning up at Chinawhite on my own and having to stand in the queue like a total loser? If you'd been there we could have walked straight in. How do you think I felt when Callista asked me where my boyfriend was?"

"Maybe you should have explained to Callista that your boyfriend was where we'd both arranged to be?" Will said. "You know, having dinner with my friends? As opposed to flouncing out because you'd decided you'd rather do something else?"

Her voice and manner might have changed entirely, but anger didn't make Charlotte any less beautiful. Her sapphire eyes (yes, they owed their extraordinary colour to expensive tinted contact lenses, but the effect was none the less devastating for that) flashed against the livid red of their whites. The swishy curtain into which she spent hours tonging her dark hair kept its shape even though she'd buried her sobbing face into it just minutes before. And her gym-honed figure was displayed to its best as she leaned back on one taut, long leg; her breasts outlined against her green dress, moving in a thoroughly distracting bounce as she sent the Appy trophy flying across the living room with lethal force, in the general direction of Will's head.

Not for nothing was Will a regular winner of the Tech City Ping Pong Fight Club. Instinctively he ducked left, extending his right hand and snatching the hourglass from the air. God, it was heavy. If it had made contact it would have done some serious damage to him, or to the window behind him. He crossed the room, back to Charlotte, and put a hand on her shoulder while carefully replacing the award on its shelf.

"Seriously, Charlotte, you need to calm down," he said. "You wanted to go to this thing at Chinawhite instead of seeing my friends. Fine. It just tells me what I need to know. You're not that interested in my life."

"I hate you," she hissed again, but with less conviction. "You never come anywhere with me, ever. If you loved me…"

Will sighed. This was another bone of contention in his four-month relationship with Charlotte. Not only did his brutal working hours mean that he was often forced to cancel or change their plans at short notice, but he had failed to tell Charlotte he loved her, in spite of her persistent and increasingly unsubtle hints.

He patted her shoulder. It was four in the morning and he was knackered and still a bit pissed. He realised that waiting up for Charlotte to get home from wherever she'd been in order to have The Talk with her had been a mistake. It could have waited until the morning – or better still, until Monday, when he could have dumped her diplomatically by email. But that was the coward's way out, and Will hated cowardice.

Will was twenty-eight. His business was more successful than he'd ever dreamed possible. He'd been amazed, when he first met Charlotte, that she seemed interested in him – he'd assumed that she would be way out of his league. But his delight at her willingness to sleep with him had turned quite quickly to dismay as he realised that going out with her took more effort even than he put into his day job. And in spite of the ever-escalating rows, in spite of the fact that he had realised quite early on that they had absolutely nothing in common, every time he tried to bring their train-wreck of a relationship to a close, Charlotte turned on the tears and begged him to change his mind.

He didn't get it. He was supposed to be having fun, not having to deal with the kind of aggro he'd seen in his parents' marriage. He really didn't need this drama, he decided. In fact, he didn't need Charlotte, although he didn't want to hurt her. He hated seeing her cry. But clearly he was failing to make her happy, and the rows were no longer worth the compensation of athletic and inventive making-up shags when he eventually capitulated and apologised for things that weren't his fault. And he was all too conscious that what worried Charlotte was not so much being single as no longer having access to the money and status she enjoyed as Will's girlfriend. It was humiliating. No amount of sex was worth feeling like a mug – or indeed looking like one in front of his friends when Charlotte behaved... like Charlotte.

Ignite Digital's new head of marketing was due to start next week, so the PR function would be moving in-house – he wouldn't even have the embarrassment of seeing Charlotte in a work context any more. It was time to grow a pair, tell her it was over, and mean it.

Perhaps Stella had a point. Perhaps, after years of being single, he just didn't have a clue what he really wanted in a girlfriend. He remembered how it had been at school: the fierce competition to go out with the hot girls, and later, to sleep with the ones who were allegedly willing to sleep with you. He remembered the frantic, hormone-driven need to not be left behind, and how it led to awkward fumbles in girls' bedrooms, posters of Jared Leto or Thierry Henry sneering down on him from the wall, promising so much more than he could deliver. And then afterwards, looking at the girl and thinking, "Did I do okay? Did you like it? Do I even like you?" And suspecting that the answer to all three questions was a resounding No.

Will had never been in love. Those hasty shags at school, which he could count on the fingers of one hand, were followed by a six-month relationship with a girl called Audrey, who was sweet, clever and, once her braces came off, seriously pretty. But they'd been friends more than anything else, and they'd gone their separate ways to university with affection and without rancour.

Then, in his first year at Cambridge, he'd met Louise. He was knocked sideways by her charisma, awed by her intelligence, and kept awake at night by the image of her lush body. But Louise had other ideas, as she made very clear very quickly. She and Gavin had been together since they were fifteen, and she was very sure he was The One. For Will, she had bigger plans.

More impressive even than Louise's cleavage was her ambition. She wanted to make serious money – she knew she would, she just hadn't yet figured out exactly how. When Will told her about the software he was developing in his spare time – just for fun, when he needed a break from pure maths – she'd latched on to the idea. The app was going to be huge, she told him. She had the business acumen, he had the product.

They'd remained friends, and Louise's cast-iron confidence had been justified. Just months after she'd persuaded Will to jack in his PhD, which he'd been tinkering with increasingly haphazardly, and focus full-time on Shutterly, the business had gone supernova. Now, five years later, it was worth millions, on paper at any rate. And that meant Will was, too.

If getting the start-up going had been a plunge into the unknown and the intervening years a long, thrilling but exhausting swim with no chance to come up for air, Will had broken the surface to find himself in the midst of a swarm of wasps. Girls hadn't been particularly interested in him before – he was too geeky, he worked too hard, he had no time for fun. Now he'd apparently become some kind of poster boy for the digital age, and when he was introduced at award ceremonies and product launches as "Will Turner, you know, who founded Ignite Digital?" he found himself being mobbed by rapacious females. Flattered and bewildered, in a fit of choice paralysis, he'd picked first Melinda, a stunning blonde who was going to be an actress as soon as she got her big break, and then, when that didn't work out, moved on to Charlotte.

Well, he guessed he'd picked wrong. It was time to hit Escape.

"I'm going to order a cab for you, Charlotte," he said, in a voice that he hoped sounded kind but firm. "I'd like you to go, please. And I'd like my keys back. I'm sorry, but I don't think things are working out between us. You're a lovely person – I don't deserve you. But I can't give you what you need."

"You… Are you trying to dump me?"

"I think we should end this relationship." Will felt a deep weariness spreading over him. "I don't think it's going anywhere. I admire you, I think you're amazing, and beautiful, and we've had fun, but I don't love you. And I don't think you love me." He thought, but didn't say, you love my apartment and my bank balance, and the restaurants and clubs I can get us into, and you'd love the diamonds and the holidays you think you'd get if it lasted.

"What do you mean?" she said. "Of course I love you. I love you, like, desperately." She had started to cry again.

"I'm so sorry, Charlotte," Will said. "It's not you, it's me."

This time she was too quick for him. Cat-like, she ducked under his arm, grabbed the steel figurine again and hurled it at the window. The double-glazing barely halted its trajectory, and there was a silence that seemed to last a long, long time, but must in reality only have been a second or two, before they heard a sickening, shattering crash as it landed on the pavement twelve floors below.

CHAPTER SIX

The prince decided that, if he was to find a lady who was as pure in heart as she was fair of face, he would have to search for her in disguise. He emptied his purse of gold. He cast off his fine clothes and donned the humble garments of a shepherd. And thus attired, he set off into the world...

I woke up the next day feeling predictably vile. I hadn't had such a bad hangover since our great Farewell to Leith night out in August. My head felt like a Brazil nut at Christmas, when everyone's had a go at it with the crackers but its shell hasn't quite given in. My mouth tasted like I'd been sucking paintbrushes. I'd kicked the duvet off during the night, and I was sweaty, suffocating and freezing cold, all at once. There was no Polly to cook healing potato scones and square sausage. And worst of all, I was absolutely sure I would never be able to face Will again. What had I been thinking, putting myself in charge of his love life like that? He was Julian's friend, not mine, and I'd taken over the entire evening with my embarrassing burbling and my stupid idea. And I'd... Had I *flirted* with him? Oh God. I hadn't. Surely I hadn't.

I warily opened my eyes, adjusting slowly to the unwelcome daylight. Julian wasn't in bed but I could hear him moving about in the kitchen, and a few seconds later he came into the bedroom with a cup of his special treacly coffee.

"Morning, beautiful," he said.

"Oh shit, Julian," I mumbled, pulling the duvet up to my chin. "I'm so sorry about last night. What a total tool! I promise I won't embarrass you in front of your friends ever again."

Julian laughed. "You don't need to worry, Will likes you. How could he not? You're so funny and sweet, even if you get pissed and have daft ideas."

I sipped my coffee, winced as it hit my churning stomach and waited to see if I was going to be sick. I wasn't – in fact, I felt a bit better as the sugar and caffeine leached gently into my bloodstream.

"It was daft," I said. "Of course it was. I'm such a romantard. I blame you for turning me all soppy."

Julian got under the duvet next to me and pulled me close. "But feel how warm you are. I can forgive you for being soppy when you're this warm."

His hands moved slowly over my back and buttocks, cold at first, then increasingly hot, increasingly urgent. We didn't say anything more for a long time.

Then, later, as I lay with my head on Julian's shoulder, listening to his slowing heartbeat, he suddenly said, "It wouldn't work anyway, you know."

"What wouldn't?" I said.

"Your scheme about Turner's love life. Think about it for a second – picture the scenario. He meets some woman and says, 'Hi, I'm Will and I'm just a humble, regular bloke.' 'Lovely to meet you, Will, what is it you do for a living?' 'I have a software development start-up.' 'Really? What kind of software?' 'It's called Shutterly, it's a social media…' 'Oh, right, so you're the Will Turner whose app everyone on the planet has on their phone?' Game over."

"You're right, of course," I said reluctantly. "It did seem like a good idea, though."

"That's because you were completely shitfaced,"Julian stroked my hair, his gentle touch taking the sting out of his words. "Lots of things seem like a good idea under those circumstances. Like riding on lions, for instance."

"Stop!" I giggled, burying my face in his chest.

"Anyway, it's done now. Will won't mind, and neither do I." Julian kissed the top of my head, then pressed the button to wake up his phone, and I saw his attention slip inexorably away from me as he checked his emails. He stood up and drifted towards the door.

"I'm just… I'll be right back, okay?"

And I realised that any bright ideas I might have had about the two of us going for a picnic in the park together, maybe even out for a cheap lunch or to a museum, were going to come to nothing. Julian was working.

I picked up my phone, clicked the Facebook icon, and saw Polly was online.

"Hey, Pollster," I typed. "Wassup?"

"Finally, I can tell you!" she said. "I'm up the duff. Three months – the baby's due in March."

I stared at my phone for a moment, taking in this amazing news. Polly was going to have a baby. Polly was going to be a mum. She'd been off the booze for the last few weeks we'd lived in the flat, I remembered, but she'd dismissed that and her bouts of nausea as a stubborn stomach bug that she couldn't shake off, and I'd been too excited about my own imminent move to London to pay it much attention.

I felt a hectic jumble of emotions – joy for her, guilt that this huge change had been happening under my nose and I'd been too self-absorbed to notice, and a twinge of something else that felt a bit like regret. Nothing would ever be the same again.

"Squeeeee!" I typed. "O. M. G. I'm so excited for you. How did you manage to not say anything?"

"Mostly because if I opened my mouth I'd vom," she admitted. "I've been so sick, but now I've stopped. I've had my first scan and everything seems to be okay, and so I can start telling everyone. And I can eat again, and I'm getting fatter and fatter by the day. I look like Beth Ditto."

"NOT fat. Pregnant. Eating for two and making up for lost time. Anyway, Ditto = cool. How's the hotel?"

"Rammed with American tourists. They all want haggis and porridge even though it's still so warm, and they keep asking Angus why he isn't wearing the family tartan. But they'll pay for the new roof eventually, so I mustn't grumble. God, the smell of that haggis, though. Just thinking about it makes me want to spew again. How's London? Are you going to fabulous clubs every night with Julian?"

I didn't want to tell her that we actually never went anywhere, and the one time I'd suggested to Julian that maybe, instead of spending another Saturday night eating microwave pizza and watching telly, we might go into town and dance, he'd looked at me as if I'd suggested popping to Mars for the night, and said truculently that he didn't dance, never had and never would.

"I cooked dinner for his best mate last night. Remember, you gave me the recipe for Carbonara à la Polly? It was delish. I got hammered and made my name arse."

"Waaah! What did you do?"

"Best mate is extremely rich but his girlfriend was a psycho biatch from hell. Truly vile, you would hated her even more than I did. But he is v nice. So I had a stupid idea."

I filled her in on the Frog Prince scheme, and what a fool I felt for having suggested it.

There was a pause. I could see her typing away, and then her reply flashed up on my screen.

"But Stella, that is fucking genius! Of course he must do it. It would be so funny. And I bet it would work, too. It's not like lying to make yourself look better than you are – lying to look worse is totes different. It would be brilliant and you have to talk him into it. I'm counting on you."

"No way. It's a rubbish idea. Julian says so. It wouldn't work, and anyway, he'd have to meet these girls to even tell them the frog story, and he never meets anyone except at work, and they're all geeks like on *The Big Bang Theory*."

"Geeks shag too. Don't they? Never watched *BBT*. Anyway, durrr, this is 21ˢᵗ century. Hello? Online dating? There are millions of women out there desperate for relationships with nice men. Get him set up with a profile saying he's… dunno, a butcher or something, then wait for offers to flood in."

I sent a 'rolling on the floor laughing' icon. "Not going to happen. Have seen error of ways. I hit peak matchmaking with you and Angus, it's time to hang up Cupid bow and arrows."

Polly said, "Fiiine, whatevs. Here am I stuck in the sticks with only rich Americans and stash of tablet for company, piling on a stone a week, and you won't even be interesting."

"Sorry, Poll. Am worst friend ever. I'll try and come and stay, though, as soon as I've got some money."

Polly said she couldn't wait, then sent a final panicky message saying she had to go, it was time to serve the guests their morning tea.

"They want scones, then they don't eat the lemon sodding curd," she said. "So I do, out of jar with spoon. LARDY."

We exchanged kisses and she signed off.

Almost immediately, Facebook sent me a new alert. To my amazement, it was a friend request from Will. However much of a fool I'd made of myself, he seemed to be willing to forgive and forget. Awash with relief, I accepted, and a few seconds later, he sent me a message.

"Thanks again for last night, Stella. I had a blast and the food was delicious – you're a fantastic cook. I must return the favour some time, although Waitrose ready-meals are about the limit of my attainment in the kitchen."

I replied, saying it had been a pleasure and it was lovely to get to know Julian's friends better. My finger was hovering over the keyboard, about to type an apology for being a drunken, interfering git, when another message from him flashed up.

"I'm sorry to be a pain, but I think I left my other phone at yours – the Android one I use for work. Would it be okay if I pop round and pick it up? Don't worry if you're going out, it's not urgent."

"It's fine – come over any time. Am paralysed by hang-over and not going anywhere!"

But Julian was. When I stumbled through to the living room on my way to have a shower, he was sliding his laptop into his satchel.

"Little star!" he said, as if he'd forgotten I was there. "I've got to go into the office. Pick up some paperwork. I'll only be gone a few hours."

"Okay," I said. "Will's coming over, though, I'm not sure when. He wants to pick up his phone."

But Julian was already halfway out of the door. "Yeah, that's fine," he said. "See you later." The door slammed closed and I heard his feet on the stairs. I felt a chill pass over me, like when a cloud crosses the sun. He hadn't kissed me goodbye. He hadn't even heard what I'd said.

Then the thump of his footsteps reversed direction and the front door opened again.

"I love you," Julian said, flashing his amazing smile at me before turning again and thundering down the stairs again, even faster this time.

I shrugged off my dressing gown, left it in a heap on the floor, and went into the bathroom. "God, Stella, you look a right sight," I said to my reflection in the mirror. It was true – I hadn't cleaned my make-up off the night before and as a result had lumps of congealed mascara in the corners of my eyes and a spot erupting on my chin. My hair was a lank, matted mess. My nail polish was chipped from all the washing-up. And if I was a state, the flat was worse – there were pans still soaking in the sink, a forest of empty bottles were lined up waiting to be taken to the recycling bin, and a layer of sticky gunk had appeared on every surface in the kitchen I'd scrubbed the day before, as if the grease fairies had popped in overnight.

I might as well get it all sorted, I thought, then Julian could come home to his girlfriend and his home looking respectable. And, of course, when Will turned up, he wouldn't think I was a minger as well as a pisshead. I stepped gingerly under the feeble spray of the shower, scrubbed my face with a flannel and worked up a satisfying turban of shampoo lather. As the water sluiced away the last of my hangover, it occurred to me that maybe Polly had a point. Maybe what I'd suggested to Will wasn't such a terrible idea after all. I'd sound him out again about it, very diplomatically, just to see what he thought. And if he agreed with Julian that it was utterly daft and so was I, then that would be that. We'd never speak of it again.

An hour later, when I heard Will's knock, I'd straightened my hair, removed a clanking carrier bag of empty bottles and hidden the washing-up in hot, soapy water. I'd just finished painting my nails, so I used my wrists to turn the doorhandle.

"Sorry about this," I said, flapping my hands in the air as he kissed me on both cheeks. "Essential repair and maintenance is under way. I don't want to smudge them."

Will took my left hand and peered at my nails. "Pretty," he said. "Orange?"

"Coral," I corrected. "One of the key shades of the season, innit? Your phone's on the sofa where you left it, come in."

"I won't stay," he said. "You'll have had enough of me after last night."

"Have a cup of tea, at least. You'll have make it, though – I'm incapacitated for the next twenty minutes or so."

We went through to the kitchen and Will leaned against the countertop while the kettle roared slowly into action.

Will said, "So, anyway, about last night. I'm really sorry about how Charlotte... how she did a runner. It was really rude. Inexcusable."

"It's okay," I said. "Stuff happens. Sometimes people change their minds about things."

There was no point, I decided, in telling Will what I really thought about Charlotte and the way she'd behaved. Either he'd see sense and chuck her, or he wouldn't.

As if he'd read my thoughts, he said, "I finally ended it with her last night. I should have done it ages ago, but I kept putting it off because I knew it would be messy. And it was. It was grim."

And he told me how Charlotte had gone ballistic and twatted his Appy trophy through the window of his flat.

"It almost decapitated some bloke going past on his early-morning run," he said. "But luckily it missed him and hit my neighbour's BMW instead."

"Blimey," I said. "That's a bit of an over-reaction, isn't it? I mean, no one likes being dumped but normal people don't go around chucking things through windows."

"There's normal, and then there's Charlotte," Will said. "Never knowingly under-reacted. Anyway, I reckon that jogger's not the only one who had a lucky escape. So I'm back on the market, so to speak."

I cleared my throat and said, "You know, I was chatting to my friend Polly earlier. On Facebook – she lives up in the Highlands – and anyway, I told her about that crazy idea I had. About you."

Will poured boiling water on to teabags. "Milk and sugar? You mean the dating thing?"

"Just milk, please. Yeah, that. The thing is with Polly, I introduced her to Angus, her other half. He was in my art history class at uni – he's interested in art, because his family have this massive stately home, except now Angus and his brother Gray run it as a hotel, because otherwise they couldn't afford to keep it. The family used to have loads of really valuable antiques and family portraits and stuff before Angus's uncle Andrew flogged them, so he kind of grew up surrounded by art, and being interested in it. And my flatmate Polly – well, she was my flatmate then, she isn't any more, obviously – is gorgeous and ultra-posh, and I thought she and Angus would be perfect for each other. So I set them up on a date and now they're getting married and Polly's having a baby in spring."

I realised I'd been burbling away like a total idiot, and took a gulp of boiling tea to shut myself up.

Will was looking rather bemused. "Er, okay," he said. "Wow, that's a great story. Romantic."

"I wasn't just telling it randomly, I promise," I said. "The thing is, because of her and Angus, Polly thinks I'm this ace matchmaker. And she's not totally wrong. I mean, I did get her and Angus together."

"So you did." Will's face was deadpan, but I caught the faintest twitch at the corner of his mouth, and suspected he was about to start laughing at me.

"Okay! I'll stop trying to be tactful, I'm crap at it. So I told Polly about you, and the idea I had, and she thinks it's genius, and we – you – should totally do it."

"Wow," he said. "That was quite a sales pitch. Were you an estate agent in a previous life?"

I thought of the oily little man who'd given Julian and me the keys to our flat, assuring us that it was a charming, sun-filled little gem, newly decorated and with a land-lord who lived down the road and sorted out any prob-lems within a day. "No! How can you even suggest such a thing?"

"Sorry, Stella. That was below the belt," Will said, and we both laughed. "Anyway, I totally get what you're suggesting. But I can't imagine how it would work. It's not like you've got a whole portfolio of single girls and one of them would be perfect for me."

"Well, no," I said. I didn't want to admit to Will that since I'd moved to London, my circle of friends had dwindled to the size of a pinprick. "I mean, you'd probably get on really well with my friend Isabella, but she's away travelling at the moment. But that's what the internet is for. What we do is, you register on a couple of dating sites with a profile that's accurate, except we change your job to something really ordinary and not that well paid. Polly thought maybe you could be a butcher."

"I could so not be a butcher," Will said. "I was a vegetarian for ten years. I'm a total wuss about blood. I'd be a crap butcher."

"Okay, maybe not a butcher then," I said. "Polly does all the orders for the hotel, I expect she'd been buying mince or something just before we spoke, and it was on her mind. Something else, then. Something not glamorous, but a bit worthy. A nurse?"

"Too specialised," Will said. "Imagine if I was on a date with a girl and she choked on a burrito or something, and expected me to know what to do. I wouldn't have a clue."

"Fair point," I said. "Firefighter? No, that's way too glamorous. If someone liked your profile because she had a thing about rugged risk-takers in uniform, she'd end up disappointed."

"Thanks," said Will. "I can see this is going to be brilliant for my ego."

"I didn't mean that! I mean, you're… like, really good looking, and everything. But you're not the firefighter type. Firefighters are more…"

"More what? Manly? Less software-developery? Go on, Stella, dig that hole a little deeper." Now he really was laughing at me. I started to laugh, too.

"Sorry," I said. "That came out all wrong. So not a firefighter. How about a teacher?" I thought of the meagre wage Julian earned in academia, in spite of his PhD, his planet-sized brain and all the years he'd spent studying.

"Hmmm. That could work. There's this thing called Code Club that Louise, my business partner, makes us all do. She's really into giving back to the community. So we go into schools for a couple of hours every week or so and teach the kids basic programming. It's good fun. I could be a computer science teacher. I've been DBS checked and everything," he added proudly.

"Result! Worthy, not glamorous, with added non-child molester credentials. Perfect." I inspected my manicure, and discovered that the polish was dry and smudge-free. "You see? It would be really simple. It's just a question of taking the plunge, being open to new experiences. And it would be fun, too. I could help. I'd do the research for you, help weed out unsuitable candidates. I'd be a firewall in human form. We could have strategy meetings."

"That sounds like it might be a bit more fun than our weekly team meetings at work," Will admitted, smiling.

I flicked on the kettle. "Go on! Please say you'll do it? Best case scenario, you meet some beautiful, sweet girl who loves you for yourself. Worst case scenario, you go on a few dates and nothing comes of them. In fact, very worst case scenario, you put your profile up and no one responds at all. So either you get something amazing out of it, or you're back where you started. What could possibly go wrong?"

CHAPTER SEVEN

Princess Stella's fairy godmother could see that all was not well with her. 'Do not be sad,' she said. 'For I can help you.' And she waved her wand...

"So, yeah, like I said, I'm not really looking for waiting staff at the moment," Martha said. "But if... hold on one second."

She stood up, leaving me alone with my cup of organic hot chocolate and my chicken and tempeh salad. I took advantage of her absence to have a good look around the room. The café was small, tucked between a gift shop and an estate agent on the high street – I'd almost walked past it before I spotted the sign, which said 'Martha's Place' in curly gold script. Inside were about a dozen wooden tables and an assortment of chairs that looked like they'd been salvaged from skips. But they'd all been lovingly painted in pastel colours, and the room was flooded with sunlight.

Although it was a weekday, the place seemed to be doing a roaring trade in stone-ground wholemeal sandwiches and gluten-free muffins. Seated at the tables were groups of women – almost all women, I counted two men in the place: the chef, who Martha had introduced as Dan, and a bearded bloke with a baby in a sling. Most of the women had children with them, too – tiny ones in buggies, toddlers with chocolate moustaches from their babyccinos, preschoolers crunching on carrot sticks.

Martha was standing by one of the tables, which had just been occupied by a mother and her two children, a little boy in a Batman onesie and his sister, who was a few years older and wearing a One Direction T-shirt and a supercilious expression.

"I'm very sorry," she said, "But this is a restaurant, and we really can only permit food that's been purchased on the premises to be eaten here."

I'd noticed, above the aroma of freshly baked bread, coffee and vanilla, a smell I knew well from my bus journeys in south London. I inched my chair around slightly and took a closer look. Just visible, almost concealed by the woman's squashy green leather handbag, was a familiar red cardboard box.

"Mummy! Chicken!" demanded the little boy.

"Just a minute, Archie, I'm talking to this lady," his mum said. "I fully intend to order food, and eat it on the premises. But my child has special dietary needs."

"I'm sure he does, madam," Martha said. "But we're not able to accommodate his need to eat KFC in my restaurant."

"KFC!" said Archie.

"Oh, do shut up," his sister said. "You're, like, so embarrassing. And KFC is totally gross."

"That's enough, Tatiana," the mum said. "Drink your smoothie and don't be unkind to your little brother. As I was saying, we are paying customers, and we expect to be made welcome."

"And you are welcome," Martha said. "You're welcome to order anything from the menu. But we can't have food brought in from other restaurants. Please feed your son his chicken elsewhere."

The women began to protest again, but Martha was holding open the door, a steely smile on her face. Muttering darkly about how many followers she had on Twitter, the woman gathered up her bag and Archie and Tatiana, and left.

I still didn't know why Martha had asked me to come and meet her, but I was beginning to feel extremely relieved that a waitressing job here wasn't on the cards.

"God," Martha sat down again. "Sorry about that. We get quite a bit of it. Entitled parents with a great line in special pleading. Corporate law sometimes seems like a walk in the park compared to dealing with this."

"So what made you decide to start a café?" I asked. "If you were a lawyer before?"

"The usual," Martha said. "I had my kids and suddenly I wasn't the shining star any more. I got passed over for promotion too many times for it to be just coincidence. And I was working stupid hours, and hardly ever saw Mia and Harry, and although our nanny is amazing, I found myself really resenting her – not the amount I paid her, but the time she got to spend with our children. So I decided to take a few years off and do something else, and this shop was vacant, and I thought, why not? And here I am. I miss going into the office every day, and I still hardly see the kids, so I don't know if it was the brilliant move I thought it was, but it's something new and, for the moment, it's fun. What do you think?"

"The food's great," I said. "I didn't expect it to be, to be honest."

She laughed. "People don't. They come because we're family-friendly and close, or just because we're new, and then they come back for the cake. Dan's a genius. It's still quite zeitgeisty, the whole organic, locally-sourced, low-impact thing. I'm hoping the place will turn into a bit of a community hub, you know, with parents hosting kids' parties here and mindfulness workshops and people selling craft and stuff. And that's where you come in."

"What do you mean?" I said.

"There," Martha gestured casually to the far wall. "I'd really love a piece of art there. A mural. Something really quirky and beautiful. Wizzy says your paintings are stunning, and I wondered if you'd be interested in doing something for me?"

I looked over. It was a perfectly ordinary wall, white-painted, splashes of sunlight throwing shadows on the slightly uneven plaster of its surface. But, suddenly, to me, it was remarkable. A canvas, a thing of infinite possibility. I could see how a landscape could take shape there, an entire world, from tiny details of flowers and insects down by the skirting boards, to puffy clouds and soaring birds where the wall met the ceiling. And beyond.

"Could I paint the ceiling too?" I blurted out.

Martha laughed. "So you like the idea. Fab. Would you be able to come up with an initial concept for me, say by this time next week, and if it works for both of us we can crack on? I'll pay you, obviously, although not much, but I'll cover the cost of your materials too. You'll just need to hang on to the receipts whenever you buy anything. But I'm hoping that when people see it, they might commission more work from you, for their children's bedrooms. We could even do T-shirts and mugs and stuff. But that's all for a bit further down the line."

I nodded. I was itching to paint – literally, I couldn't keep my hands still. I could see them twisting in my lap, knowing how it would feel to be smoothing a blank sheet of paper, squeezing pigment from a tube, stroking the bristles of a clean, new brush.

"I was thinking a sort of fairy-tale landscape," I said. "I'm sure Wizzy told you, that's always been my thing. But not cutesy and cartoonish, more classic. Even a bit dark. I always wanted to be an illustrator, but there's not much of a market for that sort of thing. Everyone expects princesses to look like Disney ones now. I'm a bit down on Disney, can you tell?"

"Yeah, me too," Martha said. "You can't escape it, though. I tried for ages with Mia but now I've given up and accepted the tyranny of pink. And I expect when Harry's old enough to start asking for toy guns I'll decide not to fight that battle, either. Anything for a quiet life."

"Give me a good old-fashioned knight in shining armour any day," I said. "You knew where you were with them. Off fighting holy wars, oppressing peasants, laying waste to great civilisations, treating women like chattel…"

She laughed again, an infectious, croaky laugh that was almost exactly like Wizzy's. We grinned at each other across the table and I had the warm, excited sense that I'd made a new friend.

On my way home, I stopped and bought a sketchpad, charcoal and a box of coloured pencils. Once Martha had approved my design – if she didn't hate it, or change her mind – I'd need to spend money on primers, specialist acrylic emulsion, brushes, varnishes – but all that would have to wait. Martha had promised to reimburse my expenses, but I hadn't told her that the state of my finances was such that she would have to pay them upfront: I had less than a hundred pounds left of my savings and had started resorting to my credit card to buy groceries.

But I pushed that gloomy thought from my mind and put up the easel Julian had given me, using one of the kitchen chairs to sit on and another to hold my pencils.

The low afternoon sun poured through the window on to my sketchpad, illuminating the motes of dust in the air and reminding me that I hadn't cleaned the flat that morning. But, today, I didn't care.

My head was full of visions of princesses, prancing horses (I hoped I'd still be able to draw them) and running stags (which I'd never attempted before). I could see shadowy forests, distant purple mountains, a silver river where swans would swim. There'd need to be an enchanted castle, I decided, perhaps surrounded by a thicket of thorn bushes. And I'd include a pond, too, with a frog on a lily pad, as a little joke for Will (and for Julian, who'd reacted with total incredulity when I smugly told him Will had agreed to my scheme).

I blocked out the dimensions of the wall on one page, roughly sketching in where all the elements might go. Then, turning the page, I began to outline the details of my imaginary world. I worked until the sun disappeared behind the rooftops opposite, then I stretched my aching shoulders, made a cup of tea, switched on the lights and carried on.

I'd been working for hours when Julian got home, and I was so engrossed I didn't hear his key in the lock. His voice startled me, and I jumped like the stag at bay I'd been trying to draw.

"Hey, little star," he said. "You've been busy."

"Haven't I?" I said proudly. "You won't believe it, I've got a commission. My first one ever. It's for a café down the road – Martha's Place. Look, there's going to be a river and princesses and deer and…" I burbled happily on, leafing through the pages as I showed him my sketches.

"Pretty," he said. "Wow. They're gorgeous. Almost as beautiful as their creator." He lifted my hair and kissed the back of my neck. "I didn't realise you were so talented."

"I've missed this so much," I beamed at him, feeling the familiar glow of fatigue and contentment work gave me. "I just hope Martha likes them. Do you think she will?"

"If she doesn't, she's wrong," he said. "I'm starving, aren't you? What's for dinner?"

"Dinner?" I hadn't thought of food since my long-ago salad lunch, and realised I was hungry too. "No idea. Have we got any eggs?"

Julian went through to the kitchen. I heard the fridge open and close. "Only two," he said.

I thought about walking to Tesco, scouring the shelves for whatever was on offer, coming home again and doing the washing-up from last night before I started to cook.

"You know what, I can't be arsed," I said. "Let's go out. It's a celebration, after all."

So we went to the Turkish restaurant next to Hussein's shop and ate lamb chops and hummus and salad, and had a bottle of wine, and I chattered excitedly about my ideas, and told him about Archie and his sister and the contraband KFC, and I barely noticed that his responses became less and less enthusiastic.

"And the day after tomorrow I'm meeting Will," I said. "He suggested Tate Modern, so I can look around there first. I can't wait, it's ages since I've been to a gallery. Even though it's not the same sort of art as mine, at all – and much better, obviously – it's going to be amazing to see. He said he'll buy me lunch, and we're going to put up his online dating profile, which should be a good laugh."

Our waitress brought the bill and put it in front of Julian. He looked at it for a bit.

"I'll get this," I said, imagining my credit card cowering at the prospect, and waiting for Julian to object. But he didn't, so I paid, and to my relief my card wasn't declined.

"Let's go," Julian said. "It's late."

We walked home, and I noticed he didn't take my hand as usual. But after we had sex I fell asleep straight away, without thinking what his silence might have meant.

Chapter Eight

With trepidation in his heart, the prince renewed his search for a princess to share his kingdom. He entered the enchanted forest where the ladies waited, each one frozen by the spell from which only his words could release her. But how would he know which of them would be his? Here was a dusky damsel with a haughty smile; here a fair maiden with tears in her eyes; here a laughing shepherdess with flowers in her hair. The prince walked among them until he was footsore and weary...

"Hi, I'm Will. I'm a 29-year-old teacher (computer science, since you ask!) living in London. I'm easygoing with a good sense of humour. I enjoy movies, going out, staying in..."

"Fuck!" I hit the delete key and watched my anodyne words vanish from the screen. This profile creation malarkey was harder than it looked, but in the end, in my enthusiasm to persuade Will to agree to my scheme, I'd promised to do the legwork myself and present him with the completed text for him to sign off. But, given that writing has never been one of my core skills and I didn't even know Will all that well, it was proving to be a tougher challenge than I'd anticipated.

Now, if I could draw him... I thought of his height, his untidy fair hair, his easy grin that displayed slightly crooked front teeth. A picture would be so much easier. But it didn't work like that, his profile had to be written, and written today. I'd been so engrossed in my sketchbook all afternoon, I hadn't got around to starting it, and Will was expecting to be able to give it the go-ahead so we could start checking out potential dates. And I'd been sitting here for ages, drinking coffee and writing and deleting descriptions and getting nowhere.

Frustration aside, it felt bloody amazing to have something to do with my time that wasn't cleaning the flat and answering ads in the *Guardian* for jobs I wasn't going to get. I'd analysed the online dating market and prepared a list of sites for Will, with facts and figures about each one. I'd checked out the most popular profiles to give him an idea of the competition, and made a few notes for myself based on what their descriptions said.

But, I realised, it had all just been procrastination, putting off the moment when I was actually going to have to describe Will in a way that would sound modest and unassuming, yet bring women flocking to his inbox. I tried again.

"Hello there, I'm Will, and I'm looking for someone kind and compassionate with a great sense of humour to share fun nights out, quiet nights in…"

Bollocks. There it was again. "There are no other kinds of night, Stella, you cretin," I said aloud. "Where the hell would he be if not in or out? Hovering on the threshold? Sheltering under a bivouac?"

It was time to call in the cavalry. I logged on to Facebook, hoping desperately that Wizzy would be online, and – result! – there she was. It would be early morning in Bali, I realised – I was lucky to have caught her.

"Wizzeee, help meee!" I typed.

"Hey you! What's up? Can't decide what filling to put in Julian's jacket potato tonight?"

"Waaah, you cow! I haven't degenerated totally into a domestic drudge, you know. And I'll have you know it's spinach and chickpea curry for tea, I'm branching out. No, I need help with something else."

I quickly filled her in on the situation and gave her a brief description of Will. "So I hoped your fine writing mind, honed by years of putting together marketing plans for detergent, would hold the answer," I finished.

"Wait. So you want me, from six thousand miles away, to write an online dating profile for some random bloke I've never met?"

"Yes. Except he's not random, he's actually quite..."

"No problem. Give me five."

I waited impatiently, for five minutes, then, when there was no response from Wizzy, got up and made my sixth cup of coffee of the day. I was sipping it, staring impatiently at the screen, when she replied.

"Bazinga! Geek seeks soulmate. Could you be Penny to my Leonard? 1 to my 0? Software to my hardware?"

She went on to describe Will in words that made him sound charmingly goofy, yet sane and solvent. She hinted at handsomeness without making him seem vain. She told of his search for a woman who was strong-minded but loving, kind and also clever, who'd make him happy and be adored in return. And she did it all comfortably within the two-hundred-and-fifty word limit.

"Isabella Reid, you are a total genius! Bloody hell, I want to date him myself after reading that."

"Yes, so do I, rather," she said. "It's a sure sign of good copy, when you fall for your own hype. Anyway, if you don't need any other acquaintances' love lives sorting, I'm off to the beach."

The next day, I left the flat shortly after Julian and spent a few contented hours wandering around Tate Modern before meeting Will. It was months since I'd properly immersed myself in a gallery, I realised – I'd missed it. The silence, the vast, light-flooded spaces, the amazing, mesmerising collection of work – no one could ever be unhappy here, I thought as I strolled around, blissfully zoned out, imagining that one day, pictures I'd painted might hang in a place like this.

The time passed so quickly that I was almost late for lunch. Although Will had promised me that the top-floor restaurant was special, part of me was still expecting a bog-standard gallery canteen, in the likes of which I'd eaten countless soggy sandwiches and slices of nameless quiche in my time. But this was seriously gorgeous – a sleek, monochrome room with no clutter to distract from the view over the river, which took my breath away and reminded me irresistibly of that first night I'd spent with Julian in Will's apartment.

I ordered a fizzy water and took out my phone, posting a photo of the view across to St Paul's to my Shutterly account. A couple of minutes later Will came rushing up to our table, breathless from running up the stairs.

"Hi, Stella, I'm so sorry I'm late," he said. "Is this okay? I asked them for a table by the window. Have you had a chance to look round? I don't know anything about art, but it's nice, isn't it?"

He must be nervous, I realised – he had the same way of burbling on when he didn't know what to say as I did.

"This is for you, just to say thanks for your time. It's why I was late – I couldn't decide what you'd like." He thrust a carrier bag from the gift shop into my hands, and I opened it to find a gorgeous framed print of a Picasso drawing.

"That's beautiful," I said. "You really didn't have to get me anything, this was all my idea and I've had fun thinking what to say about you, and anyway the profile might be crap."

Will laughed. "It won't be crap. Now, shall we have a Bloody Mary while we decide what to eat? Normally I wouldn't drink at lunchtime, but I've got no meetings this afternoon."

So much for the curling sandwich and cup of weak tea I'd been imagining. "Go on then," I said. "Just to keep you company."

When Will ordered a steak, I told myself it would only be polite if I did, too – although actually it was out of sheer greed, and it was delicious, properly bloody and rare the way I like it, with a huge pile of rustly chips. I realised I was starving, and tore into it as if I hadn't eaten for a week.

When we'd finished and ordered coffee, Will took out his laptop and said, "Okay, so let's have a look at this thing you've written." We'd been chatting quite easily away to each other while we ate, about the food, the view, my favourite artists – anything, but nothing in particular. I felt as comfortable with him as if we'd been friends for ages and not known each other for just a few weeks. But now the atmosphere had become distinctly awkward, and I realised how thoroughly cringy it must be for him to have his best mate's other half running his online search for a girlfriend. I decided not to tell him that I'd also involved Wizzy in the project.

I said, "It seems a bit ridiculous since we're sitting right next to each other, but why don't I email you the copy from my phone?"

"Hey, that's business as usual for me," he said. "At work we send emails across the room all the time – when people are coding they don't like being disturbed. Let's have a read."

I watched his expression go from amused, via diffident, to absolutely mortified as he scanned the text. When he'd finished, he actually buried his face in his hands, and I could see from the back of his neck that he was blushing.

"Oh God," he said. "Do I have to say all that stuff about myself? I sound like a vain cock."

"You don't sound like a cock at all," I said firmly. "You've got to market yourself, haven't you? If you put up a profile saying, 'I'm Will and I'm all right, I suppose,' you'll never get anywhere. Modest, but not too modest is the way forward, surely?"

Will looked dubious, but he said, "All right then, I'll get on with uploading it."

I helped him select a few photos, one showing him finishing a ten kilometre run for charity, one of him wearing a QPR shirt and drinking a beer, and one of him walking a very cute yellow labrador, which he said belonged to his sister, Cathy. There was one of him in a morning coat at Cathy's wedding, but that was as glamorous as it got. I vetoed photos of Will skiing, Will in San Francisco with the Golden Gate bridge in the background, and Will on the balcony of his fabulous flat.

"Think regular bloke," I said. "Do regular blokes go to California? No, they don't."

"Bloody hell, you're harsh," he said. "It was only a work trip."

I laughed. "If a thing's worth doing, it's worth doing properly. Want to have a look and see if there's anyone interesting online?"

"Okay. So what am I looking for? Women between twenty-two and twenty-eight?"

"What? Why has she got to be younger than you? Twenty-two-year-olds don't want relationships, they're just up for casual shags. What's wrong with older women?"

"What's wrong with casual shags?" Will countered. For a second, our eyes met, then I looked away, back to the screen, pushing away the fleeting thought that flashed through my mind: *what the hell just happened there?*

"Between twenty-five and thirty-two, maybe," I suggested.

"Fine. But if someone younger gets in touch, and she's a total babe..."

"Then you'll remember where dating total babes has got you so far," I said. "Look at her, she looks nice. Zoë, the one with the red hair."

"Charlotte's best friend is called Zoë. Well, when I say best friend, they're more like each other's number one frenemy. She's a nightmare. I don't think I could go out with anyone who reminded me of her. Sorry, Stella, Zoë gets a no from me."

"Fair enough. Sorry, Zoë, no handsome prince-kissing for you. Let's look at Nancy."

Will clicked on the artfully posed, carefully lit image of Nancy, who had beach-tousled hair and was wearing loads of red lipstick.

"If I had to pick one word to describe myself, it would be Driven. I am determined to make a success of every aspect of my life. I have a gorgeous flat in Bayswater, a brilliant career in fashion, and a fabulous circle of friends. When I'm not working, socialising, or working out in the gym (I didn't get this bod by accident!), I love travelling to exotic destinations and cooking gourmet meals. My friends tell me I have a great sense of humour and am one of the most intelligent, successful women they know. I am also a very spiritual person, and aim to spread good karma and happiness wherever I go. I'm looking for a man with similar interests."

"Similar interests!" I hooted with laughter. "So, basically, a man who finds her as fascinating as she finds herself. Not. Going. To. Happen. Nice try, Nancy. Let's look at Melissa."

I'd suggested Melissa because she looked a bit like Charlotte – a glossy-haired brunette wearing a tight white T-shirt. If Will was going to be put off by a woman with the same name as his ex's friend, how would be feel about someone with the same body as the ex herself?

"She's pretty." Will clicked on the photo.

"Hi guys! I'm Melissa. I love high heels, cupcakes and drinking cosmopolitans with my besties. Yes – my favourite TV show ever is *Sex and the City* and I'm looking for my very own Mr Big! Could that be you? If you like driving fast cars, going to cool places and treating a girl like she's your very own princess, you could be the man for me. Go on – get in touch!"

I looked at Will. This was a test. His reaction to princessy Melissa would tell me a lot about what he really wanted.

"Jesus," he said. "Epic fail. Melissa, I believe Prince Harry's still single and looking, but Will the maths teacher isn't going to be your Mr Big. Whoever he is. No, don't tell me, Stella, I'm not sure I want to know."

I felt the knot of tension in my stomach ease. It was going to be okay. Will would find a normal, lovely person, even if it took a while. He'd passed the diva test. I breathed a silent 'thank you' to high-maintenance Melissa, and hoped her besties would talk some sense into her.

Somewhere out there, amongst the Kylies and the Gemmas and the Sarahs, was the girl who'd become Will's girlfriend, my friend, the final corner of the foursome I imagined we'd form together. She'd never replace Polly and

Wizzy, of course – no one could – but she'd be a mate, my London buddy. We'd go for girly nights out while Will and Julian wrestled with intractable theorems. When Will eventually proposed, I'd organise her hen night…

"Someone's sent me a message," Will said.

"No way! Let me see!"

"Here we go." He clicked on a picture of a slim, heavily made-up blonde girl, who didn't look a minute over eighteen. She was wearing something strappy and lacy, and making a Kim Kardashian-style duck face over her shoulder for the camera.

"Are you sure you haven't found your way on to Barely Legal Babes by mistake?" I said.

"No! Honest, look, her name's Bonnie." He clicked on the profile. "Doesn't say very much. 'I'm a slim, curvaceous blonde looking for fun with like-minded men in central London.' Okay."

"Never mind the like-minded bit, what does her message say?"

"'Hi Will. U have lovely eyes, I think your hot. Id like to get to know you better. Msg me? We can talk on WhatsApp?' Blimey, she's not backwards in coming forwards. I'm a bit scared."

"Well, she's confident, I suppose. Outgoing. That's a good thing, right? Why not message her and see what happens?"

"I don't know," Will said. "It feels kind of… weird."

"Go on! What's the worst that can happen?"

"Right then. I'm going in. And you're taking full responsibility," Will said. "Hold on, I'm just going to create a new WhatsApp account – I don't want to use my regular work ID."

He tapped away at his phone for a few seconds. Although I turned my head discreetly away while he entered his new password, I couldn't help noticing that the first few characters were random numbers and punctuation marks, and it crossed my mind that he, like Julian, must have a unique and meaningless password for everything, remembered as easily as I remember people's names. Whereas I've used the same one for everything since I got my first email account when I was twelve: peanuts62, the name of my late, lamented hamster and the number of the house where I grew up. Except every now and then I get asked to include an uppercase letter or a special character and end up locking myself out of things because I can't remember whether I've gone for Peanut$62 or peaNuts62! or any number of other possible permutations, and then I get the rage and end up throwing my phone across the room. That never happened to Julian, and I supposed it wouldn't to Will, either.

"We're good to go," Will said. "I'll tell her I'm online."

I leaned over, my head almost touching his shoulder, and we peered together at the screen.

"Bonnie? You there?" Will typed.

There was a short pause. "Maybe she got sick of waiting," Will said. Then a message flashed up on the screen.

"Im here. Waitin t chat t u. Want t no wut Im werrin?"

"What's she saying?" I said. "It doesn't make sense. It's not text speak but it's not normal language either."

"Yeah, it's a thing," Will said. "I'll explain later. Do we want to know what she's wearing? I'm not sure I do."

"Go onnn," I said. "Ask her. This is hilarious. I can't believe she's doing this."

"Seriously, Stella, this is well dodge," Will said. "I could be having all my bank details hacked as we speak."

"Let's just see what she's wearing," I said. "Go on. It could be anything. Nun's habit. Plate mail armour. Anything."

"Okay, I'll ask, but after this we're stopping, okay?"

"Deal," I said.

"WAYW?" Will typed.

Seconds later, a reply flashed up. "NIFC."

Before I had a chance to ask Will what the hell that meant, the phone's little screen gave me my answer. A video flashed up, showing the blonde girl from the profile minus the lacy garment, lying back and licking her lips eagerly for the lens. The camera panned down, showing her breasts and what, in spite of the pixellation, looked like seriously toned abs.

"That's enough," Will said, but before he could end the conversation, the picture changed. The screen went blank for a second, then flashed to life again. And when I say flashed… it took me a moment to realise what I was looking at, but once I'd seen it, it could not be unseen. A fat man reclining on an unmade bed, wearing black satin underwear and lace-topped hold-ups. One hand held his phone, and the other…

I looked at Will and Will looked at me, and barely a second passed before he hit the End Call button and turned off his screen.

"Oh no," I said. "What was that?"

"A webcam, I guess," Will said. "The first bit was streamed from some porn site, but then it must have gone wrong, and we got to see the real 'Bonnie' in all his glory. Or lack of it. Or maybe he did it on purpose."

"But… I don't understand," I said. "Why go to all the trouble of setting up a fake dating account to wank when the internet's full of stuff you can wank over any time without all the hassle? Not that I'd know, obviously."

"It's rule thirty-four of the internet," Will said. "If it exists, there's porn of it. I guess we just encountered an interactive version – some sorry bastard who gets off on pretending to be a girl on dating sites, then pulling the big reveal at the crucial moment. Oh, with an added bonus of rule twenty-eight: there will always be more fucked-up shit than what you just saw."

Our eyes met again, and I started to giggle. "No way," I said. "You're having me on about rule twenty-eight."

"I'm not!" Will said. "Seriously, Google it. Everyone knows about rule twenty-eight." He was laughing too, so hard he had to close his laptop and lean his arms on it, his shoulders shaking helplessly.

"I'm so sorry, Stella," he said eventually. "I wasn't expecting that. Really I wasn't. But don't forget, this was your idea."

CHAPTER NINE

"There's just one more item on the agenda," Louise said.

Will glanced surreptitiously at his watch. Managing programmers is like herding cats, as Bill Gates once said – or is supposed to have said. Right now, although he was meant to be in charge, Will felt a bit like a cat himself – a cat who had spent the afternoon cooped up with other cats that were equally unenthusiastic about the experience.

He glanced around the meeting room. He'd never worked for the sort of firm that did things in a corporate style – never worked for anyone but himself, in fact. So he'd always been determined to run things at Ignite informally and democratically. All new members of staff were encouraged to contribute an item that meant something to them to the office décor, and the result was a haphazard collection that included posters from gigs, people's baby photos and, rather dominating the room, a giant inflatable dinosaur, christened Petronella for reasons now lost in the mists of time.

The table, a makeshift affair of an old door propped up on trestles, was littered with coffee mugs, take-away containers and various bits of tech – he counted five laptops, eight mobile phones and three tablets, and there were only five of them in the meeting.

"We need to talk about staff lunch," Louise said.

"Yeah! Let's talk about food," Tim said, instantly perking up. He was Ignite's lead developer, the first member of staff Will and Louise had actually hired, a programming genius with a PhD from Cambridge who'd gone on to work at Yahoo and Amazon before contacting Will and offering his services at a vastly reduced salary, because, he said, he wanted to experience the buzz of start-up culture.

Louise and Will had quickly realised that the minds of people like Tim and Giles, who'd joined shortly afterwards and was a specialist in cloud computing, required fuel. Coffee, obviously – huge amounts of it, and only the good stuff. But food, too. After finding too many programmers wilting over their keyboards, having been coding for twelve hours and forgetting to eat, Louise had introduced a daily lunch delivery, on the company, with each staff member getting a turn to choose what it would be.

"So I've been keeping track of the lunch orders over the past couple of weeks," Louise said. "We've had pizza five times. Burgers three times. Fried chicken twice. Okay, today was sushi – that was you, Hannah."

Hannah, the newly appointed head of marketing, nodded.

"It can't go on like this," Louise said. "I've put on a stone over the past six months. If we let people have what they want, we're all going to end up with type two diabetes. It's irresponsible."

"But I like pizza," Giles objected, swallowing the last dregs of his coffee, rolling a fag and tucking it behind his ear. He'd been chewing his biro for the past hour – its top now resembled a paintbrush, and Giles's beard was stained with green ink.

"You can have it every night at home – I'm not going to stop you," Louise said. "Fill your boots. But I think staff lunch needs to be healthier. I've found a local place that will do salads, sandwiches on wholemeal bread, vegetarian options – tasty, healthy food. So if no one objects, I'm going to switch the account to them."

As always, Will realised, Louise had timed her move to perfection. Giles was dying for a smoke and wouldn't want to get into an argument. Tim was glancing longingly at his laptop, clearly desperate to get back to work. Hannah looked like the type who'd eat salad out of choice. And Will himself had – he glanced at his watch again, less discreetly this time – twenty-five minutes to get to Bethnal Green on his bike.

"That's fine with me," he said.

"Me, too," said Hannah.

"So long as we still have Cake Tuesdays," Tim said.

"Cake Tuesday is sacrosanct," said Louise. "Fear not, it's staying, otherwise we'd have a mutiny on our hands. Giles?"

"Yeah, I guess. Whatevs," Giles said, his hand reflexively checking that his roll-up was still in place.

"Right, then, that's a wrap," said Louise. There was a chorus of scrapes as they all pushed back their chairs and drifted out, Hannah heading for the coffee machine, Louise for the ladies', Tim for his desk, Giles for the door to the fire escape and Will, rather guiltily, for the lift.

"Laters, all," he said.

Narrowly avoiding a double-decker bus as he turned his bike on to Commercial Street, Will reflected that this date might not be such a good idea, after all. But his new profile had received just a handful of views since he'd put it up a week ago, and Clemency, who he was meeting tonight, had been the first woman to contact him.

She was new to RealRomance.com, he'd noticed – she'd only joined the site that day – so clearly, in the throes of newbie enthusiasm, she was giving it some. She described herself as creative and zany – not necessarily traits Will would have looked for in a potential date. What the hell did zany mean, anyway – was it online-dating speak for 'a bit bonkers'? He had no idea.

But she was pretty, with vivid red hair and lots of eyeliner, and even if the evening's entertainment hadn't at first reading sounded like his cup of PG Tips, he was always up for trying new things.

"I've got a spare ticket for a burlesque thing tonight," she'd written. "Fancy coming along? It's alternative, a bit dark – you'll like it."

And then Louise had stuck her head round his office door and said that the monthly meeting was about to kick off, and if he didn't get his butt into the boardroom, there'd be no coffee left. So he'd hammered out a quick acceptance to Clemency's email, and now here he was, chaining his bike to a railing on a side street in Bethnal Green, where he hoped it would still be at the end of the night, and pushing open the door of The Dark Horse.

He spotted Clemency instantly – it would have been impossible not to. She hadn't said the event was fancy dress, so he guessed the skin-tight leopard-print dress, short enough to show the tops of her fishnet hold-ups, was normal attire for her. That was okay with him – a bit out there, but okay. She was also wearing thigh-high platform boots that brought her almost up to Will's height. Her hair was teased into a messy bun over her pretty face. Her lips and fingernails were painted a glossy scarlet and she had a full sleeve tattoo on one slim arm.

"Will? Hi! I'm Clem." Her voice was pure home-coun-ties-and-public-school, at odds with her appearance. "I got you a drink, it's about to start. Negroni okay? I bagsied us a table by the stage, so we'll see all the action."

Burlesque action, Will thought. Whatever that was. His knowledge of the art form didn't extend much beyond a YouTube video Giles had made them watch in the office one day, of a woman in a giant cocktail glass filled with pink feathers. He felt entirely out of his depth.

"Great," he said. "Thanks." He had absolutely no idea how to start a conversation with this girl. Her dress, her voice, her air of unshakeable self-confidence – everything about her was alien and, frankly, intimidating. Fortunately, Clem seemed happy to do the talking for both of them.

"We're over here." She led the way through the dark, packed room to a tiny table at the back of the bar, squeezed against a red velvet curtain behind which, Will presumed, would be the stage. "Take the furthest seat, if you want. There might be… splattering. Like, bodily fluids, you know. It gets quite intense some nights. I've been coming here for a couple of months now and I think it's hit peak cool but it's still in the zone. I've heard there's this new place in Deptford that's like totally sick, I'm going there next week. They have a…"

But Will was destined never to find out what made the new place in Deptford off-the-scale cool, because at that moment the lights dimmed even further and Rammstein blared from the speakers. The velvet curtains swept apart. Will took a gulp of his drink.

The stage was illuminated by a single pink spotlight. From the gloom beyond it, a woman emerged. She was clothed – if that was the right word – in dark greenish-gold body paint, and wrapped in a thick, glossy rope that made her look a bit like a female, fetishy Michelin man. Will almost laughed – and then the rope moved. Holy mother of fuck, he was watching a live show featuring a naked woman and a python. And his cocktail was finished.

Clem leaned over and whispered in his ear, "Pythagora. She's immense in Berlin."

She wasn't exactly petite in Bethnal Green, Will thought. He supposed a certain amount of subcutaneous padding was good to have if you were to avoid being squeezed to death by your scaly prop. He watched Pythagora and her snake gyrate in the rosy glow, relieved that smoke machines were pumping fog on to the stage and obscuring some of the act. If this was as bizarre as it got, he'd cope.

Once Pythagora's act reached its finale, the snake wrapped once more around her body, its tongue flicking at her rapt face, Will bought another round of drinks. He might as well immerse himself in the experience, even though he'd already decided that Clem was not the woman of his dreams.

The 'woman–python–yes it's phallic but it's ironic, duh' act was followed by a relatively tame ventriloquism-meets-taxidermy number, in which a man in a lab coat made a group of stuffed mice sing along to Michael Jackson's *Thriller*. Will bought more drinks. Clem seemed to be lapping it all up – the acts, not the Negronis, although she was getting outside those at a rate of knots too, drinking from Will's glass when her own was empty. A plate of kimchi sliders appeared on their table and Clem devoured them, although the singing mice had made Will feel strangely unhungry.

As the music changed again, to a late-nineties trance track, Will felt Clem's hand on his thigh. She shifted her stool closer to his and whispered, her breath hot against his cheek, "You're going to love this!"

A fresh blast of smoke enveloped the stage. From the ceiling, a chain was lowered, with what looked like a meat hook on the end of it. A man emerged from backstage, bare-chested, wearing a pair of emasculatingly tight leather trousers. But his body was as masculine as it got – each muscle stood out in oiled relief from his heavily tattooed skin. Even over the music, Will could hear the clink of his many, many body piercings.

Will looked at the man, the rings in his ears, nose, cheeks, shoulders, biceps… and at the metal hook, and he knew what was coming. He wasn't a wimp. He'd done a sky-dive for charity. He was ruthless at Grand Theft Auto. But the realisation of what he was about to see, combined with the increasingly hot, feral air and the strong cocktails, made him feel like he might be sick. He wanted to leave.

But Clem's hand on his thigh was insistent, and surprisingly strong. And besides, he wasn't going to show himself up. This looked like the finale, he'd avert his eyes and hope for the best.

He got through it. All of it. The clink of the hook as it entered one steel ring after another. The sight of the man's skin stretching as he was hoisted up above the stage. The look on Clem's face, rapt with what looked an awful lot like lust.

Yes, definitely lust. Because when the act finished, after what felt like years but was in reality only a few minutes, she didn't whoop and applaud with the rest of the audience – she took Will's face in her hands and started to snog him passionately.

Afterwards, Will thought of a multitude of ways he could have got out of the situation, but at the time, it was all too sudden, too bizarre, and he was frankly too pissed to avoid it. In any case, the kiss only lasted a few seconds, because that was how long it took the tattooed, pierced performer to grab a pitcher of iced water from a neighbouring table and chuck it over Will's head.

"Get the fuck off my woman!" he bellowed. Will didn't need telling a second time. He dropped Clem like she was radioactive, grabbed his bag, leaving his cycling helmet behind under the table, and legged it.

When he got out into the street, his bike had been nicked. So he spent a long, wet and chilly twenty minutes on the bus home, trying to figure out what the fuck had just happened. Just before his stop, a text from Clem arrived, giving what passed for an explanation.

"Thanks! Sorry to stitch you up. Treat 'em mean, keep 'em keen!"

CHAPTER TEN

As the year wore on and they went about their business, the wicked witch watched them. When Princess Stella sat at her spinning, she was a shadow behind the curtains. When the prince set out into the forest each day, she followed him. When they lay together at night, she was there, biding her time...

It took things changing, just a little, for me to realise how blank and featureless my two months in London had been before. It wasn't how I'd expected living with Julian would turn out, at all. I'd imagined us getting home from work, opening a bottle of wine, chatting about our days, planning holidays together, going on day trips to the seaside and exploring the city. It hadn't crossed my mind that imagined that every day would be the same, Julian going to work and coming home and then working some more, while I applied for jobs, cooked dreary meals on a tiny budget and waited and waited for something to happen.

I thought back to how I'd felt when I left Edinburgh – sad, of course, to be saying goodbye to Polly and Wizzy, but also buoyant with hope and excitement. Now things were happening, and all my enthusiasm and optimism had returned, making me realise how much I'd missed it, how close I'd been to losing something of myself.

I'd emailed Martha my initial sketches for her mural, and she'd replied almost immediately, saying she absolutely loved it, asking when I could start, and telling me to send her an invoice for the work I'd done so far. The figure we'd agreed on wasn't huge – not even a month's rent on our flat – but it was something, it was money I'd make doing something I adored, and once the painting was finished, there might be more to come. I didn't let myself think that it might lead to even bigger things, but that seed had been planted in my mind and was germinating like mad.

I dreamed about the painting every night, my sleep filled with galloping white horses, drifting swans, dancing princesses and my noble prince.

And there was another thing. Will and I had fallen into a habit of emailing each other during the day, just short one-line messages in which he kept me up to speed with the progress of his dating adventures. I could see why he was so successful at what he did – his approach was nothing if not methodical. Although his efforts didn't seem to be resulting in much success so far, his reports made me laugh and I'd pinned great hopes on the latest profile I'd sent him a link to, of a girl called Rachel.

Instead of waking up when Julian brought me coffee every morning (and sometimes not even then), I'd started pinging awake long before the alarm went off, wrapping myself in my ancient towelling dressing-gown, and sitting at my easel drawing, watching as the sky outside gradually became brighter than the unshaded bulb in our living room.

On a particularly gloomy Thursday in November, I'd been up for almost an hour, trying over and over to get the angles of my galloping horse's legs right, when my phone buzzed and an email from Will landed in my inbox. It was an account of his abortive date with Clemency, and by the time I got to the end, I was laughing so much I woke Julian up.

"What's up?" he said from the bedroom, his voice muffled by the duvet.

"Nothing," I said. "Just an email from Will. Listen." I perched on the bed with my phone and read him the story.

He laughed shortly. "Just like him to make an arse of himself," he said. "As I said, Will's always been crap with women."

I thought this was a little unfair, in the circumstances, but I didn't say anything. Will was a friend – the first friend I'd made in London – but he'd been Julian's friend first, and I didn't want Julian to feel threatened, or jealous, or like I'd ever take Will's side over him.

"Shall I put the kettle on?" I said.

"Thanks," said Julian, then added ominously, "We need to talk."

I stirred sugar into our mugs of tar-black instant coffee – I was beginning to hate the taste of it, and had promised myself that the first thing I would do as soon as Martha paid me was splash out and buy us a coffee machine – then carried them back to the bedroom.

Julian was sitting on the bed. His hair was sticking up, his face scratchy with stubble. I ran my finger down the curved rope of his spine and kissed his bare shoulder, feeling a rush of love and desire for him.

"What is it?" I said.

"I got the council tax bill through yesterday," he said. "It's fine, I can pay it without going into overdraft – just. But I don't know how much longer we can carry on like this, Stella. Have you actually looked at the budget spreadsheet I sent you?"

"Yes, of course I have," I lied. I couldn't think of a way to tell him that spreadsheets, any spreadsheets, were sources of confusion and fear to me, and one showing our – Julian's – meagre income and our terrifying outgoings was entirely unfathomable. "I transferred my share of the rent over to you yesterday." This was true – but what I didn't tell him was that it was the last of my savings and all of the deposit Martha had paid me. I took another sip of my coffee and felt it churn sourly in my stomach.

Julian stroked my hand. "You need to find a job, little star. It's important. And you haven't been looking as hard recently, have you?"

"Well, no, not really," I said. "Because of the thing I've been doing for Martha. I know it's not much money but it's something I love, and it could lead to more work. It's not like I wasn't trying before, I was, and I got nowhere. And I checked again whether I'm eligible for benefits, but I'm not, because I quit my job in Edinburgh and you earn too much."

"So you're saying you've been too busy to look for work?" Julian said.

"No – yes. I've just been doing other stuff too, recently."

"You certainly have," Julian said, very calmly. "Like emailing Will eight times a day."

"What?" I felt blood rushing to my face. It wasn't true – okay, maybe there'd been one day when we'd emailed each other loads, but that had been over a week ago, when we'd first got Will's profile up on RealRomance.com. "No I haven't."

"Don't lie to me, Stella."

Then a thought occurred to me. "Julian, have you been reading my emails?"

"So what if I have? You leave your phone lying around without a password on it. Your attitude to online security is as bad as your budgeting, little star." His pet name for me didn't sound so loving now, it just sounded patronising.

I felt my chest constrict. There was nothing, nothing at all, in my emails to Will that I minded Julian seeing. Or was there? I realised that we'd begun to fall into a tone that, while I knew it was only friendly, could be interpreted as flirtatious. All our messages finished with kisses – often more than one. Once, when he'd sent me a few links to people's profiles and asked if I'd have a quick look through them, I'd jokingly replied, "At your service, lord and master." I cringed remembering that, imagining Julian seeing it, how unnecessarily hurt and angry he must have felt. But it was his fault, wasn't it?

"Julian, I shouldn't have to password-protect my phone so my boyfriend doesn't read my private stuff – you should respect me enough to just not do it. That's how relationships work."

"Relationships work by people contributing equally to them," Julian said. "And I'm not seeing too much of that at the moment, are you?"

"I do all the housework!" I protested. "I cook your dinner every night. I'm here every day like Betty bloody Draper tidying up after you while you go off and do a job you love so much you'd do it for free." Then I remembered Betty's tranquilliser habit and affair with her riding instructor (or was it some other bloke? She'd had an affair with someone, I was sure) and wondered whether she was the best example I could have come up with.

"Really?" Julian said, and glanced pointedly around the room.

The tightness in my chest rose up into my throat so I couldn't speak. I was smarting with injustice, but at the same time I couldn't argue with what he'd said. There were dirty clothes – mine and his – spilling over the edge of the laundry basket. There was a film of dust over everything – not much, but it was there. There was two days' worth of washing up piled up in the sink. I'd meant to sort it all out, but it had just seemed so much less important than before. And, I couldn't deny it, less important than emailing Will.

"Like I said," I could hear how feeble and defensive I sounded, how much in the wrong. "I haven't had time, I've been..."

"Managing Will Turner's love life for him," Julian said. "Which, apparently, is extremely time-consuming. You might want to rethink your priorities a bit, Stella. Now I'm going to get ready for work."

He picked up his coffee mug and took a sip, then grimaced and put it down again. "This is cold," he said, as if that was my fault also, and headed for the bathroom.

I pulled my knees up to my chest and wrapped the duvet round my shoulders and sat there, shaking. Julian and I had never had a row before. Whatever else I'd doubted, I'd been certain of his love for me, his kindness and gentleness, and that we'd always be together. Without him, I realised, I'd have nothing. No money, nowhere to live. I couldn't go back to Edinburgh – there was nothing there for me any more. The only place where I could go was home to Mum, and the prospect of that filled me with horror. The idea of losing Julian was terrible – I loved him, but even more than that, I realised, I needed him.

I heard the shower switch off and hugged my knees tighter, dreading what Julian might be going to say next.

But he came back into the bedroom and put his arms around me.

"I'm sorry, little star," he said. "I don't want to hurt you. I love you so much."

"I love you too," I said, the tears I'd been holding back beginning to flow.

"Don't cry, please don't. It breaks my heart," he said. "I have to go to work now. Please don't be sad, everything will be all right. And remember, we've got my faculty drinks thing at work tonight. I can't wait for everyone to meet you and see how beautiful my girlfriend is."

After he'd gone, I cleaned the flat like it had never been cleaned before. I even defrosted the fridge and wiped the skirting boards. And when I'd finished, I spent two hours getting ready to go and meet Julian's colleagues. I didn't have time to reply to Will's email, or to return to my drawing.

"And what do you do for a living, Stella?" This was Ken, Julian's bearded, avuncular head of department, who, with his owlish spectacles and hairy tweed jacket, couldn't have been more of a cliché of a Professor of Mathematics if he'd tried. I realised that Julian's own mothball-scented jacket was a tribute to his boss's, and wasn't sure whether to dismiss this as conformity or admire it as a rather sweet fanboy gesture.

Ken hadn't been the first to ask the question. I'd had, "Are you in academia too?" from Raj, who, from what Julian had told me, was not so much a colleague as a deadly rival for Ken's esteem.

Liberty, an earnest young post-doc research assistant, asked me whether I'd met Julian while he was working in Canada. I said I had, but we'd met in London and barely seen each other in the intervening months, and she gave me an owlish stare from behind her heavy-framed glasses and said, "Oh."

Richard, who Julian had never mentioned but who reminded me, with his none-too-clean dark hair and piercing eyes, of Professor Snape, had simply barked at me, "And what's your specialism?"

And all of them, when I'd replied that I knew nothing at all about mathematics, but had a degree in fine art and had worked in a gallery in Edinburgh and was currently unemployed, had glazed over. Once they'd asked me, in a slightly panicky way, how I was liking London, they'd drifted off to talk shop with people who understood it.

I took a big gulp of warm, acidic white wine and said to Ken, "I'm not really working right now. I want to, but at the moment I'm mostly chief cook and bottle-washer for Julian."

He peered at me from beneath bushy white eyebrows. If Richard was Snape, I thought, Ken could make a passable Dumbledore. "That can't be easy."

"It isn't," I said. "Well, obviously all the hoovering and stuff isn't exactly challenging. But it's been two months now and I've been going slightly bonkers with boredom."

"And what is it you want to do?" he asked.

I realised that over the past months, my ambitions had shifted from Turner prize shortlist to National Minimum Wage. I wanted to tell him about Martha and her café and the knights and princesses, but it suddenly seemed silly and trivial.

"I've always wanted to paint," I said. "I don't know if I'm good enough to do it professionally, but I'd love to try. And I know the only way to get better at something is to practise, but at the moment I just don't seem to have any motivation at all. And I know Julian needs me to support him – not financially, although that would help, but just kind of keeping things going. Making sure he's got clean shirts, that kind of thing."

Ken said, "Make no mistake about it, my dear, academia is extremely intense and demanding. Julian's ambitious and talented and he works very hard. But he isn't a child. He's capable of solving the Vaught conjecture, therefore he's capable of switching on a washing machine. I've seen enough colleagues moving up the ranks in my time, and too many of them have had wives who've been little more than domestic drudges. It doesn't end happily for anyone."

I nodded mutely and took another sip of wine.

"I'm married to a physicist," he said. "She was made a full professor five years before I was, and we have two children. When Maria, our daughter, was born, Anthea laid down the law to me and made it very clear that I'd be doing my share of everything. And I did. I got up to settle the babies in the middle of the night, I cooked, I cleaned. And has it harmed my career? Hmmm?"

I felt exactly like I'd felt as a first-year student when my tutor had told me off for handing in an essay about abstract expressionism a day late.

"No, I suppose it hasn't," I said in a small voice.

"Exactly. And don't let Dr Mason convince you otherwise. Your time is just as valuable as his, or mine, or anyone else's."

"Thank you," I squeaked.

He laughed, the steely gaze replaced once more by a benign smile. "But you didn't come here to be lectured about your domestic arrangements by me," he said. "Let me get you another drink and you can go off and mingle."

I glugged back another glass of wine – the second one didn't taste quite as awful as the first, which I find is quite often the way with cheap wine – then I went to the loo and put on some more lipgloss. Then I stood alone in a corner for a bit, armed with yet another drink, and checked my phone. I couldn't see Julian anywhere – he'd promised that we didn't have to stay long, and assured me that the last thing he wanted to do was spend a Friday night with the people he had to see every day of the week. But either he'd found his colleagues more entertaining than he'd expected, or he'd snuck off to his office to do some work, and I had no idea where that was, so I'd just have to wait for him to reappear.

Facebook informed me that Wizzy was about to board a flight to Sydney, Polly was freezing her tits off, and Melinda Massey, who had bullied me so horribly at school but whose friend request I'd cravenly accepted, had no idea what had possessed her to marry such an utter cunt. Her husband had responded saying she wasn't exactly a catch herself, especially since she'd had that botched boob job, and the resulting airing of their dirty linen kept me fascinated, in a horribly voyeuristic way, for a few minutes.

Will was apparently on his way to Seven Dials. He'd said that he was exchanging messages with a few online dating prospects, and I wondered whether he was finally going to meet one of them, so responded to his status with a like and a row of question marks. And that was it – Facebook had nothing more to share with me. When I looked up from the bright screen of my phone, I realised almost everyone seemed to have left, and I was alone, apart from a handful of people I didn't know, with no idea where Julian was or what I was supposed to do next.

Just then, Liberty emerged from the ladies'. I was so relieved to see a familiar, if not friendly face, that I rushed over to her and said, "Hey! Are you having fun? Do you have a drink?"

"I was just leaving," she said.

Feeling like a total fool, I said, "Oh. Okay. I'm really sorry to bother you, then, but I seem to have mislaid Julian. Do you think you could show me where his office is? I think he might be hiding out there."

She blinked myopically at me and pushed her limp fringe off her forehead. "If you want," she said. "It's this way."

I followed her through a door, along a corridor, down a flight of stairs, round a corner and along another corridor, past rows of closed doors with plastic nameplates on them. At last we came to one that said 'Dr J Mason'. I felt a little fizz of pride.

Liberty tapped on the door, but there was no response. "If he's not here, it'll be locked," she said.

But when she tried the handle it opened. The room was empty. I say empty, but it wasn't, of course. There were huge piles of books on the desk and both the guest chairs, and the desk was packed with computer equipment – there seemed to be about four monitors of various sizes and orientations. But there was no Julian.

"We could try the quad," Liberty said.

"Thanks," I said. "I'm sorry to be so…" But she'd already turned away, hurrying back the way we'd come on her opaque-tighted legs.

"He might be over there," Liberty said. "There, with Francine."

Julian had mentioned Francine, the faculty administrator, to me before, but when he'd introduced her to me earlier I'd had to resist the urge to say, "Are you sure this is her?"

Ken and Richard – Professors Dumbledore and Snape, respectively – exactly fitted my mental picture of what men would look like if they'd spent their careers on a quest for knowledge of concepts most people can't even begin to understand. I'd formed a picture, too, of what a woman might look like whose job it was to organise their working lives. Mousy, I'd thought, possibly wearing badly fitting flesh-coloured tights that wrinkled over the tops of her sensible shoes. I'd added thick glasses to my mental picture, along with hand-knitted cardigans and an air of sexual repression.

A bit like I imagined Liberty would become in twenty years' time.

It's fair to say that when it came to Francine, my imagination had got it entirely wrong. She was older than me, probably in her late thirties, tall and very slim, almost gaunt. She was deeply tanned, and her face had the slightly weathered look of a habitual sunbed-user. Her eyes were a pale, bright blue, heavily ringed with liquid eyeliner that was almost, but not quite, at Amy Winehouse levels of flickiness. She had long false nails with a French manicure that looked like it had taken some punishment at her keyboard. She had highlighted blonde hair that I would have said was at attempt at the beach-tousled look, only a good inch and a half of dark roots were showing. She was wearing leather leggings with zips across the thighs and an outsize scarlet jumper, and there was a general air of slightly dissolute grubbiness about her. She looked like the sort of person who didn't floss her teeth.

I know, I know – I am sounding horribly judgy and bitchy. I'm only saying this to emphasise how truly remarkable the scene was that I witnessed out there that night on the moonlit quad, with the neoclassical pillars of the university as its backdrop.

Francine was standing there, swaying ever so slightly on her battered pink Converse trainers, a bottle of lager in one hand and a fag in the other. I could hear her croaky smoker's laugh – it sounded almost raucous in the still night. And it was followed by a sycophantic echo of mirth from the crowd of men surrounding her.

When I say crowd, there were probably no more than eight of them. And eight men to one woman in a university mathematics department is, as I was learning, entirely representative. Progressive, even. But there was an air about this gaggle of geniuses – or should that be genii? – that was fawning, almost skittish.

There they all were: lanky Raj, who according to Julian had won a Fields medal (nope, me neither, but it's evidently highly impressive and important) practically rugby-tackling the others in his eagerness to light Francine's next roll-up. Richard, looking even more reptilian as he narrowed his eyes against the billowing smoke. A couple of younger men who I hadn't met, but whose body language made it clear they were going to be first with the lighter next time if it killed them. Even my new friend Ken, puffing away on his pipe, a remote satellite to Francine's sun, utterly transfixed by whatever anecdote she was relating.

"I thought he might be here," said Liberty. "See you later, good to meet you."

Because, of course, there was Julian at the centre of the group. I walked slowly towards them, feeling more out of place than I ever had in my life. The spotlights that illuminated the facade of the building left me in shadow, but lit up Julian's face. He was laughing, his head thrown back, so I could see his perfect teeth and the column of his throat I so loved to kiss.

I was dazzled when the light hit my eyes, so for a moment I couldn't see anyone, but they must have seen me.

When I could see again, Julian had gravitated to the outskirts of the group and approached me, arms outstretched, saying, "Little star! I've been missing you, I wondered where you'd gone. Have you met everyone?"

He was clearly a bit pissed, and as he walked up to me I watched him clock the cigarette in his hand, then quickly drop it and stamp it out.

I like to think that a week before – even a day before – I'd have ripped the piss out of him about his sneaky fag.

"What's this, Doctor Lung-cancer-is-for-the-weak Mason?" I'd have said. "Get a few lagers in you and you're right there with the nicotine addicts. What's next, doing Sudoku puzzles because proper mathematics is too hard? Reading *The Economist* because you need to get out more?"

And Julian would have laughed, shame-faced but enjoying my banter, and said something about needing to put me in my place, and I'd have known exactly what he meant and felt a melting thrill of desire, and we'd have gone home to bed.

But, as I said, a lot of things had suddenly changed.

I looked at Julian, joining in with other men in admiration of this powerfully, ferally attractive woman, and I didn't feel indulgent or amused. I felt threatened. The part of me that knew he shouldn't have left me alone in a place he knew and I didn't, with people who were his friends but not mine, that it was rude, inconsiderate and selfish, was drowned out by a bigger, more strident fear that if I wasn't careful, he could slip away from me and never come back.

So I said, "Hey! I'm fine, I was chatting to Liberty for a bit. What shall we do now?"

The little mob of men around Francine seemed to have been lost its cohesion since my arrival. As I watched, they drifted away, one by one.

"Best be off," said Raj.

"Home to the missus," said Richard, looking shame-faced as he slunk past us.

"Look after yourself, Stella," said Ken, giving me a bristly, tobacco-laden kiss on the cheek.

"Oh my God, my babysitter's going to fucking fire my arse," said Francine, and dashed past us on her stilt-like legs, dropping her cigarette at my feet in a shower of sparks. I discovered a charred, irreparable hole in my favourite suede boots the next day.

"Little star, shall we go home to bed?" said Julian, and I agreed, even though I was starving and not tired at all.

The next day, to my astonishment, I received a Facebook friend request from Liberty. It wasn't that I hadn't liked her – she'd seemed perfectly nice. What she hadn't seemed was the tiniest bit interested in being friends with me. I stared at her profile for a bit, bemused. We seemed worlds apart – she liked classical music and baking, read the *New Scientist* and spent her holidays camping in the Lake District. Whereas even the most cursory glance at my own profile would have shown her that I liked YouTube tutorials on how to do leopard spots on your fingernails, played CandyCrush, and that my idea of a perfect holiday was lying on a sun-lounger with a cocktail and *Heat* magazine.

Clearly we had nothing in common apart from the fact that she worked with Julian. I studied her Facebook page more closely, and then had a lightbulb moment. Liberty's education history revealed that she'd grown up in Devon, been to Durham university and done her PhD at Warwick. She'd arrived in London at about the same time as Julian and I had – and so, like me, could probably count her real-life friends here on the fingers of one hand. In fact, I would have been able to do that had I been a three-fingered sloth.

I thought of the almost exclusively male environment at the UCL maths department – Liberty was the only woman I'd met there, apart from Francine. And Francine didn't strike me as the kind of person with whom Liberty would be able to enjoy a bit of cosy bonding over a salad in the canteen. She was lonely – she needed friends. And, I had to be honest, so did I.

So I accepted her request, then sent Polly and Wizzy an email describing the events of the evening before, not holding back in my description of Francine and how the men of the faculty responded to her.

"Honestly," I wrote, "I think she's some kind of bloke-whisperer. You know, like a horse-whisperer? All these men with IQs bigger than my bank balance, and she made them *simper*. It was most bizarre – she must be nearly forty! Strange or what? Anyway, I must go – I've got princesses to paint."

And I signed off and returned to my drawing, dismissing Liberty from my mind.

But later that afternoon, when I'd finished painting for the day and was wondering whether I'd have time for a run before it got too dark, I saw she'd sent me a message suggesting we meet for lunch next week, and I accepted. After all, it wasn't like my social diary was exactly packed, and I felt a bit sorry for her – this lonely girl, who according to her relationship status was single and even on Facebook only had forty-three friends.

Perhaps I could introduce her to Will, I thought fleetingly – she was as different from high-maintenance Charlotte as it was possible to get. Even though looks-wise Liberty might only rate a six out of ten, if I was being generous, whereas Will was a high eight, stranger things had happened in the world of relationships – after all, Julian fancied me and Julian was a ten, in my eyes at least.

And so I found myself sitting opposite Liberty in Prêt a Manger a few days later, eating a chicken and avocado sandwich and assessing her potential as a girlfriend for Will and a friend for me.

She was prettier than I remembered, but scruffier. Her eyes were a beautiful, clear blue and she had the sort of high-cheekboned, pointy face that could have looked alluringly elfin with the right haircut. But her hair was limp and shapeless, like her clothes. Her cardigan was done up on the wrong buttons, and there was a fingerprint on one lens of her thick glasses. I thought what fun it would be to take her shopping, let the girls at the MAC counter loose on her, and effect a bit of a transformation – but then, maybe she was someone who deliberately didn't bother about external appearance. Maybe when you were as clever as her, such things just weren't important.

"So… er, where in London do you live?" I asked, deciding to go for a safe conversation-opener.

"Finsbury Park," she said. "I've got a room in a shared house with four other girls. I found it on Gumtree. It's okay, I guess. It's convenient for work. I don't go out much really. London's so big, isn't it?"

I agreed that London was, indeed, big.

"I get lost all the time," she confessed. "Even with the Tube. I constantly find myself going in the wrong direction when I come out of stations. Like, you should have a one in two chance of going the right way, even if it's completely random, but I seem to get it wrong almost every time. It's against all the laws of probability."

"But you go hiking and stuff," I said. "How do you find your way up and down mountains if you get lost on the underground?"

"Mountains are easy." She sighed. "You know where you are with them. Literally. I do, anyway. I'd love to live on top of a mountain, maybe with a view of the sea. In Wales, or somewhere like that. But for now, Finsbury Park it is."

"But think of the shops," I said. "I had a look round Topshop on my way here and the winter stuff is just amazing. I didn't buy anything – I'll have to wait for the sales – but I saw this red coat that was just, like, so gorgeous. It had ultra-wide lapels and a belt, and it looked just like Moschino, only for forty quid! You wouldn't get that on a mountain in Wales."

"Really?" she said. "I'm always concerned about the ethical side of high-street fashion. The exploitation of labour in the Third World, so consumers in the West can buy cheap, disposable garments. Highly questionable from a moral point of view."

She took a bite of her hummus sandwich. Clearly a cosy chat about where to shop on a budget wasn't going to happen, and nor was a make-over at a cosmetics counter. I had another go.

"But even if you don't like London, you must be totally loving your job," I said. "Julian says it's an amazing place to work, really exciting and, like, on the cutting edge of everything."

She brightened. "It certainly is. It's a really inspiring environment. I'm learning every day – from Professor Noakes and my colleagues and even from the students."

"What's Julian like to work with?" I couldn't resist asking. I realised I envied her, being able to share a side of him that I never could – the side that kept him engrossed in whatever was on his laptop screen, late into the night, long after we'd had sex and I'd gone to sleep.

"He's brilliant, academically," she said. "But then everyone in the department is. It's hugely stimulating, as I said, but friendly and challenging too."

Clearly she wasn't to be drawn further on the subject of Julian – and I couldn't blame her, really. If she didn't get on with him, I was the last person she'd say that to.

"And what about the other people? Ken seems really nice, he was the only person at that drinks thing who really wanted to talk to me about me. And Francine?"

Liberty brushed a shower of crumbs off her cardigan. "I wonder if Francine wouldn't be more at home in a more informal environment. Not that I know her particularly well. But she seems to get things wrong rather a lot. We had a meeting the other day and when I checked the minutes afterwards, several of the points I'd made had been totally omitted. I'd have asked her to revise them but I didn't want to make a fuss, being new. Although everything Julian had said was on there. Maybe she just doesn't like women."

"Maybe she just likes Julian," I suggested, watching Liberty's face closely, not wanting to miss any nuance of her reaction.

"They do seem to get on well," she said. "As I said, it's a friendly environment. But tell me some more about yourself. How did you and Julian meet?"

Apparently Liberty wasn't willing to engage in any more gossip about Francine, either. I told her the story of Wizzy and the lion, and ending up in A&E with Julian, and how we'd fallen for each other almost at first sight. Although she laughed in all the right places, she didn't seem particularly interested – I suppose when you're single, hearing about other people's blissful loved-upness is never much fun.

We finished our sandwiches and Liberty said she'd better get back to work, but we must do it again soon, and I agreed. Even though I'd found her quite hard work, it felt like a real achievement to have actually been out for lunch with someone, met another new person who might become a friend. She was just shy, I told myself, she probably had hidden depths. Next time, I'd suggest we meet up in the evening and have a glass of wine, and maybe then she'd loosen up a bit. It would be worth a try, anyway.

"I'll walk back towards the university with you," I said. "I was going to head down to the Strand, there's a fashion design exhibition at Somerset House I'd quite like to see."

I'd thought that the René Grau illustrations, with their exaggerated proportions and vivid colours, would provide some inspiration for Martha's painting, and besides, if I was with her, Liberty would be less likely to get lost on the five-minute walk back to the building where she and Julian worked.

Also, although the idea was so pathetic and soppy I didn't want to admit it to myself and certainly wouldn't admit it to Liberty, walking through the buildings where Julian spent his days, where he worked and thought and drank coffee and had meetings, gave me a small thrill of intimacy, a feeling of closeness to the man I loved.

While we walked, Liberty took it upon herself to give me a potted history of the university and its buildings, pointing out various architectural highlights and telling me which of the dignitaries whose statues were dotted around was which. I wondered whether Julian knew them as well as she did, whether he, too, had a favourite route to take, pausing to admire the last few golden leaves on a chestnut tree as Liberty did. Somehow I doubted it – he was always in too much of a rush, always running late for something.

"Right, I'll say goodbye here," Liberty said. "It was lovely to get to know you better. I'll drop you a message in the next few days."

"Great!" I said, with an enthusiasm I didn't feel.

Then I caught sight of a familiar tweed jacket, hurrying through the crowds of students to get to the building. It was Julian – even at that distance, I couldn't mistake his long legs, his broad, stooped shoulders – nor the even longer legs and untidy blonde hair of the woman next to him.

"Looks like Julian and Francine have been out to lunch too," Liberty said. "That makes a change – normally he has a bacon roll at his desk. He works ridiculously hard. But you don't need me to tell you that."

I forced a laugh. "No, I certainly don't. Bye then, have a good afternoon."

I didn't make it to Somerset House that day. Instead, I went to Oxford Street and spent ages looking at all the beautiful clothes and shoes I couldn't afford to buy, and wondering if Julian would love me more if I could. Then I got the bus home and spent a thankless and stalkerish half-hour looking at pictures of Francine on Facebook. Then I redid all my sketches of the wicked witch for the mural, giving her long, skinny legs and a serious case of root growth.

It was stupid, I knew, and spiteful, but I thought it would make me feel better.

Newsflash: it didn't.

CHAPTER ELEVEN

"It's going to be a rout!" said Giles.

"A massacre!" agreed Tim. "We will reclaim the Iron Throne, take what is our due, destroy our enemies!"

"We'll lay waste to their lands. Take possession of their gold. Rape their women."

"Steady on," said Hannah, looking up from her laptop. "Less of the rapeyness, if you don't mind."

"Sorry." Giles paused, then resumed the war dance he'd been performing around the water cooler. "Rape their men, then! Steal their horses!"

"You don't have to rape anyone," Hannah said. "It's just a ping pong tournament, for God's sake."

"What do you mean, 'just'?" said Tim. "It's deadly serious. Our honour is at stake."

"Will, please tell these boys they need to get out more," Hannah said.

"Ha! You'll get nowhere with the boss," Tim said. "His thirst for blood is legendary. One look at the blue baize and he goes berserk. Last time he played Davina Jones he was like Gandalf facing down the Balrog."

"She still won, mind," Giles said. "But not tonight! Tonight we will have revenge. Right, Will?"

Will cleared his throat. He felt awful, letting his team down like this. The weekly Tech City ping pong tournament was a huge deal. Start-ups from all over London sent their best players, their skills honed by years of bitter rivalry. It was even rumoured that the recent annexation by a rival firm of Ivan Chan, one of Ignite's lead developers, wasn't so much a testimony to his stratospheric IQ and phenomenal coding skills, but because he had the best backhand in the business.

"I'm really sorry, dudes," Will said. "I'm not going to be able to make it tonight. I've got other plans."

"What? What could be more important than wiff waff?" said Tim.

"And last week you weren't here for Cake Tuesday," Giles said mournfully. "You missed my Victoria sponge. It's my nan's recipe and it's gnarly. I gave myself the worst wanker's cramp creaming the butter but it was worth it, wasn't it, Hannah?"

"Total mouthgasm," Hannah said. "So what's up, Will? Tell us. What out-trumps cake?"

"Ping pong, LDO," Tim said. "Unless you've got a meeting with Steve Wozniak, there is no excuse for bailing out on tonight. None."

"Unless he's got a hot date," Hannah said. "Is that what it is, Will? Go on, share it with the group."

Will allowed himself to imagine, just for a second, what it would be like to be the sort of CEO who didn't have to put up with this kind of shit. A manager who struck terror into the hearts of his subordinates, and said things like 'Step into my office', 'Your P45 is waiting', and 'Stop arsing around and do some work'. But he wasn't. He'd found himself, almost by accident, managing a team of forty-five of the brightest minds in software engineering. Between them, they had dozens of PhDs and thousands of IQ points. They were in the business because they loved it – most of

WHO WANTS TO MARRY A MILLIONAIRE?

them had been coding since before they had a 1 in front of their ages, and he sometimes thought they hadn't grown up much since then.

But, with competition for talent (not to mention mad skills at the ping pong table) so fierce among the hundreds of start-ups that populated the Silicon Roundabout, keeping staff sweet was essential. Hence the cake, the company's dizzyingly high monthly coffee bill, and the relaxed approach to management.

"Yeah, okay, if you must know," he said. "I do have a date."

"Oooh!" all three of them chorussed.

"Where did you meet her?" Hannah asked.

"Is she banging?" Tim said.

"Never mind that, have you banged her?" said Giles.

God, this was beyond cringy. Will really didn't want to discuss his foray into online dating with his colleagues – especially the bit about the made-up profile and pretending to be a low-paid computer science teacher. It was ridiculous, he knew, and it wasn't like any of them had sex lives to boast about, but he felt unreasonably ashamed of the whole business.

He looked at his watch. "It's six thirty," he said. "You guys need to get your skates on if you're not going to miss the draw."

"Fuck! No time to waste," Giles said. "Coming, Hannah?"

"Yeah, all right," said Hannah.

"Just gotta take a smellfie." Tim sniffed his armpit. "Yeah, I'm good. Tonight is the night I kick Davina Jones's arse, and then I'm going to ask her out."

"Sayonara, Will," said Giles.

"So long," Hannah said.

"And thanks for all the fish," said Tim, and they trooped off, joining the stream of others hurrying for the door.

Normally there were people at their desks until close to midnight, and through until the morning if they were working on a project with collaborators in Seoul or San Francisco, but on Wednesdays all bets were off. Rule one of Ping Pong Fight Club was you didn't miss Ping Pong Fight Club.

Will watched them go with a twinge of regret. It would be so easy to tell this Rachel he couldn't make it, plead pressure of work and spend the evening in the familiar bear pit with his paddle in one hand and a beer in the other. But he hated letting people down. Cancelling at the eleventh hour would be downright cunty behaviour, and besides, he'd promised Stella that he'd give this online dating thing his best shot. Okay, his best shot had been that winning smash against the guy from Spotify a few months ago – his second-best shot would have to do.

He went for a piss, washed his hands and ran his damp fingers through his hair while he checked his reflection in the mirror above the basin in the gents'. He'd shaved that morning, he was wearing a new shirt from Opening Ceremony, there wasn't spinach stuck in his teeth from the spelt salad they'd served for team lunch.

He looked okay, Will supposed. He'd never given much thought to his appearance. As a child, he'd always been the one who was picked last for football, the weedy, brainy kid with pebble glasses. Then, at about thirteen, he'd suddenly started growing, and growing, and growing, and become chronically self-conscious about the bony wrists and ankles that seemed to protrude from his clothes all the time, because his mum couldn't keep buying him new stuff, it would bankrupt her.

So he'd opted out – let the cool kids get on with it, and focussed on the stuff he understood: numbers, code, games.

His fate as a nerd had been sealed. And now, even though his body had filled out a bit and his daily cycling commute to work kept him in decent shape, and the distorting NHS spectacles had been replaced with designer frames his optician had insisted made him look like Gaspard Ulliel, part of him still expected girls to shout, "Eeuuw, spacker!" as he walked past.

Well, he didn't have to worry about that with Rachel, at least. She was a teacher, according to her profile, at a school for children with additional needs. Her photos showed a smiling, fresh-faced woman with a glossy fall of dark hair and an enticing cleavage, and in the few messages they'd exchanged, she'd seemed bright and funny. She was a couple of years older than him, but that was cool. He just hoped she wasn't going to ask too many tricky questions about Ofsted ratings, or his cover would be blown.

When she'd asked him to suggest somewhere for them to meet, Will had been through agonies of indecision. He knew the places where his colleagues congregated after work: the Vietnamese cafés on the Kingsland Road; cocktail bars in Hoxton stuffed (ha!) with taxidermy; that week's 'best coffee cart, like, ever'. None of them were exactly date material. And he knew the places Charlotte used to make him take her to, packed wall-to-wall with models and pseuds, where you were expected to fork out for a bottle of Ketel One you wouldn't drink for the privilege of getting a table within Shutterlying distance of Cara Delevigne. On a teacher's salary, he didn't think that would wash.

So he'd been relieved when Rachel had said in her last email that there was a pub near where she worked in Bermondsey that wasn't too busy and did good food, if he wasn't phobic about venturing south of the river. He'd assured her it was fine, and now he was making his way along the unfamiliar streets, hoping the map app on his phone wouldn't let him down.

No, this was it. Technology FTW, obviously. He pushed open the door and looked around. There she was, her phone on the table in front of her, looking expectantly towards the other entrance, the one he hadn't used.

"Rachel? I'm Will."

"Hello!" She stood up and there was an awkward do-we-shake-hands-or-do-we-kiss moment that ended with them squeezing each other's biceps like arm wrestlers sizing up the competition.

Will offered her a drink, and she said a glass of red would be lovely, thanks, so he went to the bar and got one, along with a pint of Guinness for himself. He didn't normally touch the stuff, in fact he hated it, but he remembered that it had been his maths teacher at school's drink of choice, and he always got choice paralysis when he was nervous.

"So…" said Rachel. "Did you find the place okay?"

Will said he had, yes, no problem. As they made a bit more small talk, about how their days at work had gone (lies! All lies!), he found himself warming to her, even fancying her. The way she pushed her glossy hair back from her face made him want to touch it himself, and learn what the pearly-smooth skin of her hand would feel like under his. There was an endearing squeaky quality to her laugh. She talked about her work with a passion Will could really relate to.

"The kids, you know," she said. "They're all over the place, most days. It's like, we lurch from one crisis to another. I got bitten today." She pushed her jumper up her smooth white arm and showed him a livid red circle, like a vampire's kiss. "That was Roderick. He's severely autistic and some-times he just loses it a bit. But afterwards, once he'd calmed down, I gave him a hug and for the first time, he really let go, and let me cuddle him. Normally he's really resistant to physical contact. I'm still on a bit of a high."

"Amazing! Sounds like a real breakthrough," Will said. "You must feel so proud."

"I do." Rachel beamed at him, showing a deep dimple in each cheek. Will melted a bit inside.

Then she said, "You know what, it's early doors but I think you get it. I think you get me, and I don't believe in wasting my time or anyone else's. So I'm going to lay my cards on the table. I like you, even though we only met an hour ago, and I don't want to mess you around."

Will nodded and took another sip of Guinness. "Go on."

"I'm thirty-three," Rachel said. "I want a family. I want two children, maybe three. Time is ticking. I reckon, a year to get to know each other, a year to conceive a child, if I'm lucky. But it might take longer, and women's fertility falls of a cliff at thirty-five. So that's where I'm coming from. If you'd be interested in maybe having a relationship with me, and I would be with you, thus far, I'd like to know your feelings about that."

Will looked at her, this warm, attractive woman who he wanted to get to know better and, quite intensely, to sleep with. His options were clear. He could tell her what she wanted to hear and get his end away. Or he could be honest.

Half an hour later, a cab deposited him outside the Ping Pong Fight Club. He raced down the stairs just in time to see Davina Jones send a lethal shot past Tim's head, and deliver an even more lethal knock-back when Tim tried to turn the post-match handshake into a kiss.

"How was the date then?" Hannah asked, appearing at his elbow with a beer.

"Non-starter," Will said. "She stood me up." Then he got drunk, even though it was a school night.

Chapter Twelve

Princess Stella weaved and she spun, wondering all the time what spell the witch might have cast. Each day she waited, fearing what news the prince would bring when he returned home…

It's funny how when something happens that jolts you out of a place where you thought you were secure and comfortable, making you think that you'll never return to the life you thought was normal, you adjust. You get on with it. You close your eyes to whatever it is that's changed, and ignore the wish that things could go back to how they were before. And it doesn't take very long before the new way becomes familiar too, new routines entrenched, and you forget that life was ever not like this.

I do, anyway. It's a skill I acquired quite early on in life, and I'm something of an expert at it now.

So after that strange day in November, when Julian and I had our first fight, when I saw how he was with Francine, when, for the first time, he made me feel uncertain about his love for me, I just quietly changed the way I went about things, in the hope that if I pretended everything was okay, it would be.

And it worked. Like I say, I'm good at this stuff. I got up early every morning and went for a run first thing, before it was properly light, and then showered, dressed, cleaned the kitchen and took Julian coffee in bed.

But I waited until he'd left for the day before starting on my work for Martha. The drawings were complete, the detailed design approved, and now I was preparing each element to what would be its finished size, ready to paint on to the actual wall. I'd never worked at this scale before, and I was frankly terrified of getting it wrong. Each of the one-hundred-and-twenty-four pages had to be perfect – Martha would be closing the café for the three days in January it would take me to do the work, so there was no time to do things over if they weren't just right.

Although I was daunted by the scale of the task, terrified of fucking it up, and very much making up the technique as I went along, my nervousness didn't detract from the sheer joy of painting. All my original ideas were coming together, and I kept having new ones too, ripping up parts of the design to incorporate them. I worked for hours, engrossed and content, but I always remembered to set the alarm on my phone so that by the time Julian got home, I'd have tidied everything away and the flat would be spotless and welcoming. After all, I told myself, it was his home, too – why should he have to come back to my mess and clutter?

I still checked my phone several times a day for messages from Will, laughed at his accounts of disastrous dates and almost-successful ones. I still replied, sending him suggestions of people to contact and commiserating when things went wrong. But now, I deleted all his emails as soon as soon as I'd read them, and my replies once they'd been sent.

I didn't like doing it. I hated feeling that I was hiding something from Julian. But it wasn't like we were doing anything wrong, I told myself – it wasn't even like Julian had objected to Will's and my friendship, only to the time I wasted on it. Still, I felt furtive and ashamed when I laughed at Will's stories and spent longer than I needed to composing replies that I hoped were equally funny.

One day early in December, I decided to treat myself to a day off. I'd go into town, wander round the shops, maybe buy something small for Julian's Christmas present. I sent Liberty a message on Facebook asking if she wanted to meet up for lunch or a drink, and when I took Julian his morning coffee, I was already dressed and had done my hair and put on make-up.

"You look nice," Julian said. "What have you got planned for the day? Meeting your lover?"

I laughed. "My lover's right here. I might be meeting Liberty, actually. Liberty from your work. I told you we had lunch a few weeks ago? I hope that's okay. She hasn't come back to me yet but I thought we might have a drink later, and I'll do a bit of shopping, maybe go to a gallery. I reckon I deserve a break."

Julian looked startled – I guess he'd got used to me being at home all the time, working. But he didn't say anything, just got up and went and showered and left for work as usual. An hour later, my phone pinged with a reply from Liberty, saying that she was sorry, but she was madly busy, and maybe we could catch up some time in the new year.

Feeling mildly deflated but determined to go ahead with my plan, I put my phone, purse and lipstick in my bag. Now, where the hell had I left my keys? Our landlord, who apparently couldn't have cared less about the state of the flat generally, judging by the peeling laminate floor, ancient oven, rising damp and all the rest, was evidently something of a security nut. The door was fitted with a fancy multiple-lever lock that meant you couldn't just slam it behind you and go on your merry way. No key meant leaving the flat unlocked, so without it, I wasn't going anywhere.

I looked in my other handbag – no keys. I looked in the Bag for Life that I kept meaning to take to the shops with me, but always forgot – no keys there, either. They weren't in the pocket of my coat, or among our shoes in the bottom of the wardrobe, or under the bed, or in the kitchen drawer where all our bits of string, defunct batteries and screwdrivers lived.

I rang Julian, but his phone went to voicemail and I remembered he was in meetings all morning. I searched the entire flat again. And finally I gave up, fighting tears of frustration, and spent the day lying in bed leafing through Julian's pile of copies of *The Economist* to distract myself from my thoughts, which were rushing round and round in futile circles like a rat on a treadmill. For the first time, I had to face up to the fact that not only did I feel trapped here, in London, by Julian and my life with him – I quite literally was.

I was still there, lying under the duvet, when he came home.

"Hi," I said.

"My God, Stella, you haven't been here all day, have you?" he said.

I nodded. "I was going to go out, like I said, but I've lost my keys."

"Really? I was sure I saw them when I came in. Hold on."

I pushed the duvet aside and sat up. My head felt heavy and fuzzy, as if I had a hangover, although I suspected that was just the after-effect of all the articles I'd tried to read about fiscal policy in the eurozone.

"Little star, here they are." Julian came back into the bedroom, my keys dangling from his finger on their silver fob. "They'd slipped down behind the bookshelf where you always leave them. You can't have looked very thoroughly."

"I did! Honestly, I looked everywhere. I spent hours searching for the bloody things."

He put his arms around me and held me close. "I've been thinking about you a lot today. I'm worried about you, Stella. I haven't been spending enough time with you. No wonder you're a bit depressed and not yourself – staying in bed all day like this, losing things, irritable. It's not healthy. You're spending too much time on those drawings of yours. We need to do more things together. Tonight I'm taking you out for a drink, and when we get back I want to make love to you."

So we did. I tried to enjoy myself, but I couldn't. It wasn't a night in our local pub I'd wanted, it was a day alone, being free, doing my own thing, exploring without the constraint of home being a few minutes' walk away. It wasn't the latest update on Julian and Raj's way of solving a problematic theorem, which made no sense to me and about which I didn't especially care, that I wanted to talk about. My mind kept being drawn back to how I'd felt that day, alone in the flat and unable to leave. It was almost certainly my fault, my mistake – but when we went home and Julian's arms enclosed me, that felt like a trap, too. I didn't move away from his embrace, though, because I couldn't see anything I could do other than what I'd been doing: trying to make Julian happy. Because he was my world.

At least, the next day, us going out for a drink was something to describe in my email to Polly and Wizzy. I always tried to make the little events that made up my days sound more exciting than they were, devoting whole paragraphs to the arrival of Hussein from the corner shop's first granddaughter (admittedly, she was ridiculously cute). So I wrote about that evening with Julian at the Five Bells in language that made it sound more like a glamorous evening in the West End than a couple of pints and a questionable burger in our local, and made sure that, as in all my emails, I told them how happy I was. I told them Will's stories, because I couldn't tell Julian.

I didn't tell them about my lost keys, partly because it was too small an incident to mention, but partly because there was a tiny, nagging doubt in my mind about what had really happened. But I dismissed it – Julian was right, I was alone too much. My mind was playing tricks on me.

Wizzy, on the other hand, was never alone, never bored. Each day brought new photos and videos on Facebook and Shutterly of her riding an elephant in the jungle, her surfing off Bondi Beach, her rock-climbing in New Zealand's South Island. I wasn't jealous – of course not, it was her dream, not mine – but her pictures and brief accounts did make me wonder how it might feel to turn away from a safe, secure existence and follow a dream, with no thought of the future bar whether tomorrow would take her white-water rafting or hang-gliding.

A couple of weeks before Christmas, an email arrived from Polly. I'd been waiting eagerly for news of her twenty-week scan – I knew she and Angus had decided not to find out whether the baby was a boy or a girl, and, although I could tell that in spite of her complaints about how fat she was getting, she was loving being pregnant, I knew this was a big thing, when they'd know for sure that the baby was okay.

But this was something different.

Hey gorgeous girl
I have news! And I have an invitation! (You know where this is going, right? But bear with me.)

So today I was poaching kippers for the guests' breakfast, like you do (life of drudgery, much?). I will never understand what they see in those smelly, bony bastards, but they love them.

Anyway, so I'm in the kitchen, and Angus walks in, looking all serious, and goes, Polly, and I go, yes, my darling, because we've got all domestic like that. And he says, I think we should get married.

I'm like, but we are getting married. Remember? Waverley Station? Durrr? You bought that platinum solitaire that I can't wear any more because my fingers have turned into sausages? And as soon as I've evicted this baby and don't look like a beached whale any more, we're going to have the wedding of our dreams. The bride will wear Versace. Or possibly Monsoon.

He flinches a bit at the Versace bit. But then he says he doesn't want to piss on my chips, and I can have my dream wedding, possibly at a later stage, like when the baby is twenty-one and I'm too ancient and crippled with varicose veins from slaving in the kitchen to dance any more. But he doesn't want our innocent child to be brought into this world a bastard, to be mocked and vilified by the humble, right-thinking folk of the Highlands.

So obviously I threaten to tear him a new one, and tell him that every girl has the right to a dream wedding, and he will take that from me over my cold, dead body.

But I kind of see his point. Well, I don't, this not being the nineteenth century and things like getting married before you have a baby not mattering a damn to anyone with any common sense. But apparently it's important to him. He wants to get hitched before we have this baby, and I've said yes. So we've settled on New Year's Eve, and you have to come. There'll be haggis! Bagpipes! I'll be wearing a tent! It's going to be shit!

Please don't say no.
All my love
Poll
PS – baby is fine. All fingers and toes present. Angus cried when he saw the scan, the big softie.

Although the tone of Polly's email was light-hearted, I could tell that she was completely serious. Although she wasn't going to get her fairytale wedding, she'd want it to be as special as it could be, tent or no tent. And Wizzy couldn't be there – Wizzy was on the other side of the world. So it was down to me.

I couldn't possibly miss my best friend's wedding. If she couldn't have the day she'd dreamed of, all I could do was be there, celebrate with them, tell her she didn't look a bit fat. And I wanted to go – of course I did, more than anything. And a couple of weeks ago, I'd have said yes without a second thought, paid for the flight on my much-abused credit card and found a way to make the repayments somehow. But now there was something else to consider. What was Julian going to say when I asked him if we could go? Because, I realised, it was going to be a question of getting his approval.

And what would he do if I went by myself? I imagined him alone in our flat, making coffee and toast, watching his favourite reruns on Netflix, working. But what else? I imagined him going for lunch with Francine – lunch that could segue into an afternoon meeting and then into a drink after work. I imagined him saying, "Well, Stella's not around, so…" and that turning into something else entirely.

I didn't want to leave him. But I didn't want to let Polly down.

I fired off a quick response to Polly telling her how overjoyed I was to hear her news, congratulating her on the baby's requisite number of digits, saying how much I loved her and that I would rather eat my own hair with chopsticks than miss her wedding. But I didn't tell her I could go, because I didn't know.

I tidied all my sheets of paper away, in the cupboard under the sink, which was the only place where they'd fit, carefully keeping them in their numbered sequence. I put a load of washing on. I sent Martha an email telling her that I was on track to start painting the mural in the second week of January, when business would be slow. I went to Tesco and bought a chicken that was on special offer because it was its best before date, and quite frankly, it didn't look like it would have been that great even in the prime of its life. I shoved half a lemon and load of garlic up its bum and put it in the oven and made a salad. I showered and blow-dried my hair.

And all the time, I was thinking. Plotting, even. How could I sell this idea to Julian, make him see that it wasn't just what I wanted, but what he wanted, too? He loved me, he wanted to make me happy – but was that going to be enough to make him come with me?

It might be. It probably would be. But what if I said, "Julian, Polly's getting married on New Year's Eve and I really want to go," and he said, "But, little star, how the hell are you going to pay for it? Especially at Christmas, with only two weeks' notice?" What if he said, "If you want to go, you must go. I'll be okay here on my own." What if he just said, "Well, that's a shame, because it's go to Polly's wedding or pay the rent."

Whichever one of those things he said, I'd have no comeback. I needed information – knowledge was power.

So, for the first time, I opened the spreadsheet Julian had emailed me all those weeks ago, when I'd asked whether it was really, really not possible for us to get out of London for a day and go to Brighton, go to Cambridge and see Julian's old college, go any-fucking-where at all that wouldn't mean me staring at the four walls while Julian sat, oblivious to my almost frantic cabin fever, working at his laptop.

"Look," he'd said then. "I'm working, Stella. While I work, look at this spreadsheet one more time and maybe you'll get it."

Seconds later, an email had landed in my inbox, and it had been almost as brief a snatch of time between my opening it, and closing it again in horror. But now I needed to pull up my big girl pants, as Wizzy would have put it, and have a look at our finances once and for all, so I could argue the case compellingly for him being there on Polly and Angus's wedding day.

So I did. I found the document, attached to that weeks-old email, and opened it. I don't know why, but I was suddenly quite sure that Julian was hiding something from me, or that he'd just got it a bit wrong, to the tune of misplacing a decimal point.

I knew how much he earned, after all. I knew how much our rent was, because I'd paid the deposit on our flat. I knew how much I spent, day to day, on food and soap powder and art supplies. It was less – way less – than I'd survived on in Edinburgh, when my salary had been meagre to say the least, and then I'd still been able to buy shoes sometimes, and go out, and even save up for a no-holds-barred holiday in Ibiza once a year.

So when I scanned the columns of figures on my phone's small screen, having to scroll across to see how the spreadsheet actually worked, there was only one thing I was really worried about. That Julian had been lying to me. That, actually, there was loads of money left over every month, and he was, somehow, for some reason I didn't understand, not wanting me to have the things I wanted.

In my head, it made sense. The Julian who'd sniped at me for not washing his clothes was someone who'd do that. The man who'd leave me alone at his work drinks party while he letched over the secretary would so do that. And the kind of woman I knew myself to be would never, ever put up with that kind of behaviour.

The spreadsheet wasn't complex. I couldn't think, now I was looking at it, what I'd been so afraid of. There were our incomings: Julian's salary, and the money I'd transferred to him in various large and smaller sums over the past few months.

There were our outgoings: the rent, the council tax – Christ, I knew it was a lot, but I hadn't realised quite how much. The gas and leccy, extortionate, but that was par for the course. Julian's travelcard to get to work and back. And there, in the outgoings column, a massive figure, every month, more than the gas and council tax combined – what the fuck?

I pulled my screen sideways to see the far-left column, and there it was. I felt like a child would feel, who'd been trying to fly by jumping off a table over and over again, with only gauzy fairy wings on her shoulders, only for her mother to say to her, "But you can't. That's gravity, that is."

Because there it was – something that he'd mentioned before in passing but I'd barely thought about – the gigantic student loan Julian was paying off. The albatross that nine years of studying had left around his neck, hundreds of pounds leaving his bank account each month – the price he was paying for the dream he'd followed. And I'd been bitching and moaning about not buying shoes, not being able to do fun stuff, feeling trapped by our relationship, when he was having to worry about this and support me, too.

There it was, in stark figures in front of me: he was right, and I'd been wrong.

I switched my phone off and curled into a sorry comma on our bed, my hands between my thighs, trembling. I'd been so angry with him, about nothing, when he'd been carrying this huge burden alone, with no help from me. I wasn't thinking about Polly's wedding any more, I was only worried about how I could explain myself to him, make him realise that I hadn't meant to be so selfish.

The sound of the smoke alarm jerked me out of my inertia. I ran through to the kitchen and saw a black cloud billowing from the oven. Amazingly, when I wrenched the door open, the chicken was a bronzed wonder of perfection, only the fat it had cooked in was unsalvageable.

When Julian came home, I'd hacked the bird into bits and was scouring the scorched grease off the roasting tin. The sound of his voice saying, "Hey little star! Have you gone supernova? I smell burning," made me dissolve in a puddle of tears, and the next thing I knew, I was telling him all about it – the spreadsheet, the student loan, Polly's wedding, all of it.

And Julian folded his arms tenderly around me and said, "Stop worrying, Stella. You won't miss the wedding. And why don't you spend Christmas with your mum, since it's on the way? I've got a ton of work to do here, I'll be fine on my own. And I'll come up and join you for New Year's. It's important to you – of course I'll be there. Money doesn't matter. Come on, why are you crying again? Did I say something wrong?"

CHAPTER THIRTEEN

It was three in the afternoon on Christmas Eve and there was a carnival, end-of-term atmosphere in the Ignite office. A couple of the junior programmers were playing ping pong across their desks with a sparkly scarlet bauble. Hannah was wearing a tinsel wreath over her headphones and singing along to *He Ain't Heavy, He's My Brother* as she set up the company's festive Twitter feed. Tim was heating up mince pies in the microwave. They were all nursing severe hangovers.

The end-of-year party the day before had been judged a resounding success. Louise, ever conscious of the need to keep the staff happy, didn't believe in stinting when it came to entertainment, so everyone had been bussed off for a day at the Science Museum, followed by unlimited food and drink at a trendy burger and cocktail bar in Shoreditch. Several people had returned to the office via the local off-licence, where they'd stocked up on vodka, and carried on the party overnight. Hannah definitely looked like she hadn't been to bed. Giles and a couple of others had ended up in a Soho strip joint, and been told off by Louise.

"But it's not misogyny if you do it, like, ironically," Giles protested, and Louise herself was feeling too fragile to labour the point, especially as Giles had volunteered to head up the skeleton team who would be working over the official close of business, fielding any urgent calls and making sure the ever-temperamental servers didn't fall over.

"So what's your plan for Christmas, Will? Louise asked. "Seeing your family?"

"Not this year," Will said. "Mum and my stepdad are in Florida with Cathy and her kids, and I'm... er... going to stay with friends. How about you?"

He didn't listen to Louise's reply, which was sure to be the same as every year – her and Gavin, a perfect team of two, together in their little blissful bubble. The main thing was, he'd deflected any further questions about his own plans.

Until the week before, he hadn't had any. He'd thought vaguely of getting a last-minute deal and flying somewhere hot for a week, even turning up at Cathy and Mark's place and surprising his nephews with age-inappropriate plastic presents. Or just hanging around the office, ostensibly making sure the skeleton staff weren't slacking off but actually slacking off with them. Or spending Christmas alone in his flat, as he had done for the last couple of years, messing about with new ideas on his laptop. Then he'd got an email from a girl he'd been chatting to online, met her for coffee to talk about what she had in mind, and accepted her invitation. Now he wondered if he was about to make the biggest mistake of his life, but it was too late to back out.

She was so nice, that was the thing. A nice woman who'd got herself into an awkward position by telling well-meaning lies. He could relate to that.

"Yes! Victory is mine!" A final shot sent the Christmas bauble whistling across the office, where it shattered against a whiteboard. It was time for Will to go.

An hour later, he was on a packed train out of Waterloo, making notes on his phone.

"So, okay, we've got your dad, your mum, your sister and her boyfriend, and your nan," Will said.

"And Muggle the cat," said Becky. "You mustn't forget about Muggle, he was a present from Nan for my thirteenth birthday. He's getting on a bit now, but I love him to bits."

"Right, got that." Will added Muggle to his list. "And remind me how we met?"

"You work with my flatmate Tania. She teaches at an academy in Peckham." Becky told Will the name of the school and he noted it down. "It'll be much easier to get stuff right given you're a teacher anyway. Dad's head of our local comprehensive so he'll want to talk shop for ages but you'll be fine with that. It's just the details that are different. Where is it you actually work, anyway?"

Will felt a flush creeping up his neck. This was a complete nightmare. Not only was he going to be lying to Becky's family, pretending he'd been going out with her since the summer, but his own cover story was as full of holes as the socks he'd packed that morning, unable to find any clean, intact ones.

"Look, are you absolutely sure you want to go through with this?" he said. "It's not too late to change your mind. I can get out at the next stop and you can tell them I've come down with flu or Ebola or something."

"I can't change my mind," Becky said, a note of panic in her voice. "You don't know what it's like. Mum's been on at me for fucking years. 'Why don't you have a boyfriend, Becky?' 'When are you going to settle down like your sister, Becky?' 'The biological clock is ticking, Becky – tick-tock, tick-tock.' All the damn time. So a few months ago I'd had enough, and I told her I'd met this amazing guy, who was a teacher. And she was so pleased. She started asking me about me and my life for a change, instead of going on and on about why I was still single. And once I'd started it just seemed easier to carry on, and then she invited him – you – for Christmas, and I said yes. It took me ages to find someone online who fitted what I'd told her about him."

Not for the first time, Will felt grateful for his own parents' diplomacy. He hadn't brought a girlfriend home since Audrey in sixth form, and they'd never asked him why. Okay, there had been an awkward few months while he was at university when his granny had got it into her head that Will was gay, and kept asking how his 'special friend' Julian was doing, but Will had had a word with his mum and she'd straightened things out, so to speak. He wondered whether his sister had ever faced the kind of pressure Becky was describing, but he doubted it.

And there was another unanswered question: why the hell was Becky single? She seemed intelligent, even if she did weird things like persuade randoms off the internet to pose as her boyfriend for a family Christmas. She was pretty, with her dark blonde bob and green eyes. She was successful – she'd told him in detail about her job in the City. He tried to think of a tactful way to ask, but he'd run out of time – the train was pulling in to Bracknell station.

"Here we are," Becky said. "Remember, the cat's called Muggle. And I don't eat sprouts."

An hour later, Will had begun to relax into his role. He'd survived the introductions to Becky's family, barring an awkward moment when he'd addressed her dad as "Sir", forgetting that he wasn't playing the role of the heroine's awkward boyfriend in an American rom-com. He'd said, "Awww, this must be Muggle, I've heard all about you," when a fat ginger moggy trotted into the room (although he suspected that Muggle might be the hardest member of the family to fool – the cat had given him a hard stare with its inscrutable yellow eyes and stalked off). He'd carried Becky's bag for her, and remembered that her sister was called Ruth.

"Now, I'll just show you where to put your things," said Becky's mum, and they followed her upstairs. "I've made up your old room, darling."

She pushed open the door with a flourish. The first thing Will noticed was the bed, lovingly covered with a fluffy white duvet, a threadbare teddybear propped up against the pillows. The double bed.

"It's new," Becky's mum said proudly. "We thought you'd be more comfortable together."

"Thanks, Mum," Becky said. She slipped her arm around Will's waist and gazed fondly up at him. "We'll be very comfortable together, won't we?"

Will said, "Yes, very," and gulped.

When he was going out with Charlotte, he'd never seen her read anything more challenging than *Vogue*. However, the bookshelf in her flat was well stocked with historical romances – fat paperbacks with lurid covers featuring women in ruffs and corsets. Driven by boredom and mild curiosity, he'd dipped into a couple of them while Charlotte conducted interminable chats with her friends on Facebook. He'd read how medieval monarchs and their brides would be put to bed by courtiers, escorted to their wedding chamber with ribald hollers in anticipation of a bloodstained sheet the next day. He'd thought at the time how barbaric it was that women were so objectified – but also, he'd felt deeply sorry for the bridegroom, faced with the prospect of getting it up and then deflowering some poor girl he'd barely met while his mates caroused wildly on the other side of the door.

It had never occurred to him that he might find himself in a similar position, but he basically was. After dinner, port and a game of charades, Becky's entire family stood at the bottom of the stairs and watched as he and his fake girl-friend ascended the stairs, turned back in the doorway and said, "Goodnight, then, merry Christmas!"

There was a pause, right there. Becky's mum made as if to bustle upstairs for something, but her husband caught her elbow just in time. Becky's sister whispered something to her boyfriend, and the two of them did a little giggly squirm together.

Will almost expected them to erupt into some sort of football chant when at last Becky closed the door, but they didn't, although he did hear an excited whisper from Becky's sister, followed by a hissed, "Shhh!" from her mum.

And then Muggle the cat, presumably casting himself in the role of yeoman of the bedchamber, scratched at the door and demanded to be let in.

"Jesus," Will collapsed on to the bed, followed closely by Muggle, who landed squarely on his diaphragm. "Ouch! That was hectic. Never, ever again. Just tomorrow to get through now. Not that they're not nice, and everything," he added hastily.

"You did brilliantly," Becky said. "I really can't thank you enough. Now, just a bit of stage dressing."

She opened her washbag and took out a box of Durex. "One for tonight." She carefully tore open the foil, tucked the condom back in with her toothbrush and moisturiser, and dropped the wrapper in the waste-paper basket. "And that leaves two for tomorrow, since it's Christmas and every-thing. Voilà."

"I think I'll sleep on the floor, if you don't mind," Will said.

His admiration for Becky's strategic planning increased steadily over the course of the next day. She produced beautifully wrapped gifts for him to give her mother and father, and one for herself.

"It's a Pandora bracelet," she said. "I've always wanted one, but it seemed a bit tragic to buy for myself. It's fine if you give it to me, though."

Later, when her dad tried to engage in an in-depth discussion of the school where Will supposedly taught, asking tricky questions about its latest Ofsted rating, Becky materialised from across the room with a bottle of champagne, asking him if he could possibly open it, because the cork was too tight for her, and then gave him a tray of glasses to fill and hand round, effectively terminating the conversation.

When Becky's sister asked whether the flatmate's chronic fatigue syndrome didn't make a teaching career difficult to cope with, Becky interjected and said that, after a course of CBT and gentle exercise, Tania's health had improved greatly, and she was doing really well now. Will was able to reply, quite truthfully, saying he'd no idea Tania even had the condition.

When Will spooned vegetables on to Becky's plate to go with her turkey, she caught his eye and silently mouthed, "No sprouts!"

By the end of the day, Will was beginning to feel almost like part of the family. He'd had a few glasses of champagne and two of port, and was feeling more relaxed than he could have dreamed possible. Even Muggle had warmed to him after Will had slipped half a chipolata sausage to the cat under cover of the tablecloth.

The more he thought about it, the more puzzled he was by Becky. In her festive red dress, flushed with wine and laughter, silver bracelet around one slender wrist, she was really quite beautiful. She trounced everyone in the friendly yet fiercely contested game of SingStar after dinner. She was tenderly solicitous of her doddery and somewhat dotty nan. This woman was a catch – so why hadn't anyone caught her?

He almost felt sad when the day was over, the last cracker pulled, the wrapping paper and party hats scrunched up for recycling, the boxes of chocolates raided to the second level, waiting for someone to say that if no one else would eat the marzipan one, they might as well.

He helped Becky's mum with the final stages of the washing up, standing next to her in the immaculate kitchen, carefully drying crystal champagne flutes.

"I'm so glad you're here, Will," she said, offering her fragrant cheek for a goodnight kiss and squeezing Will's hand fondly.

"Me, too," he said, and to his amazement he meant it.

When he opened the bedroom door, Becky was already under the duvet, her smooth white shoulders propped up against the pillows, the teddy under her arm.

"Okay?" she said.

"Great," Will said. "That went well, I thought. Avert your eyes for a second, if you don't mind." He took off his shoes and his holey socks, stepped out of his jeans, unbuttoned the crisp stripy shirt he'd worn for the occasion and pulled on a T-shirt. "Right, you can look now. Lob me a pillow, will you?"

He sat down on the carpet, ready for another slightly uncomfortable night. Fortunately the house was heated to tropical levels.

But Becky said, "Why don't you join me? It's cold out there."

Will looked up at her. Her eyes were slightly smudged with make-up. The duvet had slipped downwards, revealing the tops of her breasts. He could smell her toothpaste.

"Sure?" he said.

"Sure," said Becky.

Will got into bed and Becky turned off the light. For a moment he lay still, uncertain, keeping a polite distance between them. Then she slid across the taut sheet towards him, her warm arm snaking around his waist. He felt her hair tickle his cheek. Her body was soft, inviting, entirely desirable. He touched her hip and felt something lacy and silky.

She made a small sound that was part gasp, part giggle, and her fingers found the gap underneath his T-shirt and slipped lightly over his skin.

There was no need for Becky to secrete unused condoms in her washbag that night. When her mum brought their tea in the morning, the two of them were still asleep, curled tightly together, and the teddybear had been cast out on to the floor.

CHAPTER FOURTEEN

With dread in her heart, Princess Stella approached the cold, dark castle in the North where the queen waited. She had been alone for many years and she was growing old and bitter...

Perhaps I should have been hurt that Julian hadn't suggested joining me for Christmas at Mum's. But, to be honest, I'd been too busy trying to think of a reason why I didn't have to go myself, only I couldn't. Not apart from the obvious ones: I didn't want to leave him alone, and I didn't want to see Mum. But I also didn't want to tell him either of those things.

So I picked up my phone and called her (Mum doesn't even have a dishwasher. She certainly doesn't have email), and said I was thinking of spending Christmas with her in Dundee. She was so delighted at hearing from me and so eager for me to come that there was no way at all I could back out, and Julian was so generous about paying for my train ticket, so enthusiastic about coming to Polly's wedding afterwards, and so insistent about how much work he had to do in the meantime, that there was no way I could introduce the idea of him joining me there.

After a few months away from home, I always forgot what it was like, and begin to think that maybe going back wouldn't be so bad after all. And then I'd find myself standing at the end of our road, looking at the two identical rows of grey houses marching up the hill into the distance, and think, "Oh fuck, of course – it *is* that bad."

I felt it now, approaching Mum's house with my wheelie suitcase trundling behind me. Even though it was seven years since I left, I knew that confronting the wreckage of my relationship with Mum would be just the same as it had always been. It was as if, in the same way that her living room was frozen in the nineteen-nineties, our relationship was too. As soon as I pressed the doorbell, I knew I'd revert to being a truculent teenager, and as soon as Mum heard its chime, she'd be possessed by the urge to placate, to smother, to praise me for qualities I didn't have any more.

The door opened almost instantly, so I know she must have seen me coming and been hovering in the hall, not wanting to actually stand out in the road, because that would make her look too eager.

"My little Stella," she said. "Let me look at you. You've changed your hair."

"Hello, Mum. I haven't changed it really, I just haven't had it cut for a few months."

I followed her inside and took my bag upstairs while she put the kettle on. My bedroom was immaculate, sterile now that the posters of Nick Cave and Morrissey had been taken down from the walls, and freezing cold, as it had always been. I took as long as I could to unpack my things, hanging up the blue Coast dress I'd found in a charity shop and bought for Polly's wedding, folding my jeans and underwear and arranging them in a drawer. I texted Julian to tell him I'd arrived, and waited a few minutes for a reply, but none came. Eventually, when I couldn't delay it any more, I went downstairs.

Sitting on Mum's slippery chintz sofa, celebrating Christmas eve with a cup of dishwater-like tea and a bendy

Bourbon biscuit on my knee, I remembered why I would rather walk over hot coals in my precious Kurt Geiger stilettos than introduce Julian to Mum. I could imagine his look of horror as he gazed around the cramped living room with its mint-green carpet and floral curtains, the way he'd look at Mum, with her shapeless clothes and prematurely grey hair (why couldn't she dye it, like other women do in their fifties?), wondering if this would one day be me.

I know, it sounds awful, doesn't it? Being embarrassed by one's parents is something one's supposed to grow out of, along with spots and drinking cans of Kestrel in the park and trying to be a Goth. But I hadn't. Mostly, I suppose, because it was only when I was a teenager that Mum actually started to be embarrassing.

Bear with me. Everyone's cool with their parents until they hit a certain age, of course. But for me, things did actually change.

When I was little, Mum and Dad were quite normal. Mum cooked and cleaned and shopped, and Dad went off to work every day to the publishing company where he worked as an illustrator. You may be familiar with his work, if you're a fan of Dandy and Beano. No? Thought not. Because Dad was working in a dying industry, and now it's dead.

It was when I was about ten that I started to hear whispered conversations behind closed doors that abruptly stopped when I came into the room, and after a while, Mum got a job.

She went to work in a call centre for a few hours a week, which was fine with me – I was at school and didn't miss her, and when I came home, Dad was often there. I loved that, because we'd draw and write stories together. I don't think Mum minded having to go out to work either – in fact, she leapt eagerly into the whole business of having a job, broadening her horizons and meeting new people. And that was exactly what made things go wrong.

It was through work that Mum met Auntie Ina, and went out for coffee with Auntie Ina, and then got introduced to Auntie Ina's friends. It's Auntie Ina who I blame for chucking a grenade into my childhood.

Okay, I don't blame her, although perhaps I should. I blame Mum.

I know what you're thinking. It's what Wizzy thought when I told her the story after too much wine one night. "Oh my God, was she a lesbian?" she said. But Auntie Ina wasn't – she was a Christian.

All of a sudden, things I'd taken for granted – *Top of the Pops*, the horoscope in the *Daily Record*, even the whisky Dad liked to drink in the evenings (to be fair, he probably did like to drink a bit too much of it) – were Wrong, at least according to Mum and Auntie Ina.

In my memory, the change in our house happened almost overnight, but in reality I suppose it must have taken weeks, even months. The Sunday tradition Dad and I had of walking down to Visocchi's for ice cream stopped being a regular feature of my week, because Dad took to decamping to the pub after lunch instead. Mum stopped watching *Coronation Street* and started reading pamphlets from the church in silence on the sofa. She tried to make me read them, too, but I refused.

It was the beginning of my teenage rebellion. In retrospect, as rebellions go, mine was pretty tame, but it must have come as a shock to my parents because I'd always been a particularly biddable child. I didn't shout or slam doors or throw things – I just retreated into myself, into a world of reading and drawing, and, as my parents' rows became louder and more frequent, into my room.

I'm not sure when Mum found out that Dad was shagging the barmaid at the Ross Arms. I suppose she may have known about it for some time and hoped that he'd stop, but evidently he didn't, because she kicked him out. With no job and nothing to tie him to Dundee, Dad moved to Newcastle, Karen the barmaid in tow. And I'm not sure whether it was Mum, Karen or Dad himself who whittled his contact with me from weekly visits, to monthly, to a card on my birthday and at Christmas, to nothing.

If Mum been a different sort of woman, she would probably have taken to drink. But that was left to me. I soon realised that the counselling sessions recommended by our worthy, lank-haired pastoral manager at school could easily be bunked out of. And I realised that hanging out in the park with Teagan and Karl and the rest of them, wearing black clothes and listening to Theatre of Tragedy, was a far better way of dealing with my unhappiness than 'sharing' with Naomi the counsellor. At any rate, it was somewhere to be that wasn't home, where Mum's silence draped like a stifling blanket over everything.

I didn't go off the rails spectacularly: I'd been too well trained for that. I went off them in a very modest, low-key fashion. I listened to Joy Division, but death metal scared me, thanks to all Mum's warnings about the devil. I drank my cans of Kestrel and my cider and black, but when Karl gave me a tab of acid I only pretended to take it, and tucked it into my bra instead. And when I finished my A-levels, I was even still a virgin – my two-year romance with Karl was unconsummated, which might be explained by the fact that he's now cutting a swathe through Glasgow's gay scene, according to Facebook. I got good marks in my final exams – good enough, anyway, to get me a uni place at Edinburgh and secure me a passport away from home and the stifling misery it had come to represent.

By the time I was eighteen, the whole Goth thing had started to get a bit old. Misery had served me well for my teenage years, but I was over it now. Also, having shed the puppy fat that Mum's random cooking and comfort-eating ice cream to remind me of Dad had layered on me, I felt ready to emerge from my chrysalis of black velvet and become one of the hot girls. So I pierced my belly button, discovered that I looked good in ultra-lowrise jeans, and learned to like Franz Ferdinand and The Libertines. I might not have been entirely convinced by my own transformation, but it was enough to make Polly and Wizzy, who were firmly ensconced in the elite of the cool students in my first year, be my friends. After a bit, I found I didn't have to pretend I was cool too any more – they just liked me. It was fine. I was who I was now, and it worked. And Mum, meanwhile, had finally been persuaded by her GP that antidepressants weren't a guaranteed passport to purgatory, and started to live something of a life again. But it was too late – the damage to our relationship had been done.

"And how is Joshua?" Mum said. She would never express her disapproval of my living in sin directly – instead, she did so by 'forgetting' my boyfriends' names. Declan had become David; Simon, Samuel. Disconcertingly, she'd never got Karl's name wrong, which made me suspect that she'd known exactly how innocent our relationship had been.

"Julian's fine," I said. "Working very hard in his new job, getting used to being back in London… you know. I expect you'll meet him sooner or later."

Perhaps we could arrange for her to come down to London for the day, take her shopping, buy her lunch at John Lewis. Something like that. Eventually. But the idea of Julian here, with the inadequate central heating, the nylon carpet that gave you electric shocks when you touched any-thing, the flying ducks on the wall that had been there for as long as I could remember and the plastic Christmas tree hung with ropes of red and gold tinsel – just no.

I racked my brains for the names of a few of Mum's friends from church and asked after them, and feigned interest in the answers. I drank another cup of tea and ate another stale biscuit and resisted the urge to check my phone yet again for a text from Julian. I didn't ask her if she'd heard from Dad.

At last Mum suggested we have some supper, and heated up some soup – M&S chicken and mushroom, presumably in my honour, as she normally shops at Morrisons. Then we watched an old episode of *Downton Abbey*, and then, at nine o'clock, Mum said it was time for bed because she had to be up early for church, and asked if I'd like a hot-water bottle.

I almost said no, just out of churlishness, but I was glad I hadn't when I got into bed and found that the sheets were so cold they felt almost damp.

"Good night, Stella," Mum said, and I held my cheek obediently for a kiss. "I'll try not to wake you tomorrow until I get back from the early service, and then we can get our dinner on."

"Night, Mum," I said. My hands were almost literally itching to pick up my phone and text Julian, who, surely, would have texted me back by now.

"Would you like the light off?"

"No, it's fine, leave it." Which would mean getting out of my now tolerably warm bed into the freezing cold to turn it off myself. But fuck it, it could stay on all night for all I cared.

"Would you like me to leave the door open?"

"No! No, thanks, Mum, closed is fine."

At last she left, and I snatched up my phone like a crackhead getting her hands on a pipe after a long dry spell. But there was no text from Julian. I checked that the one I'd sent him six hours earlier had gone through, and it had. What the hell was going on? I wanted to call him, quite desperately, but I didn't want Mum to overhear our conversation.

I listened to her pottering about, doing her usual paranoid check that all the doors and windows were secured, then cleaning her teeth. Then there was a long silence, during which I knew she'd be kneeling by her bed in her calf-length, long-sleeved nightie, saying her prayers. No wonder Dad had fallen for Karen's earthy charm and crêpy cleavage, I thought – that was a passion-killer right there. At last I heard the creak of her bedsprings and click of her light-switch – sounds I thought I had forgotten, but were as familiar now as the cracks in the ceiling.

Then, at last, there was silence, and I pressed Call.

I heard the phone ring and ring, imagining Julian at the table in our flat, engrossed in work, his shoulders hunched over his laptop. I imagined him becoming conscious of the buzzing of the phone, his concentration breaking, a moment of annoyance before he realised it would be me. Then he'd jump up, looking around, still half-immersed in what he'd been doing, trying to remember where he'd left it. And just as he got a hand to it, the vibration would stop, and he'd say, "Fuck!" and immediately call me back.

I started to leave a message, confident that I would be interrupted by his incoming call, but it didn't come.

"Hey, you," I said. "I'm here at Mum's, it's pretty grim and seriously cold, and I'm missing you. I hope you're okay and not working too hard. Don't forget to eat. And have a lovely rest of the evening, if I don't hear from you – but I'm sure I will. I'm missing you. I said that already, didn't I? I love you."

I ended the call and held my phone in my hands, looking at its blank, unhelpful screen. Where was he? Perhaps he was in the shower and that's why he hadn't answered.

I went on to Facebook and sent Polly and Wizzy messages saying what a crap time I was having, and how jealous I was of Polly, making mulled wine in the hotel kitchen, and Wizzy, about to arrive in Brazil. Then I looked at the screen some more, and waited. Then I gave up, and found my old, tattered copy of *The Crimson Fairy Book* on the buckling shelf above the bed, and tried to lose myself in the stories.

It was a strategy that had worked well for me when I was twelve, but it wasn't as effective now. Every handsome prince who was seduced away from his betrothed was Julian, looking at Francine with the expression on his face that I couldn't quite fathom, but certainly couldn't forget. Every adventurer on a quest for his lady love was Will, who I remembered was spending Christmas pretending to be some woman from RealRomance's boyfriend. Every damsel in distress, imprisoned in a tower, was me, although I had to admit to myself that, as jailers went, Mum was relatively benevolent.

At last, when I was about to give up and go to sleep, my phone rang.

"Little star," Julian's voice was muffled by background noise, and, I suspected, by booze. "I'm so sorry I missed your call. I'm missing you so much. God, I can't wait to see you. I'm out with some people from work. My battery's about to…" And that was it. The call cut off before I could ask him where he was or who he was with.

The next day and the next, I spent alone with Mum. She bought me a beautiful new set of paintbrushes and a cashmere cardigan for Christmas, and I felt as guilty as hell about having only bought her a book about Desmond Tutu, which I'd found in the charity shop, and a box of Thorntons. She roasted a chicken for our Christmas lunch, and I peeled the potatoes, nuked the frozen peas and stirred boiling water into Bisto. She opened a bottle of Schloer because it was a celebration. I resisted the urge to go to the off-licence and buy all the cheap booze it would sell me, because I remembered how Mum used to sniff at me and make a cat's-bum mouth when I went out drinking as a teenager.

We didn't talk very much. I told her about Polly and Angus's wedding and the impending arrival of their baby, because I knew babies were one of the few things that made her happy. But when she said, "And are you and Jeffrey…?" I hastily changed the subject, and told her a bit about the painting I was doing for Martha, but I could tell that reminded her of Dad, so I soon shut that line of conversation down too. I didn't ask her about her life, because really, what was there for her to tell? She went to work, she went to church, she microwaved things, she prayed and slept. That was all.

As the hours went by, I found myself becoming more and more anxious. Julian texted me on Christmas Day, saying he loved me and hoped I was having fun. I clung to my pride and didn't ring him again – but that didn't stop me from thinking about him.

Where was he? What was he doing? Who was he with? And why the fuck wasn't he calling me? My worry made me even more snappy and irritable with Mum, especially when she asked, over and over again, how Justin was and whether I'd spoken to him. I can honestly say I have never been more relieved than when the day after Boxing Day arrived and it was time for me to get the hell out of there and go to Polly and Angus's and have some actual fun.

But, as I remembered had always been her way, Mum wouldn't let me go without a massive amount of fuss. Was I sure I wouldn't like another cup of tea? Had I remembered my mobile phone charger? (Okay, I hadn't.) Did I need to go to the loo?

And finally, when everything was packed and I was about to shut the door behind me, she said, "Just a minute, there's something I need to give you to take with you." And she pottered slowly out of the room and spent an interminable time rummaging around upstairs, before reappearing at last with a lumpy parcel. "Now, here you are. This is a little jumper I knitted for Polly's baby – you didn't say whether she's having a boy or a girl so I used yellow. I do hope she likes it. God bless you, Stella."

I thanked her through gritted teeth, stuffed it in my bag, kissed her with enthusiasm born of relief that I was finally getting out of there, and legged it back up the road, my bag rattling behind me like a little dog unaccustomed to walks.

CHAPTER FIFTEEN

The farewell committee that assembled in the doorway to see them off the next day was the same as the one that had gathered to see Will and Becky up the stairs on Christmas Eve, only, if anything, warmer.

"Goodbye, Will – I do hope we'll see you again soon," said Becky's mum.

"Let's catch up for a beer in London, bro," said Becky's sister's boyfriend.

"I'll send you that DVD I was telling you about," said Becky's sister.

"Why don't you come again next week, for Christmas?" said Becky's dotty nan.

"Mrooow," said Muggle the cat, twining himself around Will's legs and giving his ankle a friendly nip.

"We'd better be off, or you two will miss your train," said Becky's dad, slamming the boot of the car.

Will snapped his seatbelt closed and contemplated the back of Becky's head as she sat in the passenger seat, chatting to her father about their fictitious plans for New Year's Eve. There was going to be a party at Becky and her flatmate's place, apparently. Tania was making pulled pork and Becky was going to be in charge of cocktails. Will felt irrationally hurt, like a schoolboy hearing his classmates discussing the senior prom when he didn't have a date.

"Right, I'll drop you off here," Becky's dad said, and they went through a final little scuffle of, "No, it's all right, I can carry it myself," "Ring us soon, darling," and "Thanks so much for having me." Then the car pulled away and Will and Becky were alone.

"Well," he said. "We survived."

"We did." Becky grinned, pushing her hair back from her face with a gloved hand. "God, it's freezing. I hope that bloody train's on time. Dad's always so worried about being late that he's way too early. I've wasted hours of my life on this platform."

"What are you going to do next?" Will asked.

"Next? Stick a load of washing on when I get home, then tomorrow I might brave the sales on Bond Street, then I'm back in the office until the thirty-first."

"No, I mean about them – your family – us." He tried again, this time including imaginary quote marks with his fingers. "'Us', I mean."

"Oh." Becky turned away, looking down the train tracks. "I'll give it another couple of months, then tell them we've broken up. They like you, so I won't make you out to be a bastard, don't worry. I'll say you've been offered a deputy headship in Wales, or something. And they'll cut me a bit of slack on the basis of my broken heart, so hopefully I'll be okay for next Christmas. They don't mean to make such a big deal of it – they just want me to be happy, but their definition of happiness is a bit narrow."

Will said, "I know this wasn't part of the plan, but has it occurred to you that we could, maybe, like, give it a go for real? Because that's occurred to me."

She turned back and looked at him, unsmiling. "Will, I think you're a lovely guy. But I'm not sure you get what this was all about. I thought I'd explained but I guess I didn't.

Do you think I'm single because I can't get anyone to go out with me?"

"No! Of course not! You must be fighting guys off all the time, you're gorgeous." Will was glad of the cold wind blasting his hot face. "I just thought, maybe, you and I… we got on okay this weekend. That's all. I thought maybe we could see each other again, see what happens."

Her face softened. "Will, if I was looking for a relationship, you're the kind of person I would look for. But I'm not. I know that isn't what you wanted to hear, but there it is. I work eighty-hour weeks. I want to be managing a hedge fund before I'm thirty-five. In the last couple of years, I've seen my female colleagues drop like flies. They meet some guy and they fall in love, and the next thing they know they're having his babies and washing his socks. I don't want kids. Therefore, I don't need to waste time on a relationship right now. Once I've got where I want to be, I'll think about it. There's heaps of time. But for now – well, if I want sex, there's Tinder. And to be perfectly honest I don't want it that often – sleep is a lot more appealing most of the time."

While she made her little speech, the train had been approaching the platform. Will pressed the button to open the door and handed Becky her bag.

"Okay," he said. "I guess that makes sense. I can relate – I was kind of in that position myself." Suddenly, he really wanted to tell her that he wasn't who she thought he was, that he knew and understood the drive to succeed, to get to the top of the game. He wanted to tell her about the Frog Prince, and his fake dating profile, and see what she would make of him then.

But she said, "I think we should say goodbye now. I could do with fitting in an hour's work on the way home."

"Right," Will said. "It's been good meeting you. And Becky – you should tell your family what you've just told me. They love you, they'll understand."

"I'll think about it." She kissed him lightly on the lips, and he smelled her perfume and her toothpaste for the last time. "Bye, Will. Take care."

Will stayed on the train for a long time once it had arrived at Waterloo. He wanted to make sure Becky had well and truly gone – their parting had been awkward, but running into her again would be downright mortifying. So he waited until the flood of passengers passing the window slowed to a trickle and then stopped, and the guard came through the carriage picking up stray newspapers and gave him a funny look, then he disembarked.

He'd never noticed it before – maybe on normal, working days it wasn't true – but London was full of couples. Mums and dads laden with primary-coloured plastic paraphernalia, their children bundled up in parkas and wellies. An elderly man and his wife, dressed up for a night on the town, holding hands as they made their way to the South Bank exit. Two bearded hipster guys kissing on the platform, happily reunited after their separate Christmases. In all the years he'd been single, it had never crossed Will's mind that he might also be lonely, but he felt it now.

He thought of his flat, stylish and sterile, with its minimalist white furniture, on which Will was always too afraid to eat takeaway pizza, and its dazzling view that he barely saw, because his desk faced the other way. He could go there now, turn the desk around – why the fuck hadn't he done that months ago? – and play Minecraft and work his way through a few beers, like some cliché of a nerdy loser who couldn't get a girlfriend. He could go to a bar in Soho and buy women drinks and try to pull, but he was sure his lack of mojo would be clear for all to see. He could – he considered this seriously for a bit – ring Charlotte. But that way madness lay.

Life had been so much simpler before he'd embarked on this dating charade, he realised. Before, women had just been people; now they seemed to fall into a whole set of complex categories. There were ones he didn't fancy, ones who didn't fancy him, ones who were already taken. If this was a computer game, there'd be some puzzle that needed to be solved, some way of restoring order to things and getting them back to how they'd been before. But he couldn't see that happening, not at all.

He sent a brief text to Julian asking if he and Stella fancied a drink, waited a few moments to see if his friend would reply, then got on the Tube and went to the office.

"Yo, wassup?" Giles was slouched low in his chair, his feet on his desk. He was plugged into his iPad, but switched it off as soon as he saw Will, and Will wondered if he'd been watching porn. As long as it didn't compromise the security of their servers, he guessed it was none of his business, and he didn't have the stomach to comment on the strong smell of fag smoke in the office either. "Thought you were in Not London with some bird."

"I was," Will said. "But I came back early, wanted to make sure you weren't slacking off. At least not any more than usual."

Giles swung his legs to the floor and stood, hitching up his drainpipe jeans. "Drink?" he said.

"Yeah, go on," said Will. Giles pulled two bottles of Red Stripe out of the fridge and chucked one to Will, so when he opened it, froth gushed over his hand.

"How was your Christmas, anyway?" Will asked.

"Sweet," Giles said. "Watched some *Game of Thrones*. Played The Evil Within. Fuck, that game's sick – the agony crossbow is, like, the raddest thing ever. Shagged some women."

Will blinked. Giles was as terminally single as he was. "No shit?"

"Nah. Jokes." Giles looked forlorn. "My flatmate did though. He's down with that. He's a PUA."

"A what?" Will said.

"Pick-up artist. It's like, these dudes go around dissing women, neg-hitting them, telling them they're ugly and that, and they get all the sex. The rest of us get stuck in the Friend Zone."

"Wait, what?" Will said. "So you meet some woman and you fancy her, but you tell her you think she's a moose, and then she'll sleep with you? And what's the Friend Zone?"

"It's where you fancy a girl, but she thinks you're just a mate," Giles said. "Guys think, right, that if they make friends with women, then they can backdoor-it and get them to have sex. But it doesn't work like that. Avoid the Friend Zone at all costs, mate."

Will could relate to that. Shame he hadn't known about it several months back, though. "So hold on, you treat girls like rubbish, refuse to be their friend, and then you get laid?"

"Kind of like that," Giles said. "I'm not explaining it right. Have a gander at this."

He unplugged the headphones from his iPad, swished the screen a couple of times and handed it to Will.

Will pressed play, and music blared out of the speaker. It took a moment, but Will recognised it from the Pink Room scene from the *Twin Peaks* movie. The cameras panned through a dimly lit apartment that looked, in its sleek modernism, a bit like Will's own. A pair of high-heeled shoes, a bra and a suspender belt were lying discarded on the floor. Then the shot changed to a bedroom, where a man and a woman were sitting on a chaise-longue. She was a stunning blonde in a black dress, smiling rigidly through just-parted red lips. He was wearing an open-necked shirt, a black suit jacket and tight jeans. He had too-long, too-clean dark hair, and a habit of running his fingers through it.

"What a sleaze," Will said.

"Shut up and listen," said Giles.

"Hi," the man's accent was self-consciously neutral, his voice self-consciously husky. "I'm Clay, and today I'm going to show you some of the basic techniques you'll need to become an alpha and succeed with women."

The blonde lowered her eyes and crossed her stockinged legs.

"Phwoar," said Giles.

"First, we need to make ourselves the focus of attention," Clay said. "Wherever you are, in a bar, a restaurant, or just walking down the street, make sure you stand out from the crowd. Don't run with the herd – don't be afraid to ditch your friends. Now, you've seen a woman, and you want to get to know her. What do you do?

"Rule one: don't act needy. She needs to prove her value to you. Make it clear that you've got other options – you're talking to her because she wants you to. Say, 'I can tell that you find me attractive.'"

"Yeah, then she says, 'I can tell you to fuck off,'" Will said.

Clay gave a little 'we're all guys together' smirk at the camera. The blonde licked her lips. "But sometimes you're gonna come on too strong, and then you've shown weakness. That's when you neg her. Don't be nasty – you don't want a drink in your face – but counteract a positive with a negative. Like, you could say, 'You have a great body. I have a friend who would really fancy you.'"

Will pressed Stop. "For fuck's sake," he said. "What a load of bollocks."

"It's not!" Giles said. "It works, honest. My flatmate…"

"Is Russell Brand? Either that or he's shitting you. Come on, let's go for a pint."

As they were locking up and setting the alarm, Will noticed a text from Julian, saying that Stella was at her mother's for Christmas, but he was up for a drink. Will replied with the name of their Shoreditch local, and he and Giles made their familiar way there, ordered their familiar round, and were soon perched on uncomfortable wooden chairs at a rickety wooden table (the whole dive bar aesthetic was huge at the moment, and places like this tended to prioritise irony over comfort) drinking beer with Four Roses chasers.

Over the course of that drink and the next, they covered Ignite's changing fortunes at Ping Pong Fight Club (one of the new programmers, a girl called Lydia, was showing serious potential). They discussed the merits of sweet versus salted popcorn, of Reddit versus 4Chan, and of Jennifer Lawrence versus Kate Upton. They talked about some exciting new advances in data security software, a subject about which Giles knew considerably more than Will did, so Will's contribution to the conversation needed to be nothing much more than saying, "Hmmm, interesting," a few times and drinking more beer.

After a bit, a waitress approached their table.

"Watch this," Giles said, under his breath.

"Can I get you guys anything else?" She was quite hot, Will noticed – and would have been even hotter if she'd been wearing normal clothes instead of a tight white T-shirt and tiny hotpants that cut into her upper thighs.

"Hey, I really like your style," Giles said. "Do you work in fashion?"

The waitress stared blankly at him. "It's, like, a uniform," she said.

"I can tell you find me attractive," said Giles.

Will cringed. The waitress looked blank.

"You have an amazing body," Giles went on. "I have a friend who'd really fancy you."

The waitress looked like nothing would please her more than to tip the dregs of Giles's beer over his head, but she smiled determinedly and said, "Yeah. Whatever. That's nice. Can I get you guys anything else?"

Will ordered another round.

"See? That went really well," Giles said. "I told you it works."

"Mate, the only reason she didn't tell you to fuck off was so we'd tip her," Will said.

"Crap!" Giles protested. "I could tell she liked me. Clay explains it in one of his YouTubes – it's all about body language. Didn't you see how her pupils dilated?"

"Yeah, with rage," Will said.

"And she touched her hair," Giles went on. "That's, like, a thing."

"Only because her pencil was behind her ear and she needed it to write down our order," Will said.

He believed in taking the rational approach in almost all areas of his life: his flat had been purchased not because he liked it, although he supposed it was all right, but because it seemed a sensible investment and he had to live somewhere. The risks he took with the business were calculated ones, and almost always paid off. But he supposed he was a die-hard romantic where women were concerned, and he didn't like the idea of manipulating girls into bed. Besides, it was blatantly obvious that it didn't work – not for Giles, anyway.

Giles looked as if he was about to argue the point some more, but that was when Julian turned up, and, to Will's surprise, he wasn't alone.

Chapter Sixteen

All the guests gathered at the palace for the wedding of Princess Polly to Prince Angus. Kings and queens came from all over the land, wearing splendid clothes and bringing magnificent gifts. Princess Stella, arrayed in a gown of sapphire blue, was as beautiful as any of them. But she did not smile or laugh. Without her prince, she could not join in the rejoicing…

I made my train just in time, and collapsed into a window seat, plugging in my earphones to drown out the voice in my head that seemed determined to tell me over and over how horrible I'd been to Mum. I looked at the familiar scenery unfolding in front of me, flipped through the new *Cosmopolitan* and wished I could afford to go shopping for clothes. Then it was time to change on to a smaller, slower train, and I passed the time by eating a chilly and tasteless ham sandwich, and looking out of the window. Soon the flat, sheep-dotted fields began to give way to harsher scenery, and the light began to fade, and I slept for a bit before being woken up by the announcement that we were about to arrive.

Angus was waiting for me on the platform as he'd promised. I dashed over to him and hugged him, and, as usual, it was like hugging a garden shed. Angus is well over six feet tall, but it's not his height so much as his rugby-player's solidity that makes him so physically imposing.

"Oh my God, it's been ages since I last saw you!" I said. "Not since Edinburgh. How's life? Has Polly's cooking made you fat? And what the very fuck is with the face 'fro?"

Angus had always been clean-shaven, but now he was sporting an impressive, full-on ginger beard.

"Don't you like it, Stella? It keeps my face warm. And it confuses people – when they pass me in the street I can see them going, 'Nutter or hipster?' Hours of fun. Keeps the general population on its toes." He swung my bag into the boot of his battered Land Rover. "Jump in."

He let the clutch out and pulled off in a series of jerks. "How's Polly?"

"Fed up. She keeps saying she can't believe she's still got more than two months to go. She says she feels like a beached whale and she's sick of me having to paint her toenails for her, which is fair enough, because I'm crap at it. You'll take over, won't you, while you're here? She can't make her mind up, that's the problem. I paint them pink and then a few days later she wants them blue, then the other day she wanted yellow but she made me take it all off afterwards because she said it looked like a fungal infection."

I laughed. "Maybe in another couple of weeks she won't be able to see her toes at all, and you won't need to bother any more. I can't believe you guys are getting married, it's the most exciting thing in the world, ever. Are you nervous?"

"About the wedding? Not really. It's all going to be pretty low-key. We're got rid of the last of the paying guests tomorrow so it's just going to be family after that. I'm fucking terrified about the baby though, and Polly is too. At first she thought she'd want to be all 'woo' about the whole labour thing, with whale music playing and her in a warm bath and the rest of it, but she's changed her mind about that now, thank God. Being out in the sticks like we are, if something went wrong... I don't even want to think about it. So we're settled on a proper hospital birth with all the drugs she can eat."

"Drugs sound good," I said.

I didn't think I needed to remind Angus of Polly's notoriously low pain threshold. The one and only time she attempted a Brazilian wax, she rang me in tears from the salon, saying, "Oh my God, Stella, the woman's put boiling wax all over my fanny and she's just ripped off, like, a millimetre, and it's too sore! I need her to stop! I can't go through with it!"

Thankfully I managed to talk her down and convince her that running out into the street covered in rapidly hardening wax would be a bad idea. I rushed over to the salon armed with paracetamol and half a bottle of Smirnoff, and eventually the wax was removed, but Polly refused to let the beautician finish the job, so the first time she slept with Angus her minge looked like Cressida out of *Mockingjay*'s head.

So yeah, Polly and pain. Bad combination.

"And the hotel? How are the rich Americans?"

"Still filling the coffers. We were pretty busy over the autumn, in spite of half the place still being a building site, and we've been taking bookings for next year already. Mostly down to Polly's cooking. We're going to close now for a couple of weeks and work like mad to get the refurb finished, then reopen in February. And Gray's talking about getting a golf course built in the grounds before next summer, just nine holes..."

I stifled a giggle. I'd forgotten about Angus and his brother's obsession with golf. After their first date, Polly had told me how, in his nervous state, he'd started talking about it and been unable to stop, and how by the time his stroke-by-stroke description of his last round had reached the seventeenth hole Polly was so desperate with boredom she would have chewed her own arm off to get away, only she actually fancied him a lot and reckoned if he was snogging her then he couldn't be talking about golf. Fortunately it had been a one-off, she said, and as their relationship progressed he's spared her the worst excesses of his tales from the fairway.

So we chatted about general things for the rest of the journey, and at last the house came into view, a square, grey building, looking unbelievably beautiful with the rising moon reflected in the loch behind it. I ran inside, my feet echoing on the flagstones, calling for Polly.

"Stella? I'm up here," I heard her familiar voice coming from somewhere high up in the house, and I dashed up the stairs to the top floor, passing oil paintings of lairds with guns and hunting dogs and women with children peeping out from behind their crinolines, fat tartan-upholstered armchairs on the landings where the rich guests could presumably break the exhausting journey up to bed, and glassy-eyed stags' heads.

Polly and Angus's rooms, in contrast, were bright and homely. The sitting room where I found Polly was simple and uncluttered, and I recognised the sofa where she was lying, covered by a spotty blanket, from our old flat in Leith.

She sat up when she saw me, stretching like a cat, and I flung myself into her arms. "It's so amazing to see you!" we both said, sniffling a bit.

"Look at me, sleeping in the afternoon like someone's nan," she said. "I'm just so fucking tired all the time, it's ridiculous. And look how fat I've got! And my cankles! I'm not fit to be seen."

"Don't be ridiculous," I said. "You're gorgeous, you're glowing. And look at your bump!" Cankles or no cankles, even with the imprint of the sofa cushion on her cheek, Polly was radiant and just the same. Her hair smelled of the apple shampoo she always used, and she was wrapped in the fluffy pink dressing gown that had hung on our bathroom door for all those years. Seeing Mum had felt like visiting a stranger; seeing Polly felt like coming home.

"Come and see the nursery," she said, heaving herself up. "You're sleeping there, I hope that's okay. We're a bit short of space. The plan is to move to the gatehouse when the baby's older, but it's damp and full of spiders and Angus hasn't had time to sort it out."

"But everything else looks amazing," I said, remembering the shell the house had been the only other time I'd seen it. "Like it's all been here forever. How did you do it?"

"eBay," she said. "It turns out there's quite a market for this sort of thing. I keep getting into these massive bidding wars on taxidermy and ancestor portraits, but we're getting there. There's a painting I've got my eye on for over the fireplace in the drawing room that's the absolute spit of Angus, ginger beard and everything. We'll be able to pretend he's a great-great-great uncle or something. And for all I know he might be – it could easily be one of the family portraits Uncle Andrew flogged to pay his gambling debts. You're in here."

The nursery was all bright primary colours, with a mobile of fluffy sheep hanging above the cot. There was a futon on the floor for me, and Angus had put my bag next to it.

"This is so gorgeous!" I said. "Seriously, Polly, I can't believe you're having a baby!"

"You can't?" she gestured ironically at her tummy. "You think I've just been at the pies?"

"No! You know what I mean!" We both started to giggle, and I gave her another huge hug, and it must have woken the baby, because next thing I knew her bump kicked me in the ribs.

"My God! Does it do that a lot?" I gazed at her in awe.

"Yep, in between dancing Gangnam Style on my bladder," she said. "I tell you what, this baby had better be cute, because having it is a right arse. I sometimes wish it would just be over, then I remember what I've got to get through first, and I decide it can stay put for as long as it likes."

"Oh, I almost forgot," I said. "I've got a present for you from Mum. She made it herself, so it's probably a bit pants."

I pulled the tiny, squashy parcel out of my bag and gave it to Polly. She ripped off the paper and stroked the lacy little yellow cardigan, and started to cry.

"That's so lovely. Oh bless your Mum, it's so tiny! I can't believe I'm going to have an actual baby. Sorry, sorry, it's the hormones. When I'm not crying I'm weeing, I'm leakier than a leaky thing."

I was feeling a bit teary myself, so I said, "You must tell me what I can do to help. I want to be useful, while I'm here. Do we need to make food for the guests or anything? You know I can't cook but I can peel potatoes or whatever."

"They eat All. The. Time," she said. "Today, right, they had a huge fried breakfast, and then we gave them sandwiches to take out on their walk, and then they had a three-course lunch and two hours later they were stuffing themselves with scones. But dinner tonight's just soup and cheese and bread and stuff so it won't be too much work, and they're leaving tomorrow, and we've got Rhona and Magda to help. But we should probably go downstairs and get cracking. I'll just put on some clothes. And while we sort out supper you must tell me all about how things are going with Julian."

"Not," I said firmly, "until you've shown me your wedding dress."

And I squealed and Polly squealed and the two of us did a little dance around the nursery, giggling like maniacs.

I'd forgotten what a slave-driver my friend could be. Polly might have resigned herself to not having the wedding dress of her dreams, but she was going to have everything else just so, if it killed her (and me, Angus and Gray). Over the next few days, delivery after delivery arrived at the house: champagne, industrial quantities of candles, enough food to eradicate a famine.

"For a small wedding, you're certainly not doing things by halves," I said, looking down from the top of the ladder where I was precariously standing, trying to figure out how to attach what looked like about four miles of tartan bunting to the rock-hard oak beams of the dining room.

"I suppose we could Blu-Tack it, if all else fails," Polly said. "Anyway, yeah, about the 'small' thing. It's turned out to be not so very small. I may have got a tiny bit carried away inviting people on Facebook, and of course my entire family have dropped everything and are coming, and there are loads of them. But we've got the space to put them all up, so I thought, why not? And then I thought, we're going to want to market this place as a wedding venue next year, so it made sense to do it properly and get some decent photos for the website. How are your spud-peeling skills coming on, by the way, Stella? Because the veg man brought about half a ton of neeps and tatties and Rhona and Magda are going to have a job on their hands."

Rhona and Magda were the two blindingly efficient ladies of a certain age who helped out in the kitchen and waitressed. One of them was Scottish, obviously, and the other Polish, and I'd developed an embarrassing blind spot about which one was which, and had to wait for them to speak before I could tell the difference.

"Just keep ordering me around, it's absolutely fine," I said. "That's what I'm here for."

"You are a total star," Polly said.

It was an unfortunate choice of word, because it made me think of Julian, which I had managed not to do for the best part of an hour. Since I left London a week before, we'd only spoken three times. I know I'm sounding like a needy, clingy, pathetic wimp, but I was missing him, and his sporadic communication was making me miss him in a not-good way. Instead of anticipating his arrival happily and eagerly, I was twitchy with anxiety about why he didn't call, whether he still loved me, what he was doing back at home. I longed to feel his arms around me, hear his reassuring words about how much he adored and desired me. I'd developed a habit of checking my phone obsessively, interrupting conversations if I thought I heard it chirruping in another room.

I kept remembering Julian saying ever-so-casually that he was out for drinks with people from work. But what did that mean? Did it mean Richard and Raj, or did it mean Francine? His elusiveness was beginning to make me feel seriously insecure.

"Aha, here comes the cavalry," Polly said, and I turned towards the door, almost falling off my step-ladder, to see Gray brandishing a staple gun.

"This should do the trick with the old bunting," he said. "Want to have a go, Stella, or shall I do it?"

My shoulder muscles were burning with the effort of holding the bunting up above my head, so it was with some relief, although at the expense of my pride, that I climbed down and relinquished the ladder. I don't mind admitting that the view from the ground, of Gray's muscular denim-clad legs, was something of an incentive too.

I felt my phone vibrate against my hip in the jeans pocket, and snatched it out before the buzzing had even finished. There was a text from Julian. My heart beat faster as I opened it.

"See you later. xxx."

What did that mean? Had he changed his mind and decided to arrive a day early? I felt a surge of excitement and texted back. "Are you coming today??? Amazing!"

There was a longish pause, then a reply flashed up on my screen. "No, tomorrow, like we planned. See you then. X."

I read the messages again, puzzled. Later meant later, didn't it? It didn't mean tomorrow. And we'd made our arrangements, he knew when I was expecting him – why would he need to tell me? Was it possible that the message hadn't been meant for me, but for someone else? The thought made my stomach lurch with anxiety. I'd ask him, I decided, just come straight out and ask him, when we spoke tonight.

But I wasn't able to fret about Julian for long, because Polly said, "Right, come on, Stella, we've got place cards to write and the florist is meant to be here…" she glanced at her watch, "half an hour ago. And I'm really sorry, but I'm not sure this red on my toenails is working for me. Would you mind awfully if we try the green?"

"Polly, you're going to be wearing closed shoes," I said. "No one will get even the tiniest glimpse of your toes. But of course I don't mind."

Polly hadn't been exaggerating about the number of guests. Over the course of that day, about forty people turned up: Polly's parents and her three sisters with their husbands and children, old friends and acquaintances I hadn't seen since university, former rugby team-mates of Angus's. Rhona, Madga and I were rushed off our feet making beds for them all, and Polly cooked a great vat of boeuf en daube for dinner. It was hard to imagine how the wedding the next day would be more of a celebration than this – although, of course, it would be for me, because Julian would be there.

I was too nervous to eat much. As soon as I could, I left the table, phone in hand, and walked out into the icy night. The snow crunched under my feet as I made my way down to the loch, the sound of music and laughter from the house gradually fading away. I wrapped my scarf more tightly round my neck. It was a beautiful night – although snow had been falling steadily throughout the day, it had stopped now, and the wind had dropped. I could see thousands of stars above me in the clear sky, and the moon reflected with barely a ripple in the still water.

I tried to imagine Julian standing there next to me, his hand warm in my cold fingers. I pictured him looking at me, the way Angus looked at Polly, his face full of affection, desire and something else I couldn't quite place – certainty, maybe, or trust, or some other, deeper thing I found it hard to remember sharing with Julian. I took a deep gulp of the frosty air and picked up my phone, holding it up before me like a talisman, hoping that the force of my longing would bring him to me.

I dialled his number, and it rang and rang and went to voicemail.

I'd been anxious about Julian's silence, unsure about what it meant about his feelings for me, increasingly insecure. But now I was genuinely worried. What if something had happened to him? What if he'd been run over by a bus, or was ill, alone in bed with no one to look after him?

What if he'd been mugged, his phone and wallet stolen, and was lying in hospital unconscious and no one knew who he was? What if he needed me, and I was hundreds of miles away?

With increasingly horrible and improbable scenarios flashing through my brain, I rang Will. I'd ask him to go round to the flat, I decided, just to check Julian was okay.

He answered his phone on the first ring. "Hi Stella! How's it going? How's Scotland?"

"Scotland's good," I said. "Freezing, but good. Polly's wedding preparations have hit peak mental. It's going to be an amazing day. But, Will…"

Before I could say anything more, Will said, "So Julian's going up there to join you for Hogmanay?"

"You've seen him?" I said. "Is he all right? I was worried."

Will said, "Julian's fine, Stella. I saw him the other day, and he texted me for a Minecraft hack about an hour ago."

He sounded abrupt, annoyed even. I tried to think if I'd done anything to piss him off – we hadn't spoken for a while, but the last time I'd emailed him, before Christmas, he'd sounded like his normal self.

"Great!" I said. "It's just, he hasn't been… I've been trying to call him and he's not answering his phone. But I'm sure he's just busy. How are you, anyway? How was Christmas with whatshername? Are you going to see her again?"

"No," Will said. "We can write that one off as another non-starter."

"What happened?" I said. "Will? Go on, tell me what happened."

Perhaps another of Will's dating catastrophe stories would restore normality between us, let us laugh together like we used to, break through the invisible yet seemingly impermeable barrier I suddenly felt between us. But he said nothing about Becky, or Christmas.

"Stella, when did you talk to Julian last?" he asked.

"Um, earlier today. We didn't actually talk, but he texted me. He said he's going to be here tomorrow."

It was true, and it made me realise how stupid I sounded – how controlling, needy and neurotic. How like Mum.

"So it's okay," I added in a rush. "I'm so sorry to have interrupted your evening. He's fine. I was just being a bit mad. I've got to go."

There was a pause, then what sounded like a long exhalation. "Okay, Stella. Have a great day tomorrow, and happy New Year."

I ended the call and went back inside the house, shaking with cold, feeling as if I might start to cry. I wished I could talk to Polly, like we used to when we were both single, endlessly analysing why this man or that one hadn't rung, whether he was going to and what it meant (conversations that were usually interrupted by Wizzy saying, "It means he's just not into you. Move on. You're worth more than this."). But Polly had more important things to think about, so I said goodnight and went to bed.

"How do I look?" Polly said. "Go on, be honest. Like a walking marquee."

"Don't be ridiculous," I chorused, along with Polly's mum and her sisters. "You look amazing."

It was true. Polly had decided that there was no way she was going to wear white – attempting to look virginal in her condition would be an absurd waste of time, she said. She'd opted for red instead – a gorgeous, berry colour that made her skin look even more glowy than usual and her eyes even greener. There were red rosebuds pinned in her shiny dark hair. She looked so beautiful it made me want to cry, and her mum was crying, dabbing away tears with a tissue, taking care not to smudge her eye make-up. Everything was perfect, everything was ready – except Julian wasn't there.

I'd woken up to a text from him, saying briefly that he was sorry he'd missed my call, he'd been busy, but he'd see me today. He hadn't said what time he was going to arrive, and Gray had been on stand-by all day waiting to drive to the station and pick him up. But he hadn't called, and time was running out.

I'd stopped feeling anxious, and now I was getting seriously angry. But I couldn't show it – I had to put on a calm front for Polly.

As if she'd read my thoughts, she said, "Have you heard from him, Stella? Is he on his way? We're meant to be going downstairs in half an hour."

"Don't wait," I said. "You can't not get married because he's running late! He's on his way, he said so. It's going to be fine. He'll probably come bursting in midway through the ceremony and show me up totally. I'll go and get changed and then let's get you hitched."

Half an hour later, right on schedule, I was ready, my make-up done, my blue lace dress looking even better than I'd hoped. I posed for photos with Polly, trying to smile, glad that the lump in my throat couldn't be seen. Still, when I looked at the pictures Polly posted on Facebook a couple of days later, I looked white and tense, next to the beaming, lovely bride.

I walked down the broad staircase with Polly, trying to share her excitement, wishing I could be as happy as she was.

I followed her into the dining room, where the chairs had been arranged in rows with an aisle between them for

Polly to walk up to where Angus and Gray were waiting, tall and handsome in their kilts. I returned Angus's delighted smile when he saw his bride, watched him wipe away a tear and managed not to cry myself. I took Polly's bouquet of crimson roses, and sat down in the chair Gray had kept for me in the front row, with another empty seat next to it for Julian.

"Welcome, everyone," the registrar said. "We're gathered here today, on this joyous occasion, many of you having travelled a long way at short notice, for which I know the bride and groom are hugely grateful, to celebrate the marriage of Polly and Angus. Before we begin, may I just ask you to please make sure all your mobile phones are switched off."

That was it. My best friend was getting married, and my boyfriend wasn't going to be there.

I turned off my phone as I'd been told, and tried to force all thoughts of Julian out of my mind, and think only of how happy I was for Polly.

Julian didn't come bursting into the room in the middle of the ceremony. He didn't interrupt the photos afterwards. He wasn't there when the first bottles of champagne were opened, or when dinner was served, or when the speeches were made. He didn't see the cake being cut or Polly and Angus have their first dance.

Almost the worst thing about it was lying to Wizzy. She rang from Rio, just after her email was read out at the end of the speeches, along with all the others from people who hadn't been able to come. We chatted for about an hour, and I told her every single detail of the day, except that one. When she asked if Julian was having a good time, I said he was.

I knew she'd find out, sooner rather than later, but I wasn't ready to hear what I knew she'd say. I could imagine it, word for word. 'You don't have to put up with this, Stella. It's inexcusable. It's worse than rude – it's rude on steroids. It's gone through the rude barrier and come out the other side. There is only one thing for you to do in this situation: dump his sorry arse. As soon as he arrives, dump him. And if he doesn't turn up, go back to London and dump him there. Hand the fucker a one-way ticket to Dumpedville, population: him.'

I knew that was what she'd say, and I knew it was what I'd say to her, if she was in my position. But still, I couldn't listen to her saying it, because I knew that wasn't what I was going to do.

I'd talk to Wizzy about it all eventually, of course, but I wanted to talk to Julian first, to make him understand that he needed to change his behaviour. However unique and special our love for each other was – and it was, it was the most important thing in my life – he needed to respect my friends as well as me. He'd made a mistake, and he wouldn't do it again, I was sure, once he knew how it made me feel – how sad, alone and ashamed.

Because although Wizzy didn't know what had happened, everyone else did. That was for sure. Everyone had seen the empty chair next to mine during the ceremony, the place at the top table that Magda hastily cleared away when she served dinner and there was no one to eat that plate of smoked salmon or drink champagne from that glass. I knew they knew, because not one person said anything to me. No one asked where my boyfriend was. They all felt too sorry for me.

Julian arrived a few minutes before midnight, a few hours after I'd given up hope. The party was in full swing by then. Angus and Polly had taken a break from dancing and were holding court at the top table. Gray was slow-dancing with Carrie, one of our friends from uni. I was helping Polly's dad open a fresh battery of champagne ready to toast the New Year, new beginnings and Auld Lang Syne.

I didn't see Julian come in, but the atmosphere in the room changed subtly. There was a break in the music. The volume of chatter and laughter dropped almost to nothing. I didn't think anything of it – I thought everyone was just getting ready to count down to the stroke of twelve, or someone was going to turn on a telly so we could hear the One O'Clock Gun fire from Edinburgh Castle.

Then I heard footsteps behind me, and felt a hand on my shoulder, and I knew.

I turned around. Julian said, "Here I am," as if nothing had happened, pulled me towards him and kissed me hard. Then someone did turn the telly on, the Hogmanay Live broadcast blared out, and a few seconds later the room erupted into cheers and singing. Someone passed me Julian and me glasses of champagne, and we joined in the hugging and kissing and well-wishing, which seemed to go on for even longer than usual.

When at last it had finished, Julian said, "Little star, I need to talk to you."

I felt a hollowness in the pit of my stomach, a mixture of dread and anger. He was going to tell me what had happened, where he'd been. Either it would be bad news, or it would be nothing – some stupid thing like he hadn't bothered to check the train times, and then I was going to have to tell him how he'd made me feel.

But he didn't. He took my hand in his and looked down at me and said, "Stella, will you marry me?"

CHAPTER SEVENTEEN

Will emerged from Covent Garden Tube station a good twenty minutes ahead of schedule. He hadn't been nervous before his first date with Felicity, but he was now. More at stake, he supposed. When he'd met her two weeks ago, he'd had fairly low expectations – she'd seemed pleasant enough from her profile, a veterinary surgeon who'd recently moved to London from Manchester and was looking for 'new friends, and maybe a relationship if I meet someone special'.

Her photos had shown a pretty twenty-something woman with a big smile and great legs, and her description had mentioned that her mode of transport of choice was her bicycle, so at least they had that in common. They'd exchanged a few emails and arranged to meet for a drink, and it had gone well – really well. She made him laugh. The way she ran her fingers through her cropped platinum-blond hair was distinctly hot. She had enormous hazel eyes that he could imagine staring into for hours, ideally from very close quarters. And those legs…

So he'd been thrilled when she had agreed to a second date, this time for dinner, and he had a good feeling about tonight. Her profile said she couldn't cook to save her life but her barbequeing skills were legendary, so after wasting far too much time on research, he'd settled on an American diner that Tim from work assured him did great cocktails and the best ribs in London.

The place certainly looked the part. There were paper tablecloths that were clearly chosen to protect the furniture from frequent applications of grease. The ketchup came in retro tomato-shaped bottles. The music was old-school rock – Bon Jovi's *Living on a Prayer* was playing when he arrived and was shown to a red leather banquette.

Will ordered an Old Fashioned and checked his phone. God, he hoped she was going to turn up. He had a text from Louise – no news yet. Well, no news was hopefully good news. Anyway, it was the third of January; people were only just getting back to work, plus there was the time difference between London and San Francisco to consider... But he was glad he had his date with Felicity to distract him and stop him checking his email every two minutes.

And here she was. Even in this place, which certainly seemed to attract more than its share of fit women, she turned heads. It wasn't that she was conventionally beautiful – she was dressed casually in tight jeans, flat suede boots and a black jumper that managed to be both floppy and clingy, and she was wearing almost no make-up, apart from a slash of red lipstick on her eminently kissable mouth. But there was something about the air of assurance with which she scanned the room, her confident smile when she spotted Will, and the athletic grace of her walk across the restaurant to their table that was intoxicatingly sexy.

"Hey." She slung her leather jacket over the back of her chair. "Good to see you."

"And you." Will stood up and they exchanged kisses on both cheeks. Progress – their last date had ended without the snog Will had been hoping for.

She folded her long legs under the table and glanced around the room. "Great place! Have you been here before?"

"No, a colleague recommended it to me. He really rates the cocktails – what would you like?" A waitress was hovering, notepad in hand.

"I'd love a Grey Goose martini, wet, with an olive, please," Felicity said, without so much as a glance at the cocktail menu. Will was impressed.

"And what can I get you from the food menu?" the waitress asked. "Or do you need more time?"

"Maybe a few minutes," Will said. "I hope this is okay. It's all a bit trashy, but in a good way, I hope."

"It looks amazing," Felicity said. "Oh my God, pulled pork. Hot wings. Popovers. I don't know what those are, but I want them. I want all the things. And I want salted caramel cheesecake afterwards. Good choice!"

Will laughed. "I'm glad you approve."

"I'm sorry," she sipped her martini. "I'm not normally such a gannet. Okay, I am. But I'm training for a hundred kilometre cycle race and I'm hungry, like, all the time."

"Don't apologise," Will said. "Come on, let's order all the things."

An hour later, their table a wasteland of sauce smears, bones and empty beer bottles, Will was congratulating himself on his choice of date, and also wondering whether he'd ever be able to eat again, ever. In between stuffing themselves with food and drink, they'd chatted about music, films, travel, sport, and extensively about Felicity's cat, Buffy.

"Buffy the mouse-slayer," she said. "I adopted her when she was just a tiny kitten, and she's six now and totally the boss of me. I was so worried about moving her to London but she's settled right in. Look, here she is stalking pigeons on my balcony."

She took out her phone and showed Will a few photos of a presumably charming, but to his eyes quite ordinary, black moggy. He was more interested in the glimpses of Felicity's life the pictures gave him. Her balcony was crowded with flourishing herbs in pots. Her duvet was an expanse of snowy cotton, broken only by the furry, upside-down form of Buffy. She was a Mac user, as the photo of the cat asleep on her laptop revealed.

"I'm totally fucking this date up, aren't I?" she said. "I've shown myself up as a greedy bastard, and now you know I'm a mad cat lady, too. I just need to tell you how I sewed prawns into my ex's curtains and I'll be toast."

Will said, "No, you're not fucking it up. I've checked the dateometer, and I can confirm that you are in fact nailing it."

He smiled at her and she smiled back, and they exchanged a long, promising eye-meet. Will was a bit pissed, but he was sure it wasn't just the booze that was making him feel so elated. There was just one problem – he was there under false pretences.

As far as Felicity was concerned, she was having dinner with Will Turner, who taught computer science at a not-that-great comprehensive school in Wood Green and rented a crumbling one-bed flat in Hackney, and for whom this dinner represented a pretty significant expenditure. He had absolutely no idea what he was going to do when the bill arrived. He was all for equality, but he wanted to pay for the evening with his platinum credit card, in which it would make not even a dent, and maybe, if things were still going well, take her back to his place in a taxi. His place – his sleek apartment overlooking the river, which anyone, even if they'd only arrived in the capital yesterday, would be able to identify in a millisecond as the chunk of prime London real estate it was.

He wished he'd had the foresight to rent a shabby bed-sit somewhere, for just such an eventuality as this. But that would be sordid and horrible – that would be compounding the deceit he already regretted embarking on. When he and Stella had hatched their plan, they hadn't really thought as far ahead as when he would out himself. It had seemed so good in theory – the idea that once he'd established that he liked someone, and she liked him, it would be easy to casually mention the fact that he wasn't entirely who she'd thought he was. But now he felt trapped – he was already too far into the fiction to come clean, but not far enough to be sure of her reaction.

"So how about that salted caramel cheesecake?" Felicity said.

"I will if you will," he said, and they ordered two, and another round of Sam Adams. But when the pudding came, Will found he wasn't enjoying it as much as he should have done. He needed to say something to her, maybe give her a subtle hint that things weren't quite as she believed.

He was formulating a tactful way of beginning what had suddenly become the most awkward conversation of his life, ever, when his phone began to vibrate on the paper tablecloth. Louise. His spoon slipped out of his fingers and landed on the floor.

"Felicity, I'm really sorry, but I have to take this. It's a work thing. Be right back." He snatched his mobile and fought his way outside, struggling to hear Louise's excited words over the clamour of voices and boom of the music.

He wasn't right back. The conversation was huge – epic – and long. The news from Google was big news – the thing he'd worked and waited for years to hear. It was twenty minutes before, giddy with adrenalin, he returned to the table, where Felicity was sitting before her plate of untouched dessert, her own phone on the table in front of her.

"I'm really sorry," Will began. "It's just that…"

She cut him short. "Sorry? Yeah, so you should fucking be sorry. Will Turner. I Googled you. Teachers work long hours, right, but they don't get work calls at ten at night. I thought maybe you'd omitted to tell me you had a wife and kids at home. Then I remembered that your name was kind of familiar, and I was right. I do read the news, you know, even the financial pages, sometimes."

"Felicity, please let me…" but she was on a roll.

"What are you doing, field research for the new Grindr? Were you planning to shag me for a one-on-one focus group? Do you think I'm stupid? Because I'm not some shit-hot fucking internet entrepreneur, I'm just a piece of data who you can use for fun? Well, I'm not. I'm a person, and – in case you hadn't realised – people don't appreciate being strung along and lied to."

Will tried to explain. He muttered something about how it wasn't like she thought it was, honestly, it was just a stupid idea he'd come up with, a friend had thought it might help him to…

"Get more sex?" Felicity spat. "Convince women that it's a good idea to shag you, and lie to them, then lie and lie some more? Take it from me, it's not. I guess you're terrible with women, except the ones you can buy, so let me tell you a few things you may not know. We aren't idiots. We're not all so desperate for a man that we'll smile nicely and play games so we can get one. And we don't all think that money is the answer to everything. And before you start flashing your cash at me, I've paid the bill. If you paid for what I've just eaten I'd puke. And now I'm going to go home, and I as soon as I get there I'm going to go online and report your profile for the lying crock it is."

And she picked up her bag and her coat and walked out. Towards the end of her rant, she'd started to cry, and Will could feel tears on his face, too. He waited a few minutes, until he was sure she'd properly gone, avoiding the waitress's eye when she came to clear away the detritus of their meal. Then he left and hailed a cab as he'd imagined doing with Felicity, except now he was alone, and he was going back to the office, not home. On the way, he deleted his profile from RealRomance, after sending Felicity a brief message saying how sorry he was. Then he called Louise again, and asked her to tell him yet again about the discussions she'd had with Google. And then he booked a one-way flight to San Francisco, first class.

The Frog Prince experiment, such as it had been, was over.

CHAPTER EIGHTEEN

The prince sent heralds out all over the land, bearing his procla-
mation. They blew fanfares, unfurled banners and announced the
news that Princess Stella had accepted his hand in marriage…

The flat was in a right state when we got back to London
four days later. Left to himself, Julian had clearly
reverted to his bachelor standards of housekeeping – there
were unwashed plates in the sink, takeaway cartons over-
flowing the bin and a funny smell in the air.

"Look at this," I scolded. "I take my eyes off you for
just a few days and you start living like a student. You're a
disgrace."

Julian shuffled his feet and looked at the floor. "I'm
sorry, little star," he said. "I was so busy, I was working non-
stop, and I guess I just didn't notice it. And then when I left,
I was in such a hurry to get to you, there was no time for
cleaning."

It was the closest I was going to get to an apology for his
failure to get to Polly's wedding, and I chose to accept it.

"You're going to have to clean up your act now we're
engaged," I said.

Julian laughed. "Don't worry, I'll be a changed man.
Washing a few dishes is a small price to pay for spending the
rest of my life with you."

Because I'd said yes. Of course I had. It was the ultimate validation, the reassurance I'd been longing for that everything would be all right, that we really were going to be together always. In a second, I went from fear to elation, from misery to joy, like flicking a switch. I knew Julian could see in my face what my answer would be, even before could say anything, which was quite some time because I was crying great floods of relieved tears.

"Don't let's tell anyone tonight," he whispered. "We don't want to make your friends' big day about us, and besides, I want it to be our secret for a little while."

And so we didn't say anything that night, nor for the rest of the time we spent in Scotland, although I was dying to. Most of the guests departed on New Year's Day, leaving us alone with Polly, Angus and Gray once more. We chatted to them about quite ordinary things – the hotel, the baby, the weather.

Polly and I didn't have a chance to be alone together. In fact, I had the sense that she was… not avoiding me, exactly, but not wanting to talk about anything that wasn't easy and trivial. She was probably all talked out after the past couple of days, I reasoned, and tired too. She and Angus must be quite keen for us to leave, so they could get back to normality – what little of it they had left, before their baby was born and changed their lives forever.

So I didn't force the issue, and I was too insulated in Julian's and my little bubble of happiness to care. We went for long walks together by the loch. We lay in bed for hours, our bodies twined together, talking and touching. When I offered to help Polly in the kitchen, she said there was nothing to do, really, now everyone had gone, so, relieved, I went back to Julian.

And now we were home. After hours of travel, I was knackered and wanted nothing more than to collapse into bed, but, looking at the state of the flat, I realised that wasn't going to happen for an hour or three.

"Back to reality, little star," Julian said. "I'm afraid I've got some work to do tonight. You've been far too much of a distraction the last couple of days."

And he went off to the bedroom with his laptop.

I looked around me at the chaos, and fought down a surge of resentment – he'd left the place in this state, and now it was up to me to sort it out?

"Julian," I said, "Do you think you could give me a hand with this, before…"

But I was interrupted by my phone ringing. Martha.

"Hey Stella! Just checking you're all set for tomorrow? I've ordered all the stuff you needed, and it's arrived – the place looks more like an art supply shop than a restaurant! We can't wait to see it finished."

"Me too," I said. Although I'd barely thought about the project while we were away, now I felt my excitement and enthusiasm returning. "I'll get there first thing, will there be someone there to let me in? I reckon if I start at seven, I'll be able to get the grid done and start tracing the drawing tomorrow, and the next day I'll get on to the fun stuff – the actual painting."

"Great! If you're sure there's nothing more you need, I'll see you there at seven. I've been yapping on about it on social media, some of the customers are already asking who the artist is, and whether you take commissions. I've said you do, but you're outrageously expensive."

I laughed. "Don't put them off before I've even started! See you in the morning."

I wouldn't disturb Julian, I decided – I'd give the flat a quick once-over, then sit down and do some work myself, just to make sure that all my drawings were in order and ready for the next day. I quickly bagged up the takeaway boxes and took them down to the recycling bin, washed up the forest of coffee mugs that seemed to have taken over every available surface – I could have sworn we didn't even have that many – and put a load of washing on. Then I had a shower, made a pot of tea and put up my easel.

I opened the cupboard under the sink where I kept my drawings, and recoiled. They were wet through. Water was dripping down on to them from my recent washing-up spree, but not enough to account for this. I pulled out the stack of pages, and they disintegrated to pulp in my hands, soaked and ruined.

"Julian!" I screamed.

"What's wrong? Is there a spider?" He appeared in the doorway behind me.

"What the fuck happened while I was away? Look at this." I held out the mass of sodden paper.

"Oh, yeah," he said. "I'd forgotten about that. I was filling the kettle a few days ago and then Ken rang, and I completely forgot about it, and left the tap running for hours. The water bill's going to be epic, and it looks like we've got a leak somewhere. I'll ask the landlord to check it out. Are your drawings okay? I've been meaning to suggest you keep them somewhere else."

"They're not okay. They're ruined," I said. "Didn't you even think to check? This is, like, weeks of work, and I'm starting at Martha's tomorrow."

"Sorry," he said. "But I had no idea this was going to happen. You can't blame me, it was a bit of a dumb place to put them, wasn't it? What are you going to do?"

I knew what I wanted to do, of course. I wanted to throw the wad of soggy paper in his face and then rant at him for being so thoughtless. But what was the point? It wouldn't undo the damage, and I couldn't deny that I should have found more suitable storage. And now wasn't the time to have a row, anyway. I had – I glanced at my watch – eleven hours in which to redo weeks of work.

"I'm going to start again, I guess," I said.

I didn't go to bed that night. I sat up at my easel until my eyes were scratchy with fatigue and my shoulders ached. I'd pulled all-nighters before, at university, but this was a totally different level of pressure.

I had the images in my head as well as the photos I'd emailed to Martha, so I wasn't working from nothing. But as I drew, I found the design changing, new ideas taking shape, a different vision forming. Engrossed, lost in work, I barely noticed the hours passing, and it was only when I heard Julian's alarm go off that I realised it was morning. I'd run out of time.

"I'm so sorry I'm late," I said to Martha, arriving sweaty and breathless at the café, my rucksack heavy with a stack of new drawings.

"That's fine, I've just got here myself," she said. "Plenty of time for a coffee before you get started. Are you okay? You look all flustered."

"I am, a bit. I was up all night and I'd absolutely love a coffee. There's something I'd like to chat to you about before I start."

"Triple espresso, then," Martha said. "So long as it won't give you the shakes. And talk to me."

We stood at the counter, because all the tables and chairs had been pushed to the side of the room to make space for me to work. I felt the caffeine hit me, mixing with the adrenaline that had fuelled my marathon session at my easel. I was jittery with nervousness and eagerness to get started.

"I've gone in a slightly different direction with this," I said. "If you don't like it, I can just go back to what we agreed before. Or even paint over it and start again – the main thing is that you're happy. But here's what I was thinking."

I told her my idea, and she started to laugh.

"Genius! I love it. That's really going to get people talking. Go for it. I know it'll be brilliant."

I worked solidly for ten hours, too happy to notice how tired I was. Martha kept me supplied with strong coffee and bottles of water, and brought me a sandwich at lunchtime, which I was too wired to eat. I barely registered the passers-by who stopped and asked her what I was doing, but I became conscious that this was about the performance as much as the finished product.

By the end of the day, I'd transferred all of the image from my sheets of paper to the wall in careful charcoal outlines, following the numbers on the grid. It was painstaking work, tedious even, but at the same time thrilling to see the tiny details I'd put on paper take shape at their full size.

"This is going to be totally awesome," Martha said, when I climbed down from my stepladder for the last time, stretching my aching back. "I don't know why you didn't start doing this kind of thing ages ago. You're seriously talented."

"It's not finished yet," I said. "There's still plenty for me to cock up. But I'm loving it, I really hope you're happy with it when it's done."

"I'm so tempted to have a celebratory drink," she said. "But I suppose I'd better get back to the kids. Same time tomorrow?"

"Same time tomorrow," I agreed, and made my weary way to the bus stop.

When I got home, I was surprised to find Julian already there.

"How did it go? You look bloody shattered," he said, "and you've got charcoal on your nose. Do you need a hot bath?"

I said I couldn't think of anything I'd like more.

Lying in the warm water, I felt the tension in my body ease, although my mind was still buzzing with images and my mouth dry and sour from all the coffee.

"How about a drink?" Julian said, as if he'd read my thoughts.

I said a cup of tea would be awesome, but he said, "You're not drinking tea tonight, little star. We're celebrating."

A moment later I heard the pop of a cork, and Julian came into the bathroom with a bottle of champagne and two of our cheap, chipped wine glasses.

"No crystal goblets, I'm afraid," he said. "But I've got something else for you."

He reached into his pocket and took out a small cardboard box. "And no diamonds, either," he said. "This was the best I could do. But I thought you'd like it."

Inside the box was a ring. It was silver, with a small, golden-coloured stone. "It's only a garnet," he said. "One day, when we make our fortune, you'll have a rock the size of your head, if you want. But I wanted to make things official, and that means a ring on your finger."

He reached into the water and took my hand, which was still black with charcoal, and slipped the ring on to my third finger.

"And not only do I want you to know how much I love you," Julian said, "I want the whole world to know. Hold still."

He held his phone over my hand and took a picture. "I'm posting this on Shutterly," he said. "Engagement announcements in the digital age! There we go."

I thought about asking him to wait until I'd told Polly, Wizzy, even Mum – but he was so sweetly enthusiastic, the ring was so pretty, and I was too exhausted to protest.

"I've texted Will, too," he said. "We're meeting up tomorrow, I told him we had news, and he says he does too. You'll come out for a drink with us, won't you?"

"Of course I will," I said, thinking that I'd have to work at an even more furious pace the next day if I was to finish early enough. "This is so beautiful. It's the prettiest ring in the world. I'm never going to take it off."

"Drink your champagne," Julian said, "then come to bed. I've been thinking about you all day."

But by the time I got out of the bath and scrubbed myself dry with my scratchy towel, I practically sleepwalked to bed. I pulled the duvet over myself and plummeted down into oblivion before Julian had even finished cleaning his teeth.

Chapter Nineteen

Princess Stella waited until nightfall. Then, moving silently on slippered feet, she crept through the tower to the locked room where she knew the Prince's secret casket was hidden. He had forbidden her to open the door and see what was inside, but curiosity overcame her...

The next day, I worked even harder and faster, but I was in the zone now, able to relax and enjoy myself. As I began to apply colour inside my charcoal lines, the picture seemed to come alive. My landscape was just as I'd imagined it, the tall trees, the thicket of rosebushes, the river with its swans. It sounds pretentious, I know, but I began to feel almost as if I was there: the sun on my back, the grass under my feet, the flowers scenting the air.

It took Martha saying, "I don't want to break the flow, Stella, but it's five thirty and you said you needed to finish in good time today," to make me realise that it was her perfume I could smell, and I was in her café, on a busy south London street, rain lashing the pavement outside.

"I was miles away," I said. "Sorry. And you're right, I do need to head off. I'll work more on the detail tomorrow, and fingers crossed it'll be done the day after."

I hurried home, showered and changed. Although what I really wanted was to slump into bed and sleep some more, I got the bus into town to meet Julian and Will.

I wondered what Will's news could be, and realised I hadn't received an update on the dating situation since just after Christmas. I checked Facebook, but he hadn't posted. I looked for his profile on RealRomance to see if he'd updated anything, but I couldn't find it. That was weird. I refreshed, changed my search parameters, but there was nothing. He must have taken it down.

Had he met someone? That must be it. And to go from nothing, just a string of dates that had ended in disappointment, to taking himself off the market altogether, must mean something serious. Something like being in love.

But before I could speculate further, the bus's digital voice informed me that I'd reached my stop, and I stuffed my phone back into my bag and hurried downstairs, putting my umbrella up against the driving rain.

It was clearly Will who'd chosen the bar where we were meeting. This wasn't Julian's and my sort of place, at all. Not that we had a sort of place, really, only the Five Bells, with its down-at-heel clientele and vinegary wine. This was something else entirely. I wished I'd had time to straighten my hair and put on make-up – I felt horribly drab and out of place in my jeans, trainers and parka as I walked across the marble floor to the table where Julian and Will were waiting, a bottle of champagne in a silver ice bucket on the table in front of them.

"And here she is," Julian said, standing up to kiss me. "My beautiful fiancée."

Will had stood up too, and I saw an expression cross his face that I couldn't quite understand. He looked surprised, of course, but there was something else, too. He seemed shocked, even angry. But it was fleeting and I barely saw it, because Julian had pressed my face against his shirt front.

"Wow," Will said. "That's seriously amazing. Allow me to be the first offer my congratulations, or whatever they say. Incredible news. Have you set a date yet?"

Julian and I looked at each other. We hadn't talked about any of that – I hadn't even thought of it. The idea that we'd have an actual wedding hadn't really sunk in.

Not that I hadn't thought of it in the past. For an incurable romantic like me, wedding dreams were never far away. When I was a teenager, convinced that Karl and I were in love and would be together forever, I'd imagined us having some sort of terribly edgy, alternative ceremony – a handfasting, perhaps in a forest, both wearing black and exchanging vials of each other's blood. When I was going out with Declan, I'd briefly fantasised about hiring a room at the National Galleries for a reception that would be the talk of Edinburgh's art scene.

But somehow, I hadn't got that far with Julian. Maybe it was because what we had was proper, grown-up love, not daydreams and make-believe.

"We're not in a rush," Julian said. "But we don't want to wait ages, do we, Stella? Maybe in about three months' time we'll head down the road to Lambeth Town Hall and sign the register and then get together with some mates at the Five Bells. I despise big weddings, and we couldn't afford one even if we wanted one."

"I quite like them," I said, in a small voice. "Polly and Angus's wedding wasn't huge, but it was lovely, as you'd know if you'd been there."

"Anyway," Julian said hastily, "the main thing, mate, is we wanted you to know. And we hope you'll be there, obviously. I won't need a best man, I don't want any of that stuff."

"I… of course," Will said. "I'd love to come. And I'm sure I'll be back in the UK by then."

"Back in the UK?" I said.

"Yeah," said Julian. "Sorry, Stella, you've missed the main news of the evening. Will's off to San Francisco tomorrow for an indeterminate stay. He's hit the big time."

I looked at the champagne in its ice bucket, and felt suddenly cold, as if I'd been plunged into it.

"You have?" I said.

"Not just me," Will said. "Louise is the mastermind. She's been talking to people at Google for a while now, and it's all coming together. They want to work on deeper integration with the Android OS, maybe shipping Shutterly as standard on their phones, and potentially investing in the business. So I'm going to go out there and work with their dev team and see what we come up with. It might be nothing; it might be epic."

I said, stupidly, "My friend Wizzy is going to be in San Francisco in a couple of weeks. You two should meet for a drink."

Will laughed. "I'd love to, Stella. I'll need all the friends I can get when I'm out there. But I doubt I'll have much time for socialising. And I've pretty much decided to put my love life on ice for the time being. I don't think it's really been working out that well for me."

"Well, you need some serious congratulating too," I said, splashing more champagne into our glasses and earning a disapproving stare from our waiter, who'd been hovering by the table. "That's awesome! You must be so proud."

I think I sounded enthusiastic, but I didn't really feel it. I realised how much I'd come to depend on Will's friendship, his regular emails and Facebook updates. He was my best friend in London, apart from Julian. There was Martha, of course, and Liberty, who I'd been putting off arranging to meet for lunch again. But Will was special. Learning that he wasn't going to be around felt like walking down a flight of stairs and discovering an extra one at the bottom, which I hadn't known was there.

That day hadn't finished springing surprises on me. When Julian and I were on the bus home, I saw I'd missed a call from Mum. Unusually for her, she'd left a message – normally she just waited, passive-aggressively, for me to call her back, leaving me to put it off and put it off and feel more and more guilty until eventually I relented.

I dialled my voicemail and listened.

"Hi, Stella, it's me, Mum. I hope you had a lovely time at the wedding. I'm just calling to say... to ask if it would be possible to come and see you in London for a day or two? I'd love to meet Jason, I could do with a wee holiday, and there's something I need to talk to you about. Anyway, give me a ring when you can. I know how busy you are. Er... that's all, love. Good night."

A wee holiday? Mum didn't do holidays any more, and she'd never been to London – the extent of her globetrotting had been summer breaks in Spain with me and Dad when I was little, and a trip to Edinburgh with her church a few years ago. Something was definitely up.

"Mum wants to come and visit," I said to Julian.

"What?" He was also looking at his phone. "Oh, your mum? Okay. That's nice."

But I could tell he hadn't really been listening. Over his shoulder, I could see he was on Shutterly, looking at the picture he'd posted of my hand with his ring on it.

"Have lots of people commented?" I said. "What do they say?"

"Nothing," Julian said, and closed the app down, opening his email instead.

"Oh, go on," I said. "Let me see."

"Stella, I'm busy," he snapped, and we spent the rest of the journey home in silence.

Of course, as soon as we got home and Julian had opened his laptop and started work for the night, I logged into my own Shutterly account and found Julian's picture, which he'd tagged me on. There weren't lots of comments – in fact there was only one. It was from a user called Kristibelle89, and it said, "Well, that was quick. Or was it?"

I clicked on her profile, and discovered she was in Canada and liked taking pictures of trees. Then I went back to the post to read it again, trying to figure out what it meant. She must be someone Julian had known there, but why no cosy messages of congratulation? And why the question?

But when I looked back at Julian's timeline, the photo and the comment had gone. I looked across the room at him. He seemed engrossed by whatever he was doing on his laptop, but his phone was on the table next to him, its screen illuminated. As I watched, it flicked back to darkness.

"Julian, did you just take that photo down?" I asked.

"What? Yeah, I did. It seemed like a good idea to post it last night, but on reflection it wasn't. You want to tell your friends properly, not have them find out via social media, don't you? And maybe it's best to hold off until you've spoken to your mother, she should really be the first person you tell."

As this was exactly what I'd thought the previous night, I couldn't really argue. And I did want to share my news with Polly and Wizzy.

"Are you hungry?" I said. "I'm just going to make myself some toast. Want some?"

"No thanks," Julian said. "I ate earlier, with Will."

I imagined the delicious supper they would have had, paid for by Will, and wished they'd waited for me. Still, it was probably my fault for being late.

I shoved a couple of pieces of white bread in the toaster and opened the fridge, hoping that some kind of food-shopping magic might have happened, and there'd be something nice in there, but there was only an almost empty foil pack of butter, studded with crumbs, and a block of cheddar that hadn't been wrapped properly and was dry and cracked on the edges. When I'd finished at Martha's tomorrow, I'd have to do a Tesco run on my way home, otherwise we'd both starve.

I scraped the last couple of teaspoonfuls out of a jar of strawberry jam, put my meagre dinner on a plate and returned to the sofa and my phone.

There was a new email from Wizzy.

Hey, you two,
I've just arrived in the US of A. I'm in LA and it's totally incredible. I've teamed up with a couple of girls I met in Sydney and we're going out tonight to show Hollywood how to party. I'm going to put on a little black dress and hope that, plus my legendary blagging skills, will be enough to get us into Bar Marmont. There, I plan to pull Zac Efron, who naturally will fall madly in love with me and have passionate sex with me in his limo. I will report back on the size of his wang.

Polly, babes, I can't believe you're Mrs Sinclair now. I'm so sorry I missed the wedding but Stella told me all about it – it felt almost like I was there.

Stella, are you okay, lovely? I insist you reply to this email immediately. I haven't heard from you for ages and I'm worried.

Love you both.

I finished my toast and hit Reply all.

News flash from London,

Not in the same league as shagging Zac Efron, obvs. But Julian and I are engaged! He asked me just after midnight at Poll's wedding. I'm sorry I've waited so long to tell you both (four days! I've been bursting to say something!) but Julian wanted to wait a bit, so we compromised. I have the most gorgeous ring, with a tiny garnet in it, and we are so loved up you won't believe.

I looked at Julian again. He was bent over his keyboard, tapping intently at it, his hair flopping over his forehead. As I watched, he pushed it back with his long fingers. He was more beautiful than ever, but he felt more remote at that moment than Wizzy did, and she was on the other side of the world, not the other side of the room.

It feels kind of strange, though. Was it like that for you, Poll? Like, you're going to spend the rest of your life with someone, but you've got no idea what's going through their head? I feel a bit like that. But I suppose I've got all the time in the world to find out.

I signed off with a row of kisses.

Then I opened Shutterly again, and found Kristibelle89's profile, and looked at it for a long time. I scrolled past endless images of trees and autumn foliage, occasionally interspersed with pictures of a hamster called Barack. Kristibelle was a prolific poster but not a very interesting one, at least if rodents and maples weren't your thing.

Then, at last, I found a selfie. It showed a blonde woman, about my age. She had pale skin and perfect North American teeth. She was grinning happily into the camera, wearing a Hollister hoodie, Barack on her shoulder. In the background, I could see a kitchen counter with a microwave, a coffee machine and a row of canisters in primary colours. So presumably this was her apartment.

I selected the menu options from her photo feed to show me more of her images from the same location, but there were hardly any. One of her living room, tagged 'New couch!!!'. One of a plate of salad, tagged 'Detox day'. One of Barack snoozing on her pillow, which I thought was a bit grim, but who was I to judge? I scrolled down further. There was one more image, of what I presumed was her balcony, overlooking yet more trees, a spectacular sunset filling most of the frame. But on the left, I could see the silhouette of a man's head and shoulders, and one of his arms resting on the balcony wall. It was tagged 'J admiring the view'.

"Come on, little star, time for bed." Julian's voice made me jump, and I almost dropped my phone.

"I'm on my way," I said. "Five minutes."

I quickly tapped the message icon, and then gazed at the blank field, with no idea what I was going to write. Contacting some random Canadian woman for no reason other than that she liked autumn leaves and knew someone whose name began with a J was weird to say the least – stalkerish, even. But then, she'd commented on Julian's photo of me. She'd started it.

"Hi," I wrote. "You don't know me, but you commented on a pic my fiancé posted of me yesterday, and I wondered why. Mail me if you want. Promise I'm not a stalker." I included my email address, sent the message and went to bed.

Julian reached for me as he always did, his touch and kisses avid. But my body didn't seem to respond as it always had done. I closed my eyes and tried to switch off the tide of suspicion and mistrust washing over me, but I couldn't.

"What's the matter, little star?" he murmured, his breath hot against my neck.

"Nothing," I whispered. "I'm just a bit tired."

"Don't worry, this won't take long," he said. And it didn't. And for the first time, I had to pretend I was enjoying it.

"So, what do you think?" I stepped back from the wall, wiping my paintbrush, and devoured a slice of still-warm pizza from the huge box Martha had ordered in, because she said I was looking way too thin and needed to get outside some serious calories.

The mural wasn't finished – not quite. But its finished form was clear. The paint was still wet, and it gleamed in the spotlights Martha had hired to help me work through the gloomy January evening. Its sheen made it look even more alive to me – the horse's mane looked almost as if was swishing, the river sparkled, the armour shone. I'd need to work in some highlights to keep this vibrancy once it was all dry.

"Tomorrow I'll add the finishing touches," I said. "Then it'll need to be sealed, and Dan will have to go easy on boiling stock for a bit. But the basics are there now."

Martha shook her head. "I don't know, Stella," she said, and I quailed, expecting her to say it wasn't working for her after all, she'd changed her mind, it sucked. "I don't know how you've done this in such a short time. It's so cool – it's really subversive. It's going to give the Balham mums something to think about while they drink their chai lattes, and hopefully their daughters too, and maybe, eventually, the husbands. But that's probably too big an ask."

I laughed. "At least the princess is fit," I said. "That'll help keep the dads happy."

In my revised design, the knight on the white horse wasn't a handsome prince, but a beautiful princess, her chestnut ponytail flying out behind her as she galloped to the rescue of her friends – two women and one man, trapped in the stone turret guarded by dragons.

My princess looked like Wizzy. I couldn't wait for her to see it, and I knew Martha recognised her sister's long legs and flashing eyes, because she brushed away a tear and said, "I miss her, you know."

"Me too," I said. "But she's not dead. She's just in California. After that, there are only a few more stops on the grand tour and she'll come home."

Martha said, "I'm not sure she will, you know, Stella. My little sis has always had itchy feet, and now that she's seen a bit of the world I reckon she's going to want to conquer it all."

I thought about this for a moment. "No, she won't. She'll come home and settle down, just you watch." But I didn't feel anything like as confident as I sounded.

"Wizzy's been a law unto herself, ever since she was tiny," Martha said, "My daughter Mia's just the same. It's wonderful, but it scares the hell out of me, because I was always such a good girl, such a conformist. Shall we open a bottle of red?"

She didn't wait for me to reply, but found a bottle behind the bar and twisted out the cork. We unstacked a couple of chairs, Martha switched off the spotlights, and we finished the pizza and the wine together, chatting about Wizzy, Martha's children, our hopes and dreams.

I felt myself relaxing, enjoying the easy companionship of this woman who, although she was my client and I didn't know her terribly well, was so like her sister that she felt entirely familiar.

So, when Martha had sloshed the last of the wine into our glasses, I said, "I'm getting married to Julian. He asked me a few days ago, and I said yes. I love him, but I'm worried I'm not doing the right thing."

Martha said, "What do you mean, exactly? What do you think the right thing would be? And who decides what's right and what isn't?"

I tucked my feet up on my chair, wrapping my arm around my knees, and took another swig of wine.

"The thing is, with Julian, he's so brilliant and amazing, and he's off in his own world a lot of the time. I know he loves me – he tells me all the time he does. But…"

"Does he show it?" Martha said. "Does he really? Or does he just talk the talk? Because that's easy. When Paul and I first lived together, he was forever saying stuff and not doing it. 'Yes, Martha, I'll pick up the dry cleaning.' 'Don't worry, Martha, I'll plan our summer holiday, you're too busy at work.' He was telling me what he knew I wanted to hear, and he knew full well that if he talked a good enough line, he'd keep me sweet and he could get away with doing sod all."

"Does he really?" I asked. I couldn't imagine Martha letting anyone get away with anything.

"Does he fuck! It worked for a bit, I have to admit I was fooled by his lines. But then I realised that he thought he could get away with empty promises. And, obviously, that wasn't working for me. So we had a full and frank discussion, and I told him that if he wanted to get married and have kids – which he really, really did – that shit had to stop right there."

"And did it?"

"Yes, it did. It took a while, it took a few times when I chewed him out and reminded him that I wasn't his mother and I actually earned more than him, and if he thought he could step out of his clothes and leave them on the bedroom floor he had another think coming. But it kind of worked. And I take comfort in the fact that now, even though he's the main earner and I'm fannying around running a café for milfs, which is still operating at a loss, he respects what I do. That's why he's fed and bathed the kids tonight while I get plastered with you."

I'd hardly noticed, but Martha had opened another bottle of red while we talked, and we were progressing steadily through it.

"Julian's a bit like that," I said. "It's good to know that he could change. I'm sure he will, once we're married."

Martha said, "Stella, a word of advice from an old bird. Never, ever, marry anyone on the assumption that they'll change. Or rather, assume that they might, but that it'll be for the worse. Sorry, I sound like a horrible cynic."

"It's not like that!" I protested. The wine had gone to my head, loosening my tongue but confusing my thoughts. "Julian loves me. I know he does. And I love him. And I waited for months to be with him, and when I could be, I uprooted my whole life for him. It's got to work."

Martha didn't say anything for a bit. She looked down into her wine glass, turning the stem slowly between two fingers. At last she spoke.

"Wizzy says Polly says Julian is –" she broke off, mid-sentence.

"Is what?" I said. "Polly's only met him, like, twice."

The atmosphere had changed, very suddenly. A moment ago, we'd been chatting happily together, exchanging confidences, becoming friends. Now I felt prickly and defensive, like I'd done something wrong, or Martha had.

"Oh, Stella." Martha reached out and squeezed my hand. "I don't know. I spoke out of turn, I'm sorry. Your friends worry about you, being so far away all of a sudden. They know you love Julian. They just don't want you to get hurt."

I stood up, my head swimming a bit from tiredness and wine.

"I can look after myself perfectly well, thanks. I know Julian. I know him better than anyone, and I know he loves me. And I think it's a bit shitty that my friends have been talking about him behind my back. I told Polly and Wizzy last night we'd got engaged, and neither of them have even bothered to reply. If I have to choose between them and Julian, I know who's going to win. Thanks for the wine and the food, Martha, but I should be going. I need to get back to my fiancé. I'll come in tomorrow to finish the painting, assuming you still want me to."

I didn't kiss her goodnight as I'd done the last few days. I picked up my coat and my bag and headed out into the cold, drizzly darkness. Because I was a bit pissed, I ended up getting on the wrong bus and it was almost two in the morning before I reached the flat, and my phone had died so I couldn't ring Julian and tell him where I was.

But when I eventually got home, he was fast asleep, so, instead of his soothing assurances that we were the most important thing in the world to each other, and anyone who didn't believe that was wrong, I had to make do with a cup of tea and a quiet seethe while my phone charged.

How dare Martha, Polly and Wizzy bitch about Julian? How dare they judge me, belittle my choices? Just because their lives were so different, so perfect, they thought they were better than me. Well, they weren't, and their smugness had cost them my friendship. I was going to tell them that, right now.

I turned my phone on, already composing the email I was going to send just as soon as I could get my clumsy fingers to co-operate. Then I saw that a new message had arrived in my inbox. It was from a woman called Kristen Klingmann, who lived in Ottawa, Canada.

CHAPTER TWENTY

"Hi! I'm Mackenzie. I'm totally psyched to meet you. I'm going to show you round a bit and introduce you to some people, and then after lunch you'll be sitting down with the project team to do some real work. If that's okay?"

Will smiled and told her it sounded great. If he wasn't already reeling from jet lag and dazzled by the blazing California sun and the splendour of Google's HQ, he would have been blinded by Mackenzie's beauty, but as it was, she was just another element of stunning, shining newness. Her T-shirt was so white it almost sparkled. Her Levi's looked like they'd been ironed. Her sneakers were spotlessly clean. He'd never seen anyone with such white teeth or such shiny hair.

But he was able to resist the urge to stare at her, partly because it would have made him look like a sorry letch, and partly because there was so much else to stare at. He'd seen YouTube clips of the Googleplex, of course, but nothing could have prepared him for the sheer scale of the real thing. He was quite proud of the edgy cool of the Ignite office in Tech City, but compared to this it felt shabby and amateurish.

And, Will had to admit, he felt a bit the same about himself. His shirt was creased from his hasty packing, he hadn't shaved, and he'd realised in the taxi on the way that his socks didn't match – they were subtly but distinctly different shades of blue, and in the dim light of a London winter it wouldn't have been noticeable. Here, though, the piercing brightness exposed every flaw.

"So, we aren't going to be able to see everything this morning," Mackenzie said, with another of her megawatt smiles, "Because as you can see, it's like, ginormous. We have bikes for people to use to get around, otherwise we'd all be late for meetings all the time! But we don't have that many formal meetings – we try to encourage serendipitous interaction."

"Bikes sound good," Will said, wondering what the hell the other thing she'd said was.

"So here's one of the cafés – all the food and drink is free, and you can choose from pizza, burgers, salad, Mexican, candy, whatever. And the coffee is seriously good. Do you drink coffee?"

"I've already had four cups today," Will said.

Mackenzie nodded approvingly. "Thought so! Developers and coffee, right? Go together like… Bees and honey?"

"Gin and tonic?" Will suggested.

"Yeah!" She laughed, as if he'd said something actually clever. "Which reminds me, there's always so much social stuff happening. Drinks things, dinners, volleyball, whatever. And if you need a nap, we have sleep pods!"

She gestured to an enclosed recliner. Will thought how much he'd like to lie down there, right now. Maybe to sleep, or even better for a lie-down with Mackenzie.

But she'd walked on, continuing their tour.

"And here's one of the gyms – there are a few. Most people here work out a lot. There's this idea that if you work in tech, you're a bit of a geek, or a bit of a slob, or both. But we try to encourage our people to live well."

"Clean mind in a healthy body?" Will said.

"Yeah, exactly!" She laughed again. Will could imagine that winning her approval could become addictive. "Do you train?"

"I go running sometimes," Will said. "And I cycle a lot, and I play ping pong. I'm not as fit as I should be."

"You look great to me," Mackenzie said, with a charming wink. "And here are the massage rooms, if you pull a muscle or you're just feeling a bit stiff. We get free eyebrow shapes too but I guess you wouldn't be interested in those!"

"I don't know," Will said. "Is the metrosexual thing over, or not over? I can never keep track of trends."

"Over," Mackenzie said. "Proudly imperfect is where it's at, according to our futurology guys. But I'm not convinced, and until I am, I'm going to keep waxing these babies." She gestured with two fingers at her perfectly groomed brows and pulled a goofy face. "Now, let me show you where the actual work gets done, and then we'll have some lunch."

"Sounds good," Will said.

A couple of hours later, he'd been shown around acres of office space, divided into thousands of individual cubicles. There were meeting rooms, games rooms, a library – and everywhere, there were people, hurrying along corridors with laptops, standing in little knots chatting, making coffee. Mackenzie introduced him to a few of them, but he forgot their names almost immediately. He was also sure that, if she were to abandon him and tell him to make his own way out, he'd be found wandering the corridors weeks later. At least he wouldn't starve.

"Right, let's hit the cafeteria," Mackenzie said. "I normally go for the salad bar – when I joined I went a bit wild

216

with all the free food and piled on ten pounds, so I look after myself better now. But you have whatever you want – go crazy."

The room was filling up – there must have been several hundred people there, crowding around the food counters, carrying trays to tables where they sat and ate in familiar, laughing groups. Once again, Will had the sense that if he lost Mackenzie, he'd never be able to locate her again.

"Salad sounds good to me," he said.

They piled their plates with leaves, tomatoes and various obscure grains Will had never encountered before, and sat outside under a bright red parasol.

"So, tell me more about yourself," Mackenzie said. "Are you from London originally?"

Will gave her a potted life history: growing up in Nottingham, two parents, one sister. School, Cambridge, meeting Louise. Starting the business, discovering that it worked.

Already, after just a few hours in her company, he felt comfortable with her, able to share little details of his life. Perhaps it was because she knew who he was, so he didn't need to lie to her about anything. But also, although she'd said how excited she was to meet him, there was none of the disconcerting intensity in the way she communicated with him that he'd noticed in Charlotte and her predecessor, Melinda. Young, ambitious guys with successful businesses must cross Mackenzie's radar all the time, he realised – presumably she'd stopped being impressed long ago. It was refreshing. It reminded him a bit of the easy companionship he'd felt with Stella, although in a fundamental way it wasn't the same at all.

"And here I am," he said, concluding his potted resumé. "How about you?"

Mackenzie reciprocated with an account of growing up in upstate New York, two parents, one brother. School, MIT, internships.

"And here I am," she echoed, smiling. "So, Louise, is she, like, your life partner, as well as your business partner?"

"God, no," Will said. "Louise is married to Gavin, her childhood sweetheart. He's a great guy. A rozzer."

"Pardon me?"

"A policeman. Sorry. So anyway, she's just my business partner."

"And do you have a life partner?"

"Not right now." Will didn't want to disclose the full extent of his single status. "I was dating a bit, back in London, but nothing too serious. I met a few girls online but nothing really came of it."

"Oh my God, dating!" Mackenzie said. "Isn't it just the worst thing? There are so many rules. In New York, especially, it's a nightmare. Here on the West Coast things are a lot more relaxed. But I'm still looking for Mr Right."

She forked up some salad and sipped her fizzy water.

"Hey," she said. "A bunch of us are going to see a movie tonight. You should come along."

Will realised that his time in San Francisco might turn out to be interesting personally as well as professionally.

"I'd love to," he said.

CHAPTER TWENTY-ONE

*Her hands trembling, Princess Stella pulled the golden casket from
its hiding place and fitted the key into the lock...*

Hi Stella

Listen, I'm sorry about that message. I didn't intend to upset
you. To be totally honest I'd had a few drinks, otherwise I would
never have posted. It's just that it was only a few months ago that
Julian and I broke up and it's still kind of raw. But I hope you'll be
really happy.

Kristen

Only a few months? It must have been at least a year,
because I'd met Julian in March, and he hadn't said
anything then – or ever, now I thought about it – about a
recent break-up. It just didn't make sense, especially to my
wine-befuddled brain.

I replied to her message.

Hi there

Thanks for answering. I'm sorry you were hurt. But I'm a little
confused – Julian and I have been together for almost a year.
I know it's not the longest relationship in the world, and it was
long-distance for some of the time, but it's not like we just met or
something! Anyway, apology accepted, and I hope you're feeling
better about things.

I could afford to be magnanimous, I felt, since Julian was mine now, asleep in our bed. And it was time for me to join him.

I pressed myself up against his warm back, waiting for sleep to come. But it didn't. Although I was exhausted and the room was spinning a bit around me from all the red wine I'd drunk with Martha, I was restless and tense. I hadn't written the furious email I'd been going to send Polly and Wizzy, and I was glad I hadn't – they were my friends, I loved them, I didn't want to lose them. But I was still seething with anger and hurt, imagining them discussing our relationship, forming opinions about Julian, talking about him in a way that wasn't full of admiration.

Was it possible that other people didn't see him the way I did? That they couldn't appreciate his brilliance, didn't notice how gorgeous he was, weren't aware how incredibly lucky I was to have him? I thought about Angus, how fond I was of him, how thrilled I'd been when I introduced him to Polly and watched the two of them fall in love. It had never occurred to me that Polly might not feel the same about Julian. She didn't know him, obviously, but she knew how I felt about him – surely that was enough to make her like him?

I was trying to make sense of my jumbled thoughts, wondering whether to get up and fetch a glass of water and some paracetamol to stave off the hangover I knew would be in store for me, when my phone buzzed on the floor next to the bed.

It was another message from Kristen.

Hi Stella

There seem to be some crossed wires here. Julian and I were living together until he got the job in London. He even talked about me coming out there to join him once he'd settled in. But then he never contacted me, and he never answered my emails. I guess now I know why! Oh well, lessons learned, water under the bridge. I've moved on now – at least I thought I had, then I saw that picture and it brought it all back. Seriously, I wish you all the best, even if I am still kind of pissed at him. You take care.

K

I was wide awake now, stone-cold sober and trembling with shock. Surely she must have got it wrong, be somehow mistaken? I sat up in bed. Julian muttered something in his sleep and turned over. Should I wake him, ask him what this was all about? But I didn't want to have a huge row about my insecurity in the middle of the night, especially when I needed to be back at work in just five hours.

Then something occurred to me. What if it had all been a ridiculous coincidence? What if there were two men with the same name, who'd both worked in Ontario then moved to the UK at the same time? It was bizarre, but it might be true. I'd send her one more message, I decided, just to get things straight.

Hi Kristen

I'm confused too, but I think you must be mistaken. I met Julian (my Julian! :-)) when he came out here last March, for a conference at Imperial College. He definitely didn't have a girlfriend then. And we've been a couple ever since. We even went on holiday to New York together in June. So I guess he's a different person from your ex! I'm really sorry to have brought back bad memories, but I think we can leave this now.

Stella

I waited a few minutes, but there was no response. That was it – that was the end of it. There was no need to have worried.

I curled up again, wrapping my arms round Julian's waist, burying my face in his neck and breathing in the familiar smell of him. I felt myself drifting off into sleep, then my phone buzzed and jerked me awake again.

Up until now, the tone of Kristen's messages had been quite calm and measured, but it wasn't any more.

The bastard! I remember that trip to New York – he said it was another conference. The lying dick. I thought we had a future together. He talked about us getting married when I came to the UK, and all the time he was fucking someone else. If I can give you one piece of advice, Stella, it's to kick him to the kerb right now before he does the same thing to you.

K

PS – I've been waiting five months for closure. Now I guess I've got it. So thanks for that, anyways.

I didn't sleep that night. I lay awake, going through all the months' worth of emails on my phone from Julian to me and me to him, searching for clues. But there was nothing. All the words of love, all the longing for the day when we could be together, all the hopes and dreams and promises. And no hint, in any of them, that anything wasn't as it seemed.

Except for what wasn't there. That week-long gap when there'd been no messages at all. The longed-for birthday visit that never came. The times when he'd broken off a conversation in mid-stream with no explanation, then resumed it the next day as if nothing had happened.

Now I'd allowed these thoughts into my mind, it was like scratching an itch. I had to know more – I had to be sure. I couldn't stop, even if it meant drawing blood.

WHO WANTS TO MARRY A MILLIONAIRE?

I sent Kristen another message, giving her the dates, and asked her if they meant anything. Her reply came a few minutes later.

> Hell, yeah. That first week, we were at my brother's wedding in Vancouver. The other time – I'm not quite sure, I'd need to check – but I think that was when he said he was going on a stag weekend, but then a colleague's kid passed away and he had to cover for him at work, so he couldn't go. God, this is so hard, it's bringing it all back. I can't discuss it any more, I'm sorry. I hope you know what you need to do.

I got out of bed and went to the kitchen and drank a glass of water. My mouth was as dry as paper. I could feel my heart pounding in my chest. There was no way I could go back to bed, lie next to Julian as if everything was normal.

Out of habit, I went and sat at my easel by the window, but there was nothing for me to draw. My chest was tight with misery, but I couldn't cry. I waited, watching as the sky began to brighten, then the street lamp outside the window blinked off, then Julian's alarm went off. When I heard it, I was suddenly overcome with nausea, and ran to the bathroom and threw up again and again.

I didn't hear Julian come in, but I felt his hand on my shoulder.

"Little star, are you okay?" he said.

"Go away," I said. "Please just leave me alone."

"I'll be right outside. Poor darling, call me if you need me."

I felt a horrible heave in my stomach and was sick again. My face was damp with sweat and my teeth were chattering, grating together with acid. I waited a few minutes, hunched miserably over the toilet. Then I splashed cold water on my face, cleaned my teeth and went out.

Julian handed me a glass of water. "Too much celebrating with Martha last night?" he said.

"It's not that," I said. "It's you. I know about you and Kristen."

His face went suddenly still, and his eyes slipped away from me.

"What about her?" he said. "She's just an ex-girlfriend. She's ancient history."

"That's not what she says," I said. "Unless your definition of ancient is like six months ago."

"Stella, come on. Calm down. What's all this about?"

"Look at this," I said. "Go on, have a read and then you can tell me what the fuck this is about."

I thrust my phone into his hand.

He scrolled through the messages, his face unreadable. Then he handed my phone back to me.

"My poor little star," he said. "I'm so sorry you had to see that. Why don't I make us a cup of coffee and we can have a talk about it?"

"Just tell me what's going on! I don't want bloody coffee."

"Well, I do," he said calmly, filling the kettle and switching it on. I waited, leaning against the kitchen counter, while Julian spooned coffee into two mugs. His hands were completely steady.

"Come and sit down," he said.

I sat on the sofa, pulling my jumper over my knees. I didn't want the coffee – I'd be sick again if I drank it, I could tell – but I was grateful for the heat of the mug on my clammy, shivering hands.

"I never thought this would happen," Julian said. "If I had, I'd have warned you that it was a possibility. But I thought Kristen had moved on, and anyway she didn't know who you were until I posted that damn photo."

"She has moved on," I said. "She's moved on quite a bit, considering she only had six months since you dumped her."

"You didn't believe that, did you? Oh God, my poor Stella. I'll never forgive myself for exposing you to this. Of course it isn't true. None of it's true. Okay, wait, I did go out with Kristen, for a bit, when I first arrived in Canada. We worked together, I didn't have any friends there yet, and she just latched on to me – I didn't have a choice, really.

"Then I realised what she was like. She was crazy possessive, a real bunny boiler. She wanted to know where I was, what I was doing, who with, all the time. It was suffocating. And then it started to get scary. She hit me, a couple of times."

He hunched his shoulders, looking down at his hands. I felt hollow with shock and disbelief.

"Hit you?"

"Yeah. Nothing serious, she's not very strong." He looked up at me again and gave a small, twisted smile. "But it was enough to make me end it. The second time was, anyway. That was about a year and a half ago, long before I met you. But it wasn't that easy. She stalked me, sent me literally hundreds of emails and texts begging me to try again. It wore me down. I actually think I would have given her another chance, but then I came to London for that conference and met you."

"But all the dates – when we went to New York, when Ed's daughter died – she knew all that."

"Of course she did, Stella. We worked together, remember? She knew my schedule. She knew Ed." He reached over and took my coffee cup, setting it carefully on the floor, and wrapped his warm hands around mine. "It was such a relief, you know, being with you. Being with a woman who's so gentle and sweet, who trusts me."

I felt tears start to slip down my face.

"Julian, are you sure?" I said. "Because if what she said is true, I don't think I could be with you any more."

"It's not true. I give you my word of honour, we went out for – what – four months, almost two years ago. It was nothing to me. To her, it was a big deal, and maybe I should have realised that, not rushed into a relationship without getting to know her first. I didn't know it would turn out like that. I never dreamed that she'd end up hurting the person in the world who's most precious to me."

"Do you promise?" I said.

"I promise. And I want you to make a promise to me, too. Don't ever contact her again. And if she contacts you, please delete her messages. Let's delete the ones she's already sent, too. She's toxic, Stella. It frightens me to think of her spreading poison through our relationship. And that's how it feels."

Almost as if they were physically in front of me, I could see my two choices, like a fork in the path in a computer game, or an exam question with only two alternatives. A or B, yes or no, black or white. True or false. Right or wrong.

I could tell Julian I thought he was lying. I could say I didn't trust him any more – that this information compounded the doubts I'd had about him, about our relationship. Seeds of mistrust that had been sown weeks ago, when I saw him with Francine, and then been fed by his actions, by what Martha had said and Polly and Wizzy hadn't, and now brought above ground, teasing their shoots into light, by Kristen's emails.

If I said that, I'd have to leave, right now. But I had nowhere to go, and no money.

Or I could choose to believe him. I could believe everything he'd said about his love for me, the preciousness of our relationship, the hurt Kristen had caused him. I could choose our future together, in which I'd invested so much. I could reciprocate his promises, and then I wouldn't need to be alone ever again.

If I hadn't been so tired, battered by hangover and lack of sleep, I might have chosen the other path, the dimly lit one, the one on which I didn't know what I'd find. But I just didn't have the courage. And, looking at his hunched shoulders, his red-rimmed eyes, I felt a rush of pity for him. He was the man I loved. I wanted to protect him as well as myself.

There was just one more question I had to ask.

"Julian," I said. "Please tell me something, completely honestly. Is there anything going on with you and Francine?"

His back straightened. He stopped looking down at his hands and his eyes met mine. He shouted with laughter.

"Francine? That old slag? When I have you? Do you think I'm crazy?"

And that decided it. I believed him.

"Okay," I whispered, wiping my eyes on my jumper.

"Let's do it now," Julian said. "Get the messages off your phone, get her out of our life."

He watched as I turned my phone on and erased the emails, one by one.

"There," he said. "That's done. Now we should get off to work, or we're both going to be late. Shall I make you another coffee before we go?"

"It's okay," I said, my voice still a bit trembly. "I'll have a shower and head off and get something to eat on my way." I realised that the long night, the sickness and the tears had left me lightheaded with hunger.

When I got to the café, Martha was waiting for me. We looked at each other, awkward for a moment, then we both said together, "I'm so sorry about last night."

She put her arms out and I went to her and we had a hug.

"I'm such an interfering old busybody," she said. "It's none of my business how you live your life. But Wizzy made me promise I'd look out for you when you came to London. I thought I was doing that, but I wasn't, I was just meddling."

"You were just being a friend," I said. "I appreciate it, I really do."

I thought about telling her about Kristen, about what she'd done to Julian, about her messages. But then I remembered my promise to him, and decided he was right – to let her into our lives would damage my trust and bring back terrible memories for him. I must protect him from her. He needed me to do that. I'd made my choice, and I was going to abide by it.

"Anyway, I have exciting news," Martha said. "One of my customers popped in earlier to see how the mural was coming along. She owns the gift shop next door, and she loves your work. She's asked if you'd be interested in doing a range of greeting cards for her, and some original paintings, too. Maybe later on today we can pop round there and I'll introduce you."

So, that night, I was able to tell Julian that not only had Martha transferred the balance of the payment into my bank account – a huge amount by my standards – but I'd been commissioned to produce five more designs for Layla's shop, and she'd offered to stock my paintings, too.

He was so pleased and proud, I didn't want to spoil the mood by even mentioning Kristen. So I didn't, and I blocked her from my Shutterly and email accounts, and tried not to think about her again. Polly called that evening to congratulate us on our engagement, and we had an excited discussion of our plans for a wedding in the summer. Wizzy emailed and said she was planning to be back in the UK by then, and she'd heard rumours that I might be in need of a bridesmaid.

And then Mum called. When I saw her number flash up on the screen, I realised that it was three days since her message inviting herself to stay, and I had forgotten to ring her back. The familiar guilt swept over me, and I answered straight away.

"Hi Mum. I'm really, really sorry I didn't call you back, I've been so busy you won't believe. I've been doing some painting for Wizzy's sister, and it's just been totally hectic. How are you? When would you like to come and visit? Julian and I have some exciting news for you."

"That's so kind of you, love. But you might have to tell me your news over the phone, because my visit won't be until the summer. I'm going to have to go into hospital for a wee while."

"Hospital? Why? What's wrong?"

"I have a lump in my breast. I didn't think it was anything to worry about, but they make you go for mammograms and all sorts nowadays, and now they say they want to operate."

I thought of our Christmas together, how silent and sullen I'd been, while she held tight to her terrifying secret, which she might have shared with me if only I'd been kinder to her. And I realised that, now, I might not have another chance, because there might not be another Christmas. I felt hollow with shame.

"I know it's not your sort of thing, Stella, but say a prayer for me, please."

"I will, Mum," I promised, although I knew I wouldn't.

I ended the call and turned to Julian, shaking. "I'm going to have to go and see her," I said.

"Of course you must go," Julian said. "I'll miss you – it feels as if we just got back. But it's the right thing to do."

Chapter Twenty-Two

Princess Stella mounted her horse and galloped away from the tower as fast as she could go. The wind whipped her hair. She rode through rivers and forests, over hill and dale, until she reached the old queen's castle…

"And how is Jonathan?" Mum asked, once she'd sat me down in the chilly living room with the usual cup of weak tea and stale biscuit (I don't know how she did it. There must have been a moment when she opened a new packet of biscuits and they were fresh, but she seemed to have found some way of making them go soggy in a vanishingly short period of time).

"Julian. He's fine, thanks. He sends his regards," I lied.

Mum had already protested about my coming to see her, insisting that she was quite all right and I mustn't go to any trouble, so I didn't want to tell her that it had caused an epic row between me and Julian – that would only worry her more.

Everything had been fine until that morning, when I was packing my bag and he was getting ready for work.

"By the way," Julian said casually, "Before you go, would you transfer over the rent money?"

My mind raced through the contents of my bank account. It didn't take long. Not that I went crazy with the money I'd received from Martha, or anything – I took Julian out for a celebratory curry, had my hair cut for the first time in months, and bought some new paints, which I'd need for the work Layla had commissioned. But, by the time I'd booked a train ticket to Scotland, there wouldn't be very much left at all.

"Sure," I said. "My half, same as usual?"

"Actually, if you remember, you didn't pay your half last month. I paid it, so you could spend Christmas with your mother and go to Polly's wedding. So it'll need to be more this time," he said.

"I… Julian, I don't know if I can do that," I said. "Not if I go up to see Mum again today."

Julian was putting on his coat, winding a long scarf around his neck.

"You should have thought of that," he said. "Really, Stella, you need to plan these things better. You're terrible with money. Our financial position is precarious anyway, and you going dashing all over the country isn't helping it at all."

"Right," I said, my voice beginning to rise. "Please explain how I was supposed to plan for Mum being diagnosed with breast cancer, because I'm finding it hard to understand."

"Of course you can't plan for that," he said. "It's one of those things that happen. But you can plan your finances better, to make allowances for emergencies like this. And you are choosing to live beyond your means, which affects me too. It's selfish."

I hated how calm he was when we argued, how he tied me in knots and made me believe I was in the wrong, even when in my heart I knew I wasn't. At that moment, I hated him.

"I need that money today, Stella. The rent's got to be paid. I can't keep bankrolling you. We're meant to be partners in this relationship and frankly, you're taking the piss. If you can't pay your way with painting, you'll have to get a proper job. Waitressing, or something. Now I'm going to work. Think about what you want to do and I'll see you this evening."

He closed the door behind him. I sat down on the bed, shaking with rage. I couldn't believe how cold he'd sounded, how indifferent to me. We were supposed to be engaged, in love, but he'd looked at me and spoken to me with utter contempt.

Worst of all, he assumed that I'd do as I was told. That when he got home that evening, I'd be waiting there with his dinner in the oven, full of apologies. Well, I wasn't going to be. I was going to zip up my big girl suit, as Wizzy would've said, and do the right thing. But first, I was going to phone Polly and have a good cry.

As soon as she heard my voice, she knew something was the matter.

"Stella, sweetie, what is it?" she said, full of concern.

Of course, this set me off, and I sobbed down the phone, unable to get the story out for a few minutes. When at last I did, Polly's tone changed to outrage.

"The fucker! How can he do that to you? When your mum's ill and everything. He should be supporting you one hundred percent. He should be putting you first, and he isn't. Is he?"

"No, he isn't," I said, sniffing loudly. I briefly allowed myself to wonder whether he ever had, but it was too daunting a thought to dwell on for more than a second. "But what am I going to do? I didn't even really want to go and see Mum, you know we don't get on, but now I've said I will and I can't not."

"I'll tell you what you're going to do," Polly said. "You're going to get on that train, go and see your mum, spend a couple of days with her, and then come to us. He wants you to be a waitress, you can be one here. We've got two families arriving for the weekend, staying a week, and to be honest I'm not coping. My cankles are killing me and my back hurts all the time. We were going to advertise for a new staff member anyway, because I'll need to take a few months off when I have the baby and Magda's visiting her family in Krakow. So stay for as long as you want. And when – if – you decide to go back, he'll be properly shaken up because he'll realise you're not going to be a doormat."

"Are you sure?" I said.

"Of course I'm sure! Don't be daft, Stella. You'll be doing us a massive favour. Except we'll pay you, obviously. And you'll have time to paint, and I bet you'll be really inspired, too, by the scenery and everything."

Her positivity infected me, and suddenly this seemed like a totally reasonable course of action. Julian would miss me, he'd realise I wasn't to be trifled with. It could be the making of our relationship.

"I'll do it," I said. "Expect me on Friday."

I debated what to do about telling Julian my plans. I didn't want to ring him or text him – to be totally honest, I was too scared. So, in the end, I did the old-fashioned thing and left a note on the fridge. It took me several goes to write it – I didn't want him to be angry, but I did want him to know how much he'd hurt me. In the end, it was only worry about missing the train that made me go with the least incendiary version.

"Julian – I'm going to stay with Polly and Angus for a bit after I've seen Mum. Polly needs a hand with the hotel and stuff, and it will bring some cash in short-term. The rent money's in your account. Please don't be cross with me. I'm going to miss you terribly and I'll be home soon. I love you. LS xxx."

Of course, as soon as I was on the bus, I cursed myself for being a total wimp, and wished I'd said completely different things.

Now, sitting with Mum on the slippery sofa, I was getting seriously cold feet, and not just because the heating was set to arctic. I imagined Julian coming home, seeing my note, reacting – how? Would he be furious? Would he be sad? Would he turn up to fetch me back, like a knight on a white horse or a caveman who'd drag me home by my hair? I just didn't know.

And, of course, competing for space in my head with anxiety about Julian was worry about Mum. Throughout my childhood, I'd never known her to have any ailment more serious than flu. She'd always boasted that she had the constitution of a horse, but now I wondered whether there was more to it – whether she'd been afraid of admitting any frailty, and soldiered on through illness the way she had through her depression after Dad left.

"The thing is, I feel absolutely fine," she said, as if she'd read my mind. "I thought that when you have something seriously wrong, you'd know. But I didn't."

So far, neither of us had used the word 'cancer'. I didn't want to be the first one to say it. That would make it too real. So I tried to find out more about what was going to happen to her without actually mentioning what was wrong. It was a triumph of oblique communication – but then, we'd had years to perfect the technique.

"When are they going to – you know, when are you having the surgery?" I asked.

"Next week. They say I'll be out in a day or two, or even the same day if it all goes well. They say the prognosis is good."

"Will you need help? With things around the house? Because I can always come back, or stay for longer." The thought of nursing Mum filled me with dread, but I would do it if I had to, I decided. I'd do whatever it took, because if I didn't, and the worst happened, it would be my fault.

"You don't have to do that, love," Mum said. "I'll be perfectly all right. I have friends who'll come and help out, or even stay here with me."

"Auntie Ina?" I asked.

"Auntie Ina, yes. And other people from church."

"People from church, that's good," I said. But I didn't really believe my own words. I had Polly and Wizzy, who were as close to me as sisters. I had Julian – at least I hoped I still did. And Mum only had the vague, amorphous 'people from church'. I was practically writhing with guilt. Even though we were sitting next to each other, just inches of pale green chintz between us, the distance felt huge, unbridgeable, as it had done for years.

Not that Mum hadn't tried. I thought of all the birthday cards I'd received over the years and not thanked her for. I remembered all the missed calls I'd taken days or weeks to answer, or not bothered to return at all, because I was too busy. All the attempts she made, when I did finally cave in and go and see her, to find out more about my life, beyond the trivial details I reluctantly volunteered. And now it was too late – I'd waited too long, there had been too many years of silence. If I told her now how much I wished that things were different, she'd know it was my guilt talking, see it for the rank hypocrisy it was.

"It was good of you to come, you know, Stella," she said. "I do appreciate it."

"It's not a problem, Mum," I said. "I'm glad I'm here." I reached across and gave her hand a little squeeze, and she smiled. It wasn't a lot, but it was something.

"It's six thirty," I said. "Shall I start tea?"

"There's a fish pie in the freezer," Mum said. Then she added, "It should be enough for three. I bought a large one, as I was having company."

Auntie Ina, I supposed. Which meant a night of having the gospel preached at me, and probably a lecture about living in sin for good measure. Well, I'd have to put up with it, for Mum's sake.

"I'll put the oven on," I said.

I went through to Mum's tiny, spotless kitchen and lit her gas cooker, which was a relic from the nineteen eighties and reminded me of our horrible oven in Streatham, only it was a lot cleaner. I found some Birdseye peas in the freezer and set the table with three places. I boiled the kettle for tea, wishing there was something stronger – in my teenage years, I'd survived Auntie Ina's visits by sneaking up to my room at regular intervals and having furtive swigs from a bottle of vodka, not so much for the alcohol as for the thrill of imagining how appalled she would be if she knew (which, I realised with hindsight, she almost certainly had).

All too soon, the doorbell chimed its polite electronic 'ding-dong'.

"Shall I get it?" I called.

"I'm already up," Mum said.

I heard the door open and gritted my teeth, wondering how soon I could reasonably make my excuses and go to bed.

Then Mum's voice, sounding more up-beat than I'd heard it in years, said, "Hello! Come on in. How was your day?"

And a voice that definitely wasn't Auntie Ina's replied, "All the better for seeing you, Ailsa."

I dropped the bag of peas on my foot, which did an excellent job of shattering the frozen lump into which they'd solidified. A man? In Mum's house? For dinner?

"I'd like you to meet my daughter, Stella." Mum came through to the kitchen, followed by a short teddy-bear of a bloke in a navy blue jumper. He was carrying a bottle of wine, and he looked like he'd just been told he'd won the lottery.

"Stella, this is Trevor," Mum said. She, too, was lit up like a Christmas tree. "Trevor, Stella."

I shook his soft, warm hand, utterly dumbstruck, then gawped at the two of them as they stepped away, arm in arm, and struck a bit of a pose, gazing at each other, proud and glowing like Brad Pitt and Angelina Jolie on the red carpet.

Finally I found my voice and managed to say, "How nice to meet you, Trevor."

Honestly, during the course of that dinner I realised how mothers must feel when their adolescent child brings a boyfriend home for the first time. Role reversal, much? I sat there, eating my peas and fish pie (it was the right stuff, too, with prawns in it and tons of cream – clearly nothing was too good for Trevor), while the two of them nattered away about church and Mum sipped her way through two (two!) glasses of Riesling, as if she did this every night.

It turned out Trevor played the guitar, and was organising some sort of youth choir or other, and he was full of stories about uniting the community through music. Mum let slip that she was leading singing classes for children – news to me, because as far as I knew she hadn't a musical bone in her body.

And the two of them flirted. They actually flirted. It was bizarre. When Mum said, "More peas, Trevor?" and he said, "Just a few," and touched her hand as she passed him the dish, a jolt passed between them you could practically see. Mum tucked her chin into her neck and looked at him through her eyelashes, and he gave her a small, private smile, and she looked almost pretty. I'd like to say it put me right off my dinner, but it didn't, because it was really nice (the pie and the two of them, both).

When we'd finished, I offered to make some tea while they relaxed in the living room, and over the sound of the boiling kettle and the clatter of the dishes as I washed up, I could hear their voices rising as they laughed and chatted. When I took two mugs of tea out to them, Trevor had his hand on Mum's knee, and he didn't move it when he saw me.

We drank our tea, and I was about to beat a discreet retreat to bed when Trevor said, "Thank you both for the delicious dinner. I should be going now."

Mum stood up as if this was a ritual they often observed, and said, "I'll see you out."

I said again how lovely it was to have met him, and legged it back to the kitchen to wash up the mugs, leaving them to say goodnight in peace. There were some things I definitely did not want to see. What if they snogged? Too much information by a mile.

I carefully dried all the dishes and put them away, then poured myself a glass of water, and one for Mum. I handed it to her when she came into the kitchen.

"Thank you, Stella," she said. She looked around the room, which I'd restored to its usual, immaculate state. "Thank you for everything."

She was still a bit flushed and glowing, and the house felt much warmer than usual.

"Trevor's nice," I said, carefully casual. "I'm glad I met him."

"Oh, he's all right," Mum said, and she did the thing of tucking her chin down again, and she blushed. She was wearing make-up for the first time in ages, I noticed, wondering why I hadn't seen it as soon as I walked in – nothing major, no Nicki Minaj-style contouring or anything, just a bit of extra pink on her cheeks and maybe a hint of mascara – and her hair, which had previously been greying in the gentle, dispirited way blonde hair does, seemed to have acquired some honey-coloured streaks.

"Would you like a hot-water bottle, love?" Mum said.

"Why don't I make them?" I said. "You go up to bed. I'll be there in a second."

I boiled the kettle and filled two hot-water bottles, which were cocooned in knitted covers bought at some long-ago church fête and now threadbare and bobbled. The smell of the rubber when the hot water hit it reminded me potently of childhood, of Mum tucking me up in bed on winter nights, of Dad not being there.

But now wasn't the time to think of Dad. I carried Mum's hot-water bottle up to her room and tapped on the door. She was in bed, not kneeling by it as I'd expected, and she was reading a novel with a lurid turquoise cover.

"Danielle Steele," Mum said, after trying too late to hide the book under her duvet. "It's rather good. Have you read any of her books?"

"No, I haven't," I said. "But I'll look out for them, now you've mentioned her."

I slipped the hot-water bottle under the duvet by Mum's feet, and perched on the edge of the bed.

"Do you need anything else?"

"Nothing at all, love," Mum said, but she was looking at me, sort of hopefully.

I leaned over and kissed her cheek. She smelled lovely, a bit of roses and maybe of hairspray.

"Sleep tight, then," I said. But before I closed the door behind me, I turned back to her and said, "Why didn't you tell me about Trevor?"

"You never asked, did you?" she said.

I turned out her light and cleaned my teeth, then got into my own narrow bed, which now felt blissfully warm.

Then I remembered that I'd left my phone downstairs, so, reluctantly, I left my cosy cocoon and retrieved it from my handbag. Superstitiously, I made myself wait until I was back in bed before swiping it to life and checking for messages from Julian. There was nothing. Not a text, not an email, not a missed call – nothing.

I felt my entire body grow cold again, in spite of the warmth of my bed.

I checked Shutterly, but Julian's account was way down the trending list.

I checked Facebook, and there was nothing there either, just a status update from Wizzy saying she'd arrived in San Francisco.

I was about to send her a message suggesting she meet up with Will, when it occurred to me to check his profile too, and see how he was doing. I glanced through his posts – he'd played ping pong, he'd been to the movies, he'd eaten something called hamachi kama at a place called Tekka. He'd been introduced to hot yoga, whatever that was.

And he'd changed his relationship status. When I saw that, I felt a lurch of shock that couldn't have been more different from my reaction to Mum's startling emergence as one half of a couple.

Will was 'in a relationship' with a girl called Mackenzie. A beautiful girl called Mackenzie. A girl with a curtain of glossy dark hair and a smile that could stop traffic. A girl with a PhD from an elite university. A girl who did tai chi on the beach at dawn and shopped at Lulu Lemon. A girl so distant from this little terraced house in Dundee, she might as well have landed from a different planet.

I don't know what I'd been thinking. But somewhere inside me, there must have been a sense that if Julian – if I – if things didn't work out, when Will came home again, there might be... something. Something a bit more than friendship. I hadn't put it into words, hadn't allowed myself to identify the spark of happiness and excitement I felt every time an email from him arrived, or I drew a character who looked a bit like him. I hadn't allowed myself to think what my involvement in his search for romance might mean, wonder whether his friendliness towards me hid something deeper.

But now, with one click of a mouse on the other side of the world, everything had changed.

Once more, my world had narrowed to just two possibilities: be with Julian, or be alone. My resolve crumbled, and I sent an abject, grovelling text to Julian.

CHAPTER TWENTY-THREE

The sunshine streaming through the white chiffon curtains woke Will up, as it had done every morning for the past couple of weeks. At first he'd thought there might be a window of opportunity – a second or two, maybe as many as thirty – during which he could have turned over, dragged a pillow over his head to shut out the light, claimed an hour or more of extra sleep.

But there was no chance of that – not today, not any morning. Mackenzie's self-discipline was steely, and she embraced mornings with the joyful positivity that characterised her approach to all parts of her life.

"Hey, baby," she carolled, sitting up against the plump white pillows, leaning over to brush Will's lips lightly with hers. Her breath smelled minty-fresh; her eyes were bright and alert, her skin glowed. She smelled faintly of macaroons, a scent Will had struggled to identify until he'd realised the huge role virgin coconut oil played in Mackenzie's life. She cooked with the stuff, bathed with it, rubbed it into the ends of her hair, even used it to perform some obscure dental ritual Will had learned was called oil pulling.

"Chai latte?" she said, springing out of bed, and immediately dropping down into a deep stretch like a cat. "Oooh, my hamstrings are tight! Hand me my tablet, you adorable thing."

Will passed over the device. It was something he'd done many times each day over the past four weeks. Mackenzie was a devotee of what she called 'the quantified self' – this was a Thing, Will knew; Louise was all over it and Ignite had a team monitoring the trend for wearable devices that helped users track every element of their lives, from how far they walk to the quality of their sleep. However, as Will knew, there was a high degree of user bias affecting the whole concept.

A few months back, Ignite had trialled a calorie-counting app, which aimed to help dieters monitor their daily food intake, featuring a barcode reader so you didn't even have to type in the name of the food you were eating. He'd loved the idea, and Louise had been dead keen on it, too, as she herself was constantly trying to lose weight. But there was a fatal flaw in the concept, which was that users simply lied to the system about how much they were putting on their plates, or omitted to tell it about that extra Mars bar or glass of wine.

Mackenzie's constant quest for self-improvement meant that she sought to monitor every aspect of her life – what she wore, what she ate, how much she exercised, how happy it all made her, and, Will suspected with a degree of trepidation, how well he satisfied her between her snowy Egyptian cotton sheets.

In her case, the problem wasn't dishonesty, but her inherent absent-mindedness. She might have had a genius IQ, but it wasn't matched by a gift for organisation. She was on her fourth FitBit – the first one she'd left on the Google staff bus, the second had somehow slipped off her tiny wrist into the loo at her apartment, the third had met an untimely, miso-coated end when she'd dropped it into the wok when she was making stir-fry for dinner. And the fourth? She had no idea at all what had happened to it, and had spent three hours searching before giving up and writing off the hours as wasted in her time-management app – or she would have done, had she been able to find her iPhone.

There had been one lunchtime when he'd sat opposite her in the cafeteria, admiring her perfectly manicured hands and pearly teeth as she nibbled a salad, when her face had suddenly sunk into stricken disappointment and she'd said, "My heart-rate monitor! I forgot my heart-rate monitor, again! And I really tore through my VO2 max on the ergo earlier."

Another time, Will had found her in tears because she'd forgotten to record her target twenty-five positive thoughts for the day. He'd gone out and bought her a small, beautifully bound notebook with gold edges to its pages, so she could use the old-fashioned method of writing things down when she mislaid her phone or tablet, but of course she'd immediately lost the notebook too.

"Tight hamstrings," she mused, "What could that be? Maybe I didn't commit to my stretches after SoulCycle yesterday. I was conscious of some negativity. Were you conscious of negativity in me yesterday, baby?"

Will remembered Mackenzie's smiling face over the sumac-crusted tofu he'd made for their dinner, her ready laughter at his jokes, and her enthusiasm when they made love, albeit only once she'd finished doing all that shit in the bathroom with the coconut oil.

"You didn't seem negative to me," he said.

"Hmmm," Mackenzie perched on the bed, pulling her knees up to her chin and giving Will a dizzying glimpse of her Hollywood wax. "So, right, I did my mindfulness yesterday, right after my bikram. We cycled together to work. I logged my wellbeing really high after that." She gave Will a languorous, intoxicating wink, and he remembered that the day had begun with a sneaky early-morning shag.

"Then I did a few hours' work. My productivity was at the max then, check this out," she passed Will the tablet, and he scanned it, nodding.

"Yep, nine a.m. through midday, you were on fire," he said, wishing he felt as energetic himself.

"So, then, lunchtime, kale, almond and wheatgrass smoothie and a massage. Then a few more hours' work, but – oh my God! I see it now!"

"See what?" Will had abandoned any hope of more sleep.

"I had a cupcake," Mackenzie said, thumping her forehead against her knees, her hair cascading down her calves. "What was I thinking? Binh brought cupcakes in for her birthday and I ate two! I was working, and the plate came round and I just kind of took them. I didn't even log them! And they were peanut butter as well. I must be so toxic. The allergens in that! It will set me back days. I'm going to have to do a juice fast."

When Will and Mackenzie had started dating, before they became, as she put it, 'exclusive', he'd wondered whether her quest for perfection in all areas of life had been put on for his benefit. Now, after four weeks of spending almost every night at her apartment, he was beginning to realise that it was entirely sincere. She genuinely did long and strive to be the best she could – the hardest worker, the most successful, the slimmest, the prettiest, the kindest. She was relentless.

Will sat up in bed and put his arm around Mackenzie's slender shoulders.

"Kenz, you don't need to do a juice fast. Look at you, you're beautiful."

She smiled. "Thank you, baby." But she clearly wasn't listening to him, because when she went to the bathroom, he heard the electronic voice of the scale announcing her weight, followed by a cry of dismay.

Will pulled on a pair of jeans and went through to the tiny, tidy kitchen, where almost all of the worktop was taken up by Mackenzie's state-of-the-art coffee machine. He made a double espresso for himself and a chai tea for her, with a mountain of frothed low-fat coconut milk, the way she liked it (he'd asked her for a sip, once. Never again).

"So, what would you like to do with our Saturday?" he asked when she emerged from the bedroom, dressed in a chunky cable-knit jumper over denim hotpants. "Sightseeing? Beach? Movies?"

"I don't know, Will," she said, tipping her tea down the sink and filling the mug with hot water to which she added a slice of lemon. "I need to go to Pilates, I need to clean the apartment. I need to do my mindfulness."

"What's up?" he said. "There's something bothering you, isn't there?"

"I gained a pound," she said. "A pound. Because of two cupcakes that didn't even weigh eight ounces. How does that work?"

Thanks to Louise, Will had acquired extensive knowledge of the vagaries of human metabolism. He could have treated Mackenzie to a lecture on carbohydrates, water retention, adipose tissue and all the rest, but he knew that wasn't what she had really asked.

"Come here," he said.

She crossed the kitchen towards him, her mug of hot water in her hand, her face forlorn. He put his arms around her and pulled her to his chest.

"You're being daft, Kenz. Daft as a brush."

Her shoulders shook slightly under his hand, and he hoped she wasn't crying.

"Say that again," she said.

"What? Daft as a brush?"

She looked up, and he realised she was giggling.

"That expression is just adorable," she said. "I'm sorry, Will, I need to snap out of it. Maybe it's my hormones. Where did I put my phone, I need to check my cycle…"

She wandered out, leaving Will staring after her with exasperated affection. She was so sweet, so beautiful, she seemed to be mad about him. They had fun together – they'd been bowling, rollerblading, hiking in the mountains. They made a great team at work and in bed.

He couldn't help wishing, though, that she'd lighten up just a bit. He'd never heard her swear or fart. She never got drunk. She never got annoyed with him – even the time he spilled goji berry juice on her white sofa, she just said calmly that accidents happen and cleaned it up, then covered the stain with a scatter cushion. Although she was a bit high-maintenance, she was nothing like Charlotte.

And anyway, it was early days. No doubt after another few months together, she'd have turned into a lager-swilling harridan and he'd long for the return of the demure, gentle Mackenzie whose idea of a relaxing Sunday was volunteering at a local shelter for homeless people.

Will washed up his coffee mug, dried it and put it away. One of Mackenzie's mantras was 'tidy home, tidy mind'. She might be the ultimate scatterbrain but her apartment was immaculate, so at least she'd cracked half of it.

"Kenz? Where are you?" he called.

"Living room," she said.

He joined her on the couch, and the two of them flipped through their phones in companionable silence until it was time for Mackenzie to get changed for her Pilates class.

She got changed a lot, Will had noticed – most days she got through about five different outfits: something for her morning workout, something else for work, yet another for her lunchtime yoga class, something different if they went out in the evenings, and one of a seemingly endless collection of satin babydoll nighties in pastel colours for bed.

Now she was wearing yoga pants, a lace sports bra and a hoodie, her hair in two plaits behind her ears.

Will thought, for the billionth time, how much he fancied her, and wondered if there was any change of her sacking off the Pilates class in favour of a couple of hours in the sack with him. But there was no point suggesting it – her schedule was sacrosanct.

"See you later, baby," she said, tucking her keys into the flowery bag with her mat and water bottle, and skipping to the front door. She opened it, then paused, turned back to Will and said, "I love you."

Will was dumbstruck, but she didn't wait for an answer. It was only when the door had closed after her that he found his voice and said aloud, "Shit. That wasn't supposed to happen."

Chapter Twenty-Four

Disguised as a scullery-maid, Princess Stella made her way to the palace, where the young king and queen were waiting eagerly for the birth of their baby prince or princess…

"Recruit Griffiths reporting for duty, Sir!" I snapped a cod salute at Polly, who was curled up on her sofa, her bump huge under a gorgeous faux fur throw.

Polly laughed. "You're such a loon. But thanks so much for coming, it's totally amazing of you. We'll go down and start sorting dinner in a bit, but first you need to tell me all the news. How's your mum? What's up with Julian?"

"Mum's okay," I said. "Nervous, obviously, about the surgery. But I've left her in the capable hands of her new bloke."

"Her what?" Polly sat up, adjusting a cushion behind her back.

"You heard right." I filled her in on the Trevor situation. "He's a bit of a legend really, seriously nice. And he makes a mean flapjack. She seems really happy. We had some good chats – it's not like we're best mates or anything, but there's been a bit of a thaw. I felt really bad leaving her to come here, but then she told me Auntie Ina was coming to stay and look after her, so I got out of there sharpish. Which was just as well, because if I'd eaten much more of that flapjack I wouldn't have been able to fit through the door."

"Flapcrack," Polly said. "You'll have to get the recipe off him, it's meant to be awesome for lactating mums, according to my NCT teacher. But then if she's to be believed, having a baby is all about troughing cake. At least, that's what I chose to take away from the classes. When she got to the bit about the actual birth, Angus and I more or less stuck our fingers in our ears and went, 'Lalala, can't hear you.' I'm in denial, basically. Four weeks to go. I've decided that this baby is just going to appear in its cot without the birth bit having to happen."

"Sounds like a good plan to me," I said. "Who needs immaculate conception? That's missing out the fun bit. Immaculate birth would make much more sense."

"And Julian?" Polly looked at me, reading my expression with her usual astuteness. "You haven't, have you? You haven't gone and forgiven him?"

"That's not what it was about, at all," I said. "He's forgiven me. I texted him and said I was sorry, and he replied straight away. So it's all going to be okay."

"Hold on just one second," Polly said. "Pause, rewind. I missed the bit where you'd done something wrong that you needed to apologise for."

"But I did! I buggered off and went to see Mum, just leaving him a note. It was a really bad thing to do. But he's been lovely about it. Look, I'll show you the text if you want. He says he's thinking about me all the time, but I can stay as long as you need me."

"He says you can stay! Listen to yourself, Stella. Since when do you need permission from your boyfriend to visit your mother, to help out a friend, to do any of the normal stuff that normal, reasonable people do all the time?"

"That's not what I meant," I protested. "It's not about getting permission. Of course I can do what I want. He doesn't own me, he doesn't order me about. But he wants me to be with him, and I want to be with him, too. It's hard for him being on his own, especially when we were apart for so long when he was in Canada. He misses me."

Saying that reminded me of my surreal late-night email conversation with Kristen. But I wasn't going to mention that to Polly – I knew she'd just misinterpret it totally, find some way to imply that Julian was in the wrong. Nor did I tell her about my silly, baseless jealousy of Francine, because that just made me feel ashamed of myself.

"Come on," Polly said, to my relief. "Let's get downstairs and prepare the dining room for the arrival of the ravening hordes. We serve dinner at eight, and they're normally done by ten. Breakfast's from seven thirty, but this lot are late risers, and they eat lunch out, so you'll have masses of time to paint."

She briefed me on my duties as we set the tables with snowy linen cloths and starched napkins, arranging cutlery and glasses, salt and pepper, pots of mustard and vases of flowers.

I thought she had finished interrogating me about Julian, but she hadn't.

"Look, Stella," she said, when we back in the kitchen, Polly sautéeing mushrooms for soup and I chopping shallots, "I know you think I'm massively down on Julian. You're wrong, I'm not, and nor is Wizzy. We're just worried about you. We just want you to be happy. If he makes you happy, it's all good."

"He does!" I said. "Please believe me, Polly, he really does. And we have the most amazing sex. But you need to understand, he's a complicated person. It's because he's so clever, I guess. He's much cleverer than me, which is why it's hard to argue with him sometimes. He's always right!"

"No he isn't," Polly said. "For God's sake, Stella, if he's got you believing that…"

I interrupted her. "But, you know, deep down, I think he might be a bit insecure. You know his dad left when he was a baby. It leaves a scar on a person. I should know. So I have to keep proving to him that he can trust me, that I'm not going to abandon him. Once we're married, I know things will be better and we won't argue as much. We're so happy together, almost all the time. And he asked me to marry me! Of course he loves me!"

I could hear the pleading in my voice. I was desperate to convince her that what I felt for Julian was the real thing, was right, and that our relationship was only volatile because our love for each other was so intense. I wanted to explain that the only reason I worried about Kristen, about Francine, about the other women in Julian's past, was my own silly self-doubt and sense of inadequacy, and not anything he had done. I was trying to find a way to articulate all this, when Angus came crashing into the kitchen carrying a basket of logs for the fire.

"They're in the bar," he said. "They're drinking their cocktails, and asking hopeful questions about when dinner will be ready. How's it going, wife of my bosom? Need a hand with anything?"

"It's all under control." Polly tipped the mushrooms into a space-age food processor, added what looked like about two pints of double cream, and switched the machine on, and its roar drowned out any possibility of conversation.

Rhona picked up an armful of bread baskets, and I followed her through to the dining room with a tray of butter dishes. Behind us, Angus wheeled a trolley that appeared to hold every cheese known to man.

"All set?" Angus said.

As if summoned by some second sight – or more likely by the smell of cheese – the guests drifted through from the bar. From Polly's description of the last lot's scone-eating habits, I'd expected these to be the sort of Americans you see in documentaries about the obesity epidemic, who walk around Disney World with supersized buckets of fat coke hanging round their necks on strings. But they actually looked perfectly normal.

"Something smells good!" said one of the women, who had sleek blonde hair and was wearing a totally covetable silk shirt over skinny jeans. "I'm Miranda Shaw, I don't believe we've met?"

I shook her slim, cool hand and said I was a friend of Polly's, and she introduced her husband, James, and their daughters.

Then my waitressing instinct took over and I said, "Would you like to see the wine list? Polly's just on her way with the soup," and within a few minutes I was pouring wine for Mr Shaw to taste, and opening bottles of fizzy water for Emily and Olivia while Polly ladled delicious-smelling mushroom soup into their bowls.

"Please let us know if there's anything else you'd like," Polly said. "Angus will be along shortly to tell you all about our selection of cheese, and – oh."

She had frozen, the soup ladle hovering over Mrs Shaw's bowl.

"Are you okay, Poll?" I said.

"No." She looked like she was going to cry. I stared at her blankly, and so did Rhona and Mr Shaw and the daughters.

Mrs Shaw was quicker on the uptake. She pushed back her chair and put her arm round Polly's shoulders.

"Come with me," she said, leading her out of the room. We could all see the puddle of moisture spreading over the carpet where Polly had been standing. "Let's get you upstairs. I'm an obstetrician. I'll take care of you until we get you to hospital."

"Oh my God, gross," whispered Emily, and her sister silenced her with a glare.

I put the wine bottle down and rushed to the kitchen to find Angus.

"Fuck, I think Polly's waters have broken," I gibbered. "She's with Mrs Shaw now, and I don't know what to do. What do we do?"

"We call the midwife," Angus said, taking his mobile out of his pocket and dialling, his face white under his beard. He looked as panicked by the situation as I felt – it was a bit like something out of, well, *Call the Midwife.*

I stood in the middle of the kitchen, rooted to the spot and feeling utterly useless, while I listened to Angus's one-sided conversation.

"Yes, thirty-six weeks. We're almost an hour from the hospital and the roads aren't great. Yes, just a moment, hold on." He hurried upstairs, his phone pressed to his ear, and I followed, not knowing what else to do. Was I meant to boil water? Wasn't boiling water involved somehow? And towels? Did I need to find towels? Where were the towels? In Polly and Angus's bathroom, obviously, where Polly, Angus and Mrs Shaw were. I sat down on their bed, looking in horror at the closed door.

I could hear Angus, still talking into his phone. "Yes, yes, great, if you could get someone here as soon as possible."

There was a soothing murmur from Mrs Shaw, then I heard Polly say, "But what about my epidural?"

"Now, my dear, there's no need to worry," Mrs Shaw said. "It's very unlikely the baby will come tonight. Spontaneous early rupture of membranes isn't uncommon, and most probably you'll have your baby in a day or two, in hospital, with all the care you need. Just breathe deeply, now. There, let's get you lying down."

Polly said, "But it hurts!"

I said, "Do I need to boil some water?"

Mrs Shaw emerged from the bathroom, her arm still around Polly's shoulders. Polly was wearing a towelling dressing gown. "That's an excellent idea," she said. "We could all do with a cup of tea while we wait."

"Tea! Right, I'm on it." I hurried back downstairs, relieved to have something useful to do. Then, of course, I couldn't find where any of the tea things were, and Rhona had to show me, and I felt more useless than ever.

Eventually, I made my way back upstairs with a tray, to find Polly lying in bed with Mrs Shaw holding one of her hands and Angus holding the other. "Her contractions aren't coming regularly," Mrs Shaw was saying. "This may still be a false alarm, so there's no need to worry."

But I could see from Angus's face that he was worried to the point of panic.

"What about the cheese?" Polly said.

"Never mind about the cheese," said Mrs Shaw. "They'll be perfectly all right. Just focus on your breathing and relax."

I assured Polly that Rhona had risen to the occasion, and the guests had been fed and were watching Sky News in the sitting room, and Mr Shaw was drinking brandy. But she wasn't listening by the time I got to that bit – she'd sort of zoned out and was making a strange, keening sound. Angus looked like he was in pain, too, but that was probably because Polly had his hand in a bone-crunching grip.

Then both their faces relaxed. Mrs Shaw glanced at her watch, and for the first time, she began to look anxious.

Angus's phone rang and he answered it, saying, "Yes. Right. Okay, that's great. Quick as you can. Thanks.

"The ambulance is on its way. They reckon twenty minutes to half an hour."

"What can I do?" I said, knowing there was nothing, really – I wasn't calm and qualified like Mrs Shaw, or on hand-holding duty like Angus. I was just a useless, frightened spare part, standing by while my friend was in pain and her baby was in danger.

"You could pack a bag for Polly," Mrs Shaw said. "You'll be in hospital for a few days at least, my dear, so why not tell Stella what you'll need and where to find it, and she can get everything sorted for you."

I could have kissed her. It felt wonderful to be rummaging around in cupboards looking for nighties and toothbrushes and Polly's hair straighteners.

"And nail polish," Polly said. "I want my new Butter London nail polish. The silver one. And oh my God, I haven't bought anything for the baby yet." And then she was overwhelmed by pain again, and couldn't say anything for a while.

"I'll just go down and see if the ambulance is coming," I said.

I ran downstairs again and opened the heavy front door and stood in the blustery night, taking big gulps of cool air. At first all I could hear was the rustle of leaves, then I heard a faint wailing sound. Was it a siren? Or was it just the wind in the pine trees, or even Polly herself? Should I go back upstairs? But I waited, and soon I saw a flashing blue light in the distance, disappearing and reappearing around the bends in the road. Then there was the crunch of wheels on the gravel, and in the dazzle of headlights I saw people spilling out, and I ran over to them and showed them where to go.

And then there was nothing more to do. I went in to the kitchen and helped Rhona clean up, and we sat around the table and drank tea, and didn't talk very much, because we were all desperately listening for sounds from upstairs. For a long time there was nothing, then we heard the click of heels on the stone floor outside.

Rhona jumped up and opened the door. Mrs Shaw was standing there with blood on her beautiful silk shirt and a smile on her face.

"The baby's here," she said. "A girl. She's small, but that's to expected as she was preterm. Everything's going to be fine. They're just going to take Mom and the little one into hospital to be checked out."

A few minutes later Polly was carried downstairs on a stretcher, covered in blankets. I could just see the baby's tiny head peeping out from under her chin. Angus was walking behind them, looking like he'd just scored the winning try in the Six Nations.

"I think this calls for a drop of Laphroaig, Stella," he said.

I hugged him, kissed Polly's hot, flushed cheek, and touched the baby's warm red forehead with my finger before they were all bundled into the ambulance and driven away.

We all sat in the kitchen for a long time, and made a sizeable dent in a bottle of Angus's single malt, before a text came through from him saying that Polly and the baby were doing well, she weighed five pounds eight ounces, and they'd decided to call her Miranda. Mrs Shaw's poise deserted her entirely at that point, and she had a good old sob and smeared mascara all over her silk shirt, but said it didn't matter, it was ruined anyway. So we had another drink, and in the end I sat up all night telling Wizzy on Skype what had happened.

I stayed at the hotel for another week, until Magda came back from Poland. I made beds and waitressed at breakfast and dinner. I mastered the horribly temperamental coffee machine, and Mrs Shaw said my espresso was the best she'd ever tasted. I baked a mountain of flapjack using Trevor's recipe, and sat and chatted to Polly while she fed Miranda and ate her way through square after square of it. I cuddled the baby and bathed her and changed her nappies, and agreed with Polly that she was the cutest thing in the world, ever (although I will say that she had an impressive pair of lungs on her – none of us got much sleep).

If Polly was in love with her baby, Angus was even more smitten. I loved seeing how he fussed over Polly and little Miranda, tenderness and pride simply oozing out of him. I wondered if Julian would be the same when we eventually had a baby. I watched Angus cradling his daughter, who looked absurdly tiny when he held her, like that Athena poster from the nineteen eighties. He didn't mind when she screamed in his ear or was sick down his back; he just laughed and told her what a clever girl she was. Julian would be just the same, I told myself – no one could help loving someone so tiny and precious. But all that was a long time in the future – Julian I weren't even married yet; I wasn't going to frighten him with talk of babies.

I rang Julian every night, and every night he answered. He couldn't always talk for long, but every time he told me how much he loved me and missed me, and how happy he'd be when I was home. He even sent a beautiful bouquet of flowers for Polly.

I spoke to Mum and Trevor on the phone, and learned that Mum's operation had gone smoothly. She was in a bit of pain and taking it easy – Trevor assured me that between him and Auntie Ina, she wasn't being allowed to do anything more onerous than drink tea and read her way through Danielle Steele's back catalogue. Her doctors said she'd come through the surgery as well as could be expected and would be starting a course of radiotherapy in a couple of weeks, but for now all she needed to do was rest and recover.

I went for long runs in the snow every day, circling the loch until my legs ached and my body was soaked in sweat. I told myself I needed the exercise to burn off the huge dinners Rhona cooked every night, making up for the lack of Polly's culinary sophistication with masses of butter and cream. Actually, though, my runs became a daily meditation, a change to escape from the bustle of life in the hotel, clear my head and gain inspiration from the dazzling scenery.

Because Polly was right – I managed to find loads of time to paint, and I finished my designs for Layla's greeting cards. There were five of them, and they were all quirky takes on scenes from classic fairy tales. My favourite showed a handsome prince kissing a frog – I'd managed, rather cleverly I thought, to give my frog a pretty, feminine face.

Martha emailed to tell me that people loved the mural, and she'd had several enquiries from customers wanting me to paint their children's bedroom walls. I spent some time setting up a website showcasing my services, and posted pictures of my work in progress on Shutterly.

The Shaws went home to Massachusetts, promising to leave a glowing review on TripAdvisor. The other American family left for Edinburgh, and a group of golfers checked in. Gray was full of plans to build a spa in the old stableyard. I noticed that the days were beginning, almost imperceptibly, to grow longer.

Wizzy told us that she and Grace, the Australian backpacker she was travelling with, had embarked on a road trip to Vegas, where Wizzy assured us she planned to win a million pounds in a casino. I sent her Will's details and suggested they meet up when she arrived back in San Francisco.

I hadn't heard from Will for weeks. His silence made me sad – I missed his jokey emails more than I'd have believed possible. I wondered if he was happy with his new girlfriend, but I didn't dwell on the idea for long – when I thought of them together, my mind shied away.

At last, almost two weeks into February, I told Polly I was going home.

"Already?" she said. "Are you sure? You don't have to. You can stay as long as you like, we can always do with an extra pair of hands, since I'm permanently trapped on the sofa with this one."

She kissed Miranda's head and the baby's tiny hand stretched out like a starfish against her fluffy pink blanket.

"I'm sure," I said. "I've been here longer than I planned – more than a week. I need to get back. Julian's missing me, and I've got two bookings for murals."

"Stay another couple of days," she said. "Miranda doesn't want you to go, do you, darling?"

"I'll miss her, the little poppet, and you too," I said. "But I'll come and visit soon. I've booked a ticket back tomorrow – it's Valentine's Day, and I want to surprise Julian, so I haven't told him to expect me. I'm going to be waiting at the flat when he gets home from work and I'll be like, 'Tahdah!'."

Polly pulled Miranda closer to her, resting her cheek against her baby's.

"That's a lovely idea, Stella," she said, "I hope it works out."

All the long journey back to London the next day, I was twitchy with anticipation. I remembered travelling this way just two months ago, with Julian next to me, holding his hand, confident in his love for me. Now I was going to see him again, in just a few hours, but it felt a bit different, as if the stakes were even higher. Polly didn't think I'd listened to her doubts, but I had, and even though I didn't share them, I was going to make sure that things were right between him and me.

I'd done a lot of thinking over the past week, while I went for my runs and worked on my paintings. I knew things with Julian hadn't been perfect. I still had grave doubts about whether what he had told me about Kristen was true. But I had decided it was time to start afresh, to put my insecurities behind me, to trust that he loved me as much as he said, and move forward from a point of confidence, not one of neediness and doubt.

It would mean changing some things, of course. I'd need to try harder, to make a success of my painting business, or redouble my efforts to find a proper job. Now I had a bit more money in the bank, I could get some highlights in my hair, maybe even buy some new clothes. I'd try and make sure we had a night a week when he didn't work late, I decided, when the two of us could go out together, have a bottle of wine and talk about important things, not just about when the gas bill needed to be paid.

I'd be more adventurous in bed, more alluring, remind him why he'd fallen for me in the first place. I'd break the habit we seemed to have fallen into of making love last thing at night, when we were both too tired to enjoy it much. I'd greet him when he got home in the afternoons in sexy lingerie – not that I had much, but there were a few bits I bought ages ago at La Senza in Edinburgh that would have to have to do. I was going to make things right, reassure him that I loved him, and then he would no longer need to test me, to push me away.

The journey seemed to take forever. I had nothing to read and my phone's battery was dying, so I couldn't distract myself with Facebook. I stared out of the window as the landscape slipped past, gradually darkening until all I could see was the reflection of my own face, pale and anxious. I looked at my watch. It was five o'clock, and we were still an hour from London. Then there'd be the long bus journey to Streatham, and I desperately wanted to shower and put on some make-up before I saw Julian.

By the time I got home, I'd bitten all my nails down to the quick, a habit I thought I'd managed to break in my teens.

I unlocked the door of our flat, tentatively calling out to see if Julian was there, but there was no response, and the place was in darkness. I snapped on a light. In my weeks away, I'd forgotten how small the place was, how shabby. But it was clean, at least, and extremely tidy. I felt my spirits lift – Julian knew I was coming home soon, he'd made an effort to make the place welcoming for me.

I tipped my belongings out of my bag on to the bed. Just about everything needed washing – I'd have a shower, then shove it all in the washing machine, and by the time I'd bought a bottle of wine from the corner shop, he was sure to be home.

But the washing machine was full, its door closed. I fought down a burst of annoyance – Julian never, ever hung stuff up to dry. I pulled out the tangle of damp clothes and dragged the rickety airer out of its place behind the fridge. My shower would have to wait – I'd get this sorted first. A forest of clean washing hanging in the living room wasn't exactly conducive to romance, but it was better than a pile of my dirty stuff on the bedroom floor.

I shook out Julian's familiar clothes and draped them over the rails – the jumper he'd been wearing when I met him, the T-shirt I often borrowed to sleep in, endless socks that I could never find matching pairs for.

And something else. A garment I hadn't seen before, bright red. Julian never wore red.

I picked it up, puzzled, then realised what it was. A woman's nightie, a red satin thing with lace straps. Not even a particularly pretty one, but cheap and tawdry.

For a moment, my mind wouldn't let me see the truth. I whirled through possible scenarios, each more improbable than the last. Julian had bought it for me, at the charity shop, and decided to wash it before I wore it. It had blown from a neighbour's balcony in through our window and got mixed up with Julian's clothes somehow. Julian was a secret cross-dresser who'd been indulging his fantasies in my absence.

For a few moments, I almost managed to persuade myself to believe the last one. Would I still love him if that were true? Briefly I imagined having sex with him while he wore it, but the idea was so absurd, to patently untrue, it actually made me giggle – and then my gasp of laughter turned to tears.

Obviously, he was shagging someone else. Shagging Francine. This was exactly the kind of thing I could imagine her wearing. I could almost see the shiny fabric hanging from her collarbones, draping over her thin, rapacious body.

I grasped the straps and pulled, trying to tear the horrible thing apart, but the material was surprisingly strong. Eventually one of the straps gave way, then the other. I stopped. What the hell was I doing? It wasn't at this garment but at its owner that I should be directing my fury. No – not at her either, at Julian himself. I opened the kitchen rubbish bin and dumped the nightie on top of the contents. Let her retrieve it from there if she wanted. Then I poured myself a glass of water and sat at the table to wait, my entire body shaking.

My senses were on high alert – each time I heard the downstairs door slam I was sure it would be him. Each set of feet I heard climb the stairs, I expected to stop outside our door. But it was more than an hour before I heard his key in the lock.

I stood up, almost falling over because one of my feet had gone to sleep. The door opened. I could hear laughter – Julian's and someone else's. Someone else. Not Francine. Not Francine at all. I'd got it wrong. It was Liberty who walked through the door with Julian, her arm tucked into his, Liberty whose face fell when she saw me standing there.

CHAPTER TWENTY-FIVE

This was not a date – most definitely not. Still, Will was in a bar, waiting for the arrival of a woman he'd never met before, and he couldn't help feeling a bit of that familiar first-date nervousness. He wasn't sure why, but he was massively anxious to make a good impression.

He glanced at his reflection in the mirror above the bar. He was wearing a new shirt in a fine blue and white floral print, which Mackenzie had bought for him. She'd persuaded him to go to the salon where she had her hair done and ask for an 'updated' style, and his hair was now in a deep side parting with a quiff. On his feet were blue suede brogues, which Mackenzie said should be worn with bright green and yellow argyle socks.

He suspected he looked like a wanker. But then, looking around the bar, he saw that just about every other man in the place was similarly floral-shirted, quiffed and loud-socked. They all looked like wankers too, so at least he fitted in.

He glanced at his phone. There were no messages on Facebook, but there was an email from Louise, updating him on how things were going back at the Shoreditch office. He tapped out a quick reply, telling her that the work on integrating the Shutterly app into the Android operating system was going well. It was going extremely well, in fact

266

– Will reckoned he would need to spend another week working with the team, maybe two, and then there'd be nothing keeping him from going home.

Nothing except his own feelings, and Mackenzie. He wasn't quite sure how it had happened, but they were most definitely an item, exclusively dating, almost living together. He'd only spent about four nights in his own apartment in the past month, when she'd been away on a yoga retreat and when her mother visited from Connecticut. Okay, so, basically, they were living together.

And as a girlfriend, she was hard to fault. She was cute, sexy, kind and scarily bright. If she was a little humourless, he could forgive that – even though her look of polite incomprehension when she'd found him doubled over with laughter at the latest Flight of the Conchords video had been unsettling, it wasn't exactly a deal-breaker. Okay, her approach to life was generally a bit more serious than Will's own. He found it hard to get used to the way every hour of her day was filled with activity, most of it aimed at self-improvement. He wished she'd sometimes just spend a Sunday lying in bed in her pyjamas, playing games or having sex or eating chocolate. But Mackenzie never ate chocolate, certainly not in bed.

Will was aware that decision time was imminent. Two weeks at most, and he'd have to make up his mind about whether to go home to London, or stay in San Francisco. He and Louise had discussed in detail the business case for setting up a Silicon Valley arm of Ignite. It wasn't strictly necessary – communication could easily be carried out remotely, even if it meant some late nights to accommodate the time difference. With more business coming from Samsung and other tech giants in South Korea, a London office was as good as a West Coast one, if not better. But this was the global HQ where technology was concerned – it was where the action really centred, and there was huge status involved as well.

Mackenzie made no secret of wanting him to stay. Increasingly, she talked about their future together – casual mentions of plans for Labor Day weekend, the possibility of a holiday to Hawaii in the summer, Will meeting her mom next time she visited. And then less subtle references to friends' engagements, looking for a new, bigger apartment, and the fact that Mackenzie wanted two kids, a boy and a girl, maybe twins.

Will didn't want to string her along or mess her around. He liked her, although he hadn't told her he loved her. But the uncertainty he felt about being with her long-term was souring his enjoyment of the present. He wondered if the decent thing to do would be to end it now, remove her from the equation, so he could make his decisions without having to account for her feelings.

This was all just detail, though. There was only one real problem in their relationship, and it wasn't anything either Mackenzie or he could change.

Or perhaps he could – perhaps with a bit more time and effort, he could begin to feel the way she wanted him to feel about her. Perhaps even more distance from London and what he'd left behind was just what he needed. Perhaps he was being unfair to Mackenzie, making unfair comparisons, not allowing her into his heart because of who she wasn't, not because of the person she was.

And he was homesick. He missed the daily kamikaze thrill of cycling through the traffic to the office. He missed the easy, familiar banter with Tim and Giles. He missed the rain, and the grim faces of morning commuters, and Marmite. And most of all, he missed – he shut the thought down. He wasn't going there, no way. Will took a sip of his barrel-aged Negroni and ate some black truffle-flavoured popcorn from the bowl on the bar. It might be on the ragged edge of snack fashion, but it tasted of old socks to him. He checked his reflection in the mirror again. He longed to run his fingers through his hair, but he suspected that the quiff, once disturbed, would be impossible to restore to its current glory.

He glanced at his watch. She was fifteen minutes late. He'd wait five more and then text her, and allow her another fifteen before giving up. He was in no rush – it was a Saturday evening, and he had nothing better to do than sit here, leaning his arms on the cold pressed-copper counter of the bar, wondering what to order next from the vast cocktail menu. He might even eat some more popcorn – it could turn out to be an acquired taste.

He heard the door of the bar open behind him. The bloke on the next-door stool looked round, then nudged his friend, and they both took a long, appreciative stare. Will resisted for a second, then looked round too.

The girl who'd just walked in was worth staring at, that was for sure. She was tall, with a rangy, athletic figure and a tangle of chestnut hair that wasn't quite straight or entirely curly, but carelessly tousled as if she'd just been for a walk on a windy morning. She was wearing jeans and a grey T-shirt, too casual for this rather chichi bar, but there was no way she was going to get bounced for violating the dress code. She saw Will and came over.

"Will? I'm Isabella. Call me Wizzy, everyone does. It's a bit cringy but I'm used to it."

Will caught identical looks of disappointment cross the faces of the blokes next to him.

"Great to meet you." He stood up. Her only concession to glamorous dress was a pair of slouchy gold suede boots, so high-heeled he barely had to bend down to kiss her. "Shall we move to a table? We'll be more comfortable."

"Cool," she said.

Will gestured to the barman, who brought over his drink, a couple of menus and another bowl of the dodgy popcorn to a booth in the corner.

"I'm starving," Wizzy said, digging in. "Oh my God, it's this truffle stuff they have everywhere over here. I hated it at first, but now I can't get enough. It's…"

"An acquired taste?" Will suggested.

"I was going to say, it's like it's laced with crystal meth or something. But your version's classier."

Will laughed. "I don't often get called classy. The cocktails are great here – I'm moving on to Sazerac but the Negroni was amazing. Taste?"

He pushed his glass across the table and she took a sip.

"Lush," she said. "I'll have one of those, please. It's so fabulous being somewhere posh for a change. I've been hanging out in dive bars and backpackers' pubs, and drinking cheap beer and rancid white wine. The joys of travelling on a budget!"

"But you've been, like, everywhere, haven't you?" Will said.

She shook her head. "I feel like I've only scratched the surface. I started off in Thailand, then Bali, then Australia and New Zealand, then a bit of South America – Peru, Brazil and Mexico – and now Grace, the girl I've been travelling with for the past few weeks, and I have spent a couple of weeks exploring the West Coast."

"Blimey – impressive stuff. And what's next?"

"Grace is flying back to Melbourne in a couple of days, so I'm on my own," she said. "I was planning to stay here until Thursday, then head to New Orleans, then New York.

And then I suppose I'll have to call it a wrap and go home and find a job."

"Remind me what it is you do?" Will asked.

She told him a bit about her career in marketing. Dreaming up ad campaigns for soap powder didn't seem on the surface to be interesting at all, but she managed to make it sound not only fascinating, but funny too.

"Creativity is kind of limited," she said. "Almost all our advertising is what the agency guys call 2CK – a couple of women talking about how changing their brand of detergent has made their lives so much more fulfilled. Two cunts in a kitchen. How misogynistic is that?"

"Grim," Will agreed. "Still, I guess furthering the cause of equality isn't exactly high on the agenda when you've got fabric softener to flog. Will you go back to doing the same thing?"

"I guess so." She sipped her drink. "But I might look for something in London. Change of scenery, and stuff. And Stella's there."

"How do you two know each other?" Will knew the answer, but he didn't particularly want to change the subject, now they'd arrived at it.

"We met at uni," Wizzy said. "Freshers' week. You know how everyone advises you to be careful about what friends you make then, because you can end up spending four years shackled to some nightmare of a person who's decided they're your best friend? We were so lucky, Stella and Polly and me. We met in a bar one evening, when Polly was a bit pissed and being hit on by some arsehole. Stella and I rescued her and got her to her room, and we've been best mates ever since, even though we're so different."

"Different how?" Will asked, ever so casually.

"Polly's always been a bit of a homebody. That sounds like I'm dissing her, but I'm not. She's just incredibly kind

271

and warm and loves looking after people. And I'm a bit chaotic, really – I drove the other two mad sometimes, leaving
my stuff lying about and drinking all the milk and forgetting
to put the bins out. And Stella…"

Will ordered another round of drinks, and the barman
brought another bowl of popcorn.

"Stella had her head in the clouds most of the time.
Either thinking about art – she's seriously talented – or
mooning over some man."

"Really?" Will said.

"Yeah, she always had the most awful taste in blokes.
One useless boyfriend after another. We hated seeing her
get hurt all the time, and she just used to put up with it,
because she felt that if she didn't have a man in her life,
it meant she was – I don't know, worth less, somehow. But
hopefully that's all going to change now."

"Now she and Julian are getting married?" Will said,
keeping his voice carefully neutral.

"No! You mean he hasn't told you? I suppose he wouldn't
in the circumstances, but I thought you two were, like, best
friends."

"Told me what?" Will sipped his drink.

"He cheated on her. Look, I know he's your friend, but what
he did to Stella was pretty diabolical. And even before that, he
was just… Polly and I tried to talk sense into her but she just
wouldn't listen. Thought he was the love of her life. But now
she's finally seen the light, and dumped him. And hopefully he'll
stay dumped. She's staying with my sister, and I've given Martha
strict instructions to set the dogs on him if he turns up. They
haven't got any dogs, unfortunately – she'll have to improvise."

Will said, "I haven't spoken to Julian for weeks, and I
don't know if I will again. Not after I told him what I thought
about the girl, anyway. So I had no idea they'd split up."

Wizzy plonked her drink down on the table with more force than was necessary. "Wait, what? You knew about this other woman?"

"I didn't *know*, know. But I met Julian for a drink one night, and he brought her along. It was seriously awkward. He said she was a friend but it didn't really look that way."

"And you never said anything to Stella?" Wizzy demanded accusingly.

"I didn't. Maybe I should have done. But Julian is my mate – or he was, then. I almost told Stella – I came *this* close to telling her – but then I thought it would be better to try and talk sense into Julian. And that went well – not. I just didn't want to be the bad guy. I didn't want to mess things up between them."

"Even though Julian was doing a fucking excellent job of messing things up himself?"

"Look, I'm sorry," Will said. "I really am. I never wanted Stella to get hurt. But what would you have done, in my position? Gone barging in there and told her what was going on, and then she hates me because I'm the bearer of bad news, and Julian's furious with me because I've busted him to his girlfriend? Believe me, I wanted to say something. But I didn't, and I still think it was the right thing to do."

"Okay," Wizzy said. "I'll let you off this time. But don't do it again."

"I sincerely hope there won't be a next time," Will said. The booze was going to his head, but they ordered another round anyway, and changed the subject to other things.

While they chatted, about what to see and do in San Francisco, about Will's work and the state of the world in general, he felt his mind constantly veering off the subject. There was so much he wanted to ask, so much he wanted to tell her. Although his mind was in turmoil, one thing was becoming increasingly clear. He knew what he wanted to do – there was just the small matter of Mackenzie. The minor detail of his having a girlfriend.

Chapter Twenty-Six

Mounted on a fire-breathing dragon, the Princess Wizzy flew home. When she found Princess Stella weeping, she dried her tears and said, 'Do exactly as I say, and all will be well.' And Princess Stella obeyed...

"And so, you see, here's the beautiful princess, and she's got all these lovely clothes and a retinue of ladies-in-waiting and she lives in a glass tower with a handsome prince, but she isn't very happy," I said, pointing with my paintbrush at my easel.

"Why isn't she happy?" Mia asked, wide-eyed, conditioned as she was by Disney to believe that once you had a handsome prince, you'd never, ever be unhappy again.

We were in a corner of Martha's palatial kitchen, which she'd set up for me to work in because the spare room where I was sleeping was too small and Martha said the light wasn't good enough. What she'd have made of the flat in Streatham I could only guess. I'd been staying with Martha since my sobbing, incoherent phone call a week ago, and Mia had become my self-appointed apprentice, passing me tubes of paint, helping me clean my brushes at the end of the day and giving me advice on what colours things should be.

"She's sad because before the prince took her away to live in the castle, she lived with her daddy, who is a shoemaker." I pointed to another bit of the picture. "And she loves her daddy, and she loves beautiful shoes – not just wearing them, but making them too. She hoped that one day, when her daddy was too old to make shoes any more, she'd take over and make all the shoes, but instead she's married to the prince, and although she has a wardrobe full of expensive shoes in special see-through boxes, they're made by other people, and they remind her of her home and her friends. And it's very boring in the tower and none of the ladies-in-waiting want to talk to her, because they're jealous and they all wanted the prince to marry them."

"I get bored sometimes," Mia said. "And then Chloë takes me to play on the swings. Mummy doesn't, though. Mummy tells me to go and watch Peppa Pig because she's busy."

I stored up this gem to share with Martha later – I knew it would make her laugh. Chloë was the Australian nanny, a girl with boundless energy whom Mia and Harry adored.

"Mummy says you're sad sometimes too, Stella," said Mia. "She says when you go to your room and close the door I mustn't disturb you because you might be crying."

I sniffed, feeling tears prick my eyes – they were never particularly far away. I'd shed so many in the past few days I'd had to give up wearing eye make-up because I was having to repair it so often, and consequently I looked like a white rat.

"It's true," I said. "I have been sad. But I'm getting less sad, and I expect I'll wake up one morning and forget to be sad at all."

"When?" Mia asked.

"Soon, I hope," I said. "Now, let's have another look at this. See, here's the shop where the old shoemaker is working, and a little mouse has come to give him a message, telling him his daughter is unhappy and homesick."

"Why are you sad, Stella?" Mia demanded.

I bit my paintbrush hard and looked up at the ceiling. I'd read somewhere once that if you looked upwards it was harder to cry – the tears drained back into your brain, or something.

"Because I was in love with someone," I said. "But it turned out he didn't love me very much."

"Why didn't he love you?"

"Well, he did. He always said he did, anyway. But I think the problem was that he loved someone else more."

"Who?"

I thought about this for a bit. I didn't want to get into the minefield of explaining infidelity to a five-year-old.

"Himself, mostly," I said.

"How can you love yourself?"

I was saved from Mia's relentless pursuit of this line of questioning by Chloë and Harry returning from Harry's baby music class. Mia abandoned me and dashed over to the nanny to claim a hug.

"Come on, you two, time for your tea," Chloë said. "Mummy will be home soon to give you your bath and read you a story."

"Stella story!" Harry said.

"No rest for the wicked." Chloë winked at me. It was true – since I'd taken to inventing stories to tell the kids at bedtime, based on what I'd been painting during the day, this had become a bit of a ritual. They were taxing my creativity to the max, exhausting my store of ideas more quickly than I could think of new ones. Stories, I was learning, took longer to invent than to tell, and a picture that took me hours to draw would be looked at for a few seconds before the kids demanded more.

"Okay, I'll do your story if Mummy doesn't mind," I said. The plotline of the little brown mouse carrying messages from the shoemaker to his daughter had promise. I'd already decided to call him Jimmy Cheese.

I took a break from work while Chloë fed the kids their spag bol, pouring a glass of wine and sitting with them at the table, half joining in the conversation while I checked my phone.

There were no new messages from Julian. That was progress, at least. The first night – thinking about it made me want to cry again, but I took a gulp of wine and resisted. The first night was pretty awful. Seeing Julian and Liberty standing there, seeing in a second what I hadn't been able to see for months – the idea I'd tormented myself with made real, but in a horrible and unexpected way – literally turned my stomach. I ran to the bathroom, thinking I was going to be sick, but only coughed and sobbed. After a bit I heard Julian in the doorway behind me.

"Are you okay, Stella?"

"No, of course I'm not fucking okay! Why would I be okay when you've been shagging someone else behind my back?"

"Oh, my little star. You didn't think that, did you? Liberty just came back here to do some work, she and I were…"

I actually laughed through my sobs. "Yeah, right. The sort of work you do horizontally in the bedroom."

"Stella, please believe me, it's not what you think." He reached out towards me.

In that moment, I knew that if he touched me, I'd crumble. My resolve was paper-thin; one brush of his hand would tear through it.

"Don't come near me," I hissed, so vehemently he recoiled and backed away.

"Why don't we sit down? Have a cup of tea? You're upset."

"Damn right I'm upset, and I'm not drinking tea with you. I'm leaving."

"But you've got nowhere to go," he said, and when he said it he actually smiled, a bit gloatingly, and that made me angry enough to renew my strength.

"Yes I have. Now please get out of my way." I went back into our bedroom and stuffed a few clean clothes into my bag, leaving the dirty ones on the floor. "I'll let you know when I'm coming to pick up the rest of my things."

I slammed the door and walked down the stairs, and only when I'd reached the corner did I ring Martha. If she'd been out, or hadn't been willing to have me, I don't know what I would have done. Made my sorry way back to King's Cross and caught the train back to Scotland the next morning, I suppose, and presented myself on Polly's doorstep again. But thankfully it didn't come to that. Martha was there, and she gave me her home address and told me to get in a taxi straight away, and didn't ask any questions.

Julian's messages started arriving that night. He insisted that I was wrong, there was nothing going on between him and Liberty, I could ask her if I didn't believe him. I ignored them all, but it wasn't through strength of mind – I longed to reply, to tell him that as long as he promised never to see her again, we would try again. But as it happened I'd run out of credit on my phone, and I was shaking so much I mistyped the password to my account three times and got locked out.

The next day, Julian's tone changed. He sent me a long email saying that he needed to explain what was going on.

Nothing had happened. Nothing at all. But yes, they were attracted to each other, they'd thought about sleeping together, talked about it, but they resisted, because of me. And Julian's being attracted to her in the first place, wanting to take it further? You guessed it – that was because of me, too. Because I'd been emotionally distant, and physically distant too. Because since I'd started the work for Martha, I'd drawn away from him, left him feeling unwanted. And he and Liberty had this deep connection, intellectually and emotionally.

I read this out to Martha the next day, sitting at her kitchen table drinking coffee. I'd slept – God knows how, but I had – and had a shower, and sorted out my phone's password, and I was ready to compose a reply. But Martha wouldn't let me.

"Seriously, Stella, I know it's not my place to tell you what to do. But this is textbook stuff. He's following the script. He'll admit to the bare minimum, make out that it was nothing, blame you, and if you fall for it and go back, he'll just do the same thing again. You know what he did – you found proof. He's just trying to make you doubt yourself."

And much as I longed for her to be wrong, I knew she was right. So I ignored that message, too.

"Just you wait," Martha said. "In a couple of days, he'll be admitting having had sex with her, just once, in a moment of madness. He'll say it was a terrible mistake, and he'll beg you to forgive him. Trust me, he will."

And, almost to the letter, she was right again.

When Julian's next email arrived, it actually came as a relief. Now he'd admitted to sleeping with Liberty – just the once, of course – I could focus on that, the ultimate betrayal. And once I did, everything else sprung into focus too. I could see that there was more to it than him being unfaithful; that Liberty was, as Julian swore she was, a symptom and not a cause.

But a symptom of what? Not of me having not been a good enough girlfriend, that was for sure. Even though my self-esteem was in tatters, I could see that. Of the way Julian had treated me all through our relationship.

I talked to Martha about it after the children were in bed, working my way through shameful amounts of her red wine as I tried to make sense of what had happened.

"Why, though?" I pleaded. "Why did he do that, keep saying he loved me, but lying to me? I'm sure he lied about Kristen, the girl in Canada, too. I knew at the time he was talking bollocks, but I let myself believe him. I'm such a fool."

"You didn't see it because you trusted him," Martha said. "You loved him. You're not the fool here, Stella. If relationships were about doubting everything a person says, we'd all be single, or private detectives, or both."

Patiently, she let me bang on and on, unpicking it all until I'm sure she never wanted to hear Julian's name again, passing me tissues when I cried, filling up my glass over and over. But last thing at night, when I stumbled off to bed, a tearstained, pissed wreck, she said, "Why don't I keep hold of your phone, Stella? Just in case?"

And it had worked – I'd managed not to respond to any of Julian's messages for six nights. I felt almost proud. I was painting like mad, filling the days with work, loving Mia's company when Chloë brought her home from school in the afternoons and taking Harry out to the park when cabin fever threatened to overwhelm me.

Now, sitting at the table in the warm, homely kitchen, I felt almost serene. I would need to contact Julian and arrange to collect the rest of my stuff – and I'd need to do it quite soon, because I had only brought two T-shirts with me and one bra, and it was red and the T-shirts were both white. Also, I was missing my hair straighteners almost as much as I missed Julian.

I heard the sound of keys in the front door and Martha calling, "I'm home!"

The children dropped their forks and ran to the door, calling, "Mummy! Here's Mummy," and soon Martha appeared, carrying both of them in her arms.

"Oof, you two are getting too big for this," she said, passing Harry to Chloë, who tucked him back in his high chair. "Now finish your dinner. I've got something exciting to tell you all."

"What?" Mia said. "Tell us now!"

"Biscuits!" said Harry, banging his spoon on the tray.

"No, not biscuits," Martha said. "We only have biscuits on Saturdays, as you know full well. Eat up."

"I'm not hungry any more," Mia said. "I'm too excited to be hungry."

"They've had loads," Chloë said. "Why don't I clear up?"

"I'll give you a hand," I said, and we scraped the leftovers off the Peter Rabbit plates and stacked them in the dishwasher while Martha made herself a gin and tonic.

"So," she said, "today I spoke to your Auntie Wizzy on the phone, all the way from New York. And do you know what she said?"

"What?" Mia and I chorussed together. Since she'd been travelling, Wizzy had assumed near-mythical status in her little niece's eyes, and I'd told and retold the legends of her travels by way of a bedtime story, making up the details I didn't know and leaving out the ones that I knew Martha would consider too racy.

"She's coming home," Martha said. "And she's not going to go back to Scotland, she's going to come here and live with us for a bit."

"Cool!" Mia breathed.

"Not for long, mind. Just until she can get a job and find a flat somewhere."

"That's amazing news," I said, but I felt a bit hollow inside. It was a reminder that I, too, wouldn't be able to impose on Martha and Paul forever; I, too, would have to find somewhere more permanent to live. And, although my income from the mural I was designing for a customer of Martha's and the cards that were selling well in Layla's shop was enough to keep me in paint and buy Martha the occasional bottle of wine (she'd refused to let me pay any rent), it wasn't anything like enough for a deposit on a flat.

"Martha," I said. "I suppose I really have to think about what I'm going to do next."

"There's no rush," she said. "You and Wizzy will have to share your room for a bit, but you won't mind that, will you? And she's already sent off a bunch of CVs – she's pretty sure she'll find work quickly. And when she does, maybe the two of you could live together."

"Maybe we could." It was an alluring prospect – the idea of Wizzy and I being flatmates again, getting dressed together before heading out on the pull, having parties. But at the same time, it felt like a step backwards from the adult life I thought I was embarking on when I moved in with Julian.

"Anyway, don't decide anything just yet. She's getting home in a week's time, and then we can all sit down and make longer-term plans. You really are welcome here, Stella."

"I want Auntie Wizzy and Stella to live with us forever," Mia said.

"Story!" said Harry.

"Okay, I'll do your story in a minute," I said. "But first, I need to send Julian a message, and arrange to go round and get my stuff. I paid the deposit on that flat, too, so even if he's staying there he can bloody well pay it back, because I'm going to need the money whatever I do."

"Good for you," Martha said. "That's the right attitude."

"You go, girl," said Chloë. "Right, I'll head off then, if there's nothing more you need me to do this evening?"

We said goodnight to her and Martha ran the children's bath, and I checked Facebook to see if there was any news from Polly.

There wasn't. But there was a relationship status update from Liberty. Martha ended up reading Harry his bedtime story that night, because I was up in my room crying.

After that, for the sake of my sanity, I imposed a social media blackout on myself. I blocked Julian and Liberty on Facebook, then logged out of my account and stayed logged out. I avoided Shutterly like the plague. I asked Polly to send me photos of Miranda on email. I didn't communicate much with the outside world at all. Even when I received a text from Will saying that he was coming back to London, I was too dispirited to respond.

I tried not to think of Julian and Liberty together – of her having the life with him I'd imagined. I tried, but I failed. All the bad things had faded from my memory – Julian's silence, his selfishness, how lonely I'd felt so much of the time. All I could remember were his words of love, the passionate sex we'd had, the future I imagined we'd have together.

Martha said, "You mark my words, he'll do the same thing to her. They always do."

I had no doubt that she was right, but I couldn't stop the thoughts coming.

The day Wizzy was due to arrive home, I said to Martha, "Right, I'm going to go round to the – to Julian's – to Streatham, and pick up my stuff."

She looked alarmed. "Are you sure you don't want me to come with you? Only I've said I'll fetch Wizzy from the airport…"

"No. I'll be all right. He won't be there, anyway, and I have to do this sometime, so it may as well be now. Are you sure you don't mind if I bring back a few clothes, books, paintings, things like that? I feel so bad cluttering up your house with all my junk."

"I don't mind a bit about that," Martha said, but she still didn't look very happy.

As the bus made its familiar way past the common, crawling through the traffic, I started to feel sicker and sicker. (And the bloke sitting next to me eating fried chicken didn't help matters.) I couldn't help remembering all the other times I'd made the journey – when I first arrived from Edinburgh, giddy with joy at the prospect of seeing Julian. When I was full of love and pride, eager to tell him Martha had offered me a job. When I got home that rainy evening and he gave me the engagement ring.

It wasn't anticipation or excitement churning inside me now – it was fear. What would I do if he was there? What would I do if Liberty was there? But they wouldn't be, there was no way. In all the months I'd lived with him, Julian had never once been home at half past four on a weekday afternoon, and I was sure Liberty's working hours would be just as long.

I got off at the familiar stop, my legs trembling so much I could hardly walk down the stairs of the bus. I walked blindly along the high street towards the corner of our road, focussing on breathing, keeping my legs moving, doing what I had come to do.

"Stella!" I almost jumped out of my skin at the familiar voice, but it was only Hussein, arranging apples in the crates outside his shop.

I stopped and turned around.

"How are you? Long time, we haven't seen you. Have you been away?"

I paused, not wanting to lie to this man, who'd always been kind to me, but not wanting to tell the truth either. "Yes, I've been away. I've been to see my mother in Scotland. How's your granddaughter? She must be getting really big now."

"Come in," he said. "I'll show you photos."

He got out his phone, and was about to embark on a marathon session of showing off the newest member of his family when a customer came in to do what seemed like an entire weekly shop, so I had to wait. Then the phone rang and he embarked on a lengthy, heated argument with a supplier. Then someone else arrived to top up their Oyster card and didn't have any cash, so Hussein had to give them directions to the closest ATM.

Once I'd finished giving the photos of little Damla the admiration they deserved, almost an hour had passed, and I was more jittery than ever.

"I really must go," I said. "I'm so sorry, I'd love to stay and chat, but…"

Fortunately another customer was waiting, looking impatiently at his watch.

"Okay, okay," Hussein said. "But I will see you soon, yes, Stella?"

WHO WANTS TO MARRY A MILLIONAIRE?

"I don't think so," I said sadly. "I'm moving away, to stay with a friend in Balham. But I'll come and see you when I can, and find out how Damla's getting on, and buy baklava."

"Take some now," Hussein insisted, and when eventually I arrived at the flat, I was carrying a white box filled with sticky pastries.

Balancing it in one hand, I dug in my bag for the keys. Fuck, where were they? I rummaged, encountering old tissues, lipsticks, loose change – finally my fingers gripped the metal of my keyring. But then the strap of my handbag slid off my shoulder and the contents tumbled out on to the landing.

So I was down on all fours, collecting up stray tampons and scraps of paper, when Julian came up the stairs.

He stopped dead when he saw me, and I froze too, looking up at him from the floor. He held out his hand and helped me to my feet.

"Come in," he said. "Drink?"

"No, I don't want to stay." My heart was hammering in my chest. "I didn't think you'd be here. I just wanted to get some things, I was going to leave the keys."

"You didn't want to say goodbye."

"No. I didn't want to talk to you. You know that. I still don't. I just want to pack up and get out."

"Can I at least talk to you then, and you listen?"

"Talk to me while I pack, if you must," I said.

He followed me through to the bedroom. I opened the wardrobe and there were all my clothes, washed and neatly folded. I wondered if that was Liberty's handiwork or Julian's, and suspected the former – although presumably it was only guilt that had prevented her offloading the whole lot at the Oxfam shop. I reached for my suitcase on top of the wardrobe, where it had been gathering dust all these months, but it was too high for me to grasp the handle.

"Let me," Julian said, lifting it easily down and placing it, open, on the bed.

"Thanks," I said begrudgingly.

"That's all right." Julian sat down on the bed, his head in his hands. "Stella – little star – I've made the most terrible mistake."

I grabbed an armful of jeans, shoving them into the bag, and added a haphazard pile of shoes and boots.

"Please, Julian," I said. "I don't want to hear this. I don't think it was a mistake. If things were going to work out between us, you wouldn't have – done what you did."

"It was only once," he said. "You read my email, didn't you? I explained. It was just the one time, I was missing you. I love you."

"I don't believe you," I said. "Not about it being just once, and not about you loving me. I think you lied to me in that email, like you lied to me about Kristen."

"Can't you understand?" he said. "Kristen – I was so desperate to keep you. If you'd known…"

"You were hedging your bets," I said coldly. "I do believe you wanted to keep me, yes. So you'd have sex on tap and someone to wash your fucking socks waiting for you when you moved to London. It's not going to happen, Julian. This relationship is over. And it's not me ending it – you did that a long time ago. You did it when you lied to me, and you made sure of it when you slept with Liberty."

He looked up, and I could see the expression on his face changing to anger.

"Don't blame me for this, Stella," he said. "You made it happen, you made me doubt you. The way you flirted with Will – of course I was jealous."

"I what?" I laughed, feeling a blush creeping up my neck and threatening to flood my face. "I never flirted with Will! He's your mate, I was just being polite and friendly. I was trying to set him up with other women, for God's sake! On what planet is that flirting?"

I was rushing now, frantically bundling my belongings into my bag, desperate to be out of there.

"Do you think I'm stupid?" he shouted. "I saw you with him. You were like a cat on heat. You were practically twerking. You embarrassed yourself. And that was just when I was there – Christ knows what you were like when you were alone with him."

I was done. If I'd forgotten anything I didn't care – he could have it, burn it, whatever. I was also becoming quite seriously scared, not that he'd hit me, I didn't think Julian was capable of that, but of the power his words still had to wound me.

"Julian, I'm not going to listen to this any more," I said. "I'm going to ring for a taxi, and leave the keys and wait outside. There is nothing going on between me and Will and you know it."

"Oh yeah?" his tone was mocking now. "Nothing going on between you? You'll be all right with the fact that he fucked your mate then, won't you? Or maybe not so much."

"What? Julian, I have no idea what you're talking about. I'm going now."

"You aren't going anywhere," he said, standing up, his hands on either side of the door frame. I was properly frightened now. "You aren't leaving until you've seen this."

His face, once so familiar, so beloved, looked quite different. His normally pale skin was flushed an ugly brick red that clashed with his hair. He had a weak chin, I noticed for the first time – in his anger, he looked almost weaselly. He thrust his phone at me and in spite of myself, I took it.

On the screen was the Facebook page of Will's girlfriend, Mackenzie, the woman he'd met in San Francisco. Except she wasn't his girlfriend any more, because she'd dumped him, as publicly as it's possible to dump a person, posting photos of him and Wizzy together in a bar, calling him a cheat, a liar, a love rat and a whole load of other, less printable things. She'd even got the Huffington Post to pick up the story, and linked to that on her newsfeed.

"Silicon Valley beauty's revenge on Shutterly billionaire," was the headline.

"I thought so," Julian said, leaning in close to my face. "Go on, tell me how that makes you feel."

"Fuck off," I screamed. "Just fuck off out of my life and leave me alone. I wish I'd never met you, or Will fucking Turner."

Somehow, I found the strength to lift my heavy suitcase and used it to barge him out of the way. I dragged the bag out of the front door and all the way down the steep stairs, only pausing to wipe my streaming eyes on my sleeve when I got to the bottom.

Julian didn't follow me. I rang for a taxi, my breath coming in such ragged gasps I could hardly speak to give the address. Once the car arrived, I collapsed into the back seat, heaving with sobs.

It was only when I was halfway back to Martha's that I remembered Hussein's goodbye gift to me, the box of pastries he'd carefully packed, still lying in on the landing outside the flat, and that made me cry even harder.

The entire family was in the kitchen when I got back, drinking champagne in the kitchen.

"Here she is!" said Paul.

"Auntie Wizzy's home!" said Mia, and Harry tried to say "Auntie Wizzy" too, but couldn't quite manage it.

"Stella!" said Wizzy, and dashed across the room to hug me. She looked browner and more beautiful than I'd ever seen her, even though there were dark, bruise-like shadows under her eyes from the long flight. "Come here, gorgeous girl. I've missed you so..."

But she petered out when she saw my face.

"I'm going upstairs," I said. "Sorry, Martha. Sorry, Paul."

Wizzy made a move to follow me, but Martha grabbed her hand and held her back. As I ran up the stairs I heard Paul say, "That guy really has done a number on her, hasn't he?" and Martha murmur something in reply.

Wizzy's backpack was on the second of the twin beds in the spare room, her stuff bulging out over the duvet and on to the floor. I remembered how messy she'd always been – how Polly and I had good-naturedly bitched about her breakfast dishes being left in the sink, her parcels from The Outnet and All Saints cluttering up the living room for days until she remembered to open them. I was going to have to get used to living with it again, but only for as long as it took for me to get the hell out of there and go – somewhere else. Anywhere else.

Fully clothed, I got under the covers and turned to face the wall, feeling tears running down my cheeks into the pillow. I wasn't crying over Julian any more – I was crying because I felt so terribly betrayed. But why? Wizzy hadn't done anything wrong – she'd just slept with an attractive man she'd met on her travels, one of a long list. Another notch on her bedpost, I thought bitterly, although Martha's guest beds had tasteful padded headboards that you'd have to take a Stanley knife to if you wanted to notch them. But she wasn't to know – how could she have known how I felt about Will? I hadn't even known until a few minutes before – or if I had, I'd hidden it successfully from everyone, including myself. Although not, apparently, from Julian.

I pulled the pillow over my head, wishing it could blot out my memory of Will's face, his crooked smile, the sound of his laughter. I pressed my hands against my mouth to stifle another sob, and that reminded me of his hands, his bony, elegant fingers, and how they might have looked smoothing Wizzy's bright tangle of hair as he stroked her face.

The pillow over my head must have muffled the sound of the door opening. I was jerked back to reality by the mattress shifting at Wizzy sat down, and her voice saying, "You've seen it, haven't you?"

I pushed the pillow aside and turned over, the light from the landing piercing my eyes.

"Of course I have," I said. "I'm sorry, Wizz. This isn't your fault. I'm sorry to piss on your welcome-home chips. I guess seeing Julian again freaked me out a bit."

"Stella." Wizzy's voice was stern, but her hand on my shoulder was gentle. "Please don't tell me you believed one word of that bullshit."

"Of course I did," I said, sniffing. "Why wouldn't I? There were pictures of the two of you together."

"Yeah, obviously there were," Wizzy said. "Although I have no idea who took them or how the whole story got blown up like it did. I met Will when I was in San Francisco, like you said I should. You were going on for ages about how we'd be perfect for each other, and we must meet up, so I contacted him and we did. But it didn't take me long to figure out that it wasn't ever going to happen. Stella, Will's crazy about you. And unless I'm talking out of my arse, so are you about him."

"What?" I sat up, pushing my hair away from my face.

"Look, there's no point me wanking on about this," Wizzy said. "You need to hear it from him. And there's no point telling me you don't like him, because we know you do. All those emails – Will this, Will that, and hardly a word about bloody Julian, except when you were telling us how he treated you like you were worth nothing, and how determined you were to convince yourself he was The One. As if!"

"I was in love with Julian," I said. "I really was."

"Yeah, we all make mistakes," said Wizzy. "Although what you ever saw in that rodent-faced tosspot I will never know. If I hadn't been zonked on morphine when he first asked you out I'd have put a stop to it right there. The miserable, self-obsessed little…"

"Stop!" I said. "Seriously, you can slag him off later. I might even join you. But not now, I'm all bruised."

It was true. Carrying my bag down the stairs had left some serious contusions on my calves. I pulled the duvet aside and my jeans up so Wizzy could see.

"Ouch," she said. "Nasty. So, when you see Will, you're going to have to get some major opaque-tights action going on."

"I'm not seeing Will," I said.

"Oh, yes you are," said Wizzy.

"Oh, no I'm – stop!" I said. "Have you gone mad? Madder. I've just had my heart broken by Julian, there's no way I'm going to leap straight into dating his friend, who's anyway fucked up because this Mackenzie girl has named and shamed him all over the shop."

"Stella," Wizzy said, "First of all, Julian didn't break your heart, although I suppose that's how it feels right now. He did you a favour, really. He showed you that all those daft ideas you always had about relationships were wrong. They aren't all about unrequited longing and yearning and that bollocks. Look at Polly and Angus. Do they yearn?"

"Polly yearns for Harvey Nicks," I said. "She told me she does."

Wizzy laughed. "That's different, and you know it. They love each other, they have fun together. Fun like you have with Will – remember? You filled up zillions of emails telling us how much he makes you laugh, how he took you to places he knew you'd like, all the stuff Julian never did, not once."

"Because he was too…" I began.

"Too selfish," Wizzy said, and I knew she was right. "Now, listen. Martha and Paul and the kids are waiting downstairs, all ready for my welcome-home piss-up. Why don't you come and join us? Don't think about Will, or Julian, or anyone except yourself. Have fun, get drunk and leave the rest to me."

So I did. Like I said, Wizzy's an irresistible force of nature.

CHAPTER TWENTY-SEVEN

"Right," Louise said, snapping shut her laptop. "Here we all are. Welcome back, Will, we all know you had a somewhat adventurous time stateside, but Hannah's going to fill us all in on the PR angle in just a minute. First of all – coffee?"

"Hell, yeah," Giles said. "I'm on it. Way ahead of you lot." Seconds later, Damian, one of the juniors on the Cloud Computing team, nudged the meeting room door open with his snake-like hip, a tray of coffees balanced on the other hand.

"Brilliant, thanks dude," said Giles. "I found Damian working at Costa on Bethnal Green Road, turns out his code's is as good as his coffee."

"Does he play ping pong?" Tim asked hopefully.

There was a pause while they all sipped their drinks, feeling the caffeine work its magic on their synapses. Although Will had been back in the UK for two days, his body was still on West Coast time and he felt oddly disconnected from reality. Which wasn't really that surprising, given how the last week had played out.

"So, anyway, Tim," Will said. "You've been working on the Android code. How's it been going?"

Hannah said, "There's no point talking to Tim about anything at the moment. He's obsessed with a vet."

"Yvette?" Will said. "Clearly I'm behind the times. Who's she?"

"Not Yvette, a vet," Hannah said.

Louise said, "Oh, for heaven's sake, since it appears this meeting is going to be all about our private lives and not about work at all, why don't we just get it out of the way. Tim?"

Tim looked down into his espresso and said, "Yeah, so my terrapin was poorly. Google said there was a problem with his ears and he needed to see the vet. And now," he cleared his throat, "I'm kind of seeing the vet, too. Her name's Felicity. She's amazing."

"And Tim's spending all his time talking to her on WhatsApp," Giles said.

"No, I'm not!" Tim protested. "Just… a bit of time."

"Which is fair enough, in the circumstances," Louise said. "And, speaking of time, I'll be taking some time away from the office. A year, to be exact. Gavin and I are expecting a baby in September."

There was a rush of "Awww," and "Congratulations," around the table.

Hannah said, "And I'm still single. God, this is giving me the worst FOMO."

"Don't worry, you're not the only one," Will said gloomily. "About the whole thing… You know. If I can just explain…"

"You don't have to explain," Louise said. "You made a mistake, it happens. We'll deal with it. It's tomorrow's chip paper, right, Hannah?"

"Right," Hannah said. "We can put out a statement from you if you like, refuting what she said, assuming it wasn't true."

"Of course it wasn't true," Will said. "But the problem was, I let her think it was. I met the other girl for a drink – she's a friend of a friend – and then Mackenzie, the girl I was seeing in San Francisco, found out about it and went off on one, and I didn't tell her what had actually happened – which was nothing – because I was going to split up with her anyway. Big mistake."

"Not your finest hour, it would be fair to say," Louise said.

"Yeah, thanks for that," Will said. "I was feeling totally great about it all until you pointed that out. But here's the thing. There was no reason for her to go public with it – none at all. We'd been dating a couple of months. She came out of it looking as bad as I did. None of the publicity reflected exactly well on her, did it?"

"Damn straight it didn't," Hannah said. "So if you do want to turn it into a PR war, we can do that. Not that I'd advise it, although some people would say there's no such thing as bad publicity…"

"No!" Will said. "No, I definitely don't want to do that. It's just, I was completely confused by it all, at first. Who took the photos, who persuaded Mackenzie to go massively public with it? It made no sense. I know it's a cliché but she really isn't that kind of girl."

"They're all that kind of girl," Giles said. "No word of a lie. Clay off YouTube says…"

"Anyway," Will interrupted. "I called her and asked what the fuck went down. Turns out it was Charlotte, my ex from months back, who was behind it all. When we split up, I never got around to blocking her on Facebook. She's been stalking me for months, not doing anything, just waiting for something to happen. And when she saw that Mackenzie and I were going out, but I was meeting this other woman for a drink, she persuaded a photographer mate to take pictures, then contacted Kenz and convinced her it would be a good idea to smear me."

"My God!" Louise breathed. "If she'd shown a fraction of that initiative when she was interning on our account…"

"We could always get in touch with her," Hannah said. "Ask her to send an updated resumé… Just kidding, Will. So how do you want to play it?"

"Down, I think," Will said. "Mackenzie feels awful about the whole thing now, she just wants to put it behind her. I'm meeting Isabella this evening, and I'll discuss it with her, but I think she'll agree that the less we make of it the better."

"I still can't believe you turned down the opportunity for a shag," Giles muttered.

"I didn't!" Will said. "There wasn't any opportunity… there was never any question of me… You're winding me up, aren't you?"

"Yeah, 'course I am." Giles grinned, and the atmosphere around the table relaxed.

Will said, "But now we've got that out of the way, the good news is it doesn't appear to have put Google off. They're still keen to invest in the business. In fact, they've made us an offer, and it's a serious one. Louise, given your news, this might be a good time to discuss the future of the company."

"Don't be alarmed," Louise said. "Everyone will keep their jobs. They've been very keen to emphasise that if we agree to the buy-out, we'll retain our office and our independence. And, obviously, as all the staff here have a stake in the business, financially it's extremely good news all round."

"Will I be able to buy a Porsche?" Tim said.

"Maybe not just yet," Louise said.

"You'll certainly be able to make a down-payment on one," Will said. "Why don't we take a look at the figures in more detail?"

Over the next two hours, Damian was summoned for multiple coffee orders. Louise talked them through many spreadsheets. Hannah was delighted to be offered the chance to step up to operations director while Louise went on maternity leave, and agreed to start the recruitment process for a junior in marketing. Tim only texted Felicity twice.

But Will found it hard to focus. This was huge news, obviously, but he'd had a week to take it all in. What had seemed momentous at first had become part of the fabric of his life. He also couldn't help wondering what the point was of it all.

It wasn't like he needed the money. He had more than he knew what to do with anyway, and the thing he wanted most wasn't for sale. He supposed he wouldn't be single for long – the world was full of women who'd go out with him, especially now. He wasn't going to pretend to be someone he wasn't any more, that was for sure. He was done with all that.

That was why he'd agreed to meet Wizzy. To apologise for dragging her into this mess, for not coming clean with Mackenzie in the first place, telling her that their relationship wasn't going anywhere, that his heart wasn't in it – his heart was somewhere else.

At last, Louise said, "We've covered a lot of ground this afternoon, and I think we've all had enough. We're agreed on the principle, now it's about ironing out the details. I'm speaking to Jon in San Francisco tomorrow, so I'll update you all after that."

There was the usual scrape of chairs as they all stood up.

"Don't know about you lot, but I wouldn't mind a beer," Hannah said.

"Good call," said Giles, and Tim agreed.

Will got on his bike and cycled to Covent Garden. The journey was even more hair-raising than usual – he was so distracted, his usual lightning reflexes didn't seem to be working, and to make matters worse a passing bus showered him with grimy water from a puddle.

He wasn't going to be looking his best for his drinks with Wizzy, that was for sure. Not that it mattered. But it turned out to matter very much indeed.

CHAPTER TWENTY-EIGHT

Arrayed in all her finery, Princess Stella stepped into her glass coach.
She was going to the ball – but the Prince did not know of her plans.
He was expecting a different princess to arrive.
'To The Savoy!' commanded the fairy godmother...

"**A**re you sure I look okay?" I said.

"You look amazing," Wizzy said. "He won't be able to take his eyes off you. Guaranteed. Or keep his hands off you."

I surveyed my reflection in the mirror. I was wearing my trusty backless black top, a pair of new skinny jeans and shoes borrowed from Martha that were only slightly too big but much too high.

"I'm going to fall over on the escalator getting out of the Tube," I said. "I know I am."

"No you're not," Martha said. "You're not taking the Tube in my Louboutins. Taxi all the way for you."

"You'd better get going then," Wizzy said.

Suddenly all of it, my straightened hair, my clothes, the Comme des Garçons scent Martha had squirted behind my ears, felt stupid and pointless. I was pursuing a pipe dream, chasing on the rebound after a man who'd never wanted me, and would never want me.

And why would he? Even Julian, who'd said so often how much he adored me, had ended up falling for someone else. Someone else, on the face of it, even less desirable than I was. There must be something badly wrong with me, something my closest friends weren't telling me. Whatever it was, it meant I stood no chance with Will. I needed to grow up, get real, learn to be single and sensible.

"I can't do it," I said, sitting back down on the bed. "Seriously. This is a crazy idea. Wizzy, you go. He's expecting you, and you can ask him if he likes me, and if he does we can meet up another time."

"Stella! You're not wimping out of this now, after all my cunning planning," Wizzy said. "The point is, he's had all these blind dates, wanting to meet Ms Right, and she was under his nose the whole time. Although admittedly not exactly on the market. But that's how it's going to work – he'll see you, you'll see how he reacts, you'll have a drink together. What's the worst that can happen? You two are friends, friends have drinks together."

"But what if…" I didn't want to say it. What if Wizzy had it all wrong, and all I would ever be to Will was a friend? "He goes out with models! Seriously, he's out of my league. This is stupid. I should just try and get used to being on my own for a bit."

"Your cab's here," Martha said.

"That's that settled then," Wizzy said, and the two of them marched me downstairs and bundled me into the taxi. It was like being arrested by the Gestapo.

Weirdly, once I was on my way, my nerves faded, and all I could feel was eagerness. I was going to see Will again. Even if nothing happened, even if Wizzy had got it all wrong and he only saw me as Julian's girlfriend – now Julian's ex – we'd hopefully be able to salvage something of the friendship we'd shared.

And besides, I might never get another chance to have a drink at The Savoy.

The bar was so dazzling in its mirrored, dimly lit splendour, that I didn't see Will at first. Then I spotted him, at a table for two in the corner, beyond the grand piano, a beer in front of him. He'd changed his hair, but otherwise he looked just the same, just as scruffy as usual.

He hadn't seen me – understandably, he was expecting someone else after all. I walked across the room towards him, slowly and carefully in my high heels on the deep carpet, my eyes not leaving his face. It was only when I was a few feet away that he looked up from his phone.

And in that instant, I knew how he felt. His face changed. There was a moment of shock, a moment of recognition, and then a huge smile like the sun coming out.

"What the hell did your friend put you up to, Stella?" he said.

I said, "Well, you know, sometimes people have bonkers ideas about arranging dates under false pretences. Only very stupid people, that is. People who are best avoided."

"I've been avoiding you for six months," he said. "It's time to change my approach."

He stood up and stepped around the table, holding out his arms. I moved into his embrace.

We stood like that for a long moment, the sounds of the piano, the buzz of conversation, the rattle of ice in a cocktail shaker swirling around us. My head was spinning a bit too, even though all I'd had to drink was the small glass of champagne Wizzy had foisted on me for Dutch courage.

But I didn't feel terribly confident. I wanted to give myself to the moment, relax in Will's arms, press away the small space between us, but there was a small part of me, a part that was scared but also sensible, that was telling me to step away, to wait, to reassess.

I suppose Will must have sensed it, because he didn't kiss me. He smiled down at me, and said, "I guess you didn't turn up at the most famous bar in London just for a hug. Let's sit down and get you a cocktail, and you can tell me everything that's been happening."

But although my drink was fabulous, like a Buck's Fizz only classier, I didn't get to enjoy it or Will's company for long.

Just as I was sipping it, trying not to eat all the delicious olives in the little dish and wondering how to say what I needed to in a way that Will would understand, I realised he wasn't meeting my eyes any more.

He was looking past my shoulder, and his face had gone sort of still and cold. He stood up, and I heard a familiar voice behind me.

"Your new girlfriend really needs to learn how to turn off the location services on her phone."

Instantly, my mouth felt as dry as sawdust, as if I hadn't been sipping champagne and Grand Marnier a second before. I felt a flood of adrenalin, an ancient, basic urge to run away, to hide. How had Julian found me here – and why had he come? I shrank in my chair, foolishly thinking for a moment that I could make him go away by imagining I wasn't there myself.

"Oh, come on," Will said. "What the hell is this about?"

"You know," Julian said. I was too afraid to look at him, but I could hear from his voice that he was furious, and drunk too. "You were sniffing around her like a dog. You never had the balls to do anything, you were just waiting for my sloppy seconds. But let me tell you, she's not worth it. She –"

"Shut up," Will said. "Right now. You're making a fucking idiot of yourself. Get out."

"Oh, so you're going to make me, are you?" Julian taunted.

"If I have to," Will said. His face was pale and set, and I could see his hands clenching into fists. The barman had paused, cocktail shaker frozen in mid-air, and was staring over at our table with the air of a man on the verge of calling in the heavies.

I wasn't sure my legs would be able to support me, but I stood up anyway, and looked at the two of them.

Will and Julian – men I knew for certain had never struck or felt a violent blow outside of Mortal Kombat. It was horrible, it was frightening, it was embarrassing. But it was also absurd.

Quite suddenly, my fear drained away. I felt as calm and brave as the galloping girl in my painting. I knew I could take charge.

"Look at yourselves!" I said. "You're ridiculous. For God's sake. Laptop bags at dawn! You both need to grow up. I'm not a trinket to be squabbled over, and I'm not going to get in the middle of some stupid macho stand-off. Julian, you know why I left, and it had nothing to do with Will. Will, I'm sorry, I don't think I'm ready for this."

They were both focussed on me now, their faces wearing identical expressions of sheepish shock.

"I think I'll leave you gentlemen to it. Don't worry, I can see myself out."

And I swept from the room, taking longer strides than I would have believed was possible in Martha's killer heels, and got into a waiting taxi.

Chapter Twenty-Nine

And they all lived happily ever after.

"Tell me again what you said to them," Wizzy demanded, as we wrestled the last of our boxes up the narrow stairwell to our new apartment.

I started to giggle, almost losing my grip on the slippery cardboard. We were both sweaty and dishevelled after a long morning of lugging furniture from the rented van (with the help of the driver, Rafael, a handsome Brazilian who had shed his shirt after the second journey up to the third floor to cool off and, I suspected, to give Wizzy the full benefit of his brown, sculpted torso).

"You're as bad as Mia," I said. "I'll be tucking you up in bed at night for years and you'll nod off to the tale of How Stella Told Julian and Will to Do One."

"Mind the wallpaper," Wizzy said. "Or don't, we've probably scraped the fuck out of it already. There we go, that's the lot. Seriously, though, Stella. I'll never get tired of hearing that. I wish you'd videoed it, you'd be a viral YouTube sensation. I'd give anything to have seen their faces."

"It was all a bit shock and awe," I said. "I must've been channelling you."

"Pfft! You were doing no such thing. You just harnessed your inner tiger, Or something."

"My inner tiger is more of a knackered pussycat right now," I said, flopping down on to our new Ikea sofa. "There are some beers somewhere, Wizz. Fancy one? Beer, Rafael?"

Rafael shook his head regretfully. "I still have to drive, Stella. I've got three more jobs today. Please email me, if there's anything else you need?"

But he was looking at Wizzy, not at me.

She smiled, her infectious, easy grin lighting up the room.

"I think I might just do that," she said, and Rafael almost swooned with joy.

When he'd gone, we set about putting the flat to rights in a desultory sort of way, working our way through a few beers and chatting as we unpacked and unwrapped, finding homes for old and new possessions. I set up the easel Julian had given me in a corner of the kitchen, where the morning sun would shine on my work. I didn't bear it any grudge, even though it had come from him – it was one of the good things that had emerged from the wreck of our short relationship.

"You are still talking to him, though, aren't you?" Wizzy said.

For a moment I thought she meant Julian, then I realised.

"Of course! I'm not ruling anything out with Will, but I'm not ruling stuff in either, just yet. I even gave him our new address. Like you said, we're friends."

"That's right. Friends," Wizzy said, passing me another icy bottle of Peroni and raising one eyebrow in that special way she has.

"Oh, go and shag a Brazilian," I said, and we both collapsed, giggling, on the reclaimed wooden floorboards.

Just then, the doorbell buzzed.

"He's come back," I said, wide-eyed. "He's going to say he's forgotten his spanner. This is pure porn-movie stuff."

"Shut up!" Wizzy said. "It'll be British Gas, or the Jehovah's Witnesses or something."

She picked up the intercom, and I wandered through to our sparkling new kitchen and started peeling bubble-wrap off glasses. Then there was a knock at the door.

"Get that, please, Stella," Wizzy said. "I'm bursting for a wee."

I was about to protest, but the click of the bathroom lock was definitive.

Pushing my damp hair off my face, I walked to the hallway, feeling the pleasurable anticipation you do when you admit your first caller, even if you're about to send them packing. I planned my polite-but-firm rebuff as I twisted the latch.

And then I changed my mind, because there was Will. It was like a flashback. He had roses this time, a huge, fragrant bunch of them. But the bottle of Veuve was the same, and so was he. As tall, as smiling and as unexpected as he'd been all those months ago when he'd turned up to welcome Julian and me to our new home.

"Need your oven cleaning, Stella?" he asked.

This time, I didn't hesitate, except to take the flowers and the bottle out of his hands and put them on the floor. I moved into his arms like I was always meant to be there. And even though he was so much taller than me, far more than when I was wearing Martha's shoes, I discovered that our bodies fitted together just perfectly.

Everything about him, the lean hardness of his back under my hands, the smoothness of his shirt against my cheek, the smell of him, felt right, like coming home – but also as thrilling as a blank canvas waiting to be filled with a new picture.

And when he kissed me, tentatively at first, then more urgently, I realised something else. It wasn't Will who had been under a spell, waiting to be released and allowed to reveal his true self. It was me.

When you're the age I am – mid- to late-twenties – weddings seem to happen all the time. Martha told me that a couple of years back, she and Paul went to thirty-one in twelve months. She said it almost bankrupted them and she had permanent hat hair.

So it was a bit weird that Will and I didn't go to a wedding together until we'd been going out for almost six months.

I say going out – we were a couple, we were sleeping together (and it was amazing), but I wanted to take things very slowly. I was determined not to make the same mistakes I'd made with Julian – rushing forwards, letting my heart rule my head, and then realising when it was too late that I'd got it wrong.

It helped that everything else seemed to be happening at warp speed. Wizzy was offered a brand manager role at a different giant multinational company within a few days of her return to London, with an impossibly high salary and loads of international travel.

We'd paid the deposit on our flat equally, from Wizzy's and my savings. It took a few no-holds-barred emails from me before Julian finally paid me back the money he owed me – or perhaps Liberty did. She's living there in Streatham now, with Julian. I don't know if they're happy, and it's not my business. I do hope, though, that one day Liberty will live on top of a mountain as she told me longed to do, and see how the world looks from there.

Wizzy and I don't live anywhere near any mountains, although the three-storey climb to our door feels that way sometimes. But the view from our balcony makes me happy just the same. Our flat overlooks the canal in Hackney, and quite often there are swans swimming regally past. It's just a few minutes from where Will works. Which is just as well, really, given how much time he spends at ours. Not every night – I make sure of that, saying we need what Polly says is called 'spaces in our togetherness'. And he's cool with it. But still, it gives me a wonderful glow of contentment every time I wake up in the morning and he's there, or I get home from a meeting and he's skived off work early to cook dinner for us. Often it's a microwaved pizza, but I don't care.

Yes, I go to meetings now. Martha persuaded me to write down some of the stories I told Mia and Harry, and illustrate them. I thought it was just a bit of fun, therapeutic in a way, as I worked through all my thoughts about what had gone wrong in my relationship with Julian and, more importantly, my relationship with myself, and how I could do it better this time. All through the medium of repurposed fairytales – impressive, no? Or perhaps slightly mental.

But anyway, Paul has a friend who works for a publishing company, and they're going to be bringing out a book, written and illustrated by me. I still can't quite believe it's happening, but it is.

And it's had some unexpected consequences. My publisher (I still can't write that without feeling like the biggest wanker) put out a press release about my book (still can't write that without feeling like… you get it), and a couple of days after a tiny story about it appeared in the *Guardian*, I got an email from Dad.

He's still living in Newcastle, but he's not with Karen any more. I got the sense that he's quite lonely, and that he'd like to become friends, share my success with me. I'm not entirely sure. I don't think we can ever regain the closeness we had when I was a little girl and he was teaching me to draw and buying me ice creams on Sundays. But it's made me understand that he's a person too, with his own desires and disappointments. He might have had a lot to do with how my life has turned out so far, but I'm the one who gets to decide what happens next.

A couple of weeks ago, Miranda turned half. Polly and Angus decided to celebrate their baby daughter's first six months of life with a massive party, which looks like becoming a regular summer event at the hotel. Wizzy and I are her godmothers, and so is Mrs Shaw, who came out from America for the occasion. We wished our little god-daughter all the happiness in the world, all the gifts of love, courage and resilience that she'll need as she grows up, but none of us was able to wave a magic wand and promise her blessings. Still, she's more gorgeous than ever, and Polly and Angus are even more loved up than they were on their wedding day.

Oh yes – weddings. That's where I started, so that's where I should finish, really.

The first wedding Will and I attended together wasn't that of one of our contemporaries. It was Mum's.

She kept me up to date with how she was doing after her surgery, and apparently she was a text-book recovery case. She put it down to her robust immune system, but I reckon it's love that did it. Because when she told me Trevor had, as she put it, 'popped the question', and asked if I'd be the one to give her away, she was so happy she couldn't stop giggling.

Will and I made the familiar train journey up to Dundee together. Everything was the same – the scenery, the horrible sandwich from the buffet car, the walk through the streets of grey stone houses. But it was different, too.

It was different because I was holding Will's hand, and because the night before I'd told him I loved him for the first time, and because he looked around as we walked and said, "My God, just look at that view. You're so lucky to have grown up here, Stella, it's stunning."

And I looked up, for once, instead of down, out over the firth towards Fife, and realised that he was right.

When Mum and Trevor opened the door to us – there was a suspiciously long interval after my knock, and they both looked a bit dishevelled – I returned Mum's hug willingly, and held her pillowy warmth against me for a long time.

Then she broke away and subjected my boyfriend to a long, fierce scrutiny, and said, "So this is Will."

Not Walter. Not Wayne. Not even Woyzeck (I was beginning to realise just how much creativity had gone into Mum's disingenuous mistakes).

Will.

I looked at Mum's wise, smiling face. I grinned at Trevor, all puffed up with pride. I turned to the tall, gorgeous man standing next to me, and I said, "Yes, Mum, this is Will."

It should have felt like the end of a fairytale, but it didn't.

It felt like the beginning.

ABOUT THE AUTHOR

Sophie Ranald is the youngest of five sisters. She was born in Zimbabwe and lived in South Africa until an acute case of itchy feet brought her to London in her mid-20s. As an editor for a customer publishing agency, Sophie developed her fiction-writing skills describing holidays to places she'd never visited. In 2011, she decided to disregard all the good advice given to aspiring novelists and attempt to write full-time.

Who Wants to Marry a Millionaire? is Sophie's third novel, and she also writes for magazines and online about food, fashion and running. She lives in south-east London with her amazing partner Hopi and Purrs, their adorable little cat.

Follow Sophie on Twitter @SophieRanald, or like her Facebook page for updates and random wittering about the cuteness of Purrs (there will be pics! Even videos!).

Acknowledgments

The idea for *Who Wants to Marry a Millionaire?* came to me a couple of years ago, when an old friend was visiting us in London. Will's story ended up being nothing like his, and I know he'd be mortified if he thought he'd inspired a chick-lit romance. Nonetheless, he must be acknowledged: thanks, Bouillé, for being part of this book and part of my life.

Likewise (apart from the ice-cream bits), Stella's father is nothing like my own darling Dad, to whom this book is dedicated and from whom I've learned so much about kindness, strength and humour.

I've been fortunate to find inspiration close to home, but knowledge had to be looked for further afield. Thanks to Ruth Barnett and her colleagues at Swiftkey for making me feel welcome, introducing me to the crazy world of start-up culture, and for the delicious lunch. The legendary Gil Penchina helped me make sense of the finance side of this thrilling industry – thank you. Any errors are entirely mine.

Peta Nightingale, my amazing agent (I don't care if I sound like a wanker), has been a fount of knowledge and encouragement for the last two years, together with her wonderful colleagues at LAW. Thank you for everything. Every time I think Tash Webber can't come up with a more swoon-makingly gorgeous cover design, she goes and does it

– thanks, Tash. And Catherine Baigent has once again scrutinised my manuscript and found mistakes that have made me cringe, while making the good bits even better. Mrs B, you rock.

So much of this book was written with my precious Purrs asleep on my lap, and all of it with my partner Hopi to whinge to, laugh with and bounce ideas off. You're my crew, I love you and I am so glad you're here.

If you enjoyed *Who Wants to Marry a Millionaire?*
why not discover more sparkling romantic comedies
by Sophie Ranald?

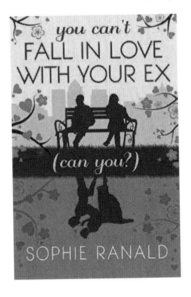

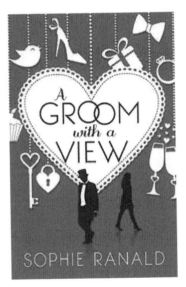

Sign up to Sophie's newsletter at sophieranald.com
to receive updates and news of future giveaways!

Made in the USA
Coppell, TX
07 September 2020

36589889R00177